THE SILVER DAGGER

THE VAMPIRES OF CRIMSON COVE BOOK 2

ALISTAIR CROSS

THE SILVER DAGGER

Brother Against Brother

Life in Crimson Cove has been good to the Colter Brothers since Gretchen VanTreese was staked and her horde of vampires scattered. Brooks is once again human, and Cade, the rare Sire Gretchen had determined to take as her mate, is in love. Then the unthinkable happens: Gretchen rises from the grave, and the brothers are torn apart, their lives - and the peace between them - shattered.

A Trail of Blood

When Cade comes into possession of an ancient ceremonial dagger he awakens a power so deadly it defies comprehension. Meanwhile, a serial killer is stalking the little mountain town, leaving a trail of blood that leads to a truth Sheriff Ethan Hunter doesn't want to face. And unknown to either of them, Gretchen is preparing to reopen her notorious nightclub, The Crimson Corset - and building an army to destroy her enemies and reclaim Cade Colter as her own.

A New Breed of Evil

The streets are no longer safe, nor are the forested paths, for a new and unknowable evil has come to Crimson Cove and everyone - vampire and human alike - must come together in order to survive.

THE PURPLE PROBE

WE DIG DEEPER THAN ANYONE ELSE DARES!

Sign up to get the Purple Probe in your inbox, and be the first to read interviews with your favorite characters! In this newspaper-style periodical, you'll also get exclusive content, sales and deals, rare Easter eggs, and a look behind the scenes that will shed new light on the Thorne & Cross Universe. Bend over and pick up your FREE subscription to the Purple Probe now at TamaraThorne.com or AlistairCross.com.

ALSO BY ALISTAIR CROSS

THE VAMPIRES OF CRIMSON COVE SERIES
The Crimson Corset

Darling Girls*

The Silver Dagger

The Black Wasp

God of Shadows

The Midnight Ripper

Darling Girls is a tie-in novel to The Vampires of Crimson Cove and The Vampires of Candle Bay

OTHER BOOKS BY ALISTAIR CROSS
Sleep Savannah Sleep

Dream Reaper

POETRY
The Book of Strange Persuasions

BOOKS BY THORNE & CROSS

THE RAVENCREST SAGA
The Ghosts of Ravencrest

The Witches of Ravencrest

Exorcism

Shadowland

Ravencrest Boxed Set -- Books 1 – 3

THE SPITE HOUSE CHRONICLES

Spite House

Spite Island

Spiteful Creatures

OTHER BOOKS BY THORNE & CROSS

The Cliffhouse Haunting

Mother

Darling Girls

NON-FICTION

Five Nights in a Haunted Cabin

PRAISE FOR ALISTAIR CROSS

The Vampires of Crimson Cove Series

"Put Bram Stoker in a giant cocktail shaker, add a pinch of Laurell K. Hamilton, a shot of John Carpenter, and a healthy jigger of absinthe, and you'll end up with Alistair Cross's modern Gothic chiller, **THE CRIMSON CORSET** - a deliciously terrifying tale that will sink its teeth into you from page one."

   - **Jay Bonansinga, New York Times Bestselling author of THE WALKING DEAD: INVASION and LUCID**

"Alistair Cross' new novel **THE CRIMSON CORSET** ... is taut and elegantly written taking us into the realms where the erotic and the horrific meet. Reminiscent of the work of Sheridan Le Fanu (CARMILLA, UNCLE SILAS) in its hothouse, almost Victorian intensity, it tells a multi-leveled story of misalliance and mixed motives. The language is darkly lyrical, and the tale is compelling. Read it; you'll be glad you did." - **Chelsea Quinn Yarbro, author of the *Saint-Germain Cycle***

"**THE CRIMSON CORSET** is a good read. There is a colorful cast of characters, a clever plot, and an intricate structure ... there are surprises and jumps and starts, sex and death, beauty and gore, something for everyone ... if you're looking for set-up and payoff, this novel will not disappoint." - **HELLNOTES**

"This drop-deadly tale of seduction and terror will leave you begging to be fanged ... "

- **Tamara Thorne, international bestselling author of HAUNTED and MOONFALL**

The Angel Alejandro

"Alistair Cross's **THE ANGEL ALEJANDRO** is an intriguing tale that pits evil against good and keeps the reader on edge with surprising shifts and changes." - **Dianna Love, New York Times Bestseller**

"**THE ANGEL ALEJANDRO** is as lush and ethereal as it is visceral and unholy. A demonic horde seeks to swallow up the citizens of Prominence made vulnerable by their weaknesses. Those who take a stand against the evil are emotionally damaged as well; particularly a sheriff who battles his personal demons in a bottle. The author had me rooting for each of them in spite of, or maybe because of their flaws. With masterful pacing, Cross brings a small mystery to a raging boil that threatens every soul in Prominence. His exquisite prose drew me into the story as if I were living it. Highly recommended." - **QL Pearce, author of the Scary Stories for Sleep-Overs series, and Spine Chillers: Hair-Raising Tales**

" ... This story caught me from the beginning and I could not put it down. It's one thing to not remember your past, but when your past is filled with mysterious powers, it's something else. The clash of good and evil, angels versus devils, it's an amazing story that keeps you on the edge of your seat ... it was magnificent! A definite must read." - **Amy's Bookshelf Reviews**

Sleep, Savannah, Sleep

"I really enjoyed **SLEEP, SAVANNAH, SLEEP** - a spooky, suspenseful tale that delves with insight into the dynamics of small towns and grieving families. It is sure to please fans of both crime fiction and horror – and anyone who appreciates a good story. Alistair Cross's deft narration and well-drawn characters will pull you in, and the pages will turn as if by magic. - **Margaret Lucke, author of Snow Angel and House of Whispers**

"Alistair Cross shows that he is a master storyteller by giving us memorable characters and a twist ending that you'll never see coming." – **HorrorAddicts**

"I read the last few pages with my jaw on the floor." – **Romi Reads**

"Sometime in October, when I list my absolute favorite Halloween night reads, this book will be way up on my list! Probably #1." – **The Novel Lady**

"The end of the book was shocking. To put it simply, I was shook." – **Paws and Paper**

PRAISE FOR THORNE & CROSS

"While "binge-reading" the clever, shocking, deliciously creepy **MOTHER** by Tamara Thorne and Alistair Cross (amid gasps, laughing out loud and muttering "Oh, my God, no…"), it dawned on me that these two should be writing for AMERICAN HORROR STORY. The authors offer up a fun, juicy, gripping thriller that's nearly impossible to put down. As I kept turning the pages, I was reminded of MISERY, ROSEMARY'S BABY, PEYTON PLACE, PSYCHO and several other classics. But this is an original—as is the main character, Priscilla "Prissy" Martin, the mother of them all. Her perfect, poised façade masks an ugly, twisted, utterly evil woman—a character you'll never forget. I think we found a spouse for Hannibal

Lecter! And I think you'll find **MOTHER** a fast-paced, delirious, heart-pounding thrill-ride." - **Kevin O'Brien, New York Times Bestselling Author**

"**MOTHER** is about as disturbing as one can get. Thorne and Cross are seriously twisted individuals who know how to horrify and entertain at the same time." - **Fang-Freakin-Tastic Book Reviews**

"A great combination of strong characters that remind me of my V.C. Andrews characters, wonderful creepy twists, and a plot that will recall Mommie Dearest in an original take that shocks and delights at the same time. This is a full blown psychological thriller worth the investment of time and money." - **Andrew Neiderman, Author of The Devil's Advocate and the V.C. Andrews novels**

"Thorne and Cross bring the goods with **THE CLIFFHOUSE HAUNTING**, a clockwork mechanism of gothic chills designed to grab the reader by the scruff and never let go until the terrifying conclusion. Atmospheric, sexy, brooding, and brutal, the book manages to be simultaneously romantic and hardboiled. Highly recommended!" - **Jay Bonansinga, the New York Times bestselling author of** *The Walking Dead: Invasion*, *Lucid*, **and** *Self Storage*.

"In **THE GHOSTS OF RAVENCREST**, Tamara Thorne and Alistair Cross have created a world that is dark, opulent, and smoldering with the promise of scares and seduction. You'll be able to feel the slide of the satin sheets, taste the fizz of champagne, and hear the footsteps on the stairs." -**Sylvia Shults, paranormal expert and author of** *Fractured Spirits* **and** *Hunting Demons*

"In this classic-style gothic, young Belinda Moorland takes a job as governess for the children of Eric Manning, whose family mansion, Ravencrest, was reassembled stone by stone after crossing over from England. Now stalked by a bevy of quirky, shady characters ... the sinister estate and its naughty nightside hijinks take center stage in this expert tale of multi-generational evil - and love. **THE GHOSTS OF RAVENCREST** will chill you and make you hot and bothered at the same time. There's nothing like a stay in a California town created by Thorne and Cross." - **W.D. Gagliani, author of** *Wolf's Blind* **(the Nick Lupo Series)**

The Silver Dagger

© 2019, 2020 Alistair Cross

All Rights Reserved

Glass Apple Press

First edition July, 2019

No part of this book may be reproduced or stored in a retrieval system, or transmitted in any form or by any means, graphic, electronic, or mechanical, including photocopying, recording, or otherwise, without written permission from the authors.

This book is a work of fiction. Names, characters, places and incidents either are products of the authors' imaginations or are used fictitiously. Any resemblance to actual persons, living or dead, events, or locales is entirely coincidental. All rights reserved.

Cover Design by Mike Rivera

*The Silver Dagger is dedicated, with love, to
Chelsea Quinn Yarbro,
whose friendship, guidance, and generosity are unparalleled.*

ACKNOWLEDGMENTS

Thanks to Q.L. Pearce for friendship, feedback, and wisdom on so many matters; Berlin Malcom at BAM Literature, who, at the end of the day, is the reason this is possible; Mike Rivera for his great art and wonderful company; Libba Campbell, the best editor in the world; my family and friends for their support and understanding; and of course, my dear friend, my collaborator, and my hero, Tamara Thorne, who always has my back and never, ever tells me, *'You can't do that.'*

I, MADMAN

Sometimes at night
    Outside my bedroom door
    I hear her whisper through the light
    That the moon casts on the floor

And in these chambers, like a grave
    Days on end I weep
    For a woman that is cold and gray
    And buried six feet deep

From *The Book of Strange Persuasions*

PROLOGUE

At the edge of the small tourist-centric town of Crimson Cove, the former nightclub known as The Crimson Corset stood vacant and alone, the silver light of a high full moon painting the face of the building, adding color to the long-dead façade like the stroke of a mortician's brush. Beyond the blackened windows, dust had settled over the club's interior, filming the unused dance floors and bars like a second skin. For months, nothing had stirred within or around the place; even the massive windmill fronting the building hadn't dared to make a move.

Tonight, as a cool September wind began to rise in the little village, growing until the pines shuddered under its command, the windmill at The Crimson Corset began to spin, creaking in slow, lazy circles at first, and then with a great fury, lending a sense of presence, of returned life, to the forgotten property.

Deeper in the village, in a cabin not far from Crimson Lake, Cade Colter slept soundly, Samantha Corbett nestled against him, the bed sheets pulled high as the first fingers of fall brought a pleasant chill to the room. In the toasty twin bed, Samantha sighed. Cade stirred and pulled her closer, relishing her warmth, her scent, and returned to untroubled, dreamless slumber.

But in the room down the hall, his older brother's sleep was thin and restless. Tonight, Brooks Colter's dreams were an army invasion of unwanted visions - visions that until now stopped haunting him in both waking and sleeping hours. In those visions he saw blood, death ... and the woman who'd nearly destroyed him.

Brooks remained under the fragile spell of that fitful sleep, wrestling with sheets soaked in sweat despite the brisk chill, and emitting the whisper-thin sounds of a low-grade terror that gained ground inside him as, beyond the cabin, at Crimson Lake, something disturbed the watery grave of Gretchen VanTreese.

1

LIFE AS WE KNOW IT

Monday morning was cold, the leaden gray sky swollen and bruised. Pounding rain crashed against the cabin's windows in heavy sheets as the wind, which had only grown stronger overnight, hissed through the trees, making the forest beyond sound like a nest of snakes.

Cade Colter stared out the kitchen window at the narrow muddy path that wound its way to Crimson Lake, surprised that Brooks hadn't woken him for their usual jog, storm be damned. Brooks was a health nut of the highest order and no mere deluge would keep him from his early morning run - and it probably hadn't; he knew his younger brother well enough to know there was no way Cade was going outside for anything today. Brooks had no doubt gone jogging without him.

And Cade was glad. He had the day off - the bookstore, Langley's Literary Labyrinth, was closed on Mondays - and he wanted nothing more than to be alone with Samantha, who had Mondays off as well.

Samantha Corbett had moved into the cabin with Cade and Brooks nearly a year ago, after what Cade now thought of as *The Dark Days* - and they had been dark. Dark and terrifying. Even now, Cade shuddered. He tried not to think about those times.

Things were better now, and that's what he tried to focus on. Even though he'd worried that Brooks might come to resent a third person in the house, Samantha's presence had proved no obstacle at all. The three of them were good friends, and a woman in the house was good for both brothers. Samantha, for all her sweetness, kept them in line. No longer was Brooks allowed to leave apple cores lying around, nor was it okay for Cade to leave his towel on the bathroom floor. Even Sir Purrcival, Cade's now-chubby black-and-white cat, was benefiting, receiving an abundance of daily treats and attention, and never having to suffer the indignity of using a less-than-freshly-scooped litter box. Cade wondered how they'd ever managed to live without Samantha.

He smiled. He was happy in Crimson Cove. He felt he'd lived here his entire life and the little mountain town seemed to feel the same way. Even the stormy days here were cozy, the smell of rained-on pine comforting. Nothing could bruise the beauty of Crimson Cove - nothing, except perhaps ...

Vampires.

The word still sent a chill through him. Even after all this time, he had trouble wrapping his mind around the reality of monsters.

But not all of them are monsters. He was thinking of local health spa proprietor Michael Ward, and Winter, his big, blond, grinning right-hand man. Winter and Michael were Cade's friends. They were the good guys, undead or not.

But the *other* vampires, those like Gretchen VanTreese ...

The name sent a surge through him and Cade shuddered, his mind involuntarily casting back to last year.

He flinched when warm hands touched his bare sides from behind.

"Why so jumpy?" Samantha rested her cheek against his back, her shower-dampened hair giving him another little shock.

"I didn't hear you come in."

"I'm in stealth-mode." Her signature scent, a lavender and night-blooming jasmine-scented perfume called *Lavande d'Amour*, blended deliciously with the soap and shampoo.

Cade turned and embraced her, kissed the top of her damp head.

"You're tense," she said.

"Am I?"

"What were you thinking about?"

"Just ... stuff."

"Ah. Stuff. And I'll bet I know what stuff that is."

"You do, do you?"

"Yep. You're thinking about vampires. You always look intense when you're thinking about vampires."

The woman knew him well. "I can't help it sometimes. It's still just so ... hard to fathom."

Samantha nodded. "It is." She was silent a moment. "Do you ever wonder what it would be like to become one?"

Cade was stunned. *Is she serious?*

After a beat, she added, "It might not be such a bad thing, you know?"

Outside, thunder muttered, a bad omen, and Cade's skin chilled. "No. I don't ever think about it." He cleared his throat. "Do *you*?"

She looked thoughtful. "Sometimes."

After everything we've gone through, she's romanticizing vampirism? Seriously? They'd nearly been killed, both of them, and Cade was about to remind her of this when Samantha raised her head, meeting his eyes. "I just like what it would mean, you know?"

"I'm not following, I guess. What do you think it would mean exactly?"

"That we could be like this forever," she said. "Young and-"

"And required to prey on the innocent, to kill people." His clipped tones surprised him but Samantha didn't seem to notice.

"They're not all like Gretchen. Michael and Winter don't kill anyone." She held his gaze. "In fact, if you and I had been vampires all along, Gretchen wouldn't have had any use for us. I mean, what good is a Sire if he's undead?"

Sire. The term for the one in God-knew-how-many-million human males with the genetic makeup that allowed him to reproduce with the undead. Cade hated the word. It made him sound like a stud horse.

"And if *I'd* been a vampire, none of them would have had any interest in my blood." And Samantha, with her rare, AB Negative blood-type, was a favorite among the undead. Together, she and Cade were a walking all-you-can-eat buffet for vampires - which was why even now, the good guys had to double up on their blood rations in order to control themselves around them.

"So, really," Samantha went on, "being a vampire is probably the safest thing to be in this town."

Cade shook his head. "No. They still have to survive on human blood. And too many of them turn bad. I'm not risking it. Besides, Gretchen's dead and gone. We're safe now, so none of that matters anyway."

"Yeah, but …we could be together forever. We'd never die. I mean, how amazing is that?"

"It's not amazing." Cade wondered if she was teasing him. "It's against nature. Dying is natural. We're *supposed* to die." He watched her, unsure how serious she was. Just to be safe, he decided to have a talk with Michael Ward as soon as the man got back from the vampires-only festival he and the others were attending in the little town of Eternity several hundred miles away. Cade didn't think they took requests, but for his own peace of mind, he wanted Michael's word that none of his men would grant Samantha that favor - should she ask.

Then Samantha smiled at him. "Don't look so serious. It's just something I think about sometimes. You know, a fantasy. I don't think I could actually *do* it."

Cade should have been relieved, but it would be a minute before the knot inside him loosened. He'd seen the look in her eyes and thought she *could* do it. Eager for a subject change, he said, "What do you want to do for the rest of the day?"

Her lips curved into a playful grin. "I think you know what *I* want."

"And what's that?"

"To stay in bed all day. With you."

Cade smiled, relieved that things were returning to normal *human* matters. "I think that's a great plan. But I need to take a shower first."

"No, don't. I like you a little stinky." She grinned.

"Gee, thanks, but-"

"We're just going to get dirty again anyway." The teasing lilt of her voice, and the fact that she wore only a towel, sent delicious shivers through Cade as her fingertips teased the waistband of his boxers - the ones she'd bought him with *RUB FOR LUCK* emblazoned on the fly. Samantha rubbed for luck. "And my work here is already half-done."

She led him down the hall to the bedroom and pulled down the cobalt quilt before helping him, slowly, out of his socks and boxers. Cade, trying to maintain self-control, let her, but when she stretched out on the sheets and lost the towel, his restraint collapsed.

As it had always been with Samantha, Cade was at first weak with need, nearly trembling with it, but once she began kissing him that nervousness passed, and soon he found the pulse of the moment and synched himself confidently to its steady, primitive rhythm.

For many minutes, their quiet murmurs rose and fell like a gentle tide, Cade raised himself, and looked into her sea-green eyes. "I love you." And he meant it. Meant it more than any words he'd ever spoken in his life.

AT THE SAME MOMENT, AT THE CRIMSON COVE SHERIFF'S STATION downtown, Sheriff Ethan Hunter tried to appear sympathetic as Myrtle McClusky, leader of the Ladies' Auxiliary and all-around pain in the ass, rehashed the details of her ongoing power struggle with her neighbor, Harold Nesbit, and his pet goat, Gonzarella.

"There must be *laws* against these things!" She was clearly upset but that wasn't why she was bellowing. Myrtle always bellowed; she was convinced that the rest of the world was going deaf right along with her.

"Actually, Ms. McClusky, as long as the goat remains in Mr. Nesbit's yard-"

"But it *isn't*, that's what I'm trying to tell you!" Her elderly head shook with elderly rage as she brought a gnarled elderly fist down on Ethan's shiny new mahogany desk. "That dirty son of a bitch can't get away with this!"

At this point, Ethan wasn't sure whether she was talking about the goat or its owner. *Probably both.* Myrtle McClusky and Harold Nesbit had been sworn enemies since sometime in the 90s when Harold had snagged up the shiny blue Grand Prix she'd had her eye on at Crimson Cove's only used car lot. For as long as Ethan had worked on the force, Myrtle had come into his office several times a month, every month, to file complaints against Mr. Nesbit that ranged from noise pollution from his television, to alleging that Harold was sneaking into her house to hide her slippers. "Ms. McClusky. We've been over this. The goat sticking its face through *Mr. Nesbit's* fence is *not* trespassing."

"It is if it's eating *my* lawn!" Cords stood out on Myrtle's wrinkled neck.

Ethan sighed. Her "lawn" consisted of a spattering of dying weeds on a patch of dirt. But there was no sense arguing with the woman. "All right. I'll talk to Mr. Nesbit. Again."

The blaze in the old woman's watery blue eyes dulled to its usual flicker of general contempt, then to one of admiration. She flashed her dentures to show that the two of them were friends once again. Myrtle was a friend to anyone who let her have her way. "I'd appreciate that, Sheriff." She stepped closer, the better to bellow at him. "You know, you young kids these days aren't *all* bad, I don't care what they say!"

Young kids? At nearly thirty-nine, Ethan couldn't help chuckling. "Thank you, Ms. McClusky. Now if you'll excuse me ..."

But the woman just stood there, jaw set, eyes hard.

Ethan sighed. "No time like the present, eh?"

Myrtle nodded, satisfied.

Ethan put away the report he'd been trying to finish, stood, and shrugged into his tan jacket. Retrieving his Smokey hat from its stand, he pulled the brim low over his eyes and said, "I'll go talk to Harold right now, how's that?"

"Oh, I suppose if you think that's best," she bellowed, practically forcing Ethan out of the office.

Outside, he hopped into the black-and-white, and headed for the offending goat-owner's house. As he made his way through the mostly-empty streets of Crimson Cove in the slashing silver rain, he wanted nothing more than a tall, cold Killian's - and a day off from the grievances of the local complaint department.

Cruising through the old-fashioned downtown district, he thought perhaps he'd stop by the mortuary on the way back and see if Sheila wanted to grab an early lunch. Passing the Old West false-fronted tourist shops, bookstores, and quaint restaurants, he smiled at the thought of her, realized he was smiling, and was surer than ever that proposing to her had been the right move. Of course, that had been over six months ago. They still needed to set a date. For a while, the engagement had been enough for both of them, but just lately, Ethan was itching to make it official. He suspected Sheila might be, too.

He wasn't sure why he was dragging his feet but he thought it might have something to do with his previous marriage.

Ethan and his ex-wife, Sydney, hadn't ended well.

But Sheila isn't Sydney. They're nothing *alike.* And that was the truth. Sydney, with her expensive tastes, high-pitched giggle, and perfectly manicured hot pink acrylic nails - *not to mention her oversized plastic breasts* - stood on the opposite end of the female spectrum from Sheila Leventis.

Sheila was easygoing. Reserved. Smart. And low-maintenance. She enjoyed splitting a bowl of microwave popcorn on the couch in front of old movies, rarely wore much makeup, and bit her fingernails to the quick. Even her hair - raven-black and loosely tied back - was a contrast to Sydney's over-bleached, hairsprayed bouffant.

He realized he was comparing the women and told himself to stop. It had been seven years since his first marriage had failed and just as long since he'd laid eyes on his ex-wife. But it had been painful and humiliating. For *him*, anyway. Sydney hadn't stuck around Crimson Cove to face the locals; before the ink had dried on the divorce decree, she'd packed up and moved to Los Angeles, leaving Ethan to answer all the awkward prying questions.

But that was ancient history. *Sydney* was ancient history. She'd since married some rich movie producer and, aside from a curt letter from her lawyers saying that she no longer required spousal support, Ethan hadn't heard a peep out of her. And he was glad.

Because Sydney had been a mistake. A big one.

But Sheila was not.

He turned down Burgundy Boulevard and by the time he neared old Harold Nesbit's property, he'd decided to talk to Sheila tonight about setting an official date.

WHISTLING AN OFF-KEY BUT INDISPUTABLY CHEERY RENDITION OF American Authors' *Best Day of My Life,* Brooks Colter slid on the creeper beneath Deputy Ryan Closter's classic red Mustang and went to work on the gasket leak. This, the dirty work, was the part of his job he enjoyed the most - not that owning his own business didn't have its perks.

When Old Man Curtis had retired and offered him a good deal on the shop, Brooks had been reluctant - fixing cars and running a business were two different things - but as time had gone on, he'd found his footing. It meant devoting almost all of his time to the shop - and dropping out of college where he'd been pursuing a degree in computer science - but Brooks had no regrets. *Computer science. What was I thinking?*

Cars, not computers, were Brooks' passion. He loved the smells of oil and engines, the ratchet of tools and the hiss of air compressors. He even liked that he could never quite get the grease out of the creases in his hands or out from under his nails.

Over all, Brooks was happy and, despite the rain, today was a good day.

Except for the nagging thoughts of Gretchen VanTreese.

Brooks had often been haunted by the vague sensation that he'd had troubling dreams the night before, but today, though the details were lost to him, he was sure he'd dreamed of her. That bothered him.

He hadn't thought of Gretchen VanTreese - or the fact that she'd very nearly succeeded in turning him into a full-on vampire - in many months. Now, he tried to shake off the thoughts. Gretchen was dead with a stake through her heart in a lead-lined coffin at the bottom of the deepest part of Crimson Lake, and Brooks had no reason to be thinking about her.

And yet he was.

The memories of last night's dreams flitted closer, but remained beyond his grasp. Brooks resumed whistling as he worked on the Mustang.

"Brooks?" The baritone drawl of Chet Wilson, Brooks' second-in-command, filtered down through the motor.

"What can I do you for, Chet?"

"I want to talk to you about my hours."

"What about them?"

The grating sound of Chet clearing his throat merged with the buzz of drills beyond. "I was just wondering if, uh, maybe next week I could start picking up a few more." He hesitated. "Or … I thought maybe, if you need a shop supervisor or something, I could, uh, do that, maybe."

Shop supervisor? Though business had grown - was booming, actually - Brooks only needed a staff of four: three mechanics and the new office girl, Jana. Since he himself was here almost all the time, he wasn't sure what Chet intended to supervise.

Brooks slid out from under the Mustang and looked up at his red-haired employee. Chet's orange freckles stood out starkly against his pale, homely face. Tall, lanky, and scarecrow-thin, he looked like the kind of guy who grew up on a farm somewhere in Minnesota, but in fact, he'd lived his entire life in Crimson Cove. "Are you asking me for a promotion?"

The freckles stood out in even greater relief as Chet's anxiety sharpened. It occurred to Brooks that a piece of straw would be right at home clamped between the guy's cheddar-yellow teeth. "I, uh, well

... it's just that ... I could really use the management experience, and ..." His slow voice trailed off.

"A man with ambition. I like that." The trouble was, Brooks didn't need a shop supervisor. Not that he wasn't impressed by Chet's work - *especially when I took time off to recover from Gretchen last year ... Gretchen. There's that name again. Stop thinking of her.*

"Is that a yes?"

"Let me get back to you on that, Chet. I think we can work something out."

Chet flashed an unattractive smile as Jana appeared in the office doorway. "Brooks!" she called above the din of tools. "There's a woman here who wants to speak with you."

A lightning bolt of inexplicable terror struck Brooks' heart. *Gretchen. What if it's Gretchen?* But of course it wouldn't be. The daylight - *and the fact that she's fucking dead!* - made that impossible.

Brooks followed Jana back into the office where Angela Dalliance - harmless, middle-aged, *human* Angela Dalliance, manager of Mystic Muffins on Ensign Avenue - stood smiling.

Shit. Despite his distaste for the woman, Brooks put on his best grin and said, "How can I help you, Ms. D.?"

She stood perhaps only five-two and wore the kind of ruffled, low-cut blouse that screamed, *Look at my tits*! To protect her mass of dyed platinum curls, she held an open rain-spattered umbrella in a coquettish pose that brought to mind the young blushing Southern belles of *Gone with the Wind.*

Except Angela Dalliance was neither Southern nor young, and the shiny tightness of her surgically-enhanced skin only emphasized her age - which was undoubtedly on the depressing side of forty.

Her heavily made-up eyes roamed over Brooks a long moment, studying his black *IMAGINE DRAGONS* t-shirt before lighting - and unapologetically remaining - on his crotch. "I was wondering if you could change my oil. It's dirty," she said with a smile. "But not today. I have somewhere to be." She sidled closer. "Thursday maybe?"

Brooks glanced at Jana who raised her brows. "Of course. Jana here can schedule you in right now. That's her job, Ms. D."

An uncomely scowl settled on the woman's unrealistically plump lips. "I'd rather *you* schedule me, thank you very much." She flashed a cold look at Jana. "*Last* time, my appointment got changed without my knowledge and I had to reschedule Alexis' appointment with the groomers."

Brooks nodded. The truth was, the woman hadn't shown up for her appointment - and that wasn't the first time it had happened. Lying about it gave her a valid excuse to deal only with Brooks, the better to eye-rape him. It was getting embarrassing. Her infatuation had become a running joke at Pinetop's.

But Brooks kept his grin intact. "Not a problem, Ms. D." He moved toward the desk, away from her, and feeling the older woman's eyes all over him, he warded off a shudder. "How's 2:30?"

"Perfect." She moved behind him, close enough he could feel her breath against his arm as she feigned interest in the ledger, practically purring.

Brooks penciled her in. "There. All done. I'll see you Thursday."

"And *I'll* see *you.*" She paused. "And perhaps I'll bring Alexis along, too. I couldn't bring her today because the poor dear is just *terrified* of the rain, but you remember how much fun she has here."

"I remember." Brooks seriously doubted that Alexis, an obese, gassy teacup poodle who was twenty-five years old if she was a day, ever had *any* idea where she was. The only thing he'd ever seen the dog do was sit in her mistress' lap, glaring with cataracted eyes in a fluffy pink sweater as she perfumed the office with the stink of rotting teeth, mothballs, and farts. Brooks forced another smile. "Alexis is welcome here any time."

"I'll let her know." Ms. D. beamed, gave him a final lingering look, then strutted out of Pinetop's and into the rain, her umbrella bouncing in time with her steps. Brooks watched as she made her way to her car and from this distance, as lightning brightened the day, the petite blond with her cinched waist, bore a startling resemblance to Gretchen VanTreese.

On the heels of *that* realization, all at once, came the vivid, horrible details of last night's dreams. Images of Gretchen and blood, sensations of sex and pain ... and then her voice:

'My little tin soldier ...'

It all came back in chilling detail, and suddenly, Brooks felt certain that something perilous was heading his way, that death hovered nearby.

When Jana cracked open a diet Coke, Brooks jumped. "That woman has no shame," said the office girl.

Brooks stared at the rain, trying to shake off his irrational fear. "Be sure and give her a reminder call on Wednesday, will you?"

"Sure thing. For all the good it'll do."

Brooks retreated back into the shop, trying his best to regain his good mood. Only when he got back under the Mustang and let his hands do the thinking did the dream memories fade and the sense of dread recede. Eventually, *Best Day of My Life*, still off-key and almost as cheerful, found its way back to his lips.

2

EXES AND BROS

That afternoon, Cade and Samantha sat at opposite ends of the tan leather couch, absorbed in their respective novels. Cade, a fan of historical romance, was lost in the words of Mary Stewart, and Samantha, whose preferences required a bit more action, clutched a paperback copy of Kevin O'Brien's *They Won't Be Hurt*, her knuckles bleached with tension, her eyes racing across the words. When she reached a chapter break, she glanced at the pendulum clock above the stone-fronted fireplace where low flames crackled lazily and lent heat to the rain-chilled living room.

"What sounds good for dinner tonight?"

A swath of chestnut hair fell over Cade's eye and he blew it from his line of sight, but he showed no signs of hearing her.

Samantha smiled, watching him. She had a hard time believing that the book he held - something called *Ivy Tree*, with a picture of, yep, a tree, on the cover - could be so riveting, but his unexpected tastes were one of the reasons she loved him. It made her feel special somehow that he no longer hid his reading preferences from her, that he allowed her access to this secret part of him. Only Brooks and the sheriff, Ethan Hunter - who, as it turned out, shared equally embarrassing tastes in literature - knew about Cade's love of gothics and bodice-rippers. When he'd first confessed to Samantha that the novel behind the Tom Clancy book jacket was actually a Regency romance, she'd felt as if she'd been admitted into a special club, made privy to top-secret information. She remembered how insecure he'd been the first time they'd read in the same room together, his eyes flitting over the top of a copy of Kathryn McLeod's *Dark Lily,* searching Samantha's face for signs of judgement.

But there was nothing insecure about him now. He'd shed his boyish innocence sometime last year and while she'd adored his almost clumsy uncertainty, she liked the changes in him. It was as if he'd fully bloomed, fully ripened. And given the terrors he'd seen - that all of them had seen - it was a wonder he hadn't turned hard and bitter.

She glanced at the framed photograph on the mantle - a teenage Cade in cap and gown - and realized the changes were physical, as well. Though less gangly, he'd looked about the same when she'd met him as he did in the photo - but now, his shoulders had broadened; he'd filled out. His face had gained sharper edges. He was handsome, very handsome, and while Cade had always felt that Brooks was the more attractive brother, Samantha disagreed. His chestnut-colored hair, in need of a cut, once again fell over his thick-lashed hazel eyes, and even in the ratty, undersized t-shirt and baggy gray sweats he wore on his days off, as far as Samantha was concerned, he could have been a movie star.

No, he was not the boy on the mantle anymore - not the boy she'd met. He was no longer a boy at all, but a man - *my man* - and Samantha was wholeheartedly and unconditionally in love with him.

And I've changed too, she realized. *We all have.* Though it hadn't shown on the surface, there was no doubt that Brooks had been changed as well. Of all of them, he had been through the worst of it.

Cade glanced up, his eyes locking onto hers. He lowered the book and said, "You're doing that thing again."

"Doing what thing?"

"That sitting-there-staring-at-me thing."

She shrugged. "If you don't want to be gawked at, then I guess you shouldn't be so damned good-looking."

Cade set the book down on the coffee table, and leaned back against the arm of the couch, legs stretched out. He grinned. "Why don't you come over here and make me?" His hazel eyes glittered suggestively under his long, dark lashes.

"Maybe I will." Samantha discarded her own book then crawled toward him, on top of him, loving the feel of his solid warm body beneath her, the beat of his heart in time with her own. The clean male scent of him. She kissed him, hard, wanting him, and knowing, as his body began to respond, that he wanted her, too. He stroked the backs of her legs, found her buttocks and massaged them as he kissed her, deep and slow.

Then the growl of an engine outside as a vehicle approached, followed by a slash of headlights through the window.

Cade broke the kiss. "Damn it. He's early."

Samantha pecked both corners of his mouth. "Then I guess we'll just have to wait. The suspense will be delectable."

Cade groaned. "Try painful."

Samantha laughed, dismounting him to resume her position on the other end of the couch. The cat, Sir Purrcival, leapt onto the sofa and happily plopped down between them, helping to create the illusion that they hadn't just been all over each other. *Thanks, kitty.* She stroked his head.

Outside, the headlamps blinked off and the motor was cut. Samantha stole glances at Cade, who was trying to appear engaged in his novel. She loved the way he looked when he wanted her. The flushed cheeks, the bright eyes, and slightly shuddery breath.

She hoped Brooks wouldn't detect the buzz of need that saturated the air.

As Brooks hopped out of his black F-150, his cell phone rang, giving him a start.

It was Ethan.

Brooks cleared his throat and put a smile on. "What's up, copper? Am I under arrest?"

"Funny. Do you think I'd call and warn you if you were?"

Brooks laughed.

"Actually, I was calling to see if you guys wanted some pizza, but if you're going to be a smartass, I can eat it alone."

"Pizza?" Brooks made his way up the steps, pausing on the front porch. "Who croaked?"

"Herbert Hindley." On the days when Sheila worked late at the morgue - meaning someone died - Ethan ate with Samantha and the Colter brothers; it had become something of a tradition. "Personally, I can't believe he lasted as long as he did. The guy must have been a hundred and five."

Brooks had no idea who Herbert Hindley was, but pizza sounded awesome. He stepped inside the cabin where Cade and Samantha were reading on the couch. Upon seeing Brooks, Sir Purrcival got up, meowed, and sauntered over in his usual slow gangsta swagger to rub himself against him. "Just let me find out what Bonnie and Clyde here want on their pizza."

Cade looked up from his book. "Pizza? Who died?"

Brooks covered the mouthpiece. "Some old dude. What kind of pizza?"

Cade looked at Samantha.

She shrugged. "Pepperoni and olives?"

Cade nodded and Brooks told Ethan.

"And veggie for you, I assume?" Ethan said.

"Yep," said Brooks. "And no cheese." He could feel Ethan's disapproval coming at him like radio waves through the phone.

"I'll never understand you, Colter."

Brooks shrugged. "The good news is, you don't have to. Now how about you quit your yapping and go get that pizza?"

"10-4. I'll see you in thirty."

In the bathroom, Brooks peeled his grease-stained clothes off and jumped in the shower. Under the pounding spray, he scrubbed away the day, but his sense of unease wouldn't wash off. That inexplicable feeling of fear, of impermanence, had followed him all day. Emerging from the shower, he cinched a towel around his waist and wiped condensation off the mirror. As he shaved, he eyed the tattoo on his left shoulder - a snake preparing to strike - and wondered if he ought to add to it. He'd gotten it in Cliffside at a place called *Wizard of Ink* and the artist was incredible.

Or maybe I'm getting too old for tattoos. Brooks would turn thirty next March, and only now did he realize he had misgivings about it. He didn't *feel* thirty - and he didn't think he looked it, either. Checking his reflection, he tried to imagine himself ten - and twenty - years from now. Would time and gravity be kind to his face? And what about his body? He tried to envision his physique gone to seed, his many hours of hard work at the gym, all for nothing as time wrinkled his skin, deteriorated his bones, ate away his muscle … disease rotting him from the inside out. *Quit with the dark thoughts. It's just a fucking birthday - and it's not even here yet! I've still got six months to be in my twenties.* But it was more than his coming birthday. He knew the cause of his black mood.

Gretchen.

The name popped into his head uninvited and he quickly cast it out.

No. It's because I'm a vain bastard who doesn't want to get old. It's normal. Everyone feels funny about turning thirty.

He decided he'd done enough thinking for one day - *for a lifetime* - and said, "Nah. Thirty's not too old for new ink. Thirty's not too old for anything." He tipped his reflection a cheesy wink and finished up, splashing on some aftershave. He yanked on a fresh pair of jeans, a clean shirt, and was slicking back his hair when he caught an eerily familiar scent that stopped him mid-comb stroke: rained-on roses.

Her scent.

"Gretchen." The name slipped from his lips as slick as satin, but it tasted foul.

He stood frozen, thinking.

Of course he smelled rain. Because it had been raining all day. And as for roses, there were plenty lingering around. The wind must have picked up the scent and-

But that smell. It was *her* scent.

Brooks shook his head, switched off the light, and joined the others in the living room. Ethan had arrived with three pizzas and they smelled glorious.

Brooks' stomach growled audibly as he swept up his cheeseless veggie and plopped down in the recliner, eager to start a movie, any movie, so long as it derailed his strange train of thought.

THE FOUR OF THEM SAT IN THE LIVING ROOM, LIGHTS OFF AND CURTAINS drawn, watching *Pet Sematary*. The book was better than the movie, and Cade said so.

Brooks reached for another slice of veggie pizza. His dark hair was still damp from the shower and he wore a tight-fitting black t-shirt boasting a rock band called *Corpsepussle*. "Why is it that when anyone reads a book, they need to tear the movie apart?" He sounded like he was trying to be chipper, but there was something dark, biting almost, underlying his tone. "Just once, I'd like to hear someone say the movie was better."

"*Psycho*," said Samantha.

"Huh?" Brooks took a bite of pizza and continued to ignore Purrcy, who, thanks to Brooks' constant sharing, had developed an affinity for vegetables.

"*Psycho*," said Samantha. "The movie was better than the book. I thought so, anyway."

"Not that the book wasn't awesome," added Cade.

"That's true. It was awesome, but the Norman in the movie was far more sympathetic."

Brooks shook his head. "Book people." In the shadows, he covertly slipped the cat a piece of spinach.

"Don't feed him that," Cade said. "I don't know if it's good for him."

"If it wasn't," said Brooks, "then he wouldn't want it." He let Purrcy finish the leaf.

From the recliner, Ethan said, "Jesus. Remind me never to go to a movie theater with you chatterboxes. We'd be eighty-sixed for talking."

Brooks flashed him a beamer. "Calm down, copper. You're liable to have a stroke with that tense disposition and poor diet of yours."

The sheriff, who was as healthy as any twenty-year-old, took an especially big bite of pepperoni pizza - with extra cheese - and flipped Brooks the bird.

Brooks laughed.

As the sun set, the movie ended and Ethan checked his phone. "Sheila's still going to be another hour."

"Mr. Dead Guy giving her hell?" asked Brooks. Purrcy trilled and he picked him up, kissed him between the ears. Purrcy laid his ears back and looked annoyed.

"Looks like." said Ethan.

"You're welcome to stay for a couple of beers." Brooks set the cat down. It seemed to Cade his brother didn't want the sheriff to leave. Something was bothering him. All through the movie, Brooks had looked faraway, troubled, lost in thought. He'd jumped at the scare-scenes, which wasn't like him. He was anxious about something and Cade's own anxiety was following suit.

Ethan yawned and stood. "Nah. I'd better hit the trail."

Brooks rose. "You sure?"

"Yep."

"I guess those sweaters aren't going to knit themselves, huh, Sheriff?"

Ethan reddened, obviously embarrassed about his not-so-secret knitting hobby.

"Oh, stop," said Samantha. "I think it's sweet." She looked at Ethan. "I *love* the sweater you made me."

Cade choked on a chuckle. He knew better. The green, yellow, and lavender-striped travesty made Samantha look like a punk-rock bumblebee. In private, she'd laughed good-naturedly about it and put the sweater in the bottom of her drawer, only wearing it when she knew the sheriff was coming over. Cade loved her for it.

"Thanks." Ethan donned his well-worn Smokey hat and dug in his pockets for his keys. "See you Thursday at Q-Balls?"

"You can count on it." Brooks stood and walked him to the door. Outside, the sky was darkening as rain continued to fall.

"You coming this week, Cade?" asked Ethan.

Cade still occasionally joined them for their weekly games of pool, but lately, he preferred to spend those evenings alone with Samantha. "I might," he said. "We'll see what's going on."

Ethan nodded, found his keys, and stepped onto the porch.

"Bring Sheila next time," Brooks said.

"Will do." Ethan trotted down the steps toward his red Wrangler, and Cade realized he was sad to see him go. He enjoyed the sheriff's company as much as Brooks did. The sheriff had become part of the family - almost a father figure, really. The parallels between Ethan and their own father weren't hard to see, the most obvious being that their dad had also been a cop.

"So now what?" Brooks asked. "I hear there's a Maisy Hart movie marathon running on the T&C Network."

While Cade was a big fan of classic horror movies, Brooks usually opted out, and again, Cade thought: *He doesn't want to be alone.* Usually Brooks went out to work on his truck or his bullet bike after dinner. Cade looked at Samantha and shrugged. "I'm game if you are."

"Sounds good to me," said Samantha. "I love Maisy Hart." She snuggled in close to Cade, who watched his brother closely.

Brooks sat down, found the movie, and zoned out again, his jaw flexing with tension. Something was definitely on the guy's mind; it wasn't just Cade's imagination.

Though Sheila wouldn't arrive for nearly an hour, Ethan was eager to get home. He couldn't stand sitting at the Colters' any longer, trying to focus on another movie. His mind was on overdrive anticipating the conversation he planned to have with his fiancée.

He made his way across town, windshield wipers slapping away the rain as the Wrangler's tires splashed through the wet streets. He wanted to take a shower and get into his civvies before Sheila arrived. Maybe even do something romantic - but nothing came to mind. *Don't overexert yourself, Hunter. You're not proposing - you already did that. You're just going to talk about setting a date. Take it easy.* But he was nervous, anyway.

He hung a quick right onto Frenchwood Lane, paying no mind to the stop sign and feeling just a little guilty about it. In the small, heavily-forested residential area, Ethan's two story cabin came into view.

And so did an unfamiliar car parked right in his driveway - a shiny Porsche that looked out of place in its humble surroundings, a gleaming renegade cherry in an apple pie.

The only man Ethan knew who might own such a machine was Michael Ward - he had an entire garage full of well-cared-for sports cars and mint-condition classics - but Ethan couldn't recall any fire-hydrant-red Porsche's among the collection. And Michael was still out of town.

Ethan pulled in beside the unexpected visitor. The car was empty. He got out and looked around. Across the street, he could see Mrs. Gelding staring out her window. She, too, was curious - but then, Gladiola Gelding was curious about everything. "Nosy old bat."

Bracing himself against the downpour, he trotted toward the porch and found his front door already unlocked. His hand instinctively moved to his Glock as he entered.

It took several moments to register what - and who - he was looking at.

A woman sat on his couch, a wadded tissue pressed to her face, tears dragging dark streaks of makeup down her cheeks. She looked up at him with red, swollen eyes.

"Sydney?"

His ex-wife stood and bumped into the coffee table, nearly knocking over the now half-empty bottle of Remy Martin he'd been saving for a special occasion. She made her stumbling way forward and fell into him, sobbing, the reek of booze surrounding her like a force field.

"What ... what are you *doing* here?"

"He left me!" Her voice cracked and trembled. "He *left* me, Ethan!" She broke into the braying, ugly tears of the utterly hopeless.

Ethan stepped back, his hands on her shoulders, looking at her. She hadn't aged a day since he'd last seen her - *Botox* - and he could tell by the way her eyes floated that she'd reached that unpredictable degree of intoxication that made all cops uneasy. "How did you get in?"

She sniffed. "I still have my *key*, of course."

"Of course." Ethan hadn't bothered to change the locks after the divorce. He'd seen no reason to do so.

Her pretty features crumpled. "And she's practically a *child*, Ethan!" She buried her face in his shoulder. "I can't believe he'd do this to me! I just can't *believe* it! It's judgment, that's what it is!" Her voice was going shrill. "Judgment for my sins! Why else would the Savior let this happen to me?"

Judgment? The Savior? Ethan's eyes slid to the dainty gold cross she wore on a chain at her throat. He'd almost forgotten she'd found the Lord and that for the last year or two of their marriage she'd been wavering precariously between healthy devotion to her church and full-on bone-rattling, snake-handling, holy-rolling. "Look, just slow down, and tell me what happened." He led her to the couch and steadied her into the seat. "Why don't we get something in your stomach?"

"I'm not hungry." She dabbed at her eyes with the corner of a tissue, then reached for the whiskey.

Ethan intervened, sliding it away. "I think you've had enough."

"Fine." Sydney huffed and leaned back into the couch. "That son of a bitch." Her bleary eyes darkened now. "I'll take him to the fucking cleaners! He won't get away with this!" She slammed a fist on the coffee table, then whimpered at the pain.

Ethan's mind reeled. Sheila would be here soon. What could he tell her? How would he explain this?

Sydney wept a moment, then looked at him, a tiny smile flickering at one corner of her smeared, puffy lips. "You look good, Ethan. Really good."

The suggestion in her tone settled the matter for him. "You can't stay here, Sydney. I've got-"

"But I don't have anywhere to *go*! I have no money, no nothing!"

"Then I'll put you up in a hotel for a few days-"

"Please, please, *please* don't kick me out. I'm so *scared*!"

As she brought the wadded tissue to her face and honked raucously, Ethan felt a deep stab of pity. "Look," he said. "I need to make a phone call. When I'm finished, you and I can talk about this. In the meantime, you need something to eat. There's plenty in the fridge and cupboards." *You already helped yourself to the liquor cabinet.* "Make yourself whatever you like. I'll be right back."

Sydney nodded, blew her nose, and collapsed into more sobs.

Ethan headed for the bedroom, concocting his story - *A headache? The flu?* Anything but the humiliating truth. *I'll cross that bridge when I get to it, I guess.* He dialed Sheila's cell.

She picked up on the second ring. Some bridges just came too damned fast.

"Hi, honey." Ethan slipped a little weakness into his voice. "I was wondering if we might cancel tonight. I'm not feeling well."

"Oh?"

"Yeah. I think it might be this bug that's been going around. I'm sorry I didn't tell you sooner but-"

"Ethan?"

"Yeah?"

"Are you sure it's a bug and not the red Porsche in your driveway?"

"Uh..." Ethan's throat turned dry. "Porsche?"

"I'm in your driveway, Ethan. I got off earlier than I expected and, um, there's a Porsche parked right next to your Wrangler. Are you aware of that?"

Ethan swallowed convulsively. "I, uh … I … well …" *Well, hell.* He sighed. "The truth is, well … I'm lying."

"You don't say."

Ethan was relieved to hear the smile in her voice. He spoke low. "It's my ex-wife. Sydney. She was here when I got home. Drunk. Apparently, she and her husband had a falling out."

"So why did you lie to me?" There was no accusation in her tone, just genuine curiosity.

"Well … that's what they always do in the movies."

Sheila laughed. "Do you need some help?"

"Yes. More than you know."

Another laugh. "I'll be right there."

3

THE FORGOTTEN AND FORSAKEN

As the rain continued its ferocious assault, night blanketed Crimson Cove. The streets were mostly emptied by the weather. On Main, in the downtown district, the town's single stoplight swayed in the wind, careening to and fro as if trying to snap free from its cable as it dutifully gave its futile commands.

Throughout the neighborhoods, lights in houses glowed and street lamps cast a ghostly pallor over the sidewalks. Aside from the pounding of rain and the wind whipping through the trees, Crimson Cove was silent. Even the wildlife had secluded itself to various shelters.

But just as the final sliver of sun sank behind the mountains, two pairs of eyes cracked wide open.

In the forest beyond Crimson Lake, in an old cavern where miners had prospected for gold over a century before, two of Gretchen VanTreese's finest, Jazminka and Scythe, came awake. It was here that they'd spent the past year and, for them, it was more than a hidden cavern - it was home.

The cave had been natural at one time, but the miners had expanded it, their picks and axes leaving the walls looking to Scythe as ribbed as a gigantic gray colon. The cave stretched about twenty feet deep before a rock slide cut it off and he often wondered if there were any bodies beyond it. He and Jazminka had regularly raided the campground by Crimson Lake and acquired air mattresses, sleeping bags, folding camp chairs and tables, blankets, and several lanterns. The lamps were strung across the low rounded ceiling on a wire and Scythe was eternally amused at Jazminka's refusal to duck, as if expecting them to raise themselves out of sheer respect.

By night, they hunted, feeding off only the lowliest of Crimson Cove residents - indigents, runaways, and sometimes, the prostitutes haunting Scarlet Street, the shady back alley that housed little more than a derelict car lot and a shut-up butcher shop where, on nights like tonight, the whores and the homeless alike took refuge.

Ah, the whores, thought Scythe. Rarely, when Jazminka's watchful eyes were not upon him, Scythe would sneak out of the cavern, slip away to Scarlet Street, and have his way with one of the women. But Jazminka wasn't easily eluded and it had been months since Scythe had gotten off. It was making him cranky.

When those low-class citizens were attacked - *or solicited* - it rarely caused so much as a blip on the radar of the law. But Crimson Cove was a small town and the well of the forgotten and forsaken was not an endless one, so many nights Jazminka and Scythe had been forced to survive on the blood of wildlife. They'd longed for the glory days when Gretchen was in charge and the blood flowed freely - and tonight, finally, they were going to bring those nights back; they were going to bring *Gretchen* back.

It was a stroke of pure luck that Michael Ward, who'd had his men keeping such watchful eyes on Crimson Lake, had left town. They'd learned of his absence last night when Scythe had been wandering the grounds of Eudemonia in search of a sleeping couple in one of the cabins rented out to tourists. It was risky, Scythe knew that - the vampires of Eudemonia hunted these grounds themselves, covertly taking sustenance from their sleeping guests by the cover of night. Scythe knew this because he'd watched them do it - that's where he got the idea. But he hadn't told Jazminka about that any more than he'd mentioned his secret visits to Scarlet Street. She would have skinned him alive - and likely made herself a nice new pair of boots out of his flesh - if she had known he'd been risking their safety.

But Scythe, tired of feeding on rabbits, squirrels, and even worse, the diseased, heroin-laden blood of Crimson Cove's underclass, had frequented Eudemonia's grounds anyway. And last night, just as he'd been working up the nerve to make an actual attack, he'd overheard a conversation between guests in one of the cabins.

The proprietor, the man told his wife, was out of town - as were several of his key employees. They weren't due back for another couple of days. Then, perhaps, the man went on, they could talk to someone who might give a shit about the mosquito problem. But the rest was of no interest to Scythe. He knew all he needed to know: Michael and his main lieutenants were gone. Gone! And that meant less eyes on Crimson Lake.

For the first time, he was glad Jazminka had demanded that they lie low - *'Eventually, they vill drop their guard,'* she'd said in her thick Slavic accent.

After hearing that Michael Ward was out of town, Scythe had sprinted back to Jazminka, and told her what he'd learned. With great caution, they'd made their way to Crimson Lake where, sure enough, no guards were posted. Then, without delay, they began their work. But the night was not on their side. By the time they'd finally located - then muscled - Gretchen's coffin from its watery depths, they'd had no time to do anything but smuggle their Mistress, still in her lead-lined box, under a deadfall and hurry back to the cavern before the sun made its deadly ascent above the eastern horizon.

But tonight, they had all the time they needed.

And finally, after what seemed an eternity, Scythe was going to get laid. That, more than anything else, was what he was looking forward to, and Vlad the Impaler, his inordinately large manhood, was joyous at the prospect as well.

Scythe smiled then looked at Jazminka, his dopey grin collapsing. "Are you ready, or what?"

"Gretchen vill need sustenance, first thing." Jazminka's voice, flat but full of iron intent, echoed through the cave. "Let us hunt."

"Can't we just unstake her first?"

Jazminka shook her head. "No. She vill need to feed."

"Where will we find enough for all three of us?"

"I do not know yet, but ve must. It vill take much time and much blood for Gretchen to recover."

Scythe thought about it, and agreed. Gretchen wouldn't be happy if they reanimated her only to let her starve. And he wanted Gretchen to be happy. *And horny.* Nothing worse than an unhappy Gretchen VanTreese - no one knew that better than Scythe. He made no argument as, together, he and Jazminka headed toward the forest, toward sustenance.

Ethan's Adam's apple bobbed. "Sydney ... this is Sheila, my, uh, fiancée."

Sydney blinked at Sheila with bleary, bloodshot eyes. *"Fiancée?"* She spoke it like a foreign word that she was trying out for the first time.

Sheila smiled and held out her hand. "Sheila Leventis. It's nice to meet you."

Sydney took her hand, her eyes flitting incredulously between Sheila and Ethan. "I ... I'm Sydney."

Ethan cleared his throat. "Why don't we all sit down and ... have some crackers or something." They sat - he and Sheila beside each other on the sofa and Sydney on the edge of the leather La-Z-Boy. On the coffee table stood a box of Ritz which Ethan slid pointedly toward Sydney. She ignored it and continued staring at Sheila. There was no malice in her eyes and for that, Sheila was glad. She wasn't sure how to go about handling jealous ex-wives. *Or even friendly ones.* For long, uncomfortable moments, Sheila and Ethan exchanged quick uncertain glances as Sydney continued to stare.

Then, with a sad smile, Sydney spoke. "Fiancée." Her features crumpled as a torrent of new tears came. "And you're *so* beautiful!" She buried her face in her hands and sobbed.

Sheila made her way over, put an uncertain hand on the woman's quivering shoulder.

Ethan sat forward, almost stood, then didn't. He looked stressed out and indecisive.

"You're so beautiful!" cried Sydney, "and I'm just old and frumpy and used up! I'm so old and ugly!"

With her perfectly-manicured bubblegum-pink nails and snug clothing stretched across her ample endowments, she looked neither old nor ugly. In fact, she was quite pretty, Sheila thought, even drunk and sobbing.

"It's no wonder I'm alone!"

"You're none of those things." Sheila crouched to level herself with her fiancée's ex-wife. "Why don't you tell us what happened and maybe we can help you figure this out."

Sydney blinked at her. "You really want to hear it?"

"Of course we do."

Without hesitation, Sydney launched into torrential and nearly incomprehensible narrative about coming home to find her husband, a man named Drake Doss, in bed with an aspiring Hollywood starlet named Misty. Misty's clothes were tossed out of the fifth-story apartment window - by Sydney - and somehow, hot wax from a burning bedside candle destroyed someone's hair weave, before the police were called and domestic disturbance charges were filed against Sydney. What followed included death-threats, a kitchen knife, a shredded feather pillow, and a custody battle over a Shih Tzu named Gloria. Apparently, Sydney's husband and his new lady friend were planning to get married, despite the fact that Sydney had yet to receive divorce papers, and having nowhere to go, she had wound up here at Ethan's, three hundred miles away. She'd arrived with nothing but what she wore, a small suitcase of God-knew-what, the Porsche, and apparently, high hopes of getting her ex-husband back.

Oddly, this last item didn't faze Sheila. She knew how Ethan felt about his ex-wife; Sheila was secure in their relationship, but she couldn't help feeling sorry for Ethan. Sydney had obviously cut him more deeply than Sheila had realized. He couldn't even bring himself to comfort the woman; he sat unmoving, watching her with icy suspicion.

As Sheila looked between the two of them - Sydney with her coiffed blond hair and glittering rings, bracelets, and earrings, and Ethan with his shadow of beard stubble, wearing a pair of loose-fitting gray sweats and an old blue t-shirt with tiny twin holes at the corner of the breast pocket - she couldn't imagine them together.

"I have nowhere to go." Sydney went on, wiping her nose. "I'm *homeless!* I'll end up on the streets! Oh, sweet, sweet Jesus! *Why?*" She rubbed the incongruous cross that hung on a delicate gold chain around her neck.

"Of course you won't be on the streets." Sheila gave Ethan a meaningful look. "I'm sure we can work something out."

Ethan caught Sheila's gaze and shook his head slowly back and forth. "Sheila? Can I talk to you in the kitchen?"

"I'll get you a glass of water," Sheila told the woman, then followed Ethan into the other room.

Alone now, Ethan raised his brows. "She can't stay here." His voice was low, nearly a growl.

"I don't know what else to do, Ethan. I guess she could stay at my place."

"It's not a matter of whose house she stays at. It's a matter of me not wanting that woman in our lives." His gray-blue eyes, which Sheila had always likened to a placid lake, were now a storm of thunder and fury, brooding like dangerous clouds. "She's like a whirlwind of drama - no, a fucking *tornado* of drama!"

"But how can we just throw her out? Like I said, she can stay at my-"

"It's not a good idea." Ethan leaned against the counter and rubbed his jaw, something he did when he was stressed. For a moment, the dry rasp of his fingers on his beard stubble was the only sound.

Sheila, too, was at a loss. "You told me yourself that she's an only child and both her parents are dead. Where is she supposed to go?"

"There are hotels and-"

"And what if her husband cuts off her credit cards? Can you pay the hotel fees, because I can't. It could take weeks, *months* even, for her to get a place of her own."

"Not our problem."

Sheila stared at him, surprised.

His mouth worked as if he were tasting unformed words. Finally, he said, "She'll try to ruin us, Sheila. She thought she could just waltz back into my life and I'd take her back. She still thinks that. You're just a bump in the road." He pushed off the counter and crossed his arms.

"I know that, but she'll realize soon enough that you aren't taking her back and then she'll be on her way. But until then … I think we have to help her, Ethan."

"Actually, we don't."

"She's terrified."

"She's drunk."

Sheila nodded and sighed. "And terrified. We can't just turn her away. It's not right."

"And what happens when she tries driving a wedge between us? Because she will. She's never been without a man, Sheila. She thinks she can't live without one. I know her. She'll try to come between us and-"

"I won't let that happen. *We* won't let that happen. I think we're strong enough to handle her, Ethan." She watched him. "Don't you?"

"Of course, but …" His words trailed off.

"Then we need to do the right thing. That doesn't mean being taken advantage of and it doesn't mean allowing her to stay indefinitely. It simply means we help her. We help her until she can figure something out. I can help her find work and a place of her own."

"No, no, no." Ethan ran his hand down his face. "You're already getting too involved, Sheila. There *must* be another way." He paused, his eyes lighting with a new idea. "Maybe Michael could put her up in one of the cabins at Eudemonia for a little while. Give her a discount, or let her work it off or something."

"Eudemonia?"

"There's no phone service there. She couldn't call us."

Sheila smiled. "But Michael's out of town."

Ethan slumped. "Right. The Biting Man Festival." He blew out a breath. He looked beaten down, exhausted.

"Until he gets back, our hands are tied." Sheila moved closer and touched his waist, looking up at him. "And who knows? Maybe her husband will take her back and none of this will amount to anything, anyway."

Ethan smirked. "Not if he has a good prenup and I'm sure he does. He won't take her back. Trust me."

"You don't know that, Ethan."

"Oh, yes, I do. And by the time she's done with us, I think you'll understand why I'm so sure of it." He paused, then sighed. "As soon as Michael gets back, I'll talk to him. And regardless of what he can or can't do for her, I'm getting her the hell out of here."

"That's reasonable."

Ethan looked at his fiancée, a crooked half-smile coming to his lips. "You're a better person than I am, Sheila."

"No, I'm not. I know you, Ethan. You would have done the right thing... eventually. All I did was speed up the process."

"I guess." He hesitated; something on his mind. "I suppose I'm just disappointed at the timing of all this. I, uh, wanted to talk to you about something tonight." He studied his hands, picked at his thumbnail.

"What is it?"

"Now isn't the right time." He tipped his head toward the living room. "For obvious reasons."

Sheila smiled at him. "Well, now you *have* to tell me."

He was silent a moment. "Well, I, uh, thought maybe it was time that we decided on a date for-"

Sydney appeared in the doorway. "I'm sorry. I don't mean to interrupt, but could I get that glass of water?" She sounded like an impatient restaurant patron. "I'm parched!"

Ethan raised his brows at Sheila - it was a look that she had no trouble interpreting: *'And so it begins...'*

Sheila stepped to the sink and poured a tall glass of water. The other woman took it with a hand that trembled a little too much to be genuine.

Ethan cleared his throat. "Sydney, you can stay in the guest bedroom tonight. We'll sort the rest out tomorrow."

Sydney widened her eyes "Oh, thank you so much! Thank you, both of you."

And when new tears spilled down her cheeks, tears of gratitude and relief, Sheila knew they'd made the right decision. She also knew that such decisions had consequences of their own. *But nothing we can't handle,* she thought as Ethan gave her an uncertain half-smile.

"And thank You, *Jesus,*" Sydney added, touching her delicate gold cross.

Ethan rolled his eyes.

4

UNSTAKE MY HEART

It was nearly two in the morning before Jazminka and Scythe returned to the woods near their cavern - and they didn't return alone. Accompanying them was a muscular nighttime grocery stocker named Rafe Santangelo; they'd found him leaving the local Peddler Puck's after his shift. While there was no telling whether or not he was actually Italian - though the name Santangelo suggested as much - he had the Latin good looks that Jazminka knew Gretchen would love. More importantly, he was big enough and strong enough to sustain Gretchen, who would be famished after nearly a year of inanimation. He would also, Jazminka thought, make a fine soldier.

Due to a generous dose of Scythe's venom, the man followed them through the woods without question or complaint, sticking close to Scythe and obeying his every command - a typical effect of the venom injection. On the long walk back, Scythe, who, after all these years, still got a juvenile kick out of controlling humans, occasionally gave the man ridiculous orders for his own amusement, cackling wildly as each command was obeyed - *'Hey, Santangelo, stand on your tiptoes and sing,* I feel pretty,' and *'Hey, Santangelo, bend over and kiss your own ass.'*

After Santangelo had nearly dislocated his own neck trying the latter, Jazminka had put a stop to Scythe's childish tricks. Now, Scythe followed behind her, sulking and silent, which was how Jazminka preferred him.

They came to the deadfall where Gretchen's coffin lay, strategically camouflaged by leaves and earth. The moon stared down at them like the milky slitted eye of a corpse, and from its position in the sky, Jazminka knew they had plenty of time to reanimate Gretchen and get enough blood into her to sustain her during the coming daylight hours.

"Should we take her to the cave first?" asked Scythe.

Though the deadfall was in the middle of the forest where Jazminka doubted any eye would see them, she nodded, thinking it best to play it safe.

Together, Scythe and Santangelo muscled the casket to the cavern where Jazminka lit the lanterns. Once settled, she stood over the coffin, the blood in her veins - the booze-laced blood of a transient - pumping hard as her excitement grew. At long last, Gretchen would be returned to her, and if Jazminka had been the type, she might have cried tears of tender joy.

But Jazminka was decidedly *not* the type for sentimental displays. "Open eet." Her clipped voice rang off the cavern walls.

As the men worked laboriously at the sealed casket, Jazminka's chest ached with anticipation until, finally, after what seemed decades, they managed it.

And there, embalmed by the dirty lake water that had filled the casket, lay Jazminka's Maker.

The putrefying body inside was scarcely recognizable. Gretchen's silvery-white hair floated around her face which now looked old and haggard. Her eyes were blessedly closed but she was grinning, her purple lips pulled back in a fixed grimace. The wooden stake protruding from her chest, from the crimson corset Jazminka had hand-crafted for Gretchen, jutted out like something obscene, something blasphemous. Her hands were curled into claws at her chest and she still wore the amethyst and onyx poison ring, though now it looked too large for her withered, knotted fingers.

The fishy smell of lake water and rot hit Jazminka like a brick wall and with a thin mewling sound she didn't know she was making, Jazminka thrust her arms into the water, hooked a hand behind her Maker's head, lifted her, and held her to her own breast for a moment, picking lake weeds and debris from the once-lustrous platinum hair. For a moment, she thought she might cry, indeed, for the face of Gretchen VanTreese was no longer beautiful. Now that face was sunken and purple-gray. The face of death.

Scythe stood at her side. "Jesus Christ. She looks fucking awful. Maybe we should just ... leave her alone and-"

Jazminka flashed her hard gaze on Scythe, who, she suspected, was only looking forward to their Mistress' return for one reason: sex. And now that Gretchen's looks had faded, Scythe had no interest. It infuriated Jazminka. "Do you vant to live like this for the rest of our existence, feeding from rabbits and chasing deer, and calling the drug-fueled blood of whores a treat? You are a traitor, and vhen Gretchen returns you vill be lucky if I do not tell her so!"

Scythe held up his hand. "I'm just saying, she might not be the Gretchen we remember." Beside him, Rafe Santangelo stood, taking in the scene before him. Only now did Jazminka realize the man's wide frightened eyes were a beautiful, jewel-toned blue - and this, she knew, would please Gretchen all the more. "You," she said to Scythe's staring supplicant. "Come here."

When he didn't move, Scythe gave him the same command. Santangelo obeyed this time, kneeling next to Jazminka without hesitation, keeping those pretty blue eyes averted from the sodden, deteriorating corpse.

Jazminka gripped the wooden stake that jutted from her Maker's heart - hating it, and hating the men who put it there - and with a scream born of fury, pulled hard.

The stake came free with a sick sucking sound, leaving behind a hollow, watery black hole.

Jazminka *was* weeping now, holding her Maker close, waiting, waiting.

Scythe stepped closer, his lip curled in disgust. "Nothing's happening."

"It vill," said Jazminka. "It vill." And she didn't care how long it took, she would not let go of Gretchen, not for an instant - not until she heard the wheezing gurgling sound of that first inhalation of breath.

But long moments passed and that sound never came.

Then, just as Jazminka began to lose hope, Gretchen VanTreese's sunken eyes popped open, milky-green and furious.

BROOKS' EYES SHOT OPEN, HIS NUDE BODY COVERED IN GREASY perspiration, and he jerked up in bed, out of breath. The rush of his own blood thrummed in his ears, roaring, blocking out all other sound. Twisting deep in his gut was a hunger. *The* hunger. The hunger for blood. And worse, the hunger for *her*. For Gretchen.

But it wasn't possible. It couldn't be. Gretchen was dead. She was ...

But what if...

No. There's no way!

And yet he knew it: Gretchen was alive. He recognized these feelings, the bone-deep craving: Brooks was back in mid-transition. Last year, Gretchen had injected enough venom into him to turn him, but before he'd consumed human blood - the final and irrevocable step in the transitioning process - Gretchen had been staked, and Brooks had reverted to full human status. Once a vampire drank human blood, the vampirism was permanent. Until then, the death of his or her Maker put the victim in retrograde - a kind of suspension between life and death. And Brooks had been in retrograde for the better part of a year, but now, it was clear that Gretchen had been reanimated. And that meant Brooks was one very tempting step from becoming a full vampire. Permanently. For all eternity.

He needed to get out of the cabin, away from Cade and Samantha, before he did something stupid, something he couldn't take back.

He stood, wiped sweat from his chest and abdomen with a t-shirt, then yanked on a pair of boxers. He glanced out the window, saw darkness. Saw the night. And he was entranced.

The night.

With no conscious thought, he left the bedroom, wanting to get to that darkness, to be surrounded by it, to be *in* it, to be part of it.

The night. He craved it deep in his bones, clear to his soul. He could smell the darkness itself, taste it on his tongue, feel it in his blood.

But in the hall, he was hit by the scent of something even more delicious. No, not *a* scent, but two scents: Blood. AB Negative - *Samantha* ... and even more tantalizing than that, Cade's blood, *Sire* blood.

Saliva exploded under Brooks' tongue, flooding his mouth, flooding it until strings of silvery drool hung from both corners. His stomach felt suddenly empty. No, not just empty, but *hollow*, as if his insides had been carved out, leaving a gaping hole within him.

He took a step down the hall, then paused. *No,* he told himself. *I have to stay away from them, I have to get away.*

But without knowing how he got there, he suddenly stood at his younger brother's bedroom door, heart hammering, fingertips trembling with need.

He could hear Cade and Samantha breathing within. He shouldn't have been able to, he knew that, but his senses had sharpened - just like before. Every sight, every sound, every taste and smell, a riot of sensation. *Just like before.*

With the silence of a moving shadow, Brooks opened the door and stared. Within, Cade and Samantha slept, unaware of anything but whatever dreams they were dreaming. Despite the dense darkness, Brooks could clearly make out their shapes and his eyes lit on two reflective orbs. Eyes. Sir Purrcival hissed and shot off the bed, disappearing beneath it where he began growling, low and steady. But Brooks wasn't interested in the cat.

The delectable scents of Cade and Samantha mingled, drawing him deeper into the room, seducing him, and now he stood over the bed, wrapped warm in the delicious aromas of skin, of blood, of breath, of *life*. He was breathing hard, noisily, and when Cade stirred, it snapped Brooks back, jolted him. He slipped into a shadow near the dresser.

Cade didn't wake, not fully, but the scare brought Brooks to his senses. He realized his younger brother wasn't safe from him. Neither was Samantha. The logical part of his mind - the *human* part - was momentarily clear. He wiped drool from his mouth, noting his own now-pointed incisors - and all doubt was shattered.

Gretchen VanTreese had returned.

Brooks remained for long moments, his mind racing, his hunger climbing, knowing he needed to leave, needed to get far away from Cade and Samantha before he hurt them, but his feet seemed immured in blocks of cement.

Finally, by sheer force of will, he left the bedroom and closed the door firmly behind him. Leaving the warm, delicious bodies within had taken more strength than he knew he had - and each step was another sharp pang of disappointment and regret - but the guilt, the fear, the *horror* of what he'd been contemplating, was stronger than all of it. What he needed, he knew, was distance. Distance from the cabin - distance from that unbearable bouquet of rare, exquisite blood.

Brooks ran, slamming out of the cabin.

He ran deep into the woods, unaware of the painful stab of dried pine needles under his pounding bare feet. He ran as hard as he could, giving himself to the night, letting it breathe its life into him.

He ran until his feet bled and his lungs burned. He ran until he forgot the hunger.

But no matter how hard, fast, or far he went, there was one thing he couldn't outrun: memories of Gretchen VanTreese. She wasn't just idly crossing his mind now. She was holding it down, screaming, demanding its full attention. '*My little tin soldier ... come to me.*' He heard her voice as clearly as if she'd whispered it in his ear, and he knew that if only he attuned himself to her with his new senses he could find her and that just being near her would make the pain stop, make the hunger stop.

But, no. He couldn't do that. *Wouldn't* do that. Gretchen was deadly. No one knew that better than he did. *Except maybe Cade.*

So he pushed her futilely from his mind, hating her, wishing her gone, and telling himself he would not go to her. Not tonight, not ever. No matter how strong the need to be with her became.

He just needed to keep running - running off the lust for blood and the lust for Gretchen, and only when he was slowed by the rise of the sun, only when Cade and Samantha were safe, would he set foot back in the cabin.

GRETCHEN - OR THE HIDEOUS THING THAT USED TO BE GRETCHEN - HAD already taken enough blood from Rafe Santangelo to leave the man looking woozy and weak, but it had done nothing to improve her appearance. Her stringy broken hair concealed some of her waxy complexion, but not enough of it. Her eyes, covered in cataracts, bulged from her emaciated face. Her skin was wrinkled and cracked, her lips thin and blue.

Pacing, wishing he hadn't so easily agreed to reanimate her, Scythe watched her feed from the other man, thinking she looked like a squirming albino leech fastened on the skin of an unwilling host.

Jazminka, like a tender lover, held back Gretchen's hair as their Maker suckled hungrily, sloppily, at Santangelo's arms and bared chest. And probably, thought Scythe, she *did* want to be Gretchen's lover. God knew *he'd* never been able to get the giant Slav to put out. Scythe shuddered, remembering how, just hours ago, he couldn't wait to nail Gretchen again. *What will I do if she wants me? I'm not fucking her while she looks like this*! He thought of how she'd always loved his donkey-sized schlong - it was the reason she'd turned him back in 1957, and it was she, in fact, who'd named it *Vlad the Impaler.*

He watched, grimacing, as the writhing white Gretchen-thing fastened her lipless mouth just above Santangelo's left nipple, bit, and suckled like a hungry piglet. It was enough to make Scythe's balls shrivel right up and go into hiding.

Finally, when Gretchen's host looked just about to lose consciousness, Jazminka gently pulled her Mistress away.

"He must rest now." Jazminka dabbed at the various wounds on the man's body with pieces of torn cloth, then pressed him onto his back.

Santangelo slept.

Gretchen stared blankly around, her horrible blind eyes filled with bewilderment and hunger. Then her milky gaze seemed to lock onto Scythe's and his breath caught; he couldn't bear to be locked in that awful stare and thought he might scream or run or both - but she didn't seem to have seen him. Her eyes moved on and she brought her knees up to her chest, cradling herself.

In the guttering candle flames, she *did* look a little better. This was not the Gretchen that Scythe - or anyone else - would have recognized, not by a long shot, but maybe there was hope that enough blood would bring her back to fuckability soon.

"Brooks Colter." The name cracked out of Gretchen's throat like dried leather, startling Scythe. "They'll know I've returned. We must ..."

"Shh." Jazminka wrapped a blanket around her Maker's shoulders.

Scythe hadn't even thought of Brooks Colter until now. Once Gretchen was unstaked, he would have reverted, alerting everyone - and most importantly, Michael Ward and his group - to her reanimation.

"They'll come for us," croaked Gretchen, the words sounding thick and jumbled in her dripping, blood-smeared mouth.

Jazminka put an arm around her. "Ve are safe right here until ve can get you better."

Gretchen then did the first Gretchen-like thing that Scythe had seen so far: she scowled and shrugged from the woman's touch. "And Emeric - is he ..."

"He disappeared vith the blood slaves in the underground," said Jazminka. "Ve have seen no sign of him since that night."

And Scythe was glad for that. The old vampire - old, meaning the dude looked like death's great-grandpa - had always given Scythe the creeps. In truth, Scythe had always been a little jealous of the man. Emeric had the sole distinction of having sway over Gretchen. He'd been her business manager, but there was more to it than that. Scythe could never quite figure it out. One thing was sure, though: the old bag of bones was in love with Gretchen, probably always had been. *Not enough to keep him from bolting with all the blood slaves when the shit got real, though.*

"Palo Alto," said Gretchen.

"Vhat?" asked Jazminka.

"Emeric. He'd go to Palo Alto. He has a mansion there. We need to find him and-"

"Shhh." Jazminka patted Gretchen's hand. "Later. There vill be time for that later."

Gretchen hesitated. "How long has it been? How long was I ..."

"About nine months," Scythe said. Though he'd begun to regret bringing her back, he still felt the need for her attention and couldn't help offering an answer. That was the drag about the bond between a vampire and his Maker - the need for approval from the one who'd turned you. That need was already awakening.

But Gretchen took no notice of Scythe. She reached up and touched her face, her spindly fingers ranging over the papery gray skin that stretched precariously across the sharp edges of her cheekbones. Then her fingers moved to the still-gaping hole in her chest where the stake had been planted and her dead eyes filled with something between anger and sadness. "They ... they did this to me. Michael ..."

And then, as if the activity had exhausted her, she dropped her hand and slumped, the glazed vacancy returning to her ruined face. Gretchen rolled onto her side and slept.

"It vill take some time," Jazminka told Scythe. "Much time."

Scythe wondered if they really would seek out Emeric - and hoped not. He didn't ask. What he did wonder aloud is if he and Jazminka ought to retrieve another supplicant tomorrow night; Gretchen had just about drained Santangelo. And Scythe didn't think he could stand looking at her like this any longer than necessary - she was fucking hideous.

Jazminka was nodding. "Yes. Tomorrow night, you go find more supplicants for her. I vill stay here vith her."

And while he was at it, Scythe decided, he'd pluck a cherry from the orchard of whores that was Scarlet Street. The prospect of finally getting laid again - and then the disappointment of realizing he would definitely *not* be getting laid - was more disappointment than he, or Vlad the Impaler, could take.

AT THE SAME TIME, ROGAN AND DANTE, THE EUDEMONIA GUARDS who'd been left in charge of security while Michael and Winter were at the Biting Man Festival, did the second of their twice-nightly rounds of Crimson Lake. Winter, their direct boss and head of Security, had given the assignment with the orders that Rogan and Dante keep a log and report back any suspicious activity around Crimson Lake, where the staked body of Gretchen VanTreese had been submerged nine months ago. Should they see anything unusual, they were to report it immediately to Winter at his hotel room in Eternity. Apparently, cell service in the strange little town was shoddy.

But, as Rogan had expected, they saw nothing out of order. As the headlights of the midnight black Jeep slashed through the rain and swept across the expanse of the lake and the area surrounding it, the place looked the same as it had for the last three seasons. Rogan had little doubt that Gretchen's surviving goons, Scythe and Jazminka - or *Muscles* and *The Amazon*, as he thought of them - had fled town and that Gretchen herself would forever remain inanimate in her coffin at the bottom of the lake.

"Nothin' doing, as usual." Silhouetted in the passengers seat, with his square jaw and short hair, Dante's head looked like a perfect square. He reached up, flipped on the interior light, and rummaged for a Hostess cupcake from his stash in the glove box.

Rogan sighed. "I don't know why you insist on eating those things." He tipped his head at the little chocolate cake. As vampires, they did not need to eat solid food. They *could* eat it, of course, but the vast majority of the undead, Rogan included, saw no point in indulging.

"I don't know why you care so much, *Mother.*"

"Because it makes you gassy. You eat one fucking cupcake and I can't stand being around you for the rest of the night."

Dante laughed, undeterred, devouring the treat in two bites. Around a mouthful of chocolate goo, he said, "Shit." He drew the word out: *Sheeyit,* and added, "These things are fucking delicious."

But Rogan knew better. Human food tasted like shit, indeed. He suspected the reason Dante insisted on continuing the habit was to keep some thread of his humanity intact which, Rogan supposed, he could understand. But the smell of the thing - lab-created chocolate and cream kept unnaturally moist by way of various chemicals and preservatives - was nauseating.

Dante reached for another cupcake. "Seriously, you should try one sometime." He tongued the creamy center with vulgar devotion. "Mmm. It takes the edge off the blood cravings, too." And Dante's cravings were insatiable. They always had been.

"No thanks. It's all yours, brother."

Though they weren't actual brothers, Rogan and Dante were the next best thing. Outwardly, they didn't have much in common, but the one bond that linked them together was the strongest possible kind.

War. That was what they had in common.

Dante had been turned in 1971, after coming home from Vietnam with a big dose of PTSD and a consequent drug problem that nearly killed him. Now, all that remained of his days in Nam was the ever-present silver peace symbol pinned to his jacket.

Being turned had saved Dante's life and the same could be said for Rogan, who'd been a pilot in Operation Neptune in 1944 and badly injured when his plane had been shot down. But as he wasted away in a Veteran's hospital, awaiting death, a strange man came to him - a man who claimed he could heal him.

So death had come to Rogan indeed, but not in the form he'd expected. Death came as vampirism, and it had saved his life. Or his *unlife,* as it were.

Because of their horrific histories, Rogan and Dante had become fast friends when they met many years later and now, the bond was unbreakable.

Dante popped the last of the cupcake, reached into the glove box for yet another, and Rogan suddenly thought he understood his friend's affinity for the nasty-ass things: Dante was an addict. In all things, he was an addict, and apparently, vampirism had not remedied the problem. If he were human, he'd be as wide as he was tall. And though not as tall as Rogan, Dante was an easy six-one.

After finishing cupcake number three, Dante slid his friend a sly grin. "And speaking of cravings, what say we go get some extra rations? It's not like anything's happening here." He tipped his head at the lake.

Normally, neither of the men were rule breakers, but with Michael and Winter out of town, Rogan couldn't see the harm in hitting an extra cabin - but only one. It was easy enough to slip in and out of the tiny cabins that dotted the property undetected. That was how Michael insisted that they live. Peacefully. And that didn't bother Rogan or anyone else. Before joining up with Michael, he'd been left to fend for himself - as all vampires were - trying to survive on the streets. "Sure. Let's do it." Rogan felt the slightest pang of guilt at this breach of conduct - the rule at Eudemonia was only about two pints of blood per week per vampire - but what Michael didn't know wouldn't hurt him. "Let's just not go too crazy. One extra ration. *One.*"

"You're such a pussy." Dante grinned.

"I guess that explains why you're always trying to fuck me, huh?"

Dante's wise-guy grin collapsed and, laughing, Rogan turned the Jeep around, its headlights slicing across a mountainside just beyond the forest.

A mountainside that, unbeknownst to either of them, housed a deep cavern where their enemy, Gretchen VanTreese, was taking her first breaths and speaking her first words in many, many months.

5

ANOTHER ONE FIGHTS THE LUST

A morning person by nature, Sheriff Ethan Hunter woke in time to see the sun outside his window as it began its dusty-pink ascent over the eastern mountains. The birds were chirping, and Sheila lay curled up next to him, her head on his chest. His bladder was screaming and he tried to slip away without disturbing her. No such luck.

"What time is it?" she mumbled.

Ethan glanced at the clock. "Six-thirty. You can sleep for a while." He made his way into the adjoining bathroom where he took the world's longest leak, and when he returned, Sheila was propped up on her elbows, a sleepy smile on her face.

"You could stay in bed for a while, too," she said.

"Better not. I want to get an early start on some paperwork." Ethan slipped off his boxers then pulled on a pair of jeans.

"You're the only guy I know who goes commando except in bed," said Sheila. She laughed. "Who does that?"

Ethan gave her a grin. "Me, that's who. You got a problem with it?"

Sheila laughed. "No problem here. I happen to think it's adorable. Weird, but adorable."

"Thanks." He pulled a t-shirt over his head. "You're pretty adorable yourself. Now, how about I go start breakfast?"

Just then, the smell of frying bacon wafted into the room and his smile faded. *Sydney.* He'd forgotten all about her. "Shit."

Sheila sat up. "Smells like she beat you to it. I figured she'd be too hungover to be out of bed before noon."

Ethan sighed as a clatter of pots and pans sounded from downstairs.

Sheila got out of bed and began dressing. "I didn't take her for a kitchen-type."

"She's not, trust me. I'll go make sure she doesn't burn the place down." He trotted down the stairs and found his ex-wife facing the stove, spatula in hand, her hips and buttocks sheathed in metallic pink stretch leggings. She was swaying to the low tune on the radio Ethan kept on the counter, and in her tiny top and matching pink heels, she looked like she was heading to an audition for *Grease.*

Ethan cleared his throat.

Sydney turned and flashed him a smile, her hair and makeup flawless despite the early hour.

"Morning," he grumbled.

"Good morning! I'm making breakfast! I remember how you like your eggs." She beamed at him proudly. "Over-medium."

"Look, Sydney, you don't have to-"

"But I *do*, Ethan. I appreciate your letting me stay last night and I'd like to make it up to you ... *somehow.*" Her smile turned suggestive.

Slowly, Ethan sat, hoping Sheila would hurry.

"I never was any good at cooking, I know, but it's the *least* I can do for you."

"Better make an extra set of over-medium, then," Ethan said.

"What?"

"Sheila's eggs. She likes them over-medium, like me." *Just a friendly reminder that my fiancée is upstairs.* "We have breakfast together every morning and-"

Sydney stiffened. "Over-medium. I get it." Her chipper tone dissolved as quickly as cotton candy in a rainstorm. She cracked two more eggs over the pan. "You know ... it never occurred to me you'd be involved with someone, let alone engaged."

Of course it hadn't occurred to her. Nothing that deviated from her own plans ever occurred to Sydney. "Well, I am. Happily."

She nodded. "I know. I can see that. Sheila's a wonderful woman." Her voice was flat, soulless.

"Yes, she is." Ethan felt like Alice down the rabbit hole. Never, not in his most deranged dreams, would he have imagined he'd be in this kitchen again with his ex-wife - *while she cooks me breakfast, no less* - talking about his fiancée upstairs. It went against the natural order of things. Ethan scratched his jaw, trying to sound casual. "So ... any developments on the, uh ... situation?"

"It's a little early, Ethan. Surely, you don't think I was up all night making new arrangements. I'm going to call my lawyer as soon as his office opens."

"You have a lawyer?"

"Not exactly, but I know a guy."

"Of course." Sydney always 'knew a guy.'

"I've got to do *something*, don't I?" She flipped the eggs. "So I'll have him make a call to Dickhead, put some pressure on, and at least get me enough money to live on until I can get a real lawyer."

Ethan had already forgotten the husband's actual name - *Dirk? Darwin?* "That sounds like a good plan."

"I guess. But it isn't your problem. I just wanted you to know I'm working on it," she sulked.

"Well, that's ... real good."

Sydney scooped runny eggs, blubbery bacon, and burnt toast onto plates. "So, where's Sheila?"

"Right here." Sheila entered in sweats and a t-shirt, her hair pulled back. She sat down. "You didn't have to cook for us."

And with all the abruptness of a flipped light switch, Sydney smiled, all plastic and lies. "Oh, but I *wanted* to." She thrust a plate at Sheila, then at Ethan, and sat down.

"Thank you." Sheila looked at the plate and flicked an uncertain glance at Ethan.

He shrugged.

"It smells wonderful, Sydney. Thank you." With a look, she prompted Ethan to say thank you, and with some reluctance, he did.

Then, just as he raised his fork, Sydney folded her hands and bowed her head. *Oh, Jesus, here we go.*

"Dear Heavenly Father," she began. "We thank thee-"

"No," said Ethan.

Sydney stopped, looked up at him. "No, what?" She blinked wide innocent eyes.

"You know the rule, Sydney. If you're going to-"

Rolling her eyes, Sydney cut him off. "*'If you're going to pray, do it in the other room or silently to yourself!'*" Her gruff impersonation of Ethan made him sound like a cantankerous retiree bitching at neighborhood kids for trampling his prize-winning flowers. Sydney brayed laughter at how hilarious she was then shot Ethan a smug look. "I guess some things just *never* change," she said.

"I guess not." Ethan held her gaze. *I won't be bulldozed in my own home*, he said with his eyes, and he knew she read the message loud and clear - but, true to form, Sydney had to have the last word.

She broke the stare and with a stubborn set of jaw that he remembered not-so-fondly, she poured herself a glass of orange juice and said, "You *do* realize, Ethan, that He's listening." You could hear the capital *H* in her voice as she referred to the big guy in the sky, and Ethan almost said he didn't give a damn if the Almighty had bugged the whole house and had the devil on speed-dial.

But he didn't. He'd engaged in her little power battle enough for one morning. Ignoring his ex-wife, he shrugged and, despite his vanished appetite, began to eat.

Sheila glanced awkwardly between them as she nibbled her eggs and toast, but Sydney had switched gears again, just as neat as you please. She gave Sheila the same song and dance she'd given Ethan, complete with saccharine tones: She appreciated their hospitality, she said. She wouldn't stay long, she promised. Just one more night, maybe.

Maybe.

Ethan had never hated a word as much as he hated that one now. He fumed in silence and tuned her out, wishing like hell that Michael Ward would get his ass back to Crimson Cove and agree to take the woman off his hands.

Ethan would pay him in blood - literally - if he had to.

"My head is killing me." Samantha rubbed her temples.

Cade set a couple ibuprofen tablets on the dining table next to her coffee. "Maybe you should stay home from work," he said, thinking she looked adorable in her little black Mary Jane shoes - his favorites.

"Thanks. I'll be fine." She downed the pills.

Cade, whose breakfast, as usual, was a giant-sized spoonful of peanut butter, sat at the table. "Are you sure you don't want to eat something?"

"No. Food sounds gross in the morning."

He never understood how anyone could skip breakfast. "That might be why you get headaches."

She shook her head. "I think it's because I didn't sleep well."

"You didn't? Why not?"

"You didn't hear Brooks coming and going at all hours?"

"Brooks went out last night?"

"A few times."

An icy finger of irrational fear touched Cade's spine as memories of the previous year came back to him. He shoved them aside, set the spoon of peanut butter down on a paper towel, and looked out the living room window. Brooks' truck was still in the driveway; he hadn't gone to work.

"What's wrong?"

"He's still here." Brooks never missed work. Never.

"Maybe he's not feeling well, either."

"I'll go check on him." As Cade headed down the hall, his heart thundered. He'd spent months after the staking of Gretchen dissecting his brother's behavior, worried that she might be revived.

Only recently had he begun to relax, and somehow that exacerbated his fear - as if letting down his guard made it all the more likely to happen. He knew what it meant for Brooks if she came back.

But he was being ridiculous. Overreacting.

Still, he had to be sure.

He approached Brooks' door, rapped lightly.

No answer.

"Brooks?" After more knocks, he stepped into the room.

And his stomach did a flip. On the bed lay his brother, pale, tangled in sheets and soaked in sweat. The room was redolent of that all-too-familiar death-smell - it was the same smell that had surrounded Brooks last year when he'd been in what Michael had called "suspension." Half-alive and half-dead, Brooks' human form was, in a sense, dying, and it would only continue - and worsen - until Brooks fed. Cade remembered it all too well.

Quickly, Cade shut the door. "Shit." He didn't know what to do. *Maybe I'm wrong.* It certainly wouldn't be the first time he'd imagined symptoms of the transition in his brother - and none had proved to be more than Cade's imagination. *Please be wrong, please be wrong.* But in his gut, in his *bones*, he knew the truth.

Should I tell Samantha? No, not until I know for sure.

Putting on a casual face he returned to the kitchen, grateful to find her slipping a jacket over her clean, white blouse. "You're going in?"

"Yeah. The caffeine and ibuprofen helped." She touched his hip and leaned in to kiss him. "How's Brooks?"

"Fine." Cade tried to keep his voice steady. "He just doesn't feel well."

Samantha grinned. "Must be going around."

"Must be."

"What time are you off tonight?"

Cade couldn't think. "Um, six. Yeah, six."

"Great. I'll see you then." She gave him another kiss and Cade watched her go.

And then he was alone in the house with Brooks, with nothing but the ghostly remnants of Samantha's perfume and his own thoughts.

His very dark thoughts. He sat on the edge of the sofa, muscles locked in tension, trying to bring the situation into focus.

I'm overreacting.

Then why had Brooks gone out last night? And why was he sleeping away the daylight in typical vampire-fashion?

He's not. He's just sick or something, like Samantha said.

And what about that smell - the smell of death, of rot?

And if this was really happening, how long could Brooks resist the hunger for blood?

Not long, he knew.

Cade shook his head. No. He was being irrational. It was like looking at a suspicious mole, waiting for it to change, certain that with every glance, it had grown. But in truth, nothing had changed. Yes, he was being irrational and to prove it to himself, all he had to do was go take another look.

So why couldn't he move?

"Fuck this." He headed down the hall, and tiptoed into his brother's room, heart hammering, ignoring the subtle smell of death.

He pulled the sheets down, fully revealing Brooks' pale face, the darkened circles under his eyes hanging like half-moons. And then, with quivering fingers, he touched his brother's face.

His skin was cold. Too cold. Vampire-cold. Then he probed between Brooks' lips. No incisors - *He hasn't fed yet, it's not permanent.*

But there was no doubt that Brooks was back in suspension - hovering between two worlds: the living and the undead.

Cade knew he had to do something but wasn't sure what. He felt like a rabbit trapped in a snare, waiting for the hunter to show. His mind raced. He needed to get hold of Michael - *not possible.* He had to deal with this himself for now. *I'm not safe. Samantha's not safe.*

He thought back to what Michael had told him: There were five ways to kill a vampire. The five S's: Sunlight, starvation, silver, staking, and severing of the head. But he couldn't kill his own brother, no way. *Maybe put a stake through his heart, wait for Michael, and when they had Brooks somewhere safe, they could remove it and bring him back.*

But Cade didn't think he could bring himself to do that, either.

Sunlight wouldn't work - there wasn't much, not enough to stop him, and even if there was, the effects of sunlight on vampires was fatal. But it wouldn't be fatal to someone in mid-transition, as Brooks was. Assuming he hadn't fed yet, anyway. *Maybe that's why he went out last night - to kill someone!* Cade clipped this thought off quick.

Starvation obviously didn't apply at this point and-

Silver. A mortal wound with something silver would kill a vampire. He didn't need to *kill* Brooks with it but he could certainly keep him at bay. Yes, silver. It was the only way.

But Cade didn't own *anything* silver.

He looked at the clock. It was time to leave for work - but there was no way he could go in, not today. He slipped from the bedroom, grabbed his phone, and punched in the number for the bookstore.

His boss, Dora Langley, answered on the first ring, her voice grating through the phone. "Langley's Literary Labyrinth, this is Dora."

"Hi, Dora, it's Cade." He tried to sound nasal. "I'm afraid I won't be able to come in today. It seems I've come down with something and-"

"Well, hell."

"I'm sorry, but I don't want to get you sick, too."

She sighed. "I guess today is as good a day as any. This weather is the shits and Christ knows it'll be slow!" She gave her raucous cackling cough-laugh that always made Cade worry she might up-and-out one of her lungs. "Of course, more than this rain, I blame that goddamned new occult shop. They're taking our business! Did you know that they have the *nerve* to sell books now? What the Christ business does an occult shop have selling books? Of course, they're occult books, but this town doesn't need another goddamned book seller!"

As she prattled on, something niggled at the back of Cade's mind, something to do with the occult shop.

"-and I'll tell you another thing, young man, it's hard enough trying to run a bookstore with all these goddamned e-readers everyone's using these days. Don't people have *enough* technology in their lives? It's as if-"

Occult shop. Yes! They might have something - they have *to!* "Look, Dora, I'm sorry, but I've got to go." He made his voice deep. "I'm very sick."

"Yes, yes, of course. You just get better, young man, and I'll see you tomorrow, assuming you're up for it, of course."

"I'll be there." Cade ended the call, locked up the cabin, and climbed into his blue Land Rover. As he drove, he called Pinetop's Garage and found out that Brooks hadn't called in this morning. Cade informed the mechanic, Chet, that his brother would be out for the day, but gave him no other information. Chet assured him that Pinetop's was in good hands.

Cade turned onto Main Street, heading to the new occult shop.

HIS SLEEP WAS DEEP, VERY DEEP, AND IN HIS FRAGMENTED, FEVERY dreams, Brooks lay with his Maker, Gretchen VanTreese, in the vast circular bed in the White Room, one of the many opulent chambers in the warren beneath The Crimson Corset nightclub. He stared up, and through the gauzy haze of the sheer white canopy, saw the massive chandelier with its dozen arms and dripping beads. Tall alabaster floor vases stood sentry on the stark white carpet - carpet that lay as thick and soft as a blanket of virgin snow. All around him was white. It dazzled the eye, entranced him.

"My little tin soldier." With her cool ivory hands, Gretchen traced invisible designs across Brooks' bare chest, her crimson nails standing out in stark relief against his skin, which was paler now - vampire-white. "How I've missed you." The sound of her voice was like a balm, a liquid, silvery balm that soothed the burn of his soul. She raised her head, penetrating the deepest places within him with heart-stopping emerald eyes. "This is where you belong now. You know that, don't you?"

"Yes. This is where I belong." The words didn't seem to come from his own lips, but they were the right words, so right.

"Soon, my lover. Soon." She gave him a red smile and lay her head down on his chest, her silken white hair spilling over him, claiming him, owning him.

"Beautiful," she whispered. "You were always so beautiful." She began laying cold, velvet kisses on his skin, first around the hollow of his throat, then down, around his nipples, then lower, lower, past his navel, and lower still.

She took him in her mouth then, clamping down on him like a familiar and oddly cool sheath. It was bliss.

Brooks closed his eyes and let it happen. He knew he should stop her, knew she was dangerous, but he hadn't the energy to fight it. Even in his dreams, he was tired. Tired, and so very, very hungry.

ANCIENT WAYS WAS ONE OF THE FALSE-FRONTED OLD WEST BUILDINGS lining the tourist-centric downtown district. Wedged between *Handy Dan's Tool Supply Shop* and *Poise and Ivy Clothing*, Cade might have missed it but for the bright red *NOW OPEN FOR BUSINESS!* announcement painted on the window. He parked and headed inside where he was met with a discordant jangle of bells that set off his already wire-tight nerves.

The place was a cluttered, cramped mishmash of candles, crystals, organic oils, dried herbs, books, t-shirts, and figurines - mostly little black cats in witch hats.

It looks like a witch exploded in here. His gaze roved the room but he didn't see anything that would help him - unless of course, he was looking to cast a spell on his brother. A heavy, sinking feeling dropped in his gut.

A woman breezed in from a back room, posting herself behind a vast glass counter. "Welcome to Ancient Ways. Is there anything I can help you with?" She smiled toothily, her dry wisps of frizzled gray hair escaping the purple sun-and-moon scarf on her head to tangle in her massive silver hoop-earrings.

"I, uh ..." Cade wasn't even sure what he was looking for.

The woman swished toward him, gauzy black skirts whispering on the hardwood floor. "Eliza. Eliza Heimberger. It's a pleasure to meet you." She held out a bony hand covered in chunky gemstone rings.

Cade shook it and introduced himself.

In a voice that reminded him of a latter-day Lucille Ball, Eliza prattled on for some time, pointing out - and describing in vast, crawling detail - the items she sold and their many uses. Everything from love spells to cold remedies was right at Cade's fingertips.

Eventually, he had to cut the woman off. "I was wondering if you had any ... silver. Real silver."

"Silver?" Eliza's lips tightened like a drawstring purse. "As in ... jewelry?"

Cade felt like an idiot. "Not exactly. I was thinking ... something more like ... a weapon, maybe?" He really wished he'd planned this out better.

"Weapon?" She scowled. "I don't sell silver bullets if that's what you're getting at. I disapprove of guns."

"No, not bullets. I don't even have a gun." His words were hurried as he over-explained. "I was thinking more along the lines of-"

"Ah." Eliza nodded sagely. "Something for your altar."

"My ... altar?"

"Athames." She brushed past him toward the glass counter. "As it happens, we have several. What kind of witch would I be without them?" She gave a gravelly chuckle.

Cade followed and stared down at a modest row of daggers, some with black handles, others with wood, and one that appeared to be made entirely of bone. *Creepy.*

Eliza opened the glass case and brandished a wooden-handled six-inch blade. "This is a popular one. I own this one. It's great for all your ritual and magickal needs and it comes with its own leather sheath which-"

"Is it real silver?"

"Well, not entirely." She frowned. "But I do have one that's silver plated." She replaced the dagger and removed another one, a slightly longer one with a large crossguard that sported a little silver wasp. "This is a nine-inch medieval athame, silver-plated with an onyx handle. It runs a little more than the others, but it's a real beauty, isn't it?" She delicately turned it this way and that, the Vanna White of wicked witchery.

"You don't have any that are pure silver?"

Eliza hesitated. "No. I'm not even sure they make-"

"I'll take this one, then. How much?"

She considered, named a price that was just shy of outrageous, then quickly added, "It's a col-lect-i-ble." With a sharp-nailed, swollen-knuckled hand, she tapped out each syllable on the onyx handle for emphasis. "The sheath alone is a work of art - also silver-plated. And the wasp, well, just look at the detail. That's pure silver."

Cade glanced down at the tips of her black old-lady shoes which pointed out from under her skirt. When he hesitated, she continued, "And all first-time customers get ten percent off." She grinned and handed him the dagger.

He held it, turning it over in his hands, feeling a quiet dread needling its way into the hollows of his bones. "That'll be fine." He didn't have time to dicker with the woman. He also planned to stop at the local religious supply shop, *The Immaculate Connection,* and pick up a few holy items before heading home. He handed the knife back and reached for his wallet, sliding out his credit card.

Eliza grinned and rang him up. As she wrapped his purchase, very slowly, in a coat of delicate black tissue paper she told him, also very slowly, about her recent move from a town called Shadow Springs where, apparently, she'd had no luck getting her business running. Crimson Cove, she said, was a much better place for an occult business - the tourists and all that.

At last, she put the purchase in a black paper sack that screamed *Ancient Ways* in gold gothic letters. By the time she handed him the bag, Cade had spent the better part of an hour in the little shop. He wasn't too worried that Brooks would wake - when the same thing had happened last year, his brother spent most of the day sleeping. But in his current state, and with the stormy, sunless sky, Brooks *could* function in the day, and Cade wanted to be there if he woke. What he'd do exactly, he didn't yet know.

SAMANTHA COULD TAKE IT NO LONGER. THE OVERHEAD LIBRARY LIGHTS stabbed her eyes like icepicks. Her left temple throbbed and if she didn't get home and lie down soon, the nausea would begin.

It was a slow day at Crimson Cove Library - every day was a slow day here - and though she'd only put in just over an hour, she couldn't punish herself further.

She finished shelving a stack of books and called out to Mary Considine, head librarian.

From the other side of the wooden shelving, she appeared. Mary was a wisp of a woman with hypochondriacal tendencies and a surprisingly pretty face behind Coke-bottle glasses. "Yes?"

"If you wouldn't mind, I'd like to take the rest of the day off. I've got a terrible headache."

"Of course." Mary studied Samantha, undoubtedly already feeling a headache of her own coming on. "Lila and I will be fine." More intense staring. "How bad is it?"

"Pretty bad. But it'll pass. I just need to lie down before it turns into a full-blown migraine."

"Do you need Excedrin? I've got some in my purse." The only thing Mary Considine loved more than dispensing medication - she had pills for every imaginable ailment - was making diagnoses. To prove it, she continued, "Perhaps it's a sinus infection, or a head cold. Lack of sleep will do it, too." She lowered her voice even more. "But I sometimes get the worst migraines when I'm on my monthly. Are you-"

Samantha cut across the other woman's words. "It'll be fine, really. I just need to sleep."

"Well, then I won't keep you. I hope you feel better."

"Thanks, Mary." For all her quirks, she was a sweet woman.

Samantha gathered her things and headed out into the dark, dreary day, followed by the fretful eyes of Mary Considine, who was no doubt, at this moment, already imagining worst-case health scenarios in her head - tumors, Anthrax poisoning, brain cancer, or perhaps a new government-created virus unleashed upon the unsuspecting public for the purpose of population control.

IN HIS DREAM, GRETCHEN WHISPERED SOMETHING INTO BROOKS' EAR and though he couldn't recall her words upon waking, he knew it had been important. A command - something she wanted him to do, something she said he was *ready* to do. And Brooks did feel ready.

But ready for what?

Blearily blinking against the gray daylight that peeked through the blinds, he lay in bed, trying to remember. But for the life of him, he couldn't. All he knew now was that he was hungry. Starving.

But the thought of going into the kitchen and searching out something to eat made his stomach shrivel up. Because it wasn't food he wanted. It was-

He heard the click of the lock in the front door, then the *snick* of the door closing. Footsteps crossed the living room. A pill bottle rattled in the kitchen. It was odd, he realized, that he could even make out the sounds of someone swallowing water from this distance. Odd, too, that he knew it was Samantha. He could detect the vague scent of her perfume - *Lavande d'Amour* - and, if he concentrated, even the clean, soft sweetness of her shampoo. Her skin. And ...

Her blood. Sweet and coppery, hot and delicious.

Almost as good as Cade's.

Throwing off the sheets, Brooks sat up, breathing hard. He remembered last night - the dreams, the hunger - and going into the woods, trying to outrun the bloodlust. But it had followed him, screaming at him and goading him, making him ache with greedy hunger.

He got out of bed on trembling legs weakened by need, pulled on a t-shirt and a pair of boxers. *I need to get out of this house - away from that smell.* A quiet, almost entirely subdued part of his mind flickered across tasks of his everyday life - *I should shower, get dressed ... and work.*

Yes, I should be at work - but the main part of him, the *hungry* part, squashed those things like size-twelve sneakers crushing sugar ants.

His mouth watered and his blood turned hot. He moved to the closed bedroom door, hand poised over the knob, bathing in the delectable scent that crept into the room. It was then that he remembered what Gretchen had commanded him in his dream: *'Join me. Forever. It is time.'* And he knew what that really meant: *Drink. Kill.*

Yet some part of him refused to move. *I can't. I won't!*

But then, as Samantha made her way toward the bathroom at the end of the hall, her scent grew stronger, stronger, so strong that Brooks squeezed his eyes shut, forcing out a single tear; it slipped down his cheek and crashed on the back of his hand, firmly on the knob, tense and poised to twist.

That tear held his whole universe, his aching need, everything that he was. And what he was, he now knew, was a vampire. A vampire that no longer needed to live torn between two worlds.

It was what he'd been born to be and he no longer had the strength to fight it.

ARMED NOW WITH A ROSARY AND A POCKETFUL OF SILVER SAINT medallions to go along with the silver-plated dagger, Cade hopped into the Land Rover and left *The Immaculate Connection*, where he'd been waylaid even further by a shortness of staff and the slowest-moving salesperson in all of Crimson Cove.

He was in a near panic now; the rain seemed a bad omen, the thunder a mortal warning. Even the radio - Katrina and the Waves' *Walking on Sunshine* - seemed to have dark meaning.

As he powered the Land Rover through the rain-sodden streets, his mind flitted from topic to topic like a fly at a picnic:

He needed to tell Samantha everything when she got home from work. He needed to tell Michael Ward, too.

Brooks is a vampire and Gretchen is back.

That lady, Eliza, totally overcharged me on the dagger.

Brooks is a vampire and Gretchen is back.

Shut up, Katrina and the Waves, and sing about something that fucking matters!

Brooks is a vampire and Gretchen is back.

Brooks is a vampire and Gretchen is back!

He reached over, pulled the silver dagger from its bag, unsheathed it, and held it tightly by the hilt, comforted by the weight of it in his hand. Unconsciously, he stroked the little silver wasp with his thumb.

AT THAT MOMENT, IN A DILAPIDATED CASITA ON THE OUTSKIRTS OF Santa Fe, the woman in black opened her eyes.

6

CONSUMMATION

Brooks stepped from his bedroom just as Samantha disappeared into the bathroom. He was at the door seconds after she closed it, his hand reaching for the knob. Then he heard a low, menacing sound.

Sir Purrcival.

The cat crouched at the end of the hall, ears pinned, staring at Brooks, eyes glittering with hatred. That quavering, savage sound continued deep in his throat as he slunk closer; Brooks scarcely recognized him.

Then, with a hiss and a yowl, Purrcy lunged at Brooks' leg, latched on, and clawed his way up his body. Brooks jerked back, both arms trying to fight him off, but the cat's claws hooked deep into his chest and shoulders, his fangs sinking painfully into Brooks' neck. Brooks tried to yank him loose but couldn't; Sir Purrcival was wrapped around his throat, fastened like Velcro, claws sinking into skin like hot needles.

Tufts of fur flew as Brooks thrashed at Purrcy, trying to get hold of enough flesh to fling the screeching creature off. At last, he found the scruff of his neck and ripped him away, hurling him down the hall.

The cat hit the floor on all fours and hissed, that poisonous hate flashing in his gold-green eyes before he darted away.

Brooks felt warm blood running over his arms and chest. He looked down at himself. His t-shirt was torn. His arms and chest, even his legs, were a network of weeping bites and cuts.

"Fucking cat," he said through clenched teeth.

The bathroom door flew open. "What's-" Samantha stood before him, her eyes wide. "Are you okay? What happened? I heard..."

But Brooks didn't hear what she was saying. He was consumed by the scent of her blood. His hunger, a low, flickering flame, now roared to a blaze.

Samantha stared at Brooks, startled. He was breathing hard and his shirt and boxer shorts were slashed and tattered. Runnels of blood ran down his arms, his hands, and dripped onto the carpet. A crisscross of cruel cuts covered his throat and chest and she could see puncture wounds, tiny holes weeping blood, at the base of his neck.

He was hurt and Samantha's instinct was to help him, but something stopped her.

It was his eyes, wide, feral, and unnaturally pale.

"Brooks?" Her voice brittle and dry as an autumn leaf, she stepped back, her hand feeling for the bathroom door behind her.

She had time to think, *Vampire!* before Brooks loosed a bone-shattering cry and lunged.

Samantha swung the door shut, using it as a shield. Brooks slammed into it and it crashed open, knocking Samantha back. She flew, hit the tile floor, smacking her head on the hard surface of the bathtub. "No!" And Brooks was on her, fingers digging into her arms, teeth gnashing just inches from her face. She pistoned her knee up, hit him in the balls hard enough to break something.

Brooks screeched in pain and fury. She kneed him again, harder this time, then shoved him off. He rolled onto his side, whimpering, hands between his legs. Samantha shot up, ran past him, out of the bathroom, down the hall, toward the front door, her only thought, *Daytime! Get into the sun!* She flew out onto the porch and half-fell down the stairs, grappling for the wooden railing, legs splaying as her ass hit the bottom step with a spine-jarring crack.

But there was no sun outside, only gray sky.

She glanced at her car in the driveway. *No good!* The keys were inside the house.

In the instant it took her to right herself, she heard the thundering footsteps behind her, the low growl of rage.

She didn't look back. She ran, darting beyond the cabin into the woods. She ran, wishing she could scream for help, but unable to catch her breath. She ran, ignoring the pain in her head, the agony of her screaming, injured tailbone. She ran, darting past trees, hopping bushes, and willing her feet to move - *to move!* - as the terrible sounds of Brooks closing in grew closer, closer.

And then, suddenly, there was no sound at all. Brooks lunged through the air and a hundred and ninety pounds of blood-hungry vampire hit Samantha like a truck, knocking her down.

She clawed at the earth, tried dragging herself out from under him. Brooks bit her shoulder, sinking blunt teeth into her skin as his machine-like jaws closed and crunched, gnashing and tearing at flesh and tendon.

Finally, Samantha found her voice and screamed.

WHEN CADE PULLED UP TO THE CABIN, A NEW COLD CREPT OVER HIM, seeping into him. His heart began to hammer. "No. No, no, no." Samantha's Civic was in the drive, and the cabin's front door yawned open. He brought the Land Rover to a hard stop and, clutching the silver dagger, hopped out and darted up the steps into the house.

"Samantha?" He looked wildly around. *"Samantha?"*

No answer. He headed down the hall.

"Brooks?"

Nothing.

He flung doors open, found only empty rooms.

A menacing growl sounded from somewhere. Cade returned to the living room and saw Purrcy's eyes glittering wide and terrified beneath the sofa.

"Brooks?" he called. "Samantha?" His throat as dry as if he'd swallowed a bucket of sand, he went to the kitchen. Nothing. The only thing here was a smell - not the death-smell of vampires but a new, sickish yellow smell. He realized it was the smell of his own terror.

And then he heard the scream - *Samantha's scream!* - from outside.

Cade exploded into motion, darting out of the cabin and into the woods, the silver dagger tight in his fist.

CROUCHED OVER AND FEEDING FROM THE LIFELESS BODY OF SAMANTHA Corbett, Brooks raised his head. The walls of his stomach began to contract in a strange and pleasant-painful way. He stood, feeling all the muscles in his legs tighten and bunch as they brought him upright. The movement was like silk. He could even feel his veins and arteries expanding and compressing, his cells flickering with new life. For a moment, these sensations were Brooks' whole universe. It was wonderful, almost sexual.

But a violent muscle spasm soon seized him. He lost control of his body and fell forward, arms braced in front of him. A cramp, like a hot spike through his abdomen, squeezed his guts and brought everything in his stomach up - blood, bile, and something rank and black, something he knew he hadn't eaten. Then more pain, the mother of all pain, shot through his head, a steel-jawed trap slamming shut on his skull. Brooks screamed, hands at the sides of his head. He fell over tightening himself into the fetal position.

Slowly, the pain ebbed.

Breathing came hard.

Harder.

And then not at all.

The world turned off.

UNREALITY.

Cade brought himself to a screeching halt near a vast redwood. Unable to process what he saw, his mind digested the scene in sips, flashes, and blinks, creating an unintelligible smear.

Brooks sprawled ten yards away, lifeless in torn, bloody clothes. He lay facing Cade, his staring eyes blank, unseeing, as rain washed blood from him in crimson rivers.

A few feet from him lay another mangled heap.

Red hair.

White shirt.

Blue skirt.

And the little black Mary Janes.

Slowly, Cade began to make sense of what he was seeing - *No, it can't be* - and he was gutted, as if someone had sliced open his stomach and let his insides spill out. Shock had him in an unyielding grip and he just stood there, rooted to the forest floor as surely as the giant redwoods surrounding him.

WHEN BROOKS CAME TO, HE HAD NO SENSE OF HOW MUCH TIME HAD passed. He blinked. His skin began to buzz and hum, and his already heightened senses sharpened enough now that he could smell the water of the lake. Unable to move anything but his eyes, he glanced toward the sky. Though charcoaled by thick, dark clouds, the light scorched his corneas.

But the hunger, that vicious, angry need, was satisfied at last. He became aware of a throbbing ache in his teeth. He flicked his tongue over the new, cruel incisors. His body had changed and so had his mind; a new intelligence overtook him, fusing with his previous consciousness, making him new, making him *whole*. He was all senses

THE SILVER DAGGER

and instinct, and without having to think about it he knew what he was: *Vampire*.

Complete.

Forever.

He got unsteadily to his feet - *my new feet* - and when his gaze lit on the massacred body on the ground, the other part of him, the human part, came to, and reality, jagged and cold, broke over him like an icy, black wave.

What have I done? Oh, God, what have I done? He began to tremble. He became conscious of the slick warmth on his hands, arms, and mouth and, staring down at the mutilated corpse, he let out a thin, manic cry.

Samantha! Her eyes were open, her face the shade of candle wax. Her throat was a raw, mangled mess, and scratches covered her arms and her chest where he'd ripped her shirt. "No, no, no, no, no!" The word dominoed from his lips as he stumbled back, away from the body, away from what he'd done. *I killed her. I killed her. I killed her, I KILLED HER!*

KILLEDHERKILLEDHERKILLEDHER! His mind rocked and spiraled, his brain filled with spun glass. He slapped hands to his ears, trying to block it out, block all of it out. A desperate need to get away - away from the forest and the sun, away from of his mind, his own skin - pierced his bones and he looked wildly around for some kind of escape.

Then Brooks detected a new scent.

The Sire.

"Cade?"

THE SOUND OF HIS BROTHER'S VOICE BROKE A DAM INSIDE CADE. Molten fury pumped through his veins, poisoning his heart and mind. The bitterness of battery acid filled his mouth and Cade loosed a furious sound - an unearthly sound - and charged, the silver dagger held high, ready to strike and slash and stab and tear. And kill.

For a moment, Brooks just stood there, eyes wide. Then, suddenly, he shot into motion.

But it was too late.

Propelled by blind, unbridled fury, Cade collided into his brother. They hit the wet earth and Cade pinned Brooks, a knee on either side of him, and with the speed of a jackhammer, the silver dagger rose and fell, rose and fell, as shrieks of fury tore from Cade's throat.

Brooks writhed beneath him, twisting and turning, dodging most of the blows.

But not all of them.

The blade glanced across the flesh just above Brooks' right eye, slicing up and into his hairline. The silver hissed, burning his skin, and the smell of smoke and burnt flesh was immediate. Brooks screamed in agony as the silver did its work, then managed to knock the knife from his brother's hands.

But that still left Cade with two weapons: his fists. He brought both down hard on his brother's face, pummeling, battering, pounding.

Then, with stunning strength, Brooks shoved him off, flung him away.

Cade flew back and hit the ground, tasting wet, rotten earth as his face smacked the mud. For a moment, the lights flickered on and off and he teetered on unconsciousness, certain the dark nothingness was going to win. But it didn't. He willed the world back, blinking rapidly, trying to bring it into focus.

Within his reach, the silver dagger lay in the mud. He grabbed it, pushed himself onto his hands and knees, tried to bring air into his battered lungs. On unsteady legs, he stood and turned to face his brother.

But Brooks was gone.

Cade whirled, eyes questing.

No Brooks.

Cade screamed. Cursed. Called his brother out.

But he was alone. Alone with Samantha. With what was left of her.

He looked down at her torn body and stepped closer. Tears sprang and spilled.

She was dead.

Dead.

Cade dropped to his knees and, sobbing, pulled her cold, broken body into his arms.

7

BACK IN BLACK

*V*isions:
    Trees. A forest.
Rain.
A small, white-pine cabin.
And blood. So much blood and violence.
Death.
And that was all.

But there was no doubt now: the silver dagger - her athame - was in motion.

The black figure in the upright chair opened her eyes and looked down. Scurrying around her feet, rats nibbled at her long skirts. Spiders, some of them long-dead, had spun silken webs over the wooden chair where she sat, across her netted black veil, and in her hair. Dust had settled over her shoes and on her dress; a thick layer of it coated the backs of her smooth, porcelain hands.

It must have been ages since she'd moved. There had been no need.

But now she reached down and snatched a rat from the floor. It squealed in fear as she raised it to her lips, then in pain as she bit into its hide. The blood did its work immediately, moving through her, bringing her awake.

And for the first time in a long, long time, a light came on in the eyes of the woman within that little casita on the outskirts of Santa Fe.

The woman in black was coming back.

8

UNCOMFORTABLY NUMB

The real world was suspended. Floating just beyond the rim of awareness, Cade was in a daze, unable to reason. In the hours he spent with Samantha's torn, limp body - the longest, grayest hours of his life - he'd alternated between holding her, talking to her, lying down beside her in the rain, and simply blanking out, at times wandering circles around her, muttering formless words he'd have no memory of ever speaking. At one point, when his mind was a little clearer, he'd gone to the cabin and brought back a blanket to cover her.

But it felt dirty, as if by covering her up, he was accepting that she was dead, and he had not - *would* not - accept that.

Twice he'd removed the blanket, taken her back into his arms, and wept fresh tears, his mind floating away again like a balloon on the wind, and both times, he expected her to come back, to smile up at him and wrap her arms around his neck.

But she never did, and Cade would realize all over again that she was dead.

Finally, he lay down, pulling Samantha's cold rag-doll body close. He kissed her mouth softly, as if he were in a fairy tale and this could break the spell and bring her back - but nothing changed. Still weeping and covered in her blood, Cade began to doze off.

Then, just as he was about to slip into sleep, he remembered: *Samantha might come back as a vampire!*

But no. That wasn't right. Only now, after his first kill, would Brooks have the venom to turn anyone. And he lost her all over again. It was like being stabbed in the gut with an icicle.

Thoughts of his brother swirled black and red, and each time Cade remembered Brooks in the forest covered in blood - *Samantha's blood* - the agony spread out, invading Cade's cells like a cancer. He wanted his brother to come back. *So I can kill him.*

As the rain turned to a mist and the cloud-covered sun moved farther west, Cade once again covered Samantha and headed back to the cabin, hating that he was leaving her, but doing it anyway because the day had grown cold, so cold it soaked into his bones and made him hurt. He knew he needed to think and he couldn't think out here. As he walked, his breath was shallow, his lips and fingertips tingled, and his heart thudded an irregular defeated rhythm.

He had no memory of making it to the cabin or sitting on the couch but when Purrcy appeared and settled into his lap, Cade realized he'd come home.

And still, he did not move. The soft tick of the clock above of the mantle went unheard, as did the patter against the windows as the rain began pelting the cabin again. He didn't register his wet, bloody clothes sticking to his skin like a coat of paint, or that his feet in the rain-soaked shoes had gone so cold his toes ached.

It was his phone that brought him back. It buzzed in his pocket. He pulled it out and stared at it absently. When the caller's identity sunk in, he answered, said *Hello* around a thick tongue that was still numb with shock.

"It's Ethan. I was just wondering if either of you boys had any use for a tool set. Old Herbert Hindley's kids came and took what they wanted, said I could keep the tools, but I don't have any use for them. I've got too many of my own as it is."

Cade tried to untangle what the sheriff was saying. He couldn't.

Thoughts tumbled around his mind like heavy wet clothes in a dryer. Finally, he opened his mouth, tried to find the words, any words, to describe what had happened.

"Dead," was the only one that came.

Ethan hesitated. "Come again?"

"Dead." The word squeaked from his dry throat thin and ugly, a vulgarity. "She's dead. Samantha's dead." The truth leaked from his lips like something poisonous, something with a thousand spidery legs, and once he'd said it, it couldn't be unsaid. Now it was real. And now he had to face it all over again. And accept it.

But no, he couldn't accept it.

He *wouldn't*.

If Cade had learned anything since moving to Crimson Cove, it was that death was not what it seemed. There were ways around death.

ON ETHAN'S ORDERS, CADE WAS TO REMAIN IN THE HOUSE WITH ONE OF the deputies while he, Ethan, examined the crime scene. The deputy, Ryan Closter, was broad-shouldered and broad-faced, with shaggy light brown hair and a sprinkling of freckles across the bridge of his nose. He looked shell-shocked and pale now. Only a few years older than Cade, Closter was not the seasoned cop that Ethan was and Cade tried to understand that as the guy fluttered around him uncertainly, constantly asking how he felt, and did he need a drink of water or something.

Cade remained on the couch, Purrcy curled in his lap, thinking of the silver dagger he'd secreted in his dresser drawer before anyone arrived. Specifically, he was thinking of the damage it had done to Brooks. He hoped the son of a bitch was bleeding out somewhere alone in the woods.

"Are you cold?" Ryan Closter didn't wait for an answer before wrapping a blanket around Cade's shoulders.

Cade said nothing. He no doubt looked like a feeble old woman who'd slipped in the tub, but he was feeling better. Much better.

Because he had a plan. Samantha was going to come back.

I'll talk to Winter. He'll turn her for me before they can bury her.

And then, everything would be fine. Samantha would be a vampire, but Cade could deal with that. They'd figure that out. Together.

Purrcy's purr rumbled to life and he began to knead Cade's lap, watching with concern in his gold-green eyes.

He became aware of Ryan Closter's low voice. It was a sound that Cade's mind had unconsciously placed as the hum of the wind or maybe a power line outside. He realized now that the deputy had been speaking for some time. "What?" Cade asked.

Ryan Closter stopped, mouth open. He sat on the sofa next to him, though how he'd gotten there, Cade didn't know; it seemed only seconds ago that Closter was at the window, looking out, commenting on the rain or something. *Then he gave me a blanket, didn't he?*

"You're in shock. I ... I was just saying that maybe you ought to reconsider going to the hospital. I can take you when-"

"No. I don't need to go."

"Are you sure, because-"

"I said no. I'm fine." Cade offered a smile. It felt too big, too bright. Too sudden. The worry in Closter's eyes only deepened.

But Ryan Closter was a fool. They all were. Samantha was coming back.

Just as soon as Winter gets back from Eternity.

9

SECRETS AND SLUMBER

*E*than and Sheila decided on the most believable explanation for Samantha Corbett's death: a bear attack. With Sheila's PhD in forensic pathology, she had the power to make that call.

"Think they'll buy it?" It wouldn't be long before Photography and Forensics showed up.

Sheila, crouching to inspect the wounds, a camera in hand, nodded. "They'll have to. It's certainly more plausible than ... the truth."

Vampires. The word hung unspoken between them.

"I dare say *this* was the cause of death." Sheila pointed at the ripped-out throat of the corpse.

No. Not the corpse, Ethan amended, *Samantha Corbett. My friend.*

"You okay?" asked Sheila.

Ethan nodded. *Keep it together. Do the job.* "I'll have to put out a warning. Keep people away from the woods. We'll have a bear panic on our hands, but ... what else can we do? Until we find Brooks ..."

"People will accept the bear attack story." Sheila lifted one of Samantha's arms, inspecting it. "Livor mortis set in a while ago. She's been gone a good few hours. What took Cade so long to call you?"

"He didn't call me. I don't think he even had the wherewithal to think of that. I called him. That's when he told me."

"I wonder what he was doing in the time between."

"I doubt he'd know if you asked him. You saw the look in his eyes. The lights are off upstairs."

Sheila examined Samantha's left hand, snapped a picture, and placed it carefully back down. "Plenty of defensive wounds. She fought. Hard. Death didn't come quick. Or easy."

Ethan's stomach twisted as he came up, once again, against the stark reality. *Brooks murdered Samantha.* "Son of a bitch. I can't believe he did this." He swallowed around the lump in his throat.

Sheila stood. "I know you're angry now, Ethan, but something's going on that we don't understand. There's an explanation for this."

"Yeah. Gretchen VanTreese." Ethan flexed his fists. "I should have cut her fucking head off myself."

"But Ethan, you know what Michael said-"

"Fuck Michael. It's his peacekeeping bullshit that caused this. If he had-"

Sheila held up a hand. "Ethan, don't. Now isn't the time."

She was right.

"We'll deal with all that later, okay? Right now we've got … this to contend with." Sheila looked down at Samantha, thinking. "You're sure she won't …"

"Come back? Not unless Brooks was a full vampire - which I doubt." Reluctantly, Ethan glanced back down at Samantha. She was definitely dead. *Dead*-dead. "If she was going to come back, she would have by now." For a long moment they were silent as the misty rain whispered through the trees. "We'll call Michael when the sun sets and once he gets back in town, we'll figure out what to do about Brooks. We'll need to find him."

"Where do you suppose he went?"

Ethan shrugged. "Somewhere hidden, somewhere dark." He looked up at the cloudy sky. "Even this much light would probably be hell on him." *And that's exactly what he deserves.*

"And what about Cade? I really think he needs a doctor, Ethan."

Ethan had tried, Sheila had tried, and Ryan Closter was still trying. But Cade refused.

BECAUSE OF THE OVERCAST AND THE PROTECTIVE CANOPY OF THE TREES, Brooks was able to make his way through the forest - but barely. Despite the chill, sweat ran down his body, plastering his tattered, bloody clothes to his skin. The rain had stopped entirely and he wished for its return - not only because it would cool him off, but because it would wash away the blood, or rather, the *smell* of the blood, which nagged at him. He'd vomited up most of what he'd consumed. He was hungry. Hungry, but no longer starving, not like before.

He plodded through the rain-damp forest, his bare feet squishing through pine needles and mud, his mind playing the past hours in fragments and flashes that didn't seem real - *Samantha. Blood. Cade, raw hate blazing in his eyes.* And the dagger, the silver - he remembered that clearly. The way it had burned, still burned.

Pausing against a massive redwood, Brooks touched the wound, tenderly fingering the jagged separation of flesh that began in his right eyebrow, dragged its way up his forehead, and disappeared several inches into his hairline. The cut was still open, still weeping blood. And it burned like a bitch. The smell of charred flesh lingered and he wondered how long before it healed. The other wounds - the scratches and cat bites across his throat, chest, and down his arms - had healed immediately upon his transition. Those hadn't been inflicted by silver.

Brooks walked on, slowly now, searching for a place to lie down. He needed to rest. He felt as wilted as a flower in a heat wave. His thoughts were disjointed, out of focus, as if his brain were wrapped in a film of gauze. His arms had grown stiff, his hands no more than clumsy lumps of stone at the ends of his wrists. His head felt too heavy to hold, and the farther he went, the more his muscles cramped and burned.

But Brooks continued. At first, he'd had no idea where he was headed, not consciously, but now he knew: Eudemonia. It was the only place he *could* go. But the vampire-run resort was too far away. He couldn't make it - not today. Not until tonight.

Tonight.

Night.

The thought of darkness prickled his skin deliciously and made his mouth water. Yes, darkness. He needed darkness. The daylight was wearing him down.

Up ahead, he spotted a fallen tree. He forced his feet to keep moving and as he neared, he saw that is was surrounded by a great drift of branches that would provide protection from the gray, painful day. Like a burrowing forest creature, he hollowed out enough space beneath the deadfall to accommodate his body, crawled in, then dragged the branches and debris over himself like a blanket.

The moment he closed his eyes, his already-dreaming mind began conjuring images. He saw five or six people sitting around the television in the cabin, sharing popcorn, laughing and talking. He realized who they were: Ethan and Sheila, Cade and Samantha, and Brooks himself. But there was someone else, too; Brooks was not by himself in his La-Z-Boy.

Perched like a great white bird of prey on the back of the chair was Gretchen VanTreese, green eyes glittering, red lips whispering. At first, he couldn't hear what she said, but straining, he realized she was telling him to turn around, to go the other way. To head back to The Crimson Corset, her deserted nightclub, which sat on the opposite end of town from Eudemonia. It occurred to him that his cabin rested exactly between the two establishments - and that he had a choice: Go to Gretchen, or go to Michael.

'But the Crimson Corset is shut down,' he said in his dream-voice.

'Not for long, my little tin soldier,' whispered Gretchen. '*Not for long ...*'

And then his mind flashed on other things:

Samantha, her torn, dead body lying on the forest floor. *Did I do that?*

Cade, wielding a silver dagger, his face a twisted mask of hate. *Hate for me?*

Crimson Lake, southwest of where he now lay.

Water. So much water.

And then there was nothing.

Nothing, as the death-like sleep of the vampire came over him.

10

ALIVE AND BITING

As Sheila's assistants loaded Samantha Corbett's bagged body into the back of the hearse, Cade went into what Ethan could only describe as a psychotic break. He went wild, screaming about how she wasn't dead. He clawed, kicked, and even spat in their faces. It took both Ethan and Closter to restrain him so the assistants could complete their grim task.

Cade wasn't grasping the reality of the situation. He was in bed now, sleeping off a massive dose of tranquilizer, but Ethan wasn't sure what he'd do when Cade woke. He'd promised the attending medics he'd get Cade to a hospital if there was no improvement, but he didn't want to do that - Cade was out of his mind and Ethan feared the kid would start ranting about vampires and end up blowing the bear-attack cover. And end up in a nuthouse.

Ethan had taken the rest of the day off to stay with Cade and now, in the Colter cabin, all was silent.

The medics and Sheila's assistants had left, as did the handful of gawkers who'd gathered in front of the house, cell phones clicking and snapping in hopes of capturing an image of the dead girl. As it turned out, the spectators had gotten a lot more than they'd bargained for; Ethan had little doubt that Cade's rampage was already splashed across various social media sites.

Ethan took a deep drink from one of the bottles of Killian's that Brooks always kept in the fridge for him. He felt dirty somehow drinking the murderer's beer - but he needed it. Needed it bad. He'd sent Closter home - the young deputy looked about ready to retire from the force and go into something less stressful like nude hang-gliding over shark-infested waters - and Sheila was back at the morgue, completing her coroner duties.

No one had questioned the bear attack story, not yet, and Ethan hoped they never would. As an extra precaution, Sheila had briefly stayed to answer questions and use her profession to full advantage.

Ethan took another pull on the beer, wondering if they were doing the right thing. It felt like they were protecting a killer ... and vampire or not, that's exactly what Brooks was - a killer. A murderer. And if he'd been anything but a fucking vampire, Ethan wouldn't have hesitated to open a full-scale manhunt, find Brooks Colter, friend or not, and send his ass to prison for the rest of his life.

He sipped the Killian's and wished he had his yarn and needles handy. Knitting put Ethan's mind at ease. He looked at the clock. Just a little while till sundown, then he'd get hold of Michael Ward in Eternity.

And Michael can help me find Brooks.

Ethan was betting Colter would be making his way toward his Maker, Gretchen. Assuming she'd been unstaked. Ethan was pretty sure she had. Otherwise, Brooks had been attacked by a different bloodsucker ... and that just didn't jibe.

No. He shook his head and swallowed more beer. The only thing that made sense was that the stake that had stopped Gretchen's heart had been removed - and now she was back. Consequently, Brooks had reverted back to vampirism - or at least half-vampirism - and the bloodlust had been too sudden, too strong, and in his moments of weakness and confusion, he'd fed on Samantha, killing her in the process. That was the only thing that made sense. According to the guys at Eudemonia, baby vampires didn't have much in the way of self-control.

As he pondered this, for the first time, Ethan felt a stab of pity for Brooks. Likely, the guy was horrified by what he'd done. *That, or he'd turn into a monster like Gretchen VanTreese.*

Gretchen VanTreese.

No matter how he looked at it, it all came back to her. Gulping Killian's, Ethan wished like hell they'd removed her head in the first place. His jaw aching from tension, he drained his beer, and looked at the clock. Sundown was on its way.

He decided to go check on Cade. Again.

THE SILENCE WAS INTERRUPTED ONLY BY THE SOFT MURMUR OF THE television in the other room. Cade lay awake, staring at the ceiling as the thin gray evening light dimmed through the slender crack between his cobalt bedroom drapes.

It might have been the drugs, but he felt like he was somewhere else. Lying there beneath the sheets, his own body seemed foreign, alien, made of plastic. But his mind felt real enough. It swam with horrible things, intermittent bursts of terrible images, memories of today which he knew, even in his fugue, he would never be able to scrub from his mind. A tear - hot and heavy with nightmares and pain - slipped from his eye and disappeared into his hair. He felt as if he'd been hollowed out with a large, blunt spoon. He rolled over onto his side, facing the door.

A light tread from the other room.

Ethan. Cade knew the sound of his walk. It was one of those things you don't know how you know, but you just do. The footfalls neared and when the door cracked open, Cade didn't bother closing his eyes. He wondered how many times Ethan had made this trip in the last couple of hours. At least half a dozen, probably. That was another thing he just knew.

When the sheriff appeared in the doorway, he looked surprised. "You're awake."

Cade said nothing.

Ethan stepped into the room and closed the door quietly behind him. Then the sheriff sat on the edge of the bed. He said nothing, just sat there, and Cade was glad. He didn't want to talk. There was nothing to be said.

Cade closed his eyes and slowly drifted back to that place where today had never happened.

THE DARKNESS CAME QUICKLY, THE SUN BLINKING OUT OF EXISTENCE IN the westerly forest, and there, in the dim light of the cave, they came to life.

On his air mattress on the hard cavern floor, Scythe watched through the amber lantern light as the Gretchen-thing came awake and clambered, spider-like, toward her sustenance, Rafe Santangelo. She hunched over him and bit his wrist, startling the man, jarring him from sleep. Santangelo cried out and tried to scramble away, his face wild with fear.

Scythe burst into laughter.

Terror in his eyes, Santangelo's back met the cavern wall and he opened his mouth to scream again.

But Jazminka cut him off. "Let her feed." She appeared from the shadows, an Amazon in ratty clothing, lantern in hand.

Santangelo's gaze moved to Scythe. His lips were chapped and his skin looked sallow.

He needed water. Later, Scythe would go fill more jugs at Scarlet Falls. But not yet. He nodded at Santangelo. "You heard the woman. Let her feed."

At the sound of Scythe's words, Santangelo visibly relaxed. Scythe's venom was still in effect, but he'd need to give him more.

"But," Santangelo's voice was husky, desperate. "I need to take a leak. Can I take a leak first? I've really got to go."

Scythe looked at Jazminka.

She nodded.

"Fine."

They got to their feet and, with an effort that felt good to his unused muscles, Scythe dislodged the boulder from the mouth of the cavern. It was heavy enough that no human - namely Rafe Santangelo - could budge it. Not that the guy was likely to go anywhere. As long as the doses of venom kept coming, he was under Scythe's command - but it was best not to take chances.

The night was teeming with life, the forest thick with possibility, and Scythe's own hunger needled him. Walking Santangelo into a small clearing about a dozen yards from the cave, he could smell the wildlife through the rain-damp earth, tiny little hearts pumping hot blood through simple-minded bodies. But tonight, if he could manage it, Scythe wanted human blood. *A trip to Santa Cruz would really hit the spot. Plenty of lowlifes there that won't be missed.*

It occurred to him again that he could fang Santangelo while no one was looking, but Scythe thought better of that. If he returned him to Gretchen half-empty, Jazminka would drive the heel of one of her ridiculous thigh-highs right up his ass. He sighed. *Santa Cruz, it is.*

Santangelo stared at him, waiting for permission, and Scythe had half a mind to let him stand there another hour or two to see how long it would take for the guy's bladder to burst. He'd never understand Gretchen's penchant for human pets. Blood slaves were like dogs, always needing, always whimpering at your feet, always begging approval from their masters.

"All right," he said to the waiting Santangelo. "Drain the tank and let's go. I got shit to do."

Santangelo just stood there, blinking at him.

Scythe rolled his eyes. "Piss already!" That was the other thing about blood slaves - they were stupid as fuck.

Hands trembling with urgency, Santangelo fumbled with his belt and zipper, and loosed a current strong enough to put out a forest fire.

He couldn't be too *dehydrated,* Scythe thought.

"Scythe?" the man asked, still pissing. "Why am I here?"

"Because Gretchen needs you."

"But why? Who- who is she?" Fear edged his voice.

Scythe stuck his lip out, tilted his head, and did his best teary-eyed Julia Roberts. "She's just a girl, standing in front of a boy, asking him to feed her." He barked out a laugh, but his humor was lost on Santangelo. "And you're just the kind of boy she likes."

"What ... what do you mean?"

Scythe let out an impatient sigh. "I mean you're the kind she likes. Gretchen doesn't get out of the coffin for anything less than an AB Negative six-foot Italian. Not that it matters when she's *this* hungry." He grinned. "Hell, you could be a short potbellied Polack with asthma and a receding hairline at this point and she wouldn't know the fucking difference!" He bellowed another deep-bellied laugh.

The other man said no more, just went on hosing down the shrubs.

Just as Scythe's patience reached its end and he was about to order the guy cut it off prematurely, Santangelo pushed out the last few squirts, shook off, and tucked himself back in.

"All right, feel better? That's great. Now come on." Scythe turned on his heel and headed back to the cave, Santangelo close behind - and that's when a new scent rose on the soft night breeze.

Another vampire.

Scythe stopped suddenly and Santangelo walked into the back of him, apologizing profusely.

"Shh." Scythe raised his face, sniffed the air.

Definitely a vampire. One he didn't recognize. It was at least a mile away. Probably more. A male, he thought. *A Rogue? One of Michael's? Emeric maybe?* Maybe the old sack of bones sensed Gretchen's return and-

But no, this wasn't Emeric; Scythe knew Emeric's scent - like dust and bones - and this wasn't it. This was sweeter, younger. A baby, practically.

A stranger.

Well, fuck.

For the first time since they'd taken up residence in the cavern, Scythe became uneasy. So far, they'd been lucky and hadn't been detected - *but if another vampire got close enough ... if the wind was just right and someone sniffed them out ...*

BROOKS RAN HARDER AND FASTER THAN HE'D EVER BEEN ABLE TO before. In a few more miles he'd be there and then ... and then he didn't know what.

He slowed to a walk.

He realized he'd only assumed that Michael's group would take him in, clean him up, give him help - but what if that wasn't how it worked out?

Suddenly unsure, he paused and sat, his back against the trunk of a redwood.

Samantha was Michael's friend. What if his group hated Brooks for killing her? What if they turned him out ... or worse ... what if they ... *dispose of me?* But he couldn't see them killing him. That's not how Michael worked.

But Michael's out of town. That left only Cedric, Emmeline, and the two guards, Dante and Rogan. Brooks didn't know any of them well enough to know what they might do. He saw an image of mice frolicking freely, taking full advantage of the cat's absence.

No, he couldn't go to Eudemonia, after all. At least not until Michael was back. And Winter. Winter was a good guy, too. *But when are they coming back?* He racked his brain, trying to remember. *Some festival in Eternity ... Biting Man? ... They'd be gone ... a few days? Maybe a week ...?*

He tried to remember when they'd left, but time was a blur now. It might have been a week ago, it might have been the day before yesterday. Though his other senses were sharper than they'd ever been before, his mind was a stuck cog. And he knew it wasn't because he was a vampire - vampires had very sharp minds - it was because of what had happened. Because of what he'd done.

Samantha. Cade.

He still couldn't believe it. But it was real. Very real, and it dominated his brain, crowding everything else out. It was too big and he couldn't think around it.

"Fuck." He put his head in his hands, thinking, thinking. "Fuck, fuck, fuck!" Tears sprang and rolled down his cheeks. "Fuck!" He smacked himself in the head, bringing fresh pain to the still-unhealed silver knife wound above his eye.

"I'm so sorry, I'm so sorry, I'm so sorry."

Then, riding the wind so faint that Brooks barely registered it, came a new smell, a familiar one. The smell of others like him somewhere in the woods.

ETHAN STARTED PHONING MICHAEL'S HOTEL ROOM AS SOON AS THE SUN set. He got no answer, but he'd keep trying until someone picked up, even if it took all night. He had nothing but time; Sheila had stopped by after work and brought him his yarn and needles, and Ethan planned to finish a particularly colorful green, red, and yellow sweater he'd begun.

Cade slept through Sheila's visit, and he was still sleeping when she went home an hour later to deal with Sydney. Ethan would spend the night right here.

He tried the hotel room again, got no answer, and continued knitting, his nimble fingers moving with quick expertise, the repetition and the click of the needles lulling him into a comfortable rhythm.

11

A BONE'S THROW FROM HOME

Twice, Gretchen had fanged Santangelo, and twice, she'd vomited.

"She ees going to need more." Jazminka watched their now-sleeping Maker, then turned her pale dead gaze on Scythe. "You are going to Santa Cruz?"

How the hell does she know I planned a trip to Santa Cruz? Seated on a milk crate, Scythe leaned back against the stone walls of the cavern, arms and ankles crossed, a dried pine needle between his lips. He'd been admiring the generous bulge in his stone-washed jeans and wishing Gretchen would get herself decent soon so he could fuck the living daylights out of her.

"Vell? You are going?"

Scythe shrugged. "I thought I might. Why?"

"You vill bring back more sustenance." It wasn't a request.

Scythe sat up, spat out the pine needle. He didn't like that idea. *Create even more slaves?*

"He ees not enough. Meestress needs more blood."

Scythe glanced at Santangelo, slumped against the cavern wall, a half-drunk jug of water between his knees. The man's eyes were closed, his breath shallow, his once-olive skin now as white as bone.

The bite marks up and down his arms looked like the needle tracks of a heroin addict - *and in a way,* thought Scythe, *that's exactly what he is.* "Naw. He'll be fine. I'll give him more venom. That'll fix him right up."

"No." Jazminka shook her head. "Any more blood loss vill kill him." Her dark hair, which once spiked up like porcupine quills, now hung over her eyes. At first, it had been strange seeing her without all the hair-gel and makeup, but in the months they'd been living off the land, hair goop and cosmetics weren't on the list of necessities. "Thees man," Jazminka gestured at Santangelo, "ees not enough. Ve need another one. Maybe two more. Men. Beeg men. The kind that Meestress likes."

"I'm not bringing a group of dudes back with me all the way from Santa Cruz. Too dangerous."

"Then get them from Scarlet Street."

"That's dangerous, too. More dangerous. Missing persons get noticed in Crimson Cove."

"It cannot be helped. Get them from Scarlet Street."

"Fine." Scythe sighed. He didn't want to envenomate anyone else. He didn't need more meat puppets following him around. "Why don't *you* go? I can stay here with-"

"No." Another head shake. "Meestress needs me."

"*Mistress* is fine." Scythe's words snapped like winter twigs. "All she does is feed and sleep." *And puke.* He looked at the Gretchen-thing lying on an air mattress in a shadowclad hollow of the cavern for any signs of improvement. He saw none.

"Go." There was no bite in Jazminka's tone, just a simple command. "The more she feeds, the sooner she vill recover."

That was true. *And the sooner she recovers, the sooner I can bang her brains out.* That definitely appealed to Scythe. Not to mention, he *was* getting hungry. Hefting himself to his feet and putting more pout into it than he now felt, he said, "Fine. I'll go. But next time, it's *your* turn."

Jazminka waved him away and crouched to comfort the Gretchen-thing, who rolled over, moaned, and coughed up more blood.

"I don't see why we need more when all she does it puke it up, anyway."

Jazminka sighed. "That vill pass. Soon her body vill accept the large amounts she needs to recover."

Scythe hoped so. He moved the boulder from the cave's entrance and stepped into the night.

Outside, he broke into a sprint - a vampiric sprint - taking the side roads to Scarlet Street. As he ran, he kept an eye out for the vampire he'd sensed earlier, but he neither saw nor smelled any sign of him.

IT WAS LATE, VERY LATE, WHEN ETHAN FINALLY GOT THROUGH.

Winter answered on the first ring. Michael was on the balcony outside talking to Natasha Darling. It looked serious and Winter didn't want to interrupt.

So Ethan told him what had happened. All of it.

Long silence. Then Winter's gruff tones vibrated in the earpiece of the phone. "Well, shit."

"Yeah. I'm at the Colter cabin now, but still no sign of Brooks."

"Good. Stay with Cade. I'll let Michael know. We'll head out at nightfall."

"Can't you leave now? I'd rather-"

"It's too far. The sun will be coming up. We won't make it back in time tonight."

Ethan pinched the bridge of his nose, feeling stupid, like when you try to turn the bathroom light on during a power outage. *Of course. Daylight and vampires - they don't mix.* He'd never get used to it. "All right. I appreciate it, Winter. Sorry to ruin your vacation."

Winter chuckled but there was no humor in it. "No worries, Boss. It ended up not being much of a vacation, anyway." He paused. "Just a head's up - we've got a couple of, uh, *newbies* coming back with us."

"Newbies?"

"Yeah. Couldn't be helped."

Great. Just what Crimson Cove needs - more fucking vampires. "I trust you'll keep them in line?"

"If I thought they'd be a problem, believe me, I wouldn't bring them back."

Ethan believed him. "How many?"

"Two. A guy - Norman Keeler, and a gal, Erin Woodhouse."

"All right. They're your responsibility."

"Sure thing."

Ethan ended the call and was surprised to see Cade standing in the hallway. Instinctively, Ethan pulled a couch pillow over his yarn and needles - it was one thing for everyone to know about his hobby, but it was another to be caught in the act.

"Was that Michael?"

"Winter. They're coming back tomorrow night." He watched Cade. The kid looked tired, too tired for someone who'd slept all day, but under that, there was something else, something faraway. Something ... *removed*. "You doing okay?"

"I'm thirsty." Cade went to the kitchen and downed enough water to put flowers on a dying cactus. Thirst was a sign of shock, Ethan knew.

When he finished, Cade headed back to his bedroom, pausing in the hallway. "She might come back, you know? Maybe Brooks *did* have venom somehow, and-"

"Cade, I don't want you to count on that. You know how this works. No venom, no vampire-making abilities. And Brooks wouldn't have had any-"

"You never know. It's possible. Anything's possible."

Ethan nodded. He couldn't bring himself to rip the last thread of hope away from the kid. "Yeah. Anything's possible."

They were silent a few beats, then Cade said, "You don't have to stay here, you know. I'm okay."

"I know." Ethan casually picked up the remote, pointed it at the widescreen, and pushed buttons. "There's a great documentary on about-" he glanced at the screen "-polar bears. Care to watch it with me?"

Cade stared at him blank-faced and empty-eyed before disappearing into his room.

When he was alone, Ethan shut the TV off and sighed. He turned off the lamp, stretched out on the couch, and closed his eyes. Sleep wouldn't come easy tonight.

DURING HIS SUMMERS AS A YOUNG TEEN IN CRIMSON COVE, WHEN other boys were sneaking cigarettes and taking their older brothers' cars for joyrides, Rafe Santangelo and his buddies, Jimmy Wilson and Carl Riedelbach, had discovered a far more dangerous pastime - one that their parents, had they known, would definitely *not* have allowed. With some rope they'd found in Jimmy's basement, along with a harness, carabiners, and belay devices Carl had stolen from his uncle, Rafe and his pals made it their goal to conquer the flat-faced rock that fronted the steep eastern mountains. Specifically, Little Captain Mountain.

Rafe had caught on quickly, learning early that foot placement - and good shoes rather than high-top sneakers - were more important than handholds. Rafe, in his harness and inappropriate shoes, had at first been terrified, but they kept at it and by the end of the summer, they'd met their goal of conquering the stony face of Little Captain. They'd celebrated with a couple of Carl's father's beers - Rafe paid dearly for that last transgression later when his mother smelled booze on his breath, but that woman and her punishments were something else he didn't like to think about.

That day, and that beer, had been a rite of passage. It was the seam that stitched boyhood and manhood together, and climbing the mountain remained one of Rafe's few fond memories. It had been fun. Fun, until the first time he'd looked down, anyway. From the seat of his harness - which, for all he knew, hadn't even been properly secured - he'd taken his eyes off the climb to gauge his progress. It had been a terrible mistake. The ground was so far away the drop would have been fatal. He'd frozen then, his muscles locking up, unable to tear his eyes away, thinking only one thing: *I'm going to die, I'm going to die, I'm going to die.*

Watching Scythe leave the cavern was like that. *I'm going to die.*

One moment, Rafe had been making his way toward his beat-up silver Hyundai in the small Peddler Puck's parking lot after a long, boring shift and the next thing he knew, he'd been attacked. Attacked and ... bitten.

And now the only thing that mattered to him was the man called Scythe. This obsession, except for the absence of the sexual element, was a little like being in love. But Rafe had been in love before - *Katie, don't think of Katie* - and this was not love. It was *more* than love. It was ... everything.

He could only think of Scythe and when the man had left him alone with the two strange women, it took everything Rafe had not to fly into another panic. He didn't want to be alone with them. The tall one with the accent, Jazminka, was scary enough, but the other one, the one who bit him, the one who smelled of death, absolutely terrified him. *Gretchen.*

Now Rafe sat, his back against the hard cavern wall, as Jazminka used an old shirt to wipe up the blood the other woman had vomited. The only light in the cavern came from dim lanterns strung overhead and in the thick shadows, the blood looked black. She finished sopping it up, then informed Rafe in her thick Slavic accent that she would not wait for Scythe any longer - she was going to go find sustenance. She wouldn't be gone long.

Only after she'd disappeared from the cavern did it occur to Rafe he was now all alone with Gretchen - the biter. Scythe was a biter too, of course, but he didn't take blood from Rafe Santangelo. Instead, Scythe injected something into him, something that made Rafe feel safe. And feeling safe was something Rafe had had very little of in life.

It was something he wanted more of. Even thinking of it now, he wished Scythe would return and sink his razor-like teeth into him - deep and hard - and make him safe again.

But Rafe did not like the bites from Gretchen.

He glanced toward her.

From here, she was no more than a malignant lump of shadows, but he could smell her - that moist, moldering odor that reminded him of bad meat and the grave. And the blood, he could smell that too. *My blood*, he realized - rejected by Gretchen's stomach. That sick, fetid stink hung in the air, coppery and thick and, together with the rotted smell of Gretchen herself, the contents of Rafe's own stomach threatened to make an expedient exit.

But Rafe held down his bile. He wondered why the woman's smell - *and the biting and the blood* - hadn't bothered him more before now. It was almost as if the farther Scythe got away from him - and the longer he went between Scythe's bites - the clearer Rafe's mind became. And in Rafe's case, a clear mind wasn't exactly a good thing.

For the first time since he'd come here, he looked - *really* looked - at Gretchen. At first, all he could see was the vague lumpy outline of her body - she lay on her side, facing him on an air mattress. Focusing his gaze, squinting in the dim light, he thought he made out more. The waxy whiteness of her face. Smooth forehead and high cheekbones. But not pretty. Not pretty at all. Though the actual features were submerged in shadow, he knew that she was hideous with decomposition. His eyes moved over the shape of her and in the darkness, he sensed the slope of her shoulder.

She was still. Too still. If she was breathing, it was barely.

The lantern-light flickered and shadows danced across the shape of her. *Is she human? Are any of them human?* Rafe didn't think so. Later, it would be obvious to him, but right now, the word *vampire* wasn't even reachable. *Monster* was the closest he could come.

His gaze moved to the darkened eye sockets of the woman's face. So deep and black and hollow that she might not have had any eyes at all.

He wondered who she was and what she was doing here. She did not seem lost or frightened, nor did she seem to be here against her will. Maybe she-

Her eyes were open! Had been all along. Fixed on him with rapt, mad intensity.

No, he told himself. *She's not looking at me. I'm imagining it. It's too dark to see anything in here.* His mind was playing cruel tricks on him - it had always liked to do that.

But hadn't he just caught a twinkle in the depths of those dark hollows where her eyes would be? And couldn't he *feel* her eyes, crawling on him like lice? Couldn't he feel the *hate* that came from her? Yes. He could. It hit him like a wall, that hate. *Whatever she is, she hates me, seriously fucking* hates *me.*

The black holes - her eyes - continued to stare, and he was sure he wasn't imagining it.

He wanted to say something - *we're friends aren't we? Of course, we are. You drink my blood, that makes us more than friends. We're practically family!* - but his tongue was dry as a strip of sandpaper and stuck to the roof of his mouth as if it had been sewn in place.

Rafe thought he saw another glint of eye - there and gone - and he grew more certain that he was indeed being watched. *But why? Why would she just lie there and stare at me?* He made out the thin white edge of her nose - or thought he did - and the deepening of texture in the shadows where her mouth would be.

Say something to her!

But he could not. He was paralyzed under the weight of the crawling black waves of malevolence that emanated from her motionless, lunatic eyes; all he could do was stare. That malevolence reached out from the snarls of shadows where she lay - he could feel it on his skin.

His throat clicked as he tried to swallow and his bladder was suddenly full. But he was aware of none of this. The only thing that existed, the only thing at all, was the black patches of shadow, her eyes.

He thought he detected movement and his gaze swept down.

Yes. There it was. Something was moving - crawling slowly toward him. Her fingers. Long. Slender. White as bone. Moving like spiders' legs. Reaching out from the shadows.

Reaching for him.

A terrible hysteria overcame him - *What is she doing*! - and he heard himself asking her in a hoarse whisper what did she want, and oh, god, oh, god, please leave me alone, and then her face moved out of the shadows and for the first time he saw - *really* saw - her terrible, white, rotted corpse's face.

She was coming toward him, crawling like an insect, and without the safety harness that was Scythe, Rafe Santangelo was falling, falling. Gretchen's lips wrinkled up into a grin and Rafe felt the moorings of his sanity begin to shiver and shake. His bladder let go but he was barely aware of the spreading warmth.

As she neared, Rafe's senses filled with her smell - the wet rot, the decaying, moldering stink. And the face, all hollow-cheeked and bony, that godawful face - *I should never have looked at her!* - and her hunched body, her matted, filthy hair, and decomposing clothes.

It isn't real, it isn't real. It's a nightmare. Even as that cadaverous face leered inches from his own, Rafe's mind tried to reason out of it. But it was real, all right. As real as the cavern itself and the boulder that blocked his way to freedom.

Those eyes, red-rimmed in their deep sockets, glittered madly, and the lips, little more than a white scar across the hideous face, began to move. "Feed me." On that raspy reptilian whisper rode the stink of things long dead, hitting Rafe in the face like the back side of a shovel.

Scythe! Where the hell is Scythe? He couldn't bear even the sight - let alone the touch - of this woman without Scythe.

Gretchen's mouth yawned open, showing vicious fangs. Saliva, like spider's webs, stretched from her top to bottom teeth.

Something popped inside Rafe's head, flashed like a strike of lightning and, no longer able to bear the weight of the horror, he did something he'd only seen women do in old movies.

He passed out.

12

VERY UNSAVORY THINGS

The next morning, even before he woke, Cade was crying. Hot tears streaming, he slowly rose to the surface of consciousness, vaguely aware of a feeling that he was safer in sleep, that some real-life nightmare awaited him on the other side of slumber. He tried to turn around, to dive back down into the warm depths of unconsciousness, but he could not.

His body sensed the reality waiting for him and his fists were already tight at his sides, his tongue as thick and dry as a strip of flannel. As he opened his eyes, his jaw ached with tension, and his heart began pounding out the primal, terrified rhythm of a cornered rabbit.

The memories didn't come back in bits and pieces. They hit him all at once, as hard and fast as a knee to the groin.

Samantha ...

DEAD.

And it's my fault! If I'd told her about Brooks before she left for work, she never would have come back, never would have been in the house alone with him!

These thoughts jackknifed through his brain; it was more than he could take. Cade threw the sheets off and shot to his feet. For a moment he just stood there, glued to the floor, focusing on pushing out the thoughts, the memories, the images of Samantha in the woods. The guilt.

Water. He was thirsty, so thirsty.

He left the bedroom and stopped at the end of the hall, momentarily baffled to see Ethan Hunter in the living room, dozing on the couch. Then he remembered. "Have you talked to Sheila?"

"Yes," said Ethan. "And there's no sign that Samantha is ... uh, going to come back."

"Yet," said Cade. In the kitchen, he ran a tall cold glass of water, downed it, and drew another. After the second glass, he bent over the sink, retching, cold water shooting from his nose and mouth. He ran the back of a shaky hand across his lips and sipped some more. It stayed down this time.

"Are you all right?"

Cade turned. "When was the last time you called Sheila?"

"Not half an hour ago." In a rumpled t-shirt, Ethan stood near the bar that separated the kitchen from the living room, his hair corkscrewed every which way, eyes still puffy from sleep.

"What time is it?" Cade's voice was hoarse.

"Just after nine."

Cade's thoughts tumbled. "Work." The word croaked out of his mouth. "I have to go to work. I'm late."

Ethan shook his head. "I left a message for your boss. She isn't expecting you for a few days."

"But-"

"But nothing. I've already made the arrangements. Until we can get this figured out, you need to-"

"Arrangements? What are you talking about?"

Ethan's look said: *Has your sanity slipped?*

"I'll be fine."

Another long, uncertain look. "You don't look fine to me. You take some time off work, and at night, someone will be here with you."

"Why? I don't need a babysitter."

"It's not safe. Until it is, someone will be here with-"

"Safe from what? I don't even know what you're talking about." Cade brushed past him and sat on the couch.

Ethan sat on the edge of the La-Z-Boy. "Your brother's still out there."

Cade wanted to argue that Brooks wouldn't hurt him - but then he hadn't thought he'd hurt Samantha, either.

"And Gretchen," added Ethan.

The name was like a punch to the gut.

Ethan cleared his throat. "She's out there. This wouldn't have happened to Brooks otherwise. And chances are, she'll come looking for you. Again."

Clear to his bones, he knew Ethan was right. Gretchen would be sniffing around, and no way would she let Cade - a Sire - slip through her hands a second time.

So, on top of his grief, his shock, Cade had *her* to contend with. It suddenly seemed that there was a large band around his chest, tightening, contracting. Feeling not quite real, like a cardboard cutout of himself, Cade rubbed his eyes with his fists. *This can't be happening. Not again.*

For a moment, he thought that the threads that tethered him to sanity would snap.

But on the heels of that burgeoning panic came the sudden and complete calm of denial. *Ethan's wrong. Gretchen is dead, and Samantha will be back. She might be back right now - and if she's not, I'll talk to Winter and he'll bring her back.*

It was suddenly funny, how upset everyone had gotten when, really, things would be just fine, and abruptly, Cade laughed.

Ethan was incredulous. "Cade? Wha ... what's so funny?"

Cade, realizing his laughter had been inappropriate, cleared his throat. "Will you call Sheila again?"

Ethan nodded and punched in the numbers. After a beat, he said, "Any news?"

Cade could tell by his face nothing had changed.

When he ended the call, Cade stood.

"I'm sorr-"

"I'm really tired. I think I'll go back to bed." *And I'm not getting up until the sun goes down, until Winter gets here, and then he'll fix everything.* Cade stood and headed back to his bedroom, feeling Ethan's worried eyes on his back.

WHILE CADE SLEPT, ETHAN TOOK A TRIP TO THE MORTUARY.

"I don't know what to do about Cade, Sheila. I think he's cracking up."

"We need to get him some help." Sheila Leventis, in her white lab coat, black-rimmed glasses, and sensible shoes, stood next to a blessedly vacated examination table in the sterile, stark-white mortuary. In a town the size of Crimson Cove, the morgue was small, with only eight refrigerated body boxes. They lined the east wall, as innocuous as the drawers of a filing cabinet.

"If we take him to a hospital, I'm afraid of what he might say. If he starts in about vampires they'll ..."

She placed a hand on his arm. "He won't. We can't put off getting him help because of that. That would be selfish." She reached into her pocket and pulled out a card, handed it over. "Give him this."

Ethan studied the card. "A support group?"

"I refer clients to this grief group all the time."

Ethan doubted Cade would be willing but tucked it into his pocket. "I'll see what I can do." Clearing his throat, he said, "So, uh, still no sign of, uh ... *life*? With Samantha, I mean."

Sheila shook her head. "None. Decomposition has begun."

"Shit."

"You didn't expect her to come back, did you?"

"Not really. It's just ... Cade. He's been holding out hope." Ethan wondered which drawer housed Samantha's remains. "So she's definitely ..."

"Deceased." Sheila nodded. "In the conventional sense. For good."

For good. Ethan had figured as much. It didn't take this long for someone to come back if they were going to. "I'll contact her mother and break the news. Then Cade." He wasn't looking forward to either.

Sheila pushed aside a strand of black hair, tucked it behind her ear. "I'll have her ready for services within a couple of days. It'll have to be closed-casket, of course." There was pain in her tone, pain that chipped away at Ethan's heart. "Ethan, maybe you should have one of your deputies talk to her mother."

But Ethan shook his head. Being sheriff was an honor, he recognized that, but it came with certain responsibilities. And he couldn't bring himself to assign such a grueling task to any of his deputies; he tried to imagine Ryan Closter breaking the news to Samantha's mother, and couldn't. "No, it's something I need to do. It's just … the burden of the badge."

"I understand."

And Ethan knew she did. Her job came with its own kind of hell. What were the odds, he often wondered, that two people with such grisly jobs should come together? Pretty likely, probably. How could he, seeing the things he'd seen, relate to a real estate agent or a flight attendant? And how could Sheila, who walked through the trenches of death every day, talk to an electrician or a hotelier? What would they discuss over dinner?

He needed Sheila, he realized - needed someone who traveled the same dark circles that most people - *sane* people - spent their lives avoiding.

Sheila crossed her arms and leaned against the table. "What time is Michael getting in tonight?"

"Late. The drive's a few hours." Ethan sighed. "I hate that we're depending on him so heavily to fix this. I mean, really, what's he going to do about it?"

"I think he'll be able to help somehow. He certainly knows more about vampire matters than we do."

Ethan scoffed. "Yes, well, if it weren't for him, this wouldn't even be happening."

"He had his reasons for handling Gretchen the way he did, Ethan. Personal reasons that we don't know anything about."

Ethan said nothing and for a moment, they were silent. He realized he was procrastinating and looked at his watch. "I guess I'd better go talk to Samantha's mother." Dread, heavy as a lead ball, sank in his gut.

Sheila wrapped him in a hug. "I'm sorry about this, Ethan." Her voice cracked. "All of it."

A lump rose in his throat and he bit back hard on threatening tears. "Me too." He kissed the top of her head.

She looked up at him. "I admire you, Ethan."

"Not half as much as I admire you." He planted a kiss at the corner of her mouth and broke the embrace. Clearing his throat, he replaced his Smokey hat. "I'll stop by the house afterwards and check on Sydney." No doubt, she was on the couch, watching The God Club starring her favorite red-faced, Bible-wielding, demon-slaying, televangelist, Reverend Bobby Felcher.

"Okay." Sheila wiped her eyes with the back of her hand, offering a smile that had no sun. "She was sleeping this morning when I left. Remember, we can always move her to my place if she's getting in the way. We're practically living together as it is. We might as well make it official."

"It's something to think about." While Ethan liked the idea of living full-time with Sheila, it seemed a bit weird to move his ex-wife into his future wife's home. *A little too ... incestuous?*

With a half-smile, he turned and left the morgue. For the first time, he was reluctant to leave the place and its clean, headache-inducing chemical smells. Bracing himself for the duty ahead, he made his way into the parking lot. Thick nets of fog cloaked the day and rags of mist hovered like sleepy ghosts. It seemed to match his mood: somber and tired - so very, very tired. He hopped into his vehicle, started the engine, and spent several minutes fiddling with the radio - procrastinating again. He wasn't looking forward to this at all.

SAMANTHA'S MOTHER, JEANNIE REYNOLDS, LIVED IN A DILAPIDATED mobile home in Crimson Cove's sole trailer park.

She took the news hard.

She'd broken down completely, falling into Ethan's arms, sobbing. Even as he stood there, trying to hold himself together and allow the woman her grief, he knew he'd never, not if he lived to be a hundred and ten, forget the sounds of her pain, her pleas for God to take it back.

She didn't question the bear attack story.

Eventually, Ms. Reynolds invited him inside and though he wanted nothing more than to be done with the unpleasant business, he accepted the invitation and, for the next hour or so, listened as the grieving woman told him about her daughter through pain-wracked sobs.

He'd held back his own tears, right up until now, driving home. "Jesus Christ," he said to himself, wiping his eyes. But he realized that his own pain was no match for Ms. Reynolds'.

Mother and daughter hadn't been close - in fact, it had been months since they'd even spoken - but no matter the distance in a parent-child relationship, there was nothing worse than a mother's grief.

As he pulled into the driveway of his own home, next to Sydney's red Porsche, he noticed the still-wet tear-stains Ms. Reynolds had left on his tan uniform. He dabbed them with tissue from the glove box then killed the engine and sat there a moment, allowing himself to breathe, to simply *be*. It was hard to believe that, up until yesterday, his greatest concern was setting a wedding date with Sheila. That seemed so far away now.

With a bone-deep sigh, he hopped out and went inside.

And as if the gods of strain and exhaustion hadn't punished him enough, there sat his neighbor, Mrs. Gelding. She was stuffed as tightly as a blood sausage into his favorite chair, sipping coffee with Sydney. On the television - which was muted, thank God - Reverend Bobby Felcher was in the grip of religious fervor, holding his empty-eyed audience in sway with one of his vein-popping litanies.

Before Ethan could turn tail and slip out unnoticed, Mrs. Gelding looked up at him, her piggy little eyes sparking like polished marbles in her doughy, perpetually perspiring face. "Well, *there* you are!" She made one attempt, two attempts, three attempts to heft herself from the chair to greet him before accepting her fate as its prisoner and motioning him over with a pudgy hand.

Once Mrs. Gelding had her victim ensnared, there was nothing to be done but smile and nod while she spun her endless web of gossip and monotony. Ethan accepted his fate, removed his hat, and forced himself deeper into the room. "Hello, Mrs. Gelding."

"Gladiola." She turned to Sydney. "If I've told him once, I've told him a *thousand* times - call me Gladiola!" *Men,* said her look. *You just can't teach them anything*!

Before anyone could speak up and compromise her position at center-stage, Gladiola Gelding steamrolled on. "I was just telling Sydney how *wonderful* it is to see her again. Why, I don't think I've even laid *eyes* on her since a month before she left town!"

Sydney, who'd always taken some kind of sick delight in engaging the woman, was apparently sticking to tradition. "I know I should have stopped and said goodbye," she said, looking regretful, "but it all happened in such a hurry. Such a hurry."

Burning questions glittered in Mrs. Gelding's beady eyes and, for a moment, Ethan thought she might hold them back, that common decency might win out. He thought wrong.

"Now, you know I'm not one to pry," she pried, "but what *did* happen, dear?" Like a scandal-starved talk show host teetering on the cusp of record-breaking ratings, she placed a fat, well-meaning hand on Sydney's knee and prodded her gently onward with a concerned, unwavering gaze.

Sydney opened her mouth, her eyes darting uncertainly to Ethan, who stood there, silent audience to the unfolding drama.

He gave Sydney an indifferent shrug: *Go ahead. Tell her. No skin off my nose. I'm not the one who loused things up.*

And then Sydney was crying, her newly-enlarged breasts quivering in impressively lifelike fashion under her pink blouse.

Like two baby elephants fighting for escape.

"It's all my fault," she wailed. "It was *me*! I was wrong. I thought the grass was greener on the other side and now - now I'm all alone and Ethan has Sheila and I don't have anyone, I don't have anyone at all!"

Oh, Jesus Christ. "What I think Sydney is trying to say," interrupted Ethan, "is that we decided we're better as friends than as husband and wife." *Friends my ass.*

But Mrs. Gelding, her plump hand raised to clutch a string of pearls she wasn't wearing, wouldn't relent. She rocked several times then, with a great grunt she was out of the chair, putting an arm around Sydney, the better to coax out her anguish. "You poor dear. You poor, poor dear. It must be just *awful* for you."

"It *is!*"

Ethan had had enough. "Mrs. Gelding," he began. "I think-"

"So many young people these days have those horrible midlife crisises," Mrs. Gelding plowed on, "My Harold - you remember Harold, don't you? - he had a bit of a wandering eye. That was when we were young, of course. Later, he seemed to lose all interest. When he died it had been years - *years*! - since he'd taken his privilege with me." Now she looked pointedly at Ethan.

A privilege, indeed, he thought.

"When a woman doesn't feel appreciated," Mrs. Gelding went on, "when she doesn't feel *attractive*, it's natural for her to look elsewhere. Not that I'm advocating *fornication*, mind you." She took a moment to look scandalized at the thought, but not long enough to risk being interrupted. "In fact, I told Harold, I said, '*Harold, you can look all you want, but if you so much as* think *of laying your hand on another woman, I'll chop it off right along with your unmentionables!*' But the point is-" She paused for breath and Ethan seized the moment.

"Mrs. Gelding," he said. "I'm afraid this isn't a good time. Sydney and I have some things to discuss and-" He looked at a watch that was as imaginary as Mrs. Gelding's pearl necklace. "It's getting late."

"Oh. I see. Of course." She looked at Sydney. "You must be busy as a kitten in a yarn basket getting settled in and here I am yammering away at you!"

Sydney, now scarlet with tears and strain, looked at her hands and sniffed.

Mrs. Gelding shifted from one deceptively tiny foot to the other. "I'm making raviolis tonight and you know I can only eat a few of them, what with my lactose intolerance and all, so I'll be sure and bring a dish to you, probably not until tomorrow though because it takes *so* long to make."

Ethan led her to the door, grimacing as her lumpy, generous buttocks happily munched a considerable portion of her rose-print house dress.

"And remember." She paused at the threshold to wag a pudgy finger. "Don't *microwave* the raviolis! Just heat them in the oven at three-fifty for a few minutes. Fifteen to twenty ought to do it, though of course that depends on how much I give you. If-"

"I won't microwave it, Mrs. Gelding."

A flash of dentures beamed from her sweating pale face. "It's Gladiola, *not* Mrs. Gelding. Mrs. Gelding was Harold's mother and let me tell *you*, she was an absolute *beast*! Why, one time, do you know that she had the nerve to-"

"Of course. We'll talk to you later." Ethan thought he had her out the door - and then he saw the KCC2 news van parked out front, the reporter and a cameraman approaching.

Well, shit.

"Sheriff! Sheriff Hunter!" Jojo McFerrell, five-foot-two if he was an inch, tight-cheeked it toward him like a man in desperate need of a restroom.

Before McFerrell could identify Mrs. Gelding as a person of interest for later interrogation, Ethan shoved her back into the house and slammed the door behind him, lopping off her chronic stream of words.

"Sheriff!" The tiny, winded reporter was suddenly in Ethan's face, his lavender slim-fit seersucker suit as immaculate as his improbably fire-red greased back hair. He thrust out his massively phallic microphone like a miniature sexual-assailant intent on forcing intercourse. "Is it true that Samantha Corbett was killed by a bear? And is it true that said bear has not yet been apprehended? And isn't it *also* true that a *manhunt* is being organized?" He fired off his questions machine gun-style, as if he were competing against a dozen other clamoring reporters. Clearly, the man had been watching too much *CSI*.

As his camera man began rolling, McFerrell thrust the mic toward Ethan, his well-moisturized face so tight and shiny that Ethan thought he glimpsed his own reflection in it.

He sighed. He'd supposed this would happen sooner or later - he'd just hoped it would be later. Much later. He cleared his throat and gave the little man a brief, stiff statement:

"We believe the victim, Samantha Corbett, was in fact attacked by a bear. The Crimson Cove Sheriff's Department is on the case and we fully expect the bear to be apprehended. Meanwhile, we urge the citizens of Crimson Cove not to panic, but rather, to be proactive. Travel in groups, keep your eyes open, and if possible, stay away from the woods. That's the only information I'm able to give at this time. Our condolences to the loved ones of Ms. Corbett."

"Is it true you and the victim knew each other?" McFerrell shoved the mic at Ethan.

"Yes, Samantha was a friend of mine, and I - along with other law enforcement officers - are intent on-"

"And is it true that, in fact, she lived with two men - *brothers*, no less - Brooks and Cade Colter, in their cabin near the woods where the attack took place?"

Ethan bit back his annoyance. "Samantha was Cade's girlfriend, yes, but that has no bearing on this case." *Bear*ing. Ethan immediately regretted his word choice. "Now, if you'll excuse me, I've told you everything I'm able to at this time. Thank you." Ethan nodded at McFerrell then stepped inside the house and closed the door.

Inside, Sydney and Mrs. Gelding watched from the windows.

"I don't want either of you talking about this with anyone. It's police business."

Both women nodded.

"I mean it." Ethan looked out the window, watching as the two-man news crew, led by the ever-purposeful, tight-cheeked Jojo McFerrell, packed up and headed for the KCC2 van.

13

MY ACHY, STAKEY HEART

*E*than returned to the Colter cabin with plenty of time to spare before sundown. He was relieved to see Cade awake and on the couch watching TV - until he realized the kid was staring at a blank screen. When Cade saw him, he got to his feet uncertainly. "I've been texting you."

"I know. Why don't you sit back down?"

Ethan could tell Cade knew what was coming. Clearing his throat, he said, "I know you've been hoping that Samantha might come back. I think we all have. But, Cade," he leaned forward, hands clasped between his knees. "It's not going to happen. It's official. Samantha is gone. I'm sorry."

Slowly, Cade sat down. He was silent for almost a full minute. Then he said, "I know. I didn't think she would come back. I guess I just kind of hoped anyway, you know?" Cade stared at the floor, saying nothing, not moving at all.

The silence was so thick you could have spread it on toast. Ethan became aware of the soft tick of the wall clock, the low purr of the tuxedo cat who lay curled at Cade's side. He even thought he detected the whisper of wind in the trees outside, but it may have been his imagination, or perhaps his own blood whooshing in his ears. Twice in one day, Ethan had broken devastating news and this time, somehow, was worse than the first. Ethan reached into his pocket and pulled out the business card Sheila had given him. "Here," he said to Cade. "I want you to consider checking into this."

Cade took the card, studied it, then looked up dubiously.

"It's a support group. I think maybe it'll help you come to terms with ... everything."

Then Cade's face crumpled and his head dropped to his chest, his shoulders heaving with silent, wracking sobs.

The sight of the younger Colter brother falling apart drew Ethan from his chair. He put an arm around Cade's shoulder. Cade fell into him, weeping, and for the second time that day, tears soaked Ethan's shirt.

WITH SCYTHE NEARBY, GRETCHEN WAS SOMEHOW LESS FRIGHTENING TO Rafe Santangelo. Even as she bit into the tender flesh at his collarbone and drained blood from his tired body, the other man's nearness put Rafe at ease. As the ghastly woman sucked the life from him, he kept his eyes on Scythe, who sat in a camp chair, playing with a deck of cards.

Gretchen's fangs pinched and stung and the sucking sounds that came from her oddly-cool mouth were sickening, but as long as Rafe stayed focused on Scythe, he was safe. He watched as the other man scowled, swept the cards from their layout, then mixed them in a deft, mesmerizing shuffle, snapping their backs, cutting the deck in half. It was hypnotic.

Jazminka's tall figure loomed, overseeing Gretchen's slovenly feast while Rafe admired the bunch and bulge of Scythe's large muscles as he worked the cards, fascinated in the same way an anatomist is fascinated by the flex of tendon, the tightening and relaxing of skin, and the captivating arrangement of blue veins beneath it. *I want to be just like him,* he thought. *No, I want to be him.* Rafe had never admired another man as much, not even his own father - not that there was much to admire there.

As Scythe slapped the cards down in a new spread, the sound of Jazminka's voice broke Rafe's trance.

"That ees enough, Meestress." She tried to nudge Gretchen away, but the corpse-white woman with matted platinum hair only bore down harder on Rafe. He winced, sucking in air.

"Enough. You vill be sick if you do not stop now." Finally, Jazminka pried Gretchen off then led her mistress to her air mattress in the dark corner and laid her down, covering her with a blanket.

Rafe did not look at Gretchen. Even with Scythe right next to him, the sight of that skull-like face was too much.

"Vhen she is asleep," Jazminka told Scythe, "we vill go get fresh sustenance for her."

Rafe felt the beginnings of a panic attack. "You're both going?" It came out louder than he'd intended, echoing off the cavern walls.

Jazminka and Scythe turned to stare at him, surprised by his outburst.

"Yes." Jazminka motioned at Scythe. "It is clear that *he* cannot be trusted to follow orders."

"Oh, shut up, you stupid cow." Scythe slapped one card down on top of another, never looking up at her. "I told you there were no suitable prospects last night. If you wanted me to bring back a strung-out, ninety-pound junkie who wouldn't survive a single feeding, you should have said so. But that's not what you said, is it? No, you said, *'Men. Beeg men. The kind Meestress likes.'*" He affected her accent, making it extra high and nasal, earning a slit-eyed glare from the tall woman. "Well, there *weren't* any, so tough shit."

Rafe thought Jazminka might swing her booted foot back and give Scythe a kick to the head - he'd seen her do it before - but she remained still, frighteningly still. Then her eerily pale eyes - so pale they were almost translucent - shifted attentively, tenderly, toward the lump of shadows that was her mistress.

Rafe had to do something. He couldn't be alone with Gretchen, not again. "I don't ... I'd rather one of you stayed. M-maybe Scythe could stay here this time."

Jazminka eyed him with naked hatred. "I vill decide how ve do this, slave. Be silent."

Scythe got to his feet, slapping clouds of dust off the seat of his ratty acid-washed jeans. "Then let's get on it. I don't want to be out all night."

A familiar panic, sharp and hot, flooded Rafe. "But-"

"Don't worry about her," Scythe told him, jerking his head toward Gretchen. "She's as asleep as she can get." Together he and Jazminka headed to the exit.

Desperate, Rafe grabbed Scythe's ankle. "Wait. Please-" There was a gulp in his voice.

Scythe looked down, piercing him with dark eyes, his broad face - *his perfect, handsome, wonderful,* safe *face* - expressionless. "You just be calm and wait here like a good doggie." He patted Rafe's head, his touch momentarily soothing Rafe's body and mind. "Be a good boy and I'll bring you back something from McDonald's."

Rafe hated McDonald's but he was very hungry - and it was a gift from Scythe. Rafe would have eaten anything the man brought him. "Thank you." Slightly calmer now, he watched as the strange couple moved toward the mouth of the cavern, the woman smacking her head on the lanterns along the way. They removed the massive boulder, crouched, and exited the cave. As they replaced the boulder and disappeared from sight, the panic arose in Rafe.

And that uneasiness only grew as minutes ticked by and Scythe gained distance from the cave - and from Rafe.

Within five minutes of being alone with Gretchen, the panic was nearing full-bloom. *I have to get out of here.* He glanced into the corner, into the tangle of shadows that obscured the walking dead woman. *Before she - No, before* it *- wakes up.*

But he couldn't. He just couldn't. Scythe had told him to stay and to be calm. He'd be back, and if Rafe left now, well ... *What if I never see him again?* Scythe had become his drug, his only means of peace.

He couldn't leave. It wouldn't be right. The *right* thing, he knew, was to wait, to be with Scythe and never leave.

A thin layer of calm settled over him, but not enough. He was still stealing glances toward that darkened corner and its mass of deadly shadows.

The quiet within the cave stretched on, growing like a living thing, building to an eerie, cemetery silence.

THE HUNGER GNAWED AT BROOKS AS HE WALKED IN THE FOREST, uncertain where he was going. There was nowhere he *could* go. He couldn't face Cade. And Michael's group wasn't an option, either. As for Ethan, well, that topped the list of no-gos; Brooks was a murderer and Ethan was a man of the law.

He stopped at a shallow stream that ribboned through the woods. *Water.* It wasn't what he craved, but he thought maybe it would satisfy his thirst. He bent and his hair, which had long been in need of a trim, fell forward into his eyes. He was surprised to glimpse a streak of stark-white. He pinched the oddly pale lock and held it out, inspecting it. No, not white - silver. And only where the silver dagger had struck. He wondered if the streak would fade as the wound healed.

But the hunger - the agonizing *thirst* - was more important.

He cupped the water, bringing it to his face. It smelled fresh enough. But touching his tongue to it, he knew this would not suffice. His instincts told him that he *could* drink it, but he knew no reason why he should, so he dumped the water back into the stream then wiped his hand on the tattered leg of his boxer shorts and continued walking. He didn't know what he was looking for - perhaps a small forest creature to get him through the night.

The rain had stopped and the fog rolled in thick patches above the forest floor. He should have been cold in nothing but a shredded t-shirt and underwear, but he wasn't. Physically, he felt fine. Wonderful, in fact. Healthier than he ever had, just hungry. His senses were impossibly sharp and were it not for the misery that plagued his mind, he would have relished his ability to see so clearly in the moonless night, to hear the scurry and scamper of smaller animals yards ahead of and behind him, the warm scent of the deer he sensed deeper in the woods. He forced himself to focus on these things, taking stock of his new body and heightened senses.

He could even smell the fog - damp and fresh and powerful. It was as if he had all new adrenal glands, scientifically altered to pump some highly specialized new hormone into his blood, shooting vitality into all of his cells. Funny, he mused, that vampires were thought of as being dead when, in fact, they were more alive than anything on earth. At night, anyway.

Yes, physically, he felt fine. No, magnificent. The only thing bothering him was the wound on his forehead and even that wasn't so bad. It itched more than burned now - and that meant it was healing.

And the hunger - that was bothering him, too. The want for hot, salty blood. The thought of it brought on a fireworks burst of saliva under his tongue that filled his mouth.

He groaned and continued - he could have walked all night and never tired - on the lookout for something living. Anything living. Anything that would smother these flames of hunger. From time to time - frequently, if Brooks were being honest - his thoughts flitted to Gretchen. She was alive again, he knew it. And more importantly, she would take him in. He knew that, too.

But it was more than the prospect of shelter and companionship that drew his mind to her again and again. She was his Maker, officially, and that had bonded him to her in a way he could only compare to a child with its mother. He longed for her. Ached to be near her. If she were a magnet, he was the steel. Despite his better judgment, he wanted her, wanted her badly - and he hated himself for it.

Even though he knew that if he quieted his mind, just a little - and listened to his instincts - he'd be able to find her, Brooks couldn't go to Gretchen; the logical part of his mind wouldn't allow it. Gretchen would use him to get to Cade, just as she had done before - and Brooks would not put his brother in danger again.

So this is life as a vampire, he thought, *a whole world full of need and impossibility.* He realized with a start that he'd been unconsciously making his way toward the cabin he'd shared with Cade. He stopped. A part of him wanted to go to Cade, just check on him to make sure that he was safe. But thoughts of Cade brought thoughts of Samantha ... and what he'd done - and Brooks couldn't bear the weight of that.

Not yet.

He headed in the other direction, making his way through the fog, deeper into the woods, so deep that no one would ever find him. He decided he had to learn to live alone, to survive on his own. It was the only way.

CADE STARTED A FIRE, MORE FOR SOMETHING TO DO THAN ANYTHING else. In the past couple of hours, he'd grown restless and irritable, and the sight of Ethan Hunter, sitting there watching him with worried eyes, made Cade self-conscious and angry. He'd broken down like a child, made a fool of himself - he couldn't take the pity. Or the babysitting. It was too much like last year when Gretchen had set her sights on him - there'd constantly been some well-meaning "bodyguard" under foot. And Cade wouldn't live like that again. If Gretchen came around, wanting to use him as her personal stud because of his "rare genetic makeup," so be it. As long as he could be with Samantha again, he didn't care what else happened.

And as soon as Michael and Winter get back, I will *be with her again.*

He sat on the stone hearth, his back against the snapping fire, stroking Purrcy in silence, thinking of ways to get rid of Ethan. Cade felt fine and didn't need him here. There was no gentle way to say so, so finally, Cade simply said, "I want to be alone. I want you to leave now."

Ethan stared at him. "That's not an option. You know that. Not until Michael gets back and we figure out how to-"

Cade scoffed. "Michael. Like he's going to do anything to help. He's the reason all this is happening."

Ethan's brows rose.

"I want you to go home, Ethan. I'm not worried about Gretchen. Unlike Michael, I *will* kill her."

"And Brooks? Will you kill him, too?"

"Brooks won't come back. He'd have to face me and he won't do that. He's too much of a coward."

Ethan shrugged. "I'm not leaving."

"You have to." Cade felt the blood rising hot and furious to his face, but he kept his tone level. "This isn't your house and I'm asking you to leave." Cade felt his control slipping and it infuriated him. He needed to feel like life was normal again but Ethan's presence made that impossible.

Ethan shrugged again and, furious now, Cade stood. He picked Purrcy up for fear that if his hands were free he might smack the smug look right off the sheriff's face.

"Why don't you get something to eat," Ethan said. "You haven't had anything all day."

Cade's jaw flexed. "I'm not hungry, and stop babysitting me."

"Is that what you think I'm doing?"

"That's exactly what I think you're doing."

"Well, it isn't. I'm a cop and I have reason to believe you're in danger. I have a job to do."

"And I have a right to decide who I want in my house!"

Ethan was getting angry now, too. "It's Brooks' house and I think he'd want me to stay with you, so that's exactly what's going to happen. Now sit down and I'll get you something to eat."

"Maybe it *is* Brooks' house," Cade spoke through gritted teeth, "but I live here and you don't."

Ethan held up a hand, offering peace. "Look. I know you don't like it, but it's just the way it is. You're not safe. Until you are, I'm staying put."

"Like I said, I know how to kill vampires if any come around - and I *will* kill them. Even Brooks." The sincerity in Cade's own tone frightened him: he'd meant it. He thought of the silver dagger in the dresser in his bedroom, wishing he'd aimed it at his brother's heart.

Ethan stared. "I don't think you mean that. He's still your brother."

And that, more than the sheriff's refusal to leave, outraged Cade. "No. He is *not* my brother. Not anymore." He paused, letting his words penetrate the sheriff. He saw that they did. "And I meant it when I said I don't want you here. Now get out."

Ethan watched him.

Cade saw the glint in his eye, and thought: *He thinks I'm mad - that I've gone over the edge.* And maybe he had.

After a brief staring contest, Ethan got up from the chair. "Fine."

"Fine," Cade said in a voice that was, even to him, childish and petulant. He stood there, a villain stroking his cat as Ethan left, and waited for the sound of a starting engine and the flash of headlights. When neither came, he looked outside. Ethan's red Wrangler remained in the drive, untouched.

And Ethan himself sat on the steps of the front porch, staring down between his feet.

Cade clenched his jaw. *Oh, for fuck's sake, just leave!* But he knew Ethan well enough to know that wasn't going to happen. Just because it felt good, Cade walked over and locked the deadbolt, nice and noisy-like.

FULL PANIC TOOK HIM NOW. THE BLACK SHADOWS OF THE CAVERN HAD closed in like thick smothering curtains. The creature in the corner hadn't moved, but it was only a matter of time before she woke, hungry for more blood. There was no time to waste.

Rafe was at the boulder that blocked the exit, pushing and shoving, trying to move it the way he'd seen Scythe do so easily.

But he was not Scythe. Not even close. He'd been at it for a good fifteen minutes and hadn't budged it more than an inch. Sweat, hot and sour-smelling - *God, I need a shower* - dripped down his face and back, soaking his shirt until it stuck to him like an itchy second skin. The muscles in his arms burned and trembled, almost useless, and now, the best he could do was shove his shoulder against the massive rock and push with his legs. He might have gotten it to move if he'd been able to gain some purchase with his feet. His steel-toed work boots were great if you dropped something on your foot, but they didn't have shit in the way of traction.

Pausing to catch his breath - but far from resigned - Rafe wiped sweat from his forehead and tried to think. *I need traction.* He looked around, searching the near-darkness, and saw a stick. He used it to dig a groove into the dirt near his feet; the soil was soft enough to work in his favor. He stabbed and scraped and dragged, wearing down the stick and tossing aside small rocks that got in his way. Digging, digging, digging, like a dog trying to find its bone. Digging until blisters formed on his hands, but finally, he'd forged a groove deep enough to use as a foothold. *Not so different from rock-climbing.* Hopeful that his teenage adventures would serve some purpose after all, he placed his right foot in the little trench, tested it. It would hold. Positioning himself at a slightly-sideways angle with his shoulder and both hands against the boulder, he pushed off.

His leg muscles screamed. It was like squatting a thousand pounds at the gym - but he pushed with everything he had, his face a pained grimace as fresh sweat popped. He pushed until a high ringing came into his ears, his head began to swim, and he could almost hear the muscles in his thighs, ass, and calves tearing.

"Come ... on, you ... *bitch*," he growled through gritted teeth.

And just when he thought his legs would break, it moved. Rafe landed on his hands and knees in the dirt, half in and half out of the cave, uncertain for a moment what had happened. He looked up and almost whooped for joy. The boulder had not only moved, but rolled several feet away, leaving plenty of room.

Free. He was free. He felt like Jesus emerging from the tomb.

Well, almost.

Now that it was real, Rafe wasn't sure he could bring himself to leave. He realized he dreaded the reality of freedom almost as much as he'd longed for it.

Because ... *What about Scythe?* The thought of leaving him punched tiny holes in Rafe's chest. Scythe made him better. Scythe made him safe.

But if I don't go, I'll die here. And that, he knew, was the truth. He looked back into the cave, feeling that he at least needed something that belonged to Scythe, something to keep with him. Maybe it would somehow soothe his nerves when the fear was on him. He grabbed Scythe's deck of cards - *The last thing he touched* - and stuffed them into his pocket.

From her corner of shadows, Gretchen stirred - and this gave Rafe all the motivation he needed to get going.

Like a panicked rabbit scurrying out from under a bush, Rafe crawled from the mouth of the cave.

Outside, he shot to his feet and looked around wildly, not sure where to go, not even sure where he was. The night sky was moonless. There was nothing to indicate his location. He turned one way - *south?* - then another - *north?* He couldn't be sure.

All he knew was that he was in the woods beyond Crimson Cove - and that meant west would lead to Crimson Lake and east toward town. If he could figure out which was which, it wouldn't be too long a walk to safety. Heart trip-hammering, he took off one way, paused - *Think, think. I need to go east. Which way is east?*

He hadn't a clue.

Just go. Run, before they come back - or that thing *in the cave sniffs you out.*

So he ran, swallowed by the woods, no longer knowing or caring which way was which. If he ended up at the lake, well, at least he'd know to turn around. *Or keep going until I hit the ocean.*

And then what? Rafe hadn't a clue.

He tried not to think of Scythe. Leaving the man felt like dying, but at least he'd never see that Gretchen creature again.

And right now, that was enough to keep him running.

It had been half an hour since the sheriff posted himself on the front porch and, alone in the cabin, the silence of the place, the *emptiness* of it, began to wear on Cade. Being alone hadn't been such a hot idea after all.

Not to mention, he felt like a jerk.

I was a total jerk.

He hadn't meant to be, but he felt scraped raw.

But it wasn't Ethan's fault.

Cade made two cups of hot cocoa and stepped outside, taking a seat on the top step beside his friend. He offered one of the cups and Ethan took it and sipped.

For a while, neither spoke. They just sat, listening to the songs of the crickets, the gentle rustle of wind in the trees - a sound that always reminded Cade of a woman's long skirt whispering across a hard floor. The night *was* like a woman, he thought; deep and mysterious, holding its secrets close. Beneath the cold, quiet smell of autumn, the slightly salty scent of fog lingered like a soft perfume, and were it not for his troubled mind, it might have been perfectly peaceful, a good night for writing.

But somewhere out there, Brooks roamed the darkness and Cade couldn't help wondering where his brother was, how he was getting by. Was he sorry for what he'd done, or was he still rampaging - maybe even killing others? Cade sipped the chocolate, averting his thoughts. The cocoa was too hot, too sweet, but he drank it anyway. Taking a deep breath, he closed his eyes. He was so tired of thinking, so tired of *feeling*.

"I'm sorry, Ethan," he said. "I was a dick."

"It's okay. I get it." Ethan paused. "And if I thought I could leave you alone, I would. But I don't ... and I can't. Not yet."

"I know."

For another long moment, the only sounds were the crickets and the wind. Cade considered telling Ethan why he didn't need to be babysat - because he was going to talk to Winter and Winter would bring Samantha back, and everything would be normal again.

But he didn't think Ethan would be too keen on the idea. He, like

Michael, thought people should be given the choice of immortality. Under normal circumstances, Cade agreed, but this was different. Samantha had been taken from him. She'd *want* to come back. Winter would understand that and do what was right. Then it would be too late for anyone to say anything about it. But until then, Cade needed to keep his mouth shut.

"Why don't you take Brooks' bed tonight?"

Ethan nodded. "I'll take you up on that. Not to be rude, but your couch sucks ass."

Cade sipped his cocoa. He was getting drowsy. "It's late. I think I'll head to bed."

"Okay. I'll wait till Michael calls and do the same. It won't be much longer now until they're somewhere that has cell service."

"Will you let me talk to him when he calls?"

"Sure." Ethan sipped from his cup, making no move to stand. Neither did Cade. They remained on the porch in silence.

Cade was suddenly grateful for Ethan Hunter, grateful for someone he could be silent with, someone who wouldn't force him to talk about his feelings - or his plans.

He thought of the grief support group Ethan had recommended. Cade would not be attending. He wouldn't need to.

Michael and Winter will be back tonight and then all of this will go away because they'll turn Samantha and it will be like none of it ever happened.

Cade felt an almost delirious joy - joy that death was not an end, not in Crimson Cove, anyway - and that soon, life would be back to normal.

For me. But what about Samantha?

Doubt flickered.

Have I even thought about what she'd want? Am I being selfish? What if she doesn't really want to be a vampire and she hates me for it?

He thought of the horrible things she'd have to do for the rest of eternity.

He tried to envision her drinking blood.

Having to live a life of restraint and suppression.

Never seeing the sunlight again.

The joy died. Tears sprang to Cade's eyes and he wiped them away. *What if this isn't the right thing to do?*

"You all right?" Beneath heavy brows, Ethan's eyes were red with exhaustion and ringed in dark shadows.

"Not really."

The sheriff nodded. "Well, the good news is, you don't have to be."

Cade's voice came out as a splintered croak. "This shouldn't have happened, Ethan. And it wouldn't have if I'd warned her. I didn't know she'd come home, I didn't-"

"Stop right there, Cade. This isn't your fault. It just ... happened."

The tears came freely now. "But if I hadn't gone out. If I'd thought about it, I would have stayed home. If I would have just *thought* about it! Samantha had a headache and I should have realized she might leave work early. I should have-"

"Don't go down this road, Cade. Don't do it. There are no shoulds and this is *not* your fault."

"But it is."

Ethan shook his head. "No. No, it isn't. I dismiss the charges."

Cade wiped at his eyes. "You can't just-"

"But I can." Ethan looked at him. "I'm sheriff of this town and it's my job to catch the bad guys." He looked at Cade. "And you're not the bad guy. You're an innocent. The only thing you're guilty of is being a good man to Samantha and a good brother to Brooks." He paused. "Not to mention, a pretty good friend to me."

Cade stared down between his feet; the sheriff's words *did* make him feel a little better. "I don't think I'm any of those things."

"Then I guess you're just going to have to take my word for it, aren't you?"

"I'll try." But Cade wondered if he'd ever believe him. The guilt was unbearable. All he could think about was what he should have done differently. He hated himself and didn't think that could ever change.

Standing, he told Ethan goodnight.

"Get something to eat, Cade."

"I will." He headed inside, grabbed an apple and then, in his bedroom, was struck by the sight of Samantha's clothes hanging in the closet.

Scenes of Samantha, lifeless and bloody, flashed in his mind and he closed his eyes and took slow breaths, nearly crushing the apple in his tightening fist, as he willed the images away.

But his anger toward Brooks remained and Cade pulled open the dresser drawer and stared down at the silver dagger.

As much as he hated himself, he hated Brooks more. He reached out and, wishing he'd driven the blade straight through his brother's fucking heart, ran his hand down the razor-fine, blade, then touched the silver wasp on the dagger's hilt.

Lost in his fantasy, he took a hard angry bite of the apple and let out a yelp when something stung his lip. He looked down. A black wasp, a real one, crawled out of the fruit and flew off. "Fuck!" Grossed out, Cade hurled the apple into the trash, aware of a sudden strangeness in the room - a kind of humming electricity.

"Just the storm," he told his reflection in the dresser mirror.

"Just the storm."

The voice echoed through the battered little casita that stood alone on the outskirts of Santa Fe and for the first time, behind closed eyes, the woman in black saw the face of the man in possession of the dagger.

He was young, much younger than she'd imagined, perhaps only twenty-three or twenty-four with a slim build and chestnut hair that fell over dark-lashed hazel eyes. The woman caught only a few details of the young man's immediate surroundings - wood walls, blue drapes, a blue bed quilt and two dressers - but nothing that betrayed his location.

"*Just the storm,*" he'd said. But it could be storming anywhere.

The woman, her body still slow and stiff after decades of disuse, reached down for one of the rats snuffling at her feet. Its blood brought warmth to her stomach, and then to her limbs. And after drinking from a second rodent, her mind began to clear.

But she'd soon need more than the blood of vermin if she was ever to locate and pursue - the dagger. It was time to bring real life back into her body, and that meant taking human blood.

And she did not have to leave the casita to search for it. They would bring it straight to her.

14

DESPERATELY SEEKING SUSTENANCE

*D*eath, cruel, beautiful, and very much alive, walked the woods beyond Crimson Cove. Hungry, it stalked the shadows, its eyes watchful, its mind and body alert, ready to follow the first scent of blood, ready to pounce at the first movement in the bushes.

Famished beyond the ability to reason, Brooks Colter was as much an animal now as the wildlife he sought; he was death itself on a quest for satiation. He'd walked for hours and as the hunger grew, he'd slowly shed logic and humanity. Now, he no longer thought of anything but the hunger, the blood; all else had been driven from his mind by the pounding urgency to feed.

The fog had thickened, hanging like curtains and draping the low branches of the trees in gossamer. Brooks moved through it on quick, lithe feet, barely disturbing it. Catching a scent, he turned, nostrils flared. But as quick as it had come, it vanished, and once again he could smell only earth, fog, forest, and distant water. But he'd detected something - something alive and warm.

He continued deeper into the woods, deeper, where the trees were thickest and the shadows so complete that even the sprinkling of stars overhead couldn't penetrate the pitch-black blanket of the night. But his eyes were keen and he saw everything around him - the redwoods and ferns, the lazy flight of moths, and - most interestingly - a crooked, abandoned cabin just ahead.

In a brief flash, his human mind screamed, *Shelter*! but that tiny spark was smothered by the press of his dominant need. He tucked the cabin away into a darkened corner of his thoughts where he'd save it for later, for after he'd fed.

And then, again, he scented the blood.

From the west.

And close.

Deer. More than one.

The hunger came fully alive now, kicking and screaming, gnawing at him like a parasite. His mouth flooded with saliva as the soft, warm musk of life enveloped him, deadening him to all else.

Like a shot, he sprinted west, pushing past trees and leaping over shrubbery, chasing down the scent of life, bare feet pounding the forest floor, his own blood roaring in his head. The smell strengthened as he closed the distance - strengthened so much he could detect the gender of the deer. Female. Two of them. Maybe three, somehow, he knew that. He ran, the muscles of his legs cording and burning with effort - but it was a delicious burn.

At last, he reached them. Crouching between two tall redwoods, he stared into the small clearing some twenty yards off where the creatures grazed. Though he'd made not a sound, they looked up, ears twitching, eyes watching. Brooks slunk lower into the shadows, salivating madly, seduced by the soft tang of blood just beneath their warm hides. He waited, wanting them off their guard, his vampiric hunter's mind anticipating possibilities and mapping out plans of attack.

Then a new scent drifted toward him. It was different from the deer-smell. This smell was the *right* smell. He rose to his full height, startling the deer. They ran off, lost to the night, but Brooks didn't care about them anymore. He only cared about this new smell. The *right* smell. It was just close enough he knew he could track it.

The hunger, which he'd thought had already fully bloomed,

opened within him even wider now, impossibly wide, like a razor-winged rose, ripping at his insides and driving him over a line he thought he'd already crossed.

He ran, chasing that smell, the *right* smell, and there was nothing - no deer, not even a steel-jawed trap - that could keep him from it.

WHEN THEY RETURNED TO THE CAVE WITH THEIR CAPTIVES FROM SANTA Cruz, Jazminka and Scythe stood at the opening, staring in disbelief. The boulder had been moved.

And Rafe Santangelo had fled.

Inside the cave, Jazminka whirled on Scythe, cursing as she hit her head on a lantern. "Vhere is he?"

Scythe shoved the two prisoners to the hard cavern floor. "How did he even move the boulder?"

"Well, he did!" Jazminka pointed to Gretchen. "*She* certainly didn't help him!" She paused, eyeing Scythe with suspicion. "You gafe him venom?"

"Of course. He won't go far." But Scythe didn't meet Jazminka's eyes; the truth was, he hadn't dosed the man since last night. Sick and tired of tripping over the guy, he'd been hoping to loosen the bond a little, so he'd skipped tonight's dose. Venom lasted about twenty-four hours so there *should* have still been enough lingering in the man's system to keep him trailing behind Scythe like a lovesick puppy. Clearly, there was enough to give him the strength to move the boulder.

Well, fuck.

Jazminka was in his face. "But did you gif it to him tonight? I didn't see you."

"I did," he lied.

Her pale eyes sparked. "No. You did not dose him and now he got away, and ve may be in danger. You fool!"

"Oh, quit being so fucking dramatic." But he knew she wasn't over-reacting. If the guy found his way back to the city and disclosed their location in the woods, Scythe, Jazminka, and Gretchen were done for. He gave Jazminka an uneasy grin. "Maybe Gretchen ate him."

Jazminka was not amused. "Meestress did nothing of the sort. This ees *your* fault."

"Whatever. Gretchen probably scared him off." Scythe looked at the barely-breathing lump in the corner. "She *is* pretty scary."

"Vich vould not have happened if you had dosed him properly. You are an idiot!"

"And you're a cow. Let's just focus on the fact that we have two new sources of sustenance for Gretchen. Between them, she'll recover faster and we can get the hell out of here."

Jazminka, several inches taller than Scythe, stepped closer, looking down at him. "No. Go find heem. Now."

Her icy gaze made it clear she wouldn't take no for an answer, and Scythe stepped out into the night.

But he wouldn't go searching for the man - he refused to waste the energy. Instead, he wandered far enough away that Jazminka couldn't see him and sat down on a boulder, wishing he'd brought his deck of cards. He'd go find something to eat, then return within an hour or two claiming there'd been no sign of him.

And if the stupid motherfucker managed to find his way to town and rat them out, well, then, Scythe guessed he'd just have to kill whoever came looking.

CADE WAS LYING IN BED, STARING AT THE CEILING WHEN ETHAN TAPPED at his door. He glanced at the digital clock; it was nearly two a.m. "Come in."

"Phone call for you."

Cade shot up.

Beside him, Purrcy lifted his head, blinked, and went back to sleep.

"It's Michael," Ethan said.

"They're back?"

Ethan nodded. "I told him we're okay for the night, but-"

"Winter's not coming tonight?"

Ethan shrugged, handed Cade his phone, and left the room.

Cade switched on the lamp. "Michael?"

"I hope I didn't wake you." Michael's low, velvety voice brought a surge of anger.

This is his fault. He should have cut Gretchen's fucking head off. But, "It's fine," was all Cade said. "Is Winter coming over?"

Michael hesitated. "Since Ethan is there tonight, I'll send Winter tomorrow. We need to get settled in and-"

"But …" Cade wasn't sure what to say. If he sounded too eager, Michael would suspect something was up. And Cade knew there was no way Michael, who had a permanent stick up his ass, would be okay with turning Samantha. "I guess it'll be okay till tomorrow. I just … hope Gretchen isn't lurking around, you know?"

"Rogan and Dante are keeping an eye on the area."

Of course.

"Also starting tomorrow, I am ordering a search for your brother."

"And what happens when you find him?" *Shake your finger at him and go tsk-tsk-tsk?*

Michael was silent a long moment. "I'm not yet sure. That depends on what state of mind he is in."

"Well, I hope you'll have the good sense to cut his fucking head off on sight." The words were out before Cade had a chance to think them through.

Michael's silence spoke volumes. He cleared his throat and said, "I meant to say, I am very sorry for your loss, Cade. Samantha was a wonderful young woman."

Fresh anger clutched Cade. "Yes. She was."

Silence strained. "I'll send Winter over tomorrow night then."

Cade tried not to sound disappointed. "That's fine."

"Goodnight, Cade."

Cade got out of bed and returned the phone to Ethan. After relaying the information, he stomped back to his room, shut off the lamp, and continued staring at the ceiling. He didn't think he could stand another day of waiting. He wanted Samantha back now. He wanted her back so he could propose to her and start a new life. Maybe even start a family.

It occurred to him that vampires couldn't have children.

But I'm a Sire and Sires most certainly can *reproduce with the undead.*

Nearly giddy with exhaustion, Cade planned his and Samantha's future together. People would think Samantha was dead; Cade would have to keep her hidden. This wouldn't be easy.

For the first time since arriving last year, he considered leaving Crimson Cove. Away from Brooks. Away from Gretchen. Away from them all. There was nothing keeping Samantha and him here, was there? Samantha had no real relationship with her family anyway, and as for her job, well, she could work at any library. And what Cade had always wanted was to be a writer, and he could be a writer anywhere. They could start over somewhere else.

But if he left he'd miss Ethan. And Winter. Winter was his friend, too.

Cade flopped onto his side, stared at the shadowed wall.

Even if he moved, Gretchen would probably follow him.

And what about Brooks? Could I really leave him here alone? He didn't know the answer to that. In the past days, he'd felt everything from pity and love and worry to blatant, pitch-black hatred for his brother. Right now, Cade felt pity. He knew Brooks hadn't deliberately harmed Samantha, he just wasn't sure he cared.

And it was the vampires' fault. Well, Michael's fault, anyway.

Maybe when Winter brought Samantha back, Cade would forgive them all.

He rolled onto his other side and stared at the clock, trying to untangle and sort his thoughts. He didn't want to leave Crimson Cove, he decided. He wasn't sure he could.

Because of the cabin. Because of his mother.

Cade had come here to live with Brooks after her death. She'd been a real-estate agent and she'd found this cabin and helped Brooks buy it. She'd loved it on sight and put her life on hold to help him get it. It was, she said, the perfect place for him, and Cade agreed. So had Brooks. She'd planted the flowers outside herself and done all the interior decorating - in a way, the place was hers as much as anyone's. And Cade couldn't lose this house, too. He'd already lost her house in Gilroy to the mountain of medical bills that had come after she'd died. That's why he'd come to Crimson Cove.

He had to keep this cabin. It may have had Brooks' name on the paperwork, but Cade would do everything he could to take care of it.

And he liked Crimson Cove. It was home now. He might not fit in here as much as Brooks did, but he'd never expected to. Brooks always made a million friends after thirty seconds in a new place - he was like a rockstar that way and now, Crimson Cove was his new fan club. Brooks, with his green eyes, cleft chin, and abs up to his eyeballs was a pretty hot commodity here. Cade saw the way the women hung around Pinetop's, asking for service on cars that didn't need a thing done to them. It was disgusting.

Pinetop's Garage. Brooks' business.

Shit. There was that to contend with and Cade didn't have a clue what to do about it. *Sell it?* But then how would he afford the cabin? No, selling it was not an option. He just needed to keep the business running and he supposed that meant getting in touch with Brooks' right-hand-man, Chet Wilson.

I'll call him tomorrow and put him in charge. I'll say that Brooks is ... sick? On vacation? Out of town. A family emergency. Yes.

That would buy a few days and hopefully, by then, he'd be able to figure something else out. *One step at a time.*

Cade sighed, content with the thought.

Then: *And what happens if the shop goes to hell without Brooks there to run it?*

Then it would be up to Cade to keep the cabin's mortgage afloat. And that would require a hell of a lot more money than he made at Langley's Literary Labyrinth.

He thought of the book he'd written, the one that *The Writer's Sanctum* editor, Ian Lake, had persuaded him to finish. If he could get that published, it would help. Ian had it now and was corresponding with Cade, making suggestions to tighten the story. Once it was polished, Ian would begin shopping it to publishers.

But how long would all of that take?

For the first time in his life, Cade wished he'd chosen a more practical path - the medical field perhaps. At the time, Ian Lake's offer had been a dream come true, but now, in the shadow of the more immediate stressors, writing seemed a distant dream, a hobby at best.

Cade realized he hadn't checked his email in days. It wouldn't be long before Ian began asking after the latest round of edits.

One more thing I should do tomorrow.

When Samantha comes back, we'll figure it all out together.

Smiling, Cade closed his eyes, determined to get some sleep. Just one more day and he could talk to Winter. And Winter would understand. He wouldn't deny Cade. He lay there for some time before becoming aware of a buzzing sound.

He sat up, straining to hear.

It was like the hum of a fly - an insect at the window maybe.

The sound reminded him of the wasp that had stung his lip earlier. He'd forgotten all about it and now he touched his lip, feeling around. There was no sign he'd ever been stung at all. *Strange.*

He realized the buzzing had stopped. The room was silent again and Cade lay back down, covering his head with the pillow.

BROOKS, CROUCHING BEHIND A TREE, WAITED, WATCHING AS THE MAN walked through the darkened forest, head down, hands in his pockets.

He was tall and broad-shouldered, his dark hair cut short. He wore faded jeans, a short-sleeved shirt, and black boots. He was big - not that the guy stood a chance of outrunning Brooks, but his size would slow him down.

The hunger was infernal now and Brooks could smell the man's blood - and the closer he got, the deeper the hunger dug. There was no thought, only instinct, only survival.

Brooks tensed, prepared to strike when the moment was right.

THE SILVER DAGGER

Rafe wandered the forest until everything began to look the same and he was certain he was walking in circles. As he moved, his thoughts drifted back to Scythe. Had leaving been a mistake? Whatever Scythe had done to him had made Rafe feel better than he ever had before. Better even, than when he and his ex-girlfriend, Katie, had been happy. Or at least, when Rafe *thought* they'd been happy. He shook off the painful thoughts - *fuck her*.

He was lost. There was no denying it.

Thirsty and weak from all the blood he'd lost to Gretchen, Rafe admitted he was going to have to give it up for the night; find a place to sleep - if he *could* sleep - and start again tomorrow.

He sat down, his back against a massive redwood and looked around, wondering what kind of bed he could make from leaves, dirt, and pine needles. His eyes slid over the cold, muddy forest floor, then back up at the trees.

And that's when he saw the man's face. Their eyes clashed like swords in battle; Rafe almost heard the silvery strike of weapons.

The face seemed to hover bodiless above a thicket of foliage several feet away, staring right at him.

Rafe scrambled to his feet, heart thundering. "Who ... who are you?" He stared, his blue eyes riveted on pale green ones that held no soul.

"What do you-"

With a deep war cry, the green-eyed man sprang from the shadows, his death-white face pulled back in a feral mask.

By chance, he'd struck an artery, and as he swallowed mouthfuls of the hot coppery life, rational thought pumped back into Brooks' mind at the same rate blood pulsed and spurted from the other man's torn neck.

Stop! Don't kill him!

With great determination, Brooks pulled back, breathing hard, and looked down at the ruin before him. The man's eyes were wide and unseeing, his mouth moving as he gasped for breath, his hands curled into large claws that swiped the air in futile attempts to ward off his attacker.

The blood he'd drunk spread out in Brooks' stomach and now he could feel it traveling his veins, charging his cells. Like oxygen, it hit his brain, cleared his mind, and brought him up hard against reality. *He's dying*! Terror zigzagged through him like lightning.

The man's eyes rolled back. Thick white foam bubbled at his lips, which were growing whiter by the moment.

Panicked, Brooks put his hand over the wound, tried to staunch the flow. It spurted through his fingers, the blood so dark in the night that it looked black.

The man began to jerk and heave, convulsing in the throes of seizure, his head smacking hard onto the earth. Foam sprayed from his lips, running down both sides of his face as he sputtered and gasped.

Venom! If Brooks could give him venom, he could heal him, save him. *But I've never used venom! How does that even work?*

It happened fast. The man's body bucked hard, knocking Brooks back, then the convulsions ebbed to tremors and twitches as the blue eyes began taking on an eerie vacancy.

"No!" Brooks lunged, sank his fangs into the man's throat. He let himself go and something happened - something he instinctively understood. Delicious warmth hummed from inside his teeth, building, building. He felt it spread along his jaw, filling his mouth, his head, and within seconds, his entire body with a mounting bliss he could only liken to orgasm. Then that liquid warmth discharged strong and hot from the depths of his being, from the very marrow of his bones, tingling deliciously through his entire body as he emptied himself deep into the dying man.

Stop! Too much will turn him! But how much was too much? He had no idea how much he'd already injected. He fell onto his side, his muscles exhausted, his body buzzing. He lay on the forest floor, spent.

I did it, he thought. *I don't know how, but I did it.*

But the man beside him did not move.

Brooks sat up. He watched the man, waiting, not sure what, if anything, to expect.

The night was silent save for the trickle of small streams ribboning through the forest. No night birds took wing, not even a cricket dared chirp.

I'm too late. Too late. Panic beat dark wings against Brooks' heart as he stared down at the dead man. *Not again. I didn't mean to kill him. I can't live with this. I can't-*

A twitch in the man's fingertips. *Nerves?*

Brooks wasn't sure. He watched, breath held deep in his lungs, waiting for something, for anything, to change.

It didn't.

"Fuck!" He got to his feet, tried to walk away, but couldn't bring himself to leave the man there. *Like I left Samantha.* Someone would miss him, someone would come looking for him, and Brooks couldn't bear the thought of them finding him like this.

Eventually, Michael and Cade and the others would hear about it too, and they'd know. They'd know without doubt who was responsible. *And where they can find me.*

I need to hide the body.

Brooks stared down at the corpse, feeling removed - like an unwilling accomplice in a violent crime. *I didn't do this. I couldn't have!*

But he had.

This is murder.

Murder.

The word was black and jagged in his mind; it tore through him, poisoning him with self-hatred.

He crouched, head in his hands. "Fuck." He looked at the dead man. Had to look away. "Fuck. I'm so sorry, man. Whoever you are, I'm sorry. I'm sor-"

The body jerked.

Brooks scrambled to his feet, eyes wide.

The corpse went still again, but something was happening. He watched for a long, breathless moment, his eyes creating movement where there was none. Every shadow became motion, every rustle of wind in the trees a gasping breath. But in truth, the body wasn't moving.

Just nerves.

Then the eyes shot open. The lips pulled back and the mouth yawned wide. A scream, soul-deep and filled with pain and terror, tore from the man's lungs. The darkness came alive as night birds exploded from trees, shattering from their branches like black-winged glass.

But Brooks was rooted in place, his feet cemented to the ground, watching with wide-eyed horror as the man clutched his stomach and rolled to his side, screaming, screaming, screaming as new life claimed him. Not human life, Brooks knew that much, but that new and terrible second life. Vampire life.

Oh, God, what have I done?

15

THE BEGINNING OF ALWAYS

After feeding, Gretchen returned to her hollow, to the shadows. She was not yet her old self, not by a long shot, but as she lay dozing on the air mattress, she was aware of a slow-growing strength, a subtle but undeniable murmur in her cells as they awakened and began carrying out their duties. She'd gathered a little more momentum with each feeding, but still had a long way to go.

For the first time tonight, she noticed a heightening of her senses. Though the darkness was still impenetrable despite her vampire eyes, her vision was clearer than it had been before. She could make out the faces of the men she'd fed from - the men Jazminka and Scythe had brought back for her. Both were well-suited to her tastes, and though they did nothing for her sexually now, she knew that as she healed, she would enjoy them both.

She could smell their fear, that pungent, sour aroma that once excited her so much. They sat against the opposite wall, eyes glazed by the venom they'd been given. The scent of that fear kindled a powerful desire to recover. It fired her synapses, brought clarity to her mind, but her body was still weak. She wanted only to sleep.

She closed her eyes, wishing Jazminka would stop staring at her, that Scythe would return with the runaway slave, and that she could get her own weak, traitorous body to obey her commands. But she could not.

Still, until she was fully healed, she had no intentions of remaining idle.

So, lying there, she began to think, to plan. There was much to do. They'd need to return to the Crimson Corset - but not before building an army. Michael and his Loyals would be looking for her even now - and they would be protecting Cade, the Sire.

The Sire. This brought her eyes open. *Yes, the Sire. Cade Colter.* She remembered. He was the reason she'd ended up here in the first place. He had been - and still was - the ultimate spring upon which to build her trap; had she been smarter in the first place, had she not trusted Michael and his men, she would have already obtained the Sire. With him, she could build the ultimate army - one that was unconquerable, impenetrable, one that would last forever.

And Emeric, her old business manager. She'd need his funds. And that meant she had to find him. She knew the man well - she'd been a companion to him since the 1890s - and she was certain he'd returned to his mansion in Palo Alto. She knew he was there now, decked out in the Victorian gentleman's finery that belied his sadist's nature, satisfying his wicked needs with whomever was unfortunate enough to cross his path. *Yes, I need to find Emeric.*

But she was getting ahead of herself. She'd deal with him - and the Sire - soon enough. First, she needed to build up her numbers. She needed to heal and for that, there was nothing to be done except to continue feeding and waiting.

How long will it take? She didn't know; she wasn't even sure how long she'd been inanimate - *a few months?* - and supposed her recovery time depended on the answer to that.

When she'd first reawakened, she'd had no inkling how much time might have passed, but as her mind had cleared and she'd looked around her, she became certain it hadn't been long. She detected no change in the clothing style in the men Jazminka and Scythe had brought her - and having been around since the 1600s, Gretchen had seen many trends come and go; she'd watched the subtle shifts

THE SILVER DAGGER

between them as one gave way to another. No fashion died so much as it evolved, and she knew she was in the same era now as when she'd been staked. She glanced at her two new blood slaves.

With wide eyes, the handsome pair stared back, and Gretchen let her eyes drop to their crotches, licked her lips, and relished their terror.

Despite having just fed, her bloodlust was returning. She ignored it; if she took more this soon she'd only vomit. It would be another hour or two before she dared another feeding.

I'll take more later. Between the two men, there was plenty.

Tired, Gretchen closed her eyes and let her thoughts wander. Of its own accord, her mind traveled back, taking her down the dusty corridors of her past - her very distant past.

IT WAS STILL RELATIVELY EARLY, WITH SEVERAL HOURS UNTIL SUNRISE AS, on the grounds of the Eudemonia Health Spa and Retreat, Michael and Winter walked along one of the narrow, cobblestoned trails that lead to the guest cabins in the forested area on the vast property. "Tomorrow night, you will be posted at the Colter place." Michael spoke so quietly no human could hear. "The sheriff is with him tonight but after that I want one of our kind to stay with him." He didn't look at Winter as he spoke.

The man had been downright shifty since their trip to Eternity and Winter wondered why.

But he knew better than to ask.

"We will not be able to leave the Sire alone," continued Michael, "until we get this settled."

Winter nodded. "Sure thing, Boss." As they wound their way past one of the aromatic gardens of night-blooming jasmine, Winter watched the fairy lights that were strewn throughout the many gardens on the property twinkle and blink. It was a nice touch that gave the impression of life and motion, the irony of which was not lost on him.

Michael said, "I have my doubts that Gretchen would return to the Crimson Corset but we must be diligent. I've sent Dante and Rogan to have a look around."

"You can always count on good old Batman and Robin." Winter chuckled. "So, you don't think Gretchen will leave town?"

Michael shook his head. "I doubt it. Not with the Sire still here."

"You think she'll want to ... finish what she started?"

"If I know Gretchen, yes, she will."

And if anyone knew Gretchen, it was Michael. Winter had no doubt the man was right. He wished they'd removed the bitch's head when they'd had the chance, but he'd never say so. Especially now. Michael was already punishing himself for the choice he'd made to disanimate, rather than destroy, Gretchen. Something to do with that promise Michael had made Gretchen's mother, Astrid, Winter thought. The two had been in love many centuries ago, and Michael had vowed to look after her daughter in the event of Astrid's death.

It sounded great on paper, Winter supposed, but to his way of thinking, if said daughter turned out to be a fucking psychopath - *and Gretchen is a fucking psychopath* - that pretty much nullified the agreement.

But Michael had made a promise, and he was nothing if not true to his word.

Too true sometimes.

But that was Michael's way, and though Winter respected the man's peace-loving principles, Astrid VanTreese was long dead. Killed, no less, by her own daughter - Gretchen, the fucking psychopath herself.

I should've just lopped the twat's head off and apologized for it later. And he'd wanted to do it - oh, how he'd wanted to do it - but Winter would never have willfully disobeyed his boss. He owed Michael a lot - *a whole hell of a lot* - and despite the man's ideals, he was solid. He believed, as had Astrid, in the humanity of vampires, and while that seemed a bit counter-intuitive, if not downright preposterous on the surface, Winter knew it was possible.

He also knew what it was like to run wild, without rules or boundaries. He knew what it meant to be a Rogue. He'd lived as one before meeting Michael, and in comparison to that kill-or-be-killed world, life with Michael - and his ideals - was a sane, if not downright cozy contrast. Winter was happy at Eudemonia. It provided him a good life, and it was a beautiful place to boot. And, if business was any indication, the guests agreed.

He smiled to himself as they made their way deeper in the forest where cabins of various sizes dotted the grounds. Here, Eudemonia guests could free themselves of work and shed technology, virtually camping out in nature while still remaining close enough to civilization to enjoy themselves. There was no electricity in the cabins, only lanterns and candles. No computers, no wifi, and no television.

Winter, who was as much a slave to technology as any human, had been surprised that it had gone over so well, but Eudemonia never lacked for visitors and in fact, the place was usually booked several months out, though Michael always kept a few cabins open for last-minute reservations.

It was from those guests that Michael, Winter, and the others took their sustenance. It wasn't exactly a rigorously honest way of living, but vampires, being what they were, needed blood - preferably fresh, *human* blood - and slipping in and out of the cabins at night hurt no one. They were each allowed only about two pints per week - the bare minimum - and through calming exercises and meditation, the vampires of Eudemonia controlled their lusts. The goal, as Michael often preached, was to make oneself master to, rather than a slave of, the vampire nature. It was a lifestyle that, while initially difficult to adapt to, Winter now had no problem following.

A few feet from one of the cabins, Winter paused, raised his nose to the air. "I think I smell AB Negative, Boss." He grinned. AB Neg was any red-blooded vampire's favorite brand.

A fleeting look - *panic?* - flashed in Michael's eyes. "Let's keep walking."

"But-"

But Michael had already moved on. It wasn't like him - or *any* vampire - to walk away from the rarest and most delicious blood type, but Winter followed.

"This one." Michael paused in front of one of the smaller cabins at the rear of the property.

Winter sniffed the air - *Nothing special in there* - and shrugged. "Works for me, I guess."

Using Michael's key, the two men slipped soundlessly into the room. On the bed lay two young women, both deep in sleep.

Michael nodded his head at the woman on the left: *I'll take this one.*

Winter stepped to the right, crouched, and carefully lifted the sleeper's wrist to his lips. As always, before partaking, he injected a minuscule amount of venom - just enough to numb the area and keep the sleeper firmly immersed in his or her sweet dreams. And, with that touch of venom, the bite wounds would be healed by morning.

The blood of the young woman had an underlying bite - *too much wine* - but it worked.

After taking the proper amount, Winter was surprised to see that Michael was still imbibing, eyes closed, mouth working hungrily, a little too hungrily, at the other woman's wrist.

Afraid the woman would wake, Winter whispered, "Boss?"

But Michael didn't respond.

"Hey. Boss. You okay?"

Michael looked up and Winter caught a feral glint in his eyes, there and gone as quick as a spark. It unsettled Winter. He'd only seen that look in his boss' eyes when the man was angry or very hungry - and both were rare.

With clear reluctance, Michael set the woman's arm down, rose, and stared down at her, breathing a little too hard. In that moment, he reminded Winter of the proverbial vampire of Hollywood movies - a tall, ominous shadow looming over his victim.

Winter got to his feet. "Everything okay, Boss?"

"Of course." Michael stood. He didn't look at Winter as the two of them slipped from the cabin. As they made their way back to the main building that served as their headquarters, neither of them spoke. When they arrived, Michael announced that he had some matters to take care of in his office and wished to be alone for the night.

It was strange. Something was on the man's mind. Something heavy. Probably, he was deeply regretting not killing Gretchen.

Winter pondered this as he headed to check on Arnie, sweet, simple-minded Arnie who, while in Eternity, had accidentally turned a young woman named Erin Woodhouse in a fit of unexpected bloodlust.

Arnie's regret over that was painful to Winter. Especially since, he, Winter, felt responsible for it.

I am *responsible for it. If I'd been watching him like I should have been ...*

The young woman, Erin, now a vampire, had returned with them to Eudemonia to adapt to her new lifestyle. She appeared to be coming along well. New vampires - and of course, youthful-minded ones like Arnie - often struggled with bloodlust and had a hard time controlling their appetites - and their venom expression. In this environment though, with plenty of blood at their disposal, Erin hadn't exhibited any of the more violent baby-vampire tendencies.

Arnie, simple of mind, had been upset when it had first happened, but now he was happy to have a new friend. Erin, by all appearances, was just as content. She and Arnie had quickly forged the expected bond between a new vampire and her Maker. They seemed happy, and Winter wished this did something to ease his own conscience, but it didn't.

Guilt needled hard at him as he stood before the door to Arnie's room.

If I'd only been watching him instead of burying my sexual frustrations into the three Darling girls ... Winter's dick was his worst enemy and this wasn't the first time it had gotten him into trouble. He was a free spirit, he enjoyed playing the field, indulging in the pleasures of the flesh. As far as he was concerned, that was the best part of being undead - no risk of unwanted pregnancy, no possibility of STDs. But he'd been irresponsible, and now Arnie and Erin would pay for it.

Forever.

Winter was just glad Michael hadn't laid into him for neglecting

Arnie in the first place - and it occurred to him now how odd that had been; he'd expected a strongly-worded lecture at the very least, but Michael had said nothing about it, nothing at all. It wasn't like him.

Winter shook the thoughts off and knocked lightly on the door.

"Come in," called Arnie's gentle voice.

He stepped inside, his heart warming. Arnie and Erin sat cross-legged on the floor. In front of them was a scattering of colorful Matchbox cars and what looked like a makeshift racetrack made from books, game pieces, and popsicle sticks. Erin wore a pair of pink pajamas and matching fuzzy slippers. Arnie, too, was in his sleepwear, a pair of silky green PJs he called his *shinies*.

Arnie's eyes lit up. "Papa Winter! We're playing Racetrack!"

Winter smiled. "I see that. But isn't it a little early for your *shinies*? It's hours till sunrise, bud."

"We're having a slumber party." Arnie beamed and Winter smiled back at the perpetual child in the man's eyes. Arnie's features were frozen at about twenty years old, the approximate age he'd been when Winter had unintentionally turned him in 1801 in Sleepy Hollow, New York. Arnie had been a farmhand who'd been in the wrong place at the wrong time. He had the boyish good looks of a 1970s teen heartthrob and cheerful blue eyes, but as sure as his golden-brown hair was always in need of a cut, Arnie's mind would remain that of a child's. As his Maker, Winter felt as much like a father to Arnie as he ever would to anyone.

"A slumber party, huh?"

Arnie nodded. "Yes, sir!"

Winter glanced at Erin; she looked embarrassed. "We were bored with Connect-Four." She, unlike Arnie, was not simple-minded. She'd been a college student working on her thesis when she'd crossed paths with Arnie and for the first time, Winter realized she was quite pretty. Beautiful really, and petite - though from Winter's six-foot-six, two hundred and sixty-five-pound perspective, most people were petite.

She had the big green eyes, smooth pale skin, and dark red hair that would turn any man's head, and Winter suddenly worried about

Arnie taking a sexual interest in her - despite his childlike mind, Arnie was in full possession of a grown man's needs.

But watching them together, Winter sensed nothing that wasn't platonic, just the closeness of a Maker and his protégée. And he had a feeling that Erin could hold her own should Arnie ever get the wrong idea.

"Want to play with us?" Arnie was as giddy as a kid at the zoo. "I'm the red car and Erin is the blue one. You could be the white one if you want."

Winter looked down at the makeshift racetrack and opened his mouth to say no, but he realized it would be a good opportunity to get to know Erin. "I'd love to," he said. "If you don't mind." This he said to Erin. He didn't want to impose on valuable bonding time.

Her smile was warm. "Of course not. It's a slumber party. The more the merrier."

"But you have to wear your pajamas," said Arnie.

Winter, who slept in the nude, laughed. "Let's just pretend these are my pajamas."

Arnie scanned Winter's t-shirt and blue jeans, and sighed. "All right. We'll pretend, but next time, you *have* to wear pajamas."

"It's a deal." Winter joined them on the floor and Arnie explained the rules of the game. As they played, for the first time since returning from Eternity, Winter's guilt faded. Arnie and Erin were so obviously happy that it made it hard to wish things had turned out any differently. *In fact,* Winter thought, *this might be just what Arnie needs.*

He looked at Erin, who was laughing as she rear-ended Arnie's tiny car with her own. "Get off the track, slow-poke!"

Hell, maybe it was what all of them needed.

Suspended somewhere between sleep and consciousness, images began to flash in Gretchen's mind, long-ago memories crashing back to her.

Rome. 1679.

Though born in Sweden, she had no memory of her life there. After Queen Christina's reign ended in 1654, her mother, Astrid, had taken Gretchen, only an infant, to Rome where they'd lived - though not quite prospered - in relative happiness. In her short, young life, this was the only home Gretchen had ever known.

Times were hard in those days, especially for women, who, without benefit of a man's support, were often forced to sell their bodies to survive. But Gretchen and her mother were lucky. Astrid had been born with beauty, a sharp mind, and most importantly, the ability to draw a crowd - all of which she'd passed on to her daughter. Intent on making her own way in the world, Astrid used those talents to their greatest advantage, teaching Gretchen to do the same as soon as she was old enough to understand.

It had worked. By the time Gretchen was six years old, she had an arsenal of survival skills, and knew exactly how to use her Nordic beauty to her advantage. She knew when to bat the thick lashes of her emerald eyes and twirl a finger in her white-blond hair.

And more importantly than how, Gretchen knew who *to charm. As she'd grown into a beautiful young woman, she'd honed her social skills - often under her mother's rather overbearing tutelage - to ensure that she would never resort to offering her body to strangers in dark alleyways by cover of night.*

But as many doors as charm might open, it was rarely enough to earn a place within the room. There was no security in merely being charming, no guarantees, and so, for as long as Gretchen could recall, she and her mother had made their living as part of a local troupe of the commedia dell'arte, delighting spectators with theatrical performances that, in those days, served as one of the main sources of entertainment.

It was a mostly happy life for Gretchen, who, despite her growing boredom with supporting roles to her mother's starring ones, had never considered herself anything but fortunate. Though actors weren't exactly respected among the community, the money was steady; they never suffered for lack of work. In fact, oft times, thanks to a couple of Astrid's personal patrons, the troupe gave multiple shows a day, some of them running well into the night.

It was after one such late-night performance, at the theater of one of

Astrid's patrons, that Gretchen and her mother met the man who would change their lives forever.

The show had gone well, but Gretchen, in her customary red, white, and gold harlequin's costume, was silently furious. She felt this way more and more as she matured and found herself craving more stage presence. Astrid was the star - she was always the star - and Gretchen was outgrowing her own willingness to live in the woman's very tall shadow.

But she said nothing to her mother as, backstage in their dressing room, they changed from their costumes into their evening finery. While Astrid was well-known for her cordiality, Gretchen knew that before the kindness often came the salute to arms; the woman had a temper, and though it didn't flare often, it frightened Gretchen. She'd learned to gauge her mother's moods, suggesting, advising, and submitting her opinions with the lightest of touches, and only at the appropriate times.

And tonight was not the appropriate time to suggest that her mother might tone down her performance and allow the others more room. Gretchen wasn't sure if the time would ever be right for that.

"No, no," said Astrid as Gretchen finished lacing her white satin corset. "You can get it tighter than that." She moved behind Gretchen and began to violently tug the laces. Though petite enough to play a child in many of the troupe's performances, it seemed to Gretchen that her waist was never quite narrow enough for her mother. With each hard pull, Gretchen felt her ribs being compressed, and with every breath forced out of her, her resentment grew. It seemed fitting, somehow symbolic, that her mother should confine her, forcing the very breath from her body.

In a tarnished mirror, Gretchen watched her mother's face frown with concentration and disappointment, the pile of pale curls upon her head bobbing with her efforts to bring her daughter another half-inch closer to perfection. "Mother, I can't breathe."

"Nonsense. You don't want people to think I'm escorting a peasant home, now do you?"

Gretchen wanted to tell her, 'But Mother, we *are* peasants,' but knew it would only infuriate Astrid, who, despite their station, maintained the decorum of nobility, the swollen importance of someone far more distinguished than even a somewhat famous player in the commedia dell'arte, and insisted her daughter do the same. So Gretchen remained silent, watching as her mother's reflection grimaced and continued tightening the corset until Gretchen was sure her ribs would splinter and collapse.

Only when it was tight enough that she felt lightheaded from lack of oxygen did her mother relent. She stood back, eyeing her daughter critically. Gretchen waited for the frown that would indicate more cinching was in order, but instead, Astrid smiled one of her beautiful, bright smiles. "There, now. That's much better, don't we agree?"

"I suppose."

Astrid, gliding like a slip of silk, returned to her seat in front of her own mirror where she continued removing the last of her stage makeup. "And don't wear the satin dress. It doesn't flatter your figure." Astrid herself wore satin, white and pale pink, low-cut and off-the-shoulder, with paned sleeves and a flourish of ruffles that gathered and spilled down her figure like water. The gown was used, quite old, really, but you wouldn't know it to look at it.

Obeying her mother's wishes, Gretchen opted for something plainer because, that was what Astrid *really wanted*. So she slipped into a well-worn, poorly-cut high-shouldered dress, a lesser star trying to shine next to the sun, as Astrid eyed her from the mirror where she began powdering her already pale face. Gretchen, her face clean of makeup now save for a light dusting of powder, parted her hair in the center and put it into a low knot behind, then completed the ensemble with the beaded trinzale her mother had handpicked for her. After a nod of approval from Astrid, the two of them left the theater and went into the night, heading toward their small, third-story apartment at the inn deeper in the city.

The walk home was, as always, as much a performance as anything they did on stage. Once they retired to their chambers, of course, Astrid would change into something more suited to their surroundings, but she never allowed either of them to be seen publicly in less than their best - especially just after a show, when audience members often milled about, hoping to catch the eye of a star. And they *were* stars, Astrid insisted, and it was the duty of stars to shine whether on the stage or off.

Tonight, no admirers awaited them, but as they walked, Gretchen felt eyes upon them. Faces peered at them from doorways of tall buildings, figures paused and stared, and many of the men - especially the common ones who *became more frequent as they neared their inn at the poorer side of the city - took them in with bold, lecherous gazes. Gretchen and her mother continued, heads high, smiling at strangers and ignoring the beggars in tattered clothing who approached them, their eyes raised in supplication, hands stretched out. Some of them followed Gretchen and Astrid and when they would not relent, Astrid would turn on them, speak roughly, and the beggars would draw back, disappearing between the buildings.*

Coming to a great piazza, Astrid and Gretchen passed a cluster of people who talked, laughed, and gestured. Gretchen, who'd grown increasingly faint within the unyielding confines of her corset, paused to sit at the edge of a fountain beneath a clutch of statues staring down at them with blind eyes.

"What's wrong?" Astrid hissed, looking around in obvious fear that someone might recognize her while her daughter was having a fit.

"I just need to catch my breath, Mother."

"You'll be fine, dear. We're almost there, then you can change into something more comfortable."

"If I don't rest, I'm going to faint."

"Nonsense. Now come along and-"

"I think perhaps the young lady has a point." A new voice, a man's voice, startled them both. He seemed to have appeared more than approached. He was tall and slender in waistcoat and breeches and wore a broad smile on a narrow handsome face etched with sharp, fox-like features. "Forgive my intrusion." His voice was like black satin. "I couldn't help overhearing."

Astrid flashed him an irritated look, but he took no notice.

Instead, he removed his black copotain hat and gave a little bow. There was lace at his throat and wrists, the white of which took color from his face and stood out in great contrast to the black of his hair. "Stefano Sabatini, at your service." His smile widened to reveal teeth that were a little too white, a little too long and sharp.

After a beat of reluctance, Astrid held out her hand. "Astrid VanTreese."

He took it, touched it to his lips.

"And this is my daughter, Gretchen."

Gretchen stood and the man took her hand. Though his touch was unusually cold, it invoked warmth within her, and when his lips, also cold, touched her skin, her face flushed hot.

"A pleasure to meet you both." He sighed and sat down at the lip of the fountain, stretching out his legs and crossing one ankle over the other. Gesturing for Gretchen to sit beside him, he said, "Please. Continue your rest, signorina."

Gretchen was speechless as his gaze latched onto hers. Perhaps it was just a trick of shadows, but for a moment, his eyes - so dark they were black - seemed to be the only living thing in that pale mask of a face. Glinting with some kind of forbidden knowledge, they stirred deep things in Gretchen. She felt herself blushing and quickly looked away. "I'm fine, thank you."

He shrugged. "As you wish."

Gretchen and Astrid stood there like dumb, mute things as he closed his eyes, taking a slow deep breath. "Ah, the scent of the city, the music of the fountains." For a time, he didn't move and it appeared that the man had lapsed into some kind of sleep.

Then his eyes snapped open and found Astrid's, his grin returning.

It was so sudden, so unexpected, that a small gasp escaped her.

"Rome really is such a beautiful place, is it not?"

Astrid hesitated, looking around as if seeking escape, but Gretchen could feel her mother's intrigue, could see it holding her in place. "Yes, yes, it is a beautiful city." She paused, her cheeks pink with some unnamed emotion. "If you'll excuse us, sir, we-"

"I don't suppose I could talk you two lovely ladies into joining me for a drink at the tavern? I've been traveling, you see, and have worked up quite a thirst." His dark eyes blazed with razor-sharp interest.

Astrid watched him. "Traveling?"

"Indeed." Shifting, he stretched back into a languorous, almost suggestive pose that brought warmth to Gretchen's cheeks and throat and a rare rosiness to the exposed tops of Astrid's breasts.

Astrid stiffened. "And might I ask what brings you to Rome?"

His smile was sudden and bright. "I'm a traveling tradesman. A cobbler, to be exact. I've come from Tivoli."

"That's not so far." Though Astrid tried to appear indifferent, there was something undeniably attractive about this man - something magnetic - and Gretchen could see that her mother was not impervious to it. "And how long will you be in the city, sir?"

"Please, call me Stefano." He hopped suddenly to his feet, rising to his full height, that playful smile ghosting around the edges of his lips. "And to answer your question, that depends on how good business is."

"I see."

"Now, concerning our drink." He glanced at the many buildings surrounding the piazza. "What establishment shall we haunt? Surely, there must be a few to choose from."

There was a tavern at their inn, but Gretchen doubted Astrid would be so bold as to invite him. When Astrid shook her head and said, "I'm sorry, but we really must be on our way," Gretchen felt both relief and disappointment.

The man's laugh was a soft, touchable sound as he stepped close to Astrid, too close, one brow rising in an oddly erotic arch. "You do not wish to be seen with the likes of a lowly tradesman such as myself, eh? Even one who could furnish you with the finest and handsomest shoes in all the city?"

Astrid, appearing slightly offended, raised a hand to her throat. "Of course that's not it. And I'm sure you're very talented. It's just that the alehouses here ..." She turned and cast a glance at Gretchen, who stood just behind her, almost hiding from this rakish stranger.

"Then show me to your inn. I'm sure it has an acceptable tavern within it." In a quick move, Stefano took Astrid's hand in his own. The pale, slender fingers that peeked out from his ruffled cuff were those of a gentleman, not a working tradesman. "If it's the rowdiness of the local drunkards you're worried about, I have ways of keeping them at bay." This with a provocative glance, a gleam of those too-sharp teeth, and another soft kiss to the back of Astrid's hand.

Astrid hesitated, then squared her shoulders. "Very well. I suppose we have time for one drink."

Gretchen was astonished by her mother and equally appalled and delighted at the prospect of joining this man at the tavern. Her heart was like a little bird battering its wings against her constricted ribs.

Stefano gave another small bow. "You've made me very happy, signorina." Then he grinned and replaced his hat, tilting it over his eyes.

"Please, call me Astrid."

Gretchen remained speechless as the three of them headed toward the inn - and the tavern inside, which was a place that under any other circum-

stance, Astrid stringently avoided. It was so unlike her mother to accompany a strange man - especially a vulgar one such as this - and despite Gretchen's own inexplicable intrigue, she hadn't for a moment believed that her mother would accept his brazen invitation.

As they walked, Astrid and Stefano discussed his impressions of Rome. She listened politely as he made remarks about the buildings, the trees, and the piazzas, or the food or the statuary, or some other feature. Gretchen followed closely behind, unable to take her eyes off the mysterious man's back. And her other senses were just as firmly fastened to him: the sound of his voice, low and smooth, which streamed back to Gretchen like mist over a slow-moving river; the scent of him on the lazy breeze ... like wood smoke and pine and something else. Something feral. Dangerous, even.

They paused at the river a moment, watching it ribbon and surge, losing itself in the darkness. But Gretchen had no interest in the river. By the flickering light of a single lantern upon the bridge, Gretchen stole glances at Stefano's sharp and kingly profile, tucking it into her memory for safekeeping. Despite the frolicsome smile and twinkle of amusement that seemed never to die in those deep-set obsidian eyes, there was something proud, almost contemptuous about his countenance, as if here was a man who had seen the world, and despised the entirety of it.

Gretchen watched him, tried to absorb the essence of him and in those moments, none of them spoke; the rush of the river was the only voice. There were few people on the streets now and their own footsteps sounded hollow on the cobbled stones of the bridge. Shortly, they turned from the river and made their way toward the inn.

Conversation returned, and now Stefano looked back occasionally to include Gretchen, as if only now aware of her.

He saw me staring, *she thought*, and feels obligated to include me.

She berated herself for her bad manners and each time he turned back and spoke to her, Gretchen felt the color shoot up her neck and face to the very roots of her hair, and quickly looked down at her feet; she could not meet the man's eyes.

How ill-bred he must think me.

She spent the rest of the walk behind her mother, resisting her urge to watch him, to listen to him, to admire him.

But even so, by the time they reached the inn, she was possessed of a feeling that she'd known Stefano Sabatini all her life - and that it would be unnatural somehow, painful even, to ever be separated from him again.

And as the evening deepened, she was certain her mother felt the same way.

16

CORPUS DELICTI

Cade moved through Langley's Literary Labyrinth, going about his duties, feeling removed from himself, separate from the world. But one thing was real: He was going to talk to Winter tonight and have him bring Samantha back. It was all he could think about.

He was grateful for work - stocking books, dusting shelves, adding titles to the inventory, and helping customers, none of whom had asked about the recent tragedy involving his girlfriend. Yet.

But Crimson Cove was small, and soon, word would spread and the questions would begin. But so far, not even his boss, Dora Langley, had brought it up.

She'd been surprised to see Cade this morning and told him she'd be fine without him for a few more days until he "took care of himself," but Cade had only shrugged and gone back to work. He wanted normal life, he *needed* it.

Dora, ever the business-woman, let him, and called back clients and rescheduled the psychic readings she'd had to cancel while Cade was off. She was in the back room with one of them now, no doubt gazing into her faux-crystal ball and weaving tales of distant travels and tall, dark strangers while Cade held down the bookselling end of the fort. He liked Dora, but he relished her absence, however temporary. The woman liked to talk - a lot - and Cade was in no mood for conversation.

He'd muddled through a brief call to Pinetop's Garage first thing this morning, explaining to Chet Wilson that Brooks was out of town for an indeterminate amount of time to take care of some family business. Cade could tell the guy had wanted to ask questions but he hadn't and Cade was grateful. He asked Chet if he'd mind acting as manager and the man had agreed, assuring Cade that the shop was in good hands.

Now, Cade was at the front desk at the bookstore, entering inventory into the monstrous, outdated *Dell* when he received a text from Ethan.

How's it going?

He considered ignoring it, but didn't want Ethan to get worried and show up.

Fine, he texted back. *Just working. Everything OK with you?*

A moment later, Ethan responded. *Good here. Back on duty. I'm staying home tonight. One of Michael's guys will be over to your house after sunset.*

Winter? Cade texted back.

I think so.

Cade was glad.

After a few minutes, another text came. *Sheila says Sam's mother scheduled the funeral for 4 pm on Wednesday at St. Anthony's. Is that OK for you?*

The funeral. Somehow, Cade hadn't even thought about that.

The funeral.

Something icy-cold and sinuous worked its way through Cade's lower belly at the thought of Samantha being buried, but before it could grip him entirely, he reminded himself that Winter was back; he'd fix Samantha up. Sheila would make sure the funeral was closed-casket, and no one would be the wiser.

Tears blurred Cade's vision. Not tears of pain, he realized, but of joy. He couldn't wait to see Samantha again; he didn't care whether she was a vampire or not. And it would all be taken care of long before the funeral.

That sounds fine, he texted back.

Then, through his tears, he caught sight of someone, a woman, at the end of one of the aisles at the front of the store. She was a vague shape in a long, black dress and veiled hat. *A woman in mourning?* Two eyes - a strange shade of pale blue - seemed to stare at him through the veil that concealed her features.

Startled, Cade wiped roughly at his eyes.

And realized he'd been wrong; it was just a trick of light and tears.

A stack of books near the door had formed a phantasm; his tired, bleary mind had connected false dots.

He returned to his work, but an icy chill remained on his skin. The mirage had rattled him, and for the first time, he felt glad that Michael's men - and Ethan - would be hanging around him for a while.

"Well, shit." Ethan stared down at the mutilated corpse.

It had been dragged between two large Dumpsters in an alley between downtown shops where it now played host to a swarm of flies.

Ethan had been in his office, catching up on paperwork while enjoying a nice acrid cup of the station's famous burnt coffee, when he'd gotten the call. Another bear attack, said the frantic woman on the phone.

He knew better, but was glad the rumor had caught on.

The victim - or what was left of him - appeared to be in his thirties or forties, though it was impossible to tell given that the majority of his face looked like it had been shredded with something akin to a giant cheese-grater. There were marks and gashes all over the body, but it was the throat, laid open to expose the now-dried meat within, that made it clear this was the work of a vampire. And Ethan had a pretty good idea which one. *'Brooks Colter'* flashed in his mind like a blinking neon sign.

But this was different than what he'd done to Samantha. This was … worse. *Could Brooks be devolving this fast?* Ethan looked at the shredded flesh all the way down the victim's torso, where a swollen loop of intestine peeked out at him. Teeming flies busily dipped and buzzed. *Maybe this is the work of one of Gretchen's Loyals.*

Ethan crouched to inspect the body. The knot of rubberneckers was growing by the moment and it wouldn't be long before it became something he couldn't control. "Step back. Stay out of the alley." He was the first on the scene but medics and backup would arrive any minute and help him get things under control. Till then, he was on his own. "And put away your phones," he said to the looky-loos snapping pictures and trying to get video footage. "Get back, all of you. This is a crime scene."

Reluctantly, phones were lowered but no one moved until Ethan repeated the order, this time with a threat to charge the lot of them with obstruction. *Everyone loves a thrill,* he thought bitterly. It was no different now than in the days of public hangings; violent death as a spectator sport served as a reminder of how little the human race had evolved over the centuries.

As Ethan looked for any distinguishing birthmarks or tattoos that might help identify the victim, the voices of the growing crowd overlapped and speculated.

"Who is he?" asked a man. "A tourist? Someone local?"

"Probably a tourist," answered someone. "He doesn't look familiar to me."

"The bear got him," said a woman. "There was another attack just the other day. You heard about it, didn't you?"

Yes, everyone had heard about the bear attack.

"Bear, my ass," said a man. "No bear did this. I heard Brooks Colter left town. Considering the first girl was killed on *his* property, I think maybe the *sheriff* ought to look into *that!*"

Well, shit. Ethan had hoped it might take the town longer to start speculating on Brooks' disappearance.

He stood and faced the onlookers. "Look-"

"Brooks Colter would *not* do this!" said a woman. "It *has* to be a bear. I don't think a man even *could* do this! *Especially* not Brooks!"

"Ladies and gentlemen," Ethan said. "I'll kindly ask you one more time to step back and to keep your speculations to yourselves. We have no reason to believe that any man - or woman - is responsible for the death of Samantha Corbett *or* this man."

"So Brooks Colter isn't a suspect?" A fat man in front twisted a greasy-looking baseball cap in his hands.

"There's no reason to think this was anything but another bear attack. The coroner will be here shortly and findings will be announced once an examination has been done. Now, I need you to clear out."

Reluctantly, the crowd dispersed.

"Go on, now," said Ethan. "Let the professionals take care of it. Go on."

And then they were gone.

Ethan knew it looked suspicious that Brooks had disappeared around the time of Samantha's death but he couldn't let that rumor take root. He glanced down at the corpse and tried to imagine Brooks doing this. He couldn't.

He crouched for a closer look and that's when he saw that a bite had been taken right out of the victim's heart. He'd heard the heart blood was considered a delicacy among vampires.

It must have been one of Gretchen's who did this. It must *have been.*

Otherwise, Brooks Colter had gone full-on monster.

Ethan shuddered.

News of the bear attack traveled fast through Crimson Cove, reaching Cade before he'd left his shift at the bookstore. He first heard about it from Josephine Griffith, one of Dora Langley's regulars, who'd come in for an emergency psychic reading in hopes of finding out when - and who - the infamous, deadly bear would strike next. And she wasn't the only one talking about it - for the whole of the afternoon, he heard little else, though no one spoke of it to Cade directly. Crimson Cove still wasn't ready to talk about Samantha. Not to Cade, anyway.

But he knew there was no bear and that meant only one thing: Brooks was out of control. Cade had been texting and calling Ethan all morning, but the sheriff wasn't answering. It briefly occurred to him that it might be Gretchen and her goons - but Cade couldn't see her being so sloppy.

Brooks. It has to be. His hands shook with rage as he tried to focus on the job.

But he couldn't train his mind on anything but Brooks. The thought of his brother running around on a murderous vampiric rampage added even more pits and scars to Cade's already ruined world. Tonight, when he got off work, he'd find Ethan and demand he tell him everything he knew. He'd hunt him down if he had to.

Tonight.

Samantha.

Cade looked at the time. Nightfall - and Winter - couldn't come soon enough.

BEFORE THE MURDERED MAN'S BODY HAD A CHANCE TO GET COZY AT THE morgue, *The Crimson Cove Daily* had already reported the vicious attack under the headline KILLER BEAR CLAIMS SECOND VICTIM. Relaxing in his La-Z-Boy, Ethan breathed a sigh of relief and began reading, hopeful there would be no mention of "murder."

He was surprised to see the story was written by none other than Crimson Cove's most dogged news reporter, Jojo McFerrell. As he read, Ethan was surprised by how much information McFerrell had managed to acquire.

The victim's name was Nestor Campbell, though on the street, he was known simply as "Nessie," a fitting moniker, Ethan thought, considering the man was nothing short of a monster. The report followed Nessie on his last day on earth, beginning when, at nine in the morning, he went to work at Little Buggers, Crimson Cove's sole pest control company. The testimony of three clients placed him in their homes at his appointed times, where he provided his services with quiet, satisfactory efficiency. But over the years, more than one claimed they didn't trust the man to be left alone in their home, and one former client even alleged that she'd stopped using the exterminator's services after some jewelry had gone missing.

And off-duty, the seedy side of Mr. Campbell's life became more apparent.

After leaving work, Mr. Campbell stopped at Querida's Bakery where he sat down to eat a pastry - a *bear claw,* McFerrell pointed out in a subtle but nonetheless tasteless attempt at irony. Ethan groaned and read on.

Eyewitnesses recalled the scene.

At approximately five-fifteen, Mr. Campbell tossed down his pastry, stalked up to the counter and demanded to speak with the manager, Querida herself. Mr. Campbell alleged that he'd found a stray hair in the icing of his bear claw, and to calm him down, Querida gave him half a dozen Danish on the house. It was not, according to several staff members, the first time Mr. Campbell had made the claim, and the general opinion of the staff was that he placed the stray hair on his pastries himself to obtain free product. When asked how she felt about this transgression, owner Querida Leigh shrugged and said, "It takes all kinds. I only give him the day-old Danish that are about to be tossed out anyway."

From the bakery, Nestor Campbell made his final, and sketchiest, stop of the night.

On Scarlet Street, he commissioned the services of a working girl, a woman known as Roach Clip Rachel, who claimed that Nessie was infamous in her circles for his rather violent kinks. The prostitute, with some reluctance, followed Mr. Campbell inside one of the nearby empty buildings where, instead of engaging her in sexual intercourse, he beat her unconscious with the buckle-end of his leather belt while masturbating.

Lovely man.

Having satisfied his lusts, Mr. Campbell headed back toward his truck, which he'd left in front of Querida's Bakery. But he never made it back to his vehicle, or to the dilapidated home he shared with his alcoholic mother.

The report went on to list the many crimes of Nestor "Nessie" Campbell, which included such offenses as breaking and entering, public intoxication, indecent exposure, shoplifting, vandalism, attempting to sell wraps and stoles made of rat fur, and of course, several counts of soliciting prostitutes. At the bottom of the report was a photograph of Mr. Campbell, ante mortem, of course, and Ethan shivered as he recalled the disfigured face he'd seen just hours before; the man in the photo was unrecognizable.

Couldn't have happened to a nicer guy.

Ethan shut his laptop, relieved there'd been nothing in the article to raise the town's suspicions. If it'd been written by anyone else, Ethan would have bought the reporter a beer.

He was grimacing at the thought of drinking with Jojo McFerrell when yet another text came through from Cade.

Ethan had put him off long enough. Reluctantly, he called him back, already knowing what the kid wanted.

"It's him, isn't it?" Cade wasted no time with pleasantries.

"Him who?" But Ethan had no doubt what Cade was talking about.

"Brooks. He killed the guy, didn't he?"

Ethan sighed. "I don't know, Cade. And I'm not sure we should be discussing this over the-"

"How can you *not* be sure? Unless you think it's one of Gretchen's? Do you think it was?"

"Could be. There were some ... *differences* about this crime that make me think it might've been someone else. I can't see Brooks doing this." But he wasn't sure that was true. Maybe Brooks *could* have done it. Brooks wasn't exactly Brooks anymore, after all.

"What differences? What do you mean?"

Ethan thought of the gnawed-on heart and grimaced. "Don't worry about it, Cade. And stop panicking. It's not helping."

"I'm not panicking." But he sounded ready to crawl out of his skin.

Ethan tried to be patient with him. "Look, Cade, I don't know anything yet. But we can't assume it was Brooks." *And dear God, please don't let it be Brooks.* "There's nothing you can do about it right now anyway, so let it go, okay?"

Cade was silent.

"Okay?"

"Fine. Okay."

Ethan waited, but Cade said nothing else. *Be gentle with him. He's been through a lot.* "Do you need anything?"

"No."

"Let me know if you do. And if Winter isn't there immediately after dark, call me and I'll come over."

"I will."

Cade ended the call and Ethan sighed, pinching the bridge of his nose. He was just about to get up and grab a much-needed Killian's when Sydney stepped through the front door, a bag of fast food and three milkshakes all crushed against her prodigious plastic chest. His heart sank. When he'd arrived home to find her gone, he'd hoped she'd gone back to Los Angeles. No such luck.

"Honey, I'm home!" His ex-wife breezed into the room in a cloud of undisciplined perfume and plunked the bag on the coffee table. "Where's Sheila?"

"Working late." As soon as he said it, he regretted it.

Satisfaction glinted in Sydney's eyes. "Oh, well. I guess I'll just put her shake in the freezer." She disappeared into the kitchen, twitching her backside with a brazen flourish. "Do you want salt and pepper?" she called.

"No thanks." Ethan listened as she moved about the kitchen with the confidence of a permanent resident. He didn't like the idea of being alone with her. He didn't like it one bit.

She returned with condiments, extra napkins, a cold Killian's just for him, and a pair of alarmingly hardened nipples that he would've sworn hadn't been nearly as enthusiastic just moments before.

What the hell did she do to those things in there? "Uh, thanks." Ethan took the Killian's, averting his eyes.

Sydney pushed his milkshake toward him. "Oreo cookie for you." She winked at him. "I remember what you like." She curled up on the sofa and took a giant bite of burger, not bothering to pray first. Or maybe she'd given thanks on her way home from the fast food joint. Either way, Ethan appreciated that. As she chewed, she moaned. It was a distinctly sexual sound and it set Ethan's teeth on edge.

After swallowing and delicately dabbing at her lips, she looked at Ethan and frowned. "Not hungry?"

"Not really." He sipped his Killian's and tried not to look at her.

"Uh-oh. I know what *that* means."

"Huh?"

"It means you saw something ugly today." She grinned, took another bite of burger, and said, "I know you, Ethan. I know you inside and out."

Ethan sipped his Killian's and shifted in his seat.

"So? Am I right? Did you see something ugly?"

He cleared his throat. "There was another ... incident, yes."

"An incident?" Sydney dipped a French fry in her shake and ate it. Another habit Ethan had forgotten about - one that made him queasy. "So tell me about it. What happened?" She hadn't even taken this much interest in his job when they were married.

"Nothing to tell. Another bear attack."

Sydney drew in a startled gasp, quickly wiping her greasy fingers on a napkin before placing a manicured hand against her silky blouse, opera-diva-style. "Not *again?*"

Ethan nodded, told her the shorthand version, then changed the subject. "I thought maybe you'd gone back to LA."

Sydney shook her head and gouged her pink ice cream with another fry. "No. Of course not. I wouldn't go back *there* if my life depended on it."

"Did you hear anything from your lawyer friend yet?"

Sydney chewed, swallowed, then frowned. "Oh, Ethan. These things take time. You know that."

But how much time? he wanted to ask. Instead he picked up the bag of burgers and took one out.

"Extra-crispy this time," she said.

"Huh?"

Sydney's lips, painted a red-purple not dissimilar to "Nessie" Campbell's bloated innards, spread into a smile. "I noticed you didn't touch your bacon when I made you breakfast, then I remembered that you like it extra-crispy. You *always* liked it extra-crispy." Now she frowned. "I can't believe I forgot that."

"Yeah. Thanks." He unwrapped a burger and looked at it, wanting it, but not so sure his stomach was up for it. He'd never built a proper cop's tolerance to blood and gore; his appetite was always reduced to a shadow of its usual self in the days that followed a violent death. Noting a strip of red-brown bacon peering out the side of the bun, he was reminded again of the murdered man's insides. Swallowing a dry heave, he set the burger aside.

Sydney had no such trouble. She finished her burger in a few big bites, burrowed into her shake with fries, and smiled at him with a look that said, *Ain't this fun? Ain't this just like old times?*

Ethan wondered how long before Sheila got home.

"Mmm." Then, as Sydney slowly licked ice cream from her French fry, she slid Ethan another look, a different look, one that suggested wanton things.

Ethan knew that look too well. He was on his feet in an instant, eager to get away from her. "I've got to go shower and take care of some things."

"But ... but you didn't even eat." The girlish pout she put on might have been cute back in the days when Clinton was in office and NSYNC topped the charts, but now, all these years later, the big sad eyes and puckered lips were unseemly, embarrassing.

"I'll eat later." Ethan was already halfway up the stairs, digging his phone out of his pocket. He needed to get Sydney out of his house and now. He shut the bedroom door and called Michael Ward, praying the man would take her in.

And speaking of praying ... as he punched in the number, the television downstairs came on at full volume - or damned close to it. *The God Club.* Of course. Ethan sighed, willing Michael to pick up as Reverend Bobby Felcher's voice saturated the whole house in the 'healing love of *Jaysus Kee-rist!*'

17

TRUST, DUST, AND UNCONTROLLABLE LUST

*J*ust minutes after full sunset, Winter's giant white Hummer - *FROST*, according to the personalized plates - pulled into the drive. Cade was at the window, where he'd been waiting since twilight. He watched as the big man swung out, willing him to hurry as he slung a white gym bag over the bulk of one shoulder and, finally, made his way to the porch. Cade had almost forgotten how big the guy was - he was huge, easily six-foot-six with massive shoulders, giant hands, and enormous muscles.

Before he had a chance to knock, Cade threw the door open. "Winter, I need to talk to-"

He was cut short when Winter pulled him into a crushing bear hug. "Good to see you, Gilroy. How're you holding up?"

Jesus! Cade couldn't get the air to answer. He felt his eyes bulge and just when he thought he might hear ribs crack, Winter let him go, reached into his gym bag, and pulled something out. "Here." He handed the object to Cade. "For you."

It was a snow globe of a mountain. *Icehouse Mountain*, said the nameplate on the base. Cade had no idea why he should have this.

"From Eternity." Winter averted his eyes uncertainly. "I thought you'd like it."

Cade realized Winter was offering his condolences. "Thanks. It's ... nice." He placed the snow globe on the mantle. "Look, Winter, I need to talk to you about something."

"Hey there, big boy." Winter bent to scratch Purrcy, who'd wound himself around his ankles, purring and trilling.

"It's about Samantha."

Winter looked up.

"Look, sit down." Cade gestured and Winter set the gym bag next to the recliner and took a seat. He looked, as he always looked to Cade, too big for his surroundings. Purrcy hopped into his lap for more head-scritches. "Okay, I'm sitting. What is it?"

Cade sat stiffly on the edge of the sofa, not sure how to start. "It's ... well ... you're the only one I can ask to do this for me. I know Michael won't be willing and ... well, the thing is ..."

"Gilroy. You're rambling." Purrcy hopped down and Winter leaned forward in the recliner, reminding Cade of a grown man on a child's tricycle. "Tell me what's on your mind."

"Samantha," Cade said. "I want you to bring her back."

Winter didn't move but his frosty blue eyes, usually glinting with merriment, went flat. "Bring her back?"

"Yes." Cade leaned in, speaking quickly, a machine gun firing. "Turn her. Before the funeral. See, it's going to be closed-casket anyway because of the damage, and Sheila's the mortician, so no one will question her if-"

"No."

Cade blinked. "No?"

"No."

In one word, the world collapsed into dust and rubble. "What do you mean, *no*?"

"I mean I won't do it."

Panic. "But ... but *why*?" Cade's voice peaked with surprise.

Winter's jaw knotted. "Because that's not how it works, Cade. Once a body-"

"Not how it works?" Cade was on his feet. "Not how it *works*? If you think Samantha would rather be dead than be a vampire I can promise you, she wouldn't, so if this is about her *freedom of choice*, well, I think it's fair to say *that* was taken away from her when Brooks killed her! Just because *Michael* doesn't think it's right-"

"It's not about choices, Gilroy, and it's not about Michael."

"Then what the *hell* is it about?" Cade couldn't have been more stunned if the ground had opened up and swallowed him whole. "You *have* to bring her back! You owe it to me."

"I *owe* it to you?" Winter asked slowly.

"Yes! If you and Michael had cut off Gretchen's head when-"

"Stop." Winter stayed him with a very large hand. "You need to get this out of your head, Gilroy. It's not going to happen. I'm sorry, but … Samantha is gone."

Gone. The word reverberated down dark hallways in his mind. "But …" Cade was edging on hysteria; the breaking point was coming. "Bullshit!" Purrcy, startled by his master's tone, darted from the room. "Tell me *why*!"

Winter seemed to be debating something. Then he blew out a deep breath. "Just let it go."

"The hell I will! I don't understand." It was getting hard to breathe.

"I know you don't." Winter got to his feet, concern in his eyes. "But for now, you've just got to trust me."

"*Trust* you?" Rage was a boa constrictor cutting off Cade's breath.

"Yeah. Trust me, okay?" Winter's sleeveless t-shirt exposed arms that could have made Mr. Universe nervous about losing his title, but in that moment, Cade wanted to sock him in the jaw, consequences be damned.

But he was suddenly too dizzy, too sick, and when Winter told him, "Take it easy," and put a hand on his shoulder, the room tilted and flickered red. "Don't fucking touch me!" Cade drove a fist into Winter's abdomen; he may as well have punched a stack of bricks. Winter barely registered the blow but it was still satisfying. "Go to hell." Cade stomped off down the hall, slamming the bedroom door behind him.

The door slammed and Winter stood there, stunned. "Holy shit." He was worried about Cade. About his headspace. He hadn't looked sane.

And who could blame him?

Maybe I should tell him why I won't turn her. He almost had, but he'd stopped himself; it was a bad idea. He knew Cade, knew he wouldn't let it go. He'd insist on bringing Samantha back, no matter the consequences - and that couldn't happen.

Winter sat back down, thinking.

Cade wasn't going to let it go, he was sure of that much. He hoped like hell the kid wouldn't go to another vampire with the same request. Not that any sane one would grant it.

Winter shivered at the thought. He'd need to keep a very close eye on Cade.

The Crimson Corset looked much the same as it had in its heyday, minus the crowd, of course.

Rogan and Dante, for the second consecutive night, were given orders to check the place out, but it was clear that Gretchen and her guys hadn't returned: No cobweb had been disturbed, no footsteps sullied the layer of dust that covered the hard floors. The underground still needed to be checked, but that too was, in Rogan's opinion, an exercise in futility.

"Hey," said Dante, nodding toward the great empty aquarium beyond the massive bar. "Remember the two hotties that used to swim in there? What were their names?"

"Violet and Scarlett," said Rogan.

Gretchen's mermaids. Dressed in fins and seashells, they'd swim for the patrons' pleasure, moving and swaying to the blare of music - a kind of underwater strip show, really. And rumor had it that for the right price, a gentleman could take a girl to one of underground rooms for an hour.

"Yeah, Violet and Scarlett. I wonder where those two ended up."

Absently, he rubbed the peace symbol on his jacket. That habit - and the carnal undercurrent in his tone - made it clear that Dante's thoughts were not on the job.

Rogan sighed. He'd known it was a bad idea to sneak extra rations while Michael and Winter were away. Dante was an extremist, a bottomless pit, and the extra blood had fired up his lusts; now *all* of his appetites were raging. *As evidenced by the six Hostess cupcakes he's already eaten tonight.* "Dream on, brother. That'd be fraternizing with the enemy. Winter would have your head. Besides, Violet and Scarlett scattered last year with the rest of them so you're shit out of luck."

"I don't know what you're talking about." Dante sounded too innocent.

Rogan chuckled. "Yeah, right. Now, come on, let's keep moving. We still need to stop by the lake after this."

They headed to the office behind the bar where Rogan knew they'd find a passageway to the myriad underground tunnels that had been built in the rum running days. Those tunnels led to countless rooms - including the former quarters of Gretchen's various Loyals - but Rogan was sure they'd find no one down there now. Nor would they see any activity at the lake. Gretchen was too cunning for that. She was planning something, he was sure, and wherever it was, she wouldn't be found until she was good and ready.

He only hoped that by then it wouldn't be too late to stop her.

IN THE DILAPIDATED CABIN DEEP IN THE WOODS, BROOKS COLTER AND Rafe Santangelo sat on the rotting floor, slaking their thirsts with a pair of rabbits they'd found under some bushes.

Biting into the rabbit's throat and tearing away the tough, chewy flesh, Rafe wished he had Brooks' sharp incisors.

He sucked blood into his mouth and sighed, dissatisfied. It seemed that nothing, not even a sack full of rabbits, could penetrate his hunger. It gnashed at him, squirming in the pit of his belly like an unquenchable parasite - but the panic was gone, completely gone.

The blood was already coagulating and he set the rabbit down and looked at Brooks. "Maybe later we can go out again and find a deer or something."

Brooks wiped his bloody mouth with the back of his hand. "Maybe. But I think we ought to take it easy. I don't know how long we might have to live this way, so it's best to learn to control our appetites early on." Brooks didn't meet his eyes, but Rafe could see the regret in them. He was sorry he'd bitten him.

But oddly, Rafe didn't mind. He only wished he could be a full vampire. He wanted to ask how to make it happen, but Brooks had made it pretty clear he wasn't into extensive Q and A sessions, so Rafe doled out his questions carefully. "Well, I hope we can at least find something better than bunnies next time."

Brooks looked down at the shredded rabbit in his hands. "They're not the best, I know, but they'll do the job. And we'll adapt. We have to."

"Why can't we just find a human?" The question came before Rafe had a chance to think it out. "We don't have to kill them, do we? Couldn't we just-"

Brooks shook his head. "No. We're not doing that." He bit into his own rabbit.

Rafe watched him, unwilling - or perhaps, unable - to argue. Only a few hours ago, he couldn't shake the nagging fixation on the other man, Scythe, but Rafe no longer felt anything for him. Looking back, he couldn't understand where the need to be near him had even come from.

But the need itself had not gone away - now, it had shifted to Brooks.

It was different though, calmer.

With Scythe, it had been like an unhealthy obsession, as if being away from him would cut his oxygen supply. With Brooks, it was more natural. It was a simple feeling, a *knowing*, that it was here with Brooks that Rafe belonged. It was weird.

He continued to watch this virtual stranger with the streak of silver in his dark hair, wondering at it all and thinking: *We're nothing like the vampires on TV.* In books and on television, vampires were romantic, rich, sexy. Rafe and Brooks were hungry, dirty, and squatting in an abandoned cabin.

And surviving on bunny-blood.

Barely surviving. But at least the panic is gone.

"I just wish this fucking hunger would go away."

"You'll be fine," said Brooks. "Over time, the bloodlust mellows out. As long as you don't cater to it."

But Rafe wondered if Brooks believed his own words. It was obvious he was suffering, too - that his hunger was just as sharp. *Isn't that why he attacked me in the first place, because he couldn't control his appetite?* "And what if it doesn't?"

"It will." The hardness in Brooks' voice told Rafe the discussion was over.

Rafe stood and flung the carcass out one of the broken windows. He sat down on the floor, leaning back on his elbows, and looked at a dilapidated fireplace that probably used to be charming. Now, stones had come loose, leaving dark holes in the face. The hearth, too, was crumbling. The place was a dive. The cabin itself jutted from the earth at a precarious slant, like an old woman in need of a new hip, and when the wind blew, the framework groaned and creaked like arthritic joints. It was probably a matter of time, Rafe thought, before the whole thing collapsed - with them in it.

The glamorous lives of vampires.

He snickered.

But, he reminded himself, it was a hell of a lot better than being in the cave with Gretchen. He tried not to think about her. As soon as he'd mentioned her to Brooks it was obvious the guy knew who she was. And after what he told Rafe about his own experiences with the woman, he felt even luckier to have gotten away. Originally, he'd wanted to talk more about her, but Brooks refused, saying that the topic was too dangerous for both of them. So for now, it was enough that Rafe was safe from being sucked on and drained to the point of unconsciousness every few hours.

If not for that aching, throbbing need for blood - fresh, *human* blood - he was content here. He thought a normal person would have been dying to get back home, back to normal life, but he wasn't a normal person with a normal life. He had nothing to go back to, nothing at all. This was a new beginning. For the first time in his life, he felt like he might be okay.

And he wanted to be with Brooks - even if it was in a rickety cabin miles from civilization. Rafe was someone else now, and his former life didn't matter anymore. Not that it had mattered much when he was living it. He'd always felt there was something more for him, but he'd never been able to touch it. Now, despite the circumstances, Rafe felt he was on the brink of something greater. His existence mattered now. He counted. He was content. At last, he was content.

If only it weren't for this godforsaken blood craving!

Brooks tossed his dead rabbit out a window, then sat back down, staring into space, looking lost and uncomfortable.

"They won't come back will they?" asked Rafe. "The bunnies, I mean."

Brooks looked at him a moment. "You mean, like *Bunnicula*?" He laughed. "No. Vampirism is species-specific."

He was still chuckling when Rafe said, "Can I ask you something?"

"Sure."

"What would happen if we *did* feed from a human now? And how come you don't want to?"

Brooks sighed. "The bloodlust would get worse." He looked at Rafe. Eyes grave, he added, "A lot worse. Trust me, I know. It would become uncontrollable."

But Rafe's mouth flooded at the prospect of human blood. Not wanting to irritate Brooks, he said no more and pulled the deck of cards from his back pocket - *Scythe's cards*. He'd taken them as a means of keeping something of the man he'd so revered, but now the cards held no significance except as a way of passing time. He shuffled them. "Want to play some poker?"

"As long as it's not strip," said Brooks, looking down at his blood-stained, tattered underwear and barely-there t-shirt. "I'd lose for sure."

A ghost of a smile lifted the corner of his lips. When Rafe realized the man had cracked a joke - an actual joke - he laughed.

"You deal." After shuffling, Rafe pushed the deck toward Brooks. As Brooks dealt the cards, Rafe's hunger was momentarily forgotten.

But above all, there was no fear. It was strange to finally be free of it.

CADE LAY AWAKE STARING AT THE CEILING, HIS ANGER CHURNING LIKE molten lava in the pit of his gut. He rested a hand on his bare stomach, trying to soothe the rumbles it made. Apparently, even his stomach was pissed off.

But under that fury, he was devastated. Winter refused to turn Samantha. *Why?* It was obvious he had a reason for it, but the guy wasn't talking.

Why?

Why?

He realized he'd pinned all his hopes on Winter and now he needed a plan B. Michael wasn't an option. That guy wouldn't turn a man who was dying in a fire - not before having him fucking pray about it first and then sign consent forms or some shit, anyway.

No, Michael wasn't an option and the only other vampire Cade had any rapport with at all was Chynna - and if he were to be honest, the woman kind of frightened him. She wasn't mean - she just had a certain no-nonsense approach to things; Cade couldn't see her bending Michael's rules.

There were others - the suffragette, Emmeline, and Winter's guys, the former soldiers, Rogan and Dante, but they were out; Cade didn't know any of them well enough to ask.

Then, of course, there was Arnie, Winter's simple-minded sidekick. Asking him to do it seemed a kind of sacrilege - like taking advantage of the mentally challenged. As much as Cade wanted Samantha back, he couldn't do that.

So now what? With the funeral looming, time was of the essence; Cade's sense of urgency was growing sharper.

Vaguely, Cade heard Winter playing video games in the living room - then he caught the low buzz humming all around him. He sat up.

And then he saw the figure.

Cade froze, muscles locking in tension.

For a moment, he thought he was staring at a gathering of shadows in the corner - but looking closer, he made out the head and shoulders, the shape of a human body squatting there, watching him.

"H-Hello?"

The darkness didn't move and for what felt like an eternity, neither did Cade. His first thought was: *Gretchen*! but it didn't seem like her, didn't *feel* like her. He blinked, growing more certain he was imagining it.

Then the figure shifted.

Though there was no sound except the low buzz, he heard a clear whisper in his head: *"I am coming. I am coming for what is mine."* Cade squeezed his eyes shut, certain he was losing his mind.

"Go away," he murmured.

Only silence. And the buzzing.

"Get out of here."

And then, in slow, barely perceptible motion, the malignant lump of shadow gathered itself and grew until it loomed over him, tall and taunting.

Cade's breath caught. It was a woman. A woman in old-fashioned mourning clothes - just like he thought he'd seen at the bookstore.

Behind a netted veil, he made out the glint of eyes, eyes the color of death, the color of suffocated skin.

Cyanosis. He'd learned the term in a health class and it came to him now, unbidden.

Cyanotic blue, the color of her eyes.

Those eyes never blinked, not once, and somehow, Cade instinctively knew they could not.

"What do you want?" His words came strained and dry, edged in whispers.

Again, the funereal figure above him said without words: *"I am coming."* And then the mouth grinned, jarring Cade as if a firecracker had gone off. The sound of buzzing insects - *Wasps*! - rose to a sharp crescendo and Cade threw himself out of bed, lurched toward the switch and shot the light on.

There was nothing in the corner. Nothing over the bed. Nothing in the room with him at all. Even the buzz of the wasps had died away. His own labored breath was the only sound. Covered in an icy sweat, his legs trembling, Cade steadied himself on the edge of the mattress.

It was shadows. Only shadows.

He didn't believe it for a second.

18

AS THE WORLD CHURNS

For two days, Cade moved through life in a daze, and for two nights, he begged Winter to turn Samantha.

And he'd gotten exactly nowhere. Winter still refused to bring her back - and he still refused to tell him why. The most Cade ever got out of him was, *'One day I'll tell you my reasons.'* When Cade had asked him when 'one day' might be, Winter only shrugged and said, *'Today is not that day.'*

Samantha's funeral was tomorrow, and it still was not 'that day.'

Despondent and resigned, Cade was out of hope.

He hadn't been shaving, bathing, or eating - and that was fine by him. He saw the looks the customers at the bookstore gave him, and he knew what they were thinking - that, unable to cope with his loss, Cade had started taking drugs, probably heroin. He'd heard rumors; even Dora had asked him if he was on something. He was stone-cold sober, he told her, and it was the truth.

Ethan was still nagging him about going to the therapy group in Santa Cruz, but Cade refused. He wasn't interested in "healing." His only interest was in bringing Samantha back and since that obviously wasn't going to happen, he didn't give a damn about feeling better. He deserved to feel like shit. This was, after all, his own fault; the pain and guilt were well-deserved.

Today, after he'd messed up the inventory three times, Dora sent him home early, telling him to get some rest. Now, he sat on the couch, Purrcy in his lap, staring at nothing in particular. He wanted to hold time down and make it be still. He was dreading the funeral tomorrow, and just as much, dreading tonight. Not because Winter would come - Cade had taken to making himself scarce when Winter arrived; he couldn't stand looking at the guy - but because night was when the dreams came, the nightmares, the buzzing and stinging of wasps, the cyanotic blue eyes watching him in the darkness, the whispering without words.

He'd wake slick, wet, and shivering, too tired to stay awake and too terrified to go back to sleep. A few times, he even heard the wasps in daylight hours. It was only, he thought, the product of his overtired, overburdened mind and it, just like the guilt, was what he deserved.

When the sun began to set behind the western mountains, Cade went into his room where he was, as always, tormented by the sight of Samantha's clothes. But he wouldn't throw them out, not ever. He couldn't.

He stretched out on the bed and closed his eyes. He doubted he could sleep, but when Winter came, he wanted to be left alone. Cade would let him think he was sleeping.

And if sleep did come - and with it the night terrors - well…

Well, that's what I deserve.

ETHAN AND SHEILA WERE TAKING FULL ADVANTAGE OF THE EVENING now that Sydney was gone. Michael had put the woman up in one of his cabins and tonight Ethan felt like a teenager who'd invited his girlfriend over while his parents were out of the house.

They sat on the couch, sharing a bowl of popcorn, and watching an old black-and-white John Wayne. Ethan knew Sheila hated the movie - she hated all westerns - but she didn't complain. He loved her for it.

There'd been no more "bear attacks" since Nestor Campbell's death, but Crimson Cove remained abuzz with speculation. It didn't help that Brooks Colter still hadn't returned from his out-of-town "family business." It would have been better had Jojo McFerrell not talked to Chet Wilson at Pinetop's and extracted the whole fictional story out of him, but it kept people from thinking Brooks had fallen victim to a bear attack himself. Ethan figured they could milk out the "family business" thing as long as they needed to. For all anyone knew, Brooks was taking care of an ailing aunt who might live for weeks yet, or even months.

Months. Ethan hoped it wouldn't take that long to find Brooks. It occurred to him that Colter might have skipped town, but Ethan just wasn't buying it. No, Brooks was close by. He wouldn't leave. Ethan didn't know how he knew that, he just did.

And Ethan needed to find him. Needed to get him to Eudemonia where he could be taken care of. He'd been hoping Brooks might turn up there on his own, but no such luck.

And I need to do something about Cade, too.

Sheila pressed for group therapy. Ethan told her he couldn't make Cade do anything he didn't want to, but he was beginning to wonder if using force might be the best thing after all. The kid wasn't coping. He wasn't eating, he looked - and smelled - like hell, and even when he was right in front of you, looking right at you, he wasn't seeing you. His mind was somewhere else. Somewhere dark and dangerous.

But aside from checking in on him - which Ethan did several times a day - and trying to get him out of the house and into therapy, Ethan was at a loss. Time heals all wounds, they said, and Ethan thought that was probably true. He only wished it moved a little faster sometimes.

"What are you thinking about?" Sheila, in only panties and an oversized blue-and-yellow sweater Ethan had knitted her, looked gorgeous.

"I'm thinking about how fantastic you look in that sweater."

Sheila laughed. "I'll bet." She snuggled close, pressing herself warm against him, and the nearness of her, the heat of her, turned Ethan's mind to more pleasant things.

He leaned in and kissed her.

She kissed him back.

As much as she'd thought she'd hate the little cabin at Eudemonia - and in fact, had *tried* to hate it just to spite Ethan - Sydney Hunter-Doss could no longer pretend she wasn't happy. She was in one of the nicer cabins that fronted the grounds - one that she suspected was a kind of "suite" because it was bigger than those that spread out deeper into the trees, further from Eudemonia's main headquarters. The bedroom was small, but it had everything she needed: a closet, a tiny writing desk, a walnut dresser, and a surprisingly comfortable bed. There was a cozy living area with a cute little loveseat and chair, a small kitchenette and, praise Jesus, running water. It even had its own bathroom, and for that alone, she could have jumped for joy. The cheaper cabins, she knew, shared shower facilities, and Sydney wasn't having any of that. As it turned out, she hadn't even had to fight that battle.

With a few items she'd purchased on her credit cards, the place had gone from quaint and cute to feeling like *home*. She bought a fuzzy pink throw rug for the hardwood floors, a couple of battery-operated gooseneck lamps - also pink - some vases for the silk carnations she'd found at the cute little Peddler Puck's at the edge of town, pink polka-dot drapes for every window, and a framed portrait of the Savior, hands clasped in prayer, to mount above a rustic fireplace that burned real wood.

It had taken several days to get the place in order, and now, as she hammered in the final nail and gazed up at Jesus, she realized two things: Her little home was complete ... and Jesus didn't go with the rest of the decor. She frowned at the portrait. She didn't know why artists, if only for the sake of interior design, couldn't portray Him in something with a little more color than those drab white robes - but it would have to do. Jesus had earned His place in her home and hanging this painting was the *least* she could do for Him after He'd come into her heart and saved her. She smiled at Him. "Well, here we are, Lord."

She'd found Christ before she and Ethan had divorced, and knew that His holy presence in her life had something to do with their split. Ethan never could accept anything he couldn't see with his eyes or touch with his hands and he'd promptly turned away from the Word, refusing even to participate in prayer at supper and eventually insisting she go to the other room to give thanks. As if she were some sort of pariah.

It was no way to live.

She'd had hopes that after being Born Again her track record with men might improve but it hadn't. Not at all. In fact, it had gotten worse. Drake Doss had turned out to be an even bigger jerk than Ethan - at least Ethan could keep his pecker in his pants.

She thought of Drake's infantile new sex-partner, Misty, and frowned. *Misty. Misty Darva. What the hell kind of name is Misty Darva, anyway?* She wondered how much little Miss Hot-Lips liked her new boyfriend now that he was about to be divorced and stuck with alimony payments.

Sydney's friend, Monty the lawyer, a slick and handsome man she'd met through a mutual friend back in LA, had contacted Drake and put enough heat on him that he'd agreed to let her keep the Porsche. He'd also agreed to pay Sydney twenty-five percent of his monthly income until the divorce was official and a judge made a final, more generous, ruling.

Sydney hadn't argued. She would be happy with twenty-five percent - maybe even less if she found decent work here in Crimson Cove. With each passing day, it began to feel more like her home. It helped, too, that Eudemonia owner Michael Ward had refused to take anything for her stay at the cabin. He'd said they could discuss it further when she got on her feet - but the invitation to stay as long as she needed to was looking better and better. She found that, despite her earlier reservations, she liked the lack of cell reception, electricity, and wifi. It made life simpler, quieter. It was like Jesus' days in Bethlehem - or wherever it was He'd lived - and after a few years in LA, it was exactly what she needed. And it wasn't as if she couldn't go to Eudemonia's headquarters, which was a short - and rather beautiful - walk when she needed to use the internet or her phone. Surely, even Jesus would have taken advantage of those perks.

Sydney liked it here, and it didn't hurt a bit that Michael Ward was the biggest, juiciest piece of man-candy she'd laid eyes on since seeing Instagram sensation Brock O'Hurn tie his flowing mane of wild locks into a man bun atop his big, beautiful head. But whereas Brock had the rugged appeal of a star running back, Michael Ward was satanically handsome with a refined old-school elegance to go with the animal magnetism.

If Brock was suited to the shirtless grandeurs of romance novel cover art, Michael Ward belonged on old Gothics, in dark English tweeds with lace at his throat and wrists, beneath the lamplight of a nineteenth-century city crawling with fog where men in top hats and cloaks moved through the shadows. She could see him now, waiting for her in some darkened doorway, those arresting features, both sensitive and cruel, lighting up as she approached, his dreamer's eyes gleaming, his poet's lips curling into a lascivious, heartbreaking smile.

Sydney breathed out a sigh, pointedly avoided looking at Jesus - who, by the way, would have looked fantastic with a man bun - and wondered how much of her happiness here had to do with Michael Ward. The very prospect of seeing him had her throbbing all over, and had she known that Ethan was going to refer her to such a stunning landlord, she never would have argued. Or wasted her time trying to win Ethan back.

Michael, however, was a man of much mystery and few words. Having concocted some reason or another to speak to him, she'd gone more than once to the main building, but he was always unavailable. She'd never gotten past the reception desk. She wondered what on earth he did all day that prevented him from speaking to his guests.

He might be busy all day, she thought as she began arranging the pink carnations in their pink vases, *but he can't be busy all* night, *too.*

And that's why Sydney had bought the cookies when she'd gone out earlier. Tonight, when she was certain Michael Ward's workday would be done, she'd go to the headquarters, ask to see him, and give him the cookies as a thank you. How could anyone say no to cookies?

She looked out the window. The sun was setting.

Sighing, she wondered what Michael would be wearing. Butterfly wings brushed the edges of her heart. It was time to go get dolled up.

NO ANSWER.

Winter, in his signature white muscle shirt and faded jeans, let himself inside. He carried a large bouquet of flowers with a sympathy card from Michael. After placing them in a vase on the kitchen table, he quietly checked Cade's room - his very warm, musty room - glad to see the younger Colter brother sawing logs.

Winter closed the door quietly, crept down the hall and, not wanting to wake Cade with television or video games, went back to his Hummer for his reading glasses. No one - except Arnie - ever saw him wear them. He'd had lousy eyesight in his human life and while vampirism improved the senses, it picked and chose which ones - at least in Winter's case. He could practically detect the scent of a cigar from fucking San Francisco, but his eyesight still sucked balls.

Back inside, he sat under the light of a lamp with a book in his lap - Charles Dickens' *A Tale of Two Cities*. It was better than the other novels Cade kept around. Winter wasn't into romance, historical or otherwise.

He couldn't focus on the words - and that was no fault of Mr. Dickens. Not that the book's long-winded opening line wasn't enough to achieve full-on mind-wandering. The trouble was that his head was too full of too many things to get into the story.

Cade was beginning to really concern him. He was a mess and, Winter noted, so was his house. It needed vacuuming, dusting, and picking up. It had gotten a little worse every day and by now, Winter was disgusted enough he decided to clean it up himself. *And crack a fucking window.* The place was as hot and musty as the seventh level of hell.

Before he got to his feet, Purrcy hopped onto his lap. He arched into a long, luxurious stretch, kneaded Winter's jeans a moment, and in an inquisitive tone, meowed.

For a moment, the two stared at each other.

Another questioning meow.

"I, uh ... I'm not sure what you want, cat."

Purrcy began kneading Winter's thigh again, his claws extending and retracting, his eyes fixed on Winter's as if he were trying to communicate something of great importance.

"You hungry? Should we check your food bowl?"

Purrcy rubbed himself sinuously along Winter, mewing, purring, and trilling, begging for attention. Then with a quick leap he was on Winter's shoulder, butting his head against his cheek and rubbing his cheek along his jaw. Winter took his glasses off before they got knocked off his face.

Purrcy walked along his shoulders, behind his neck, turning one way then the other, pausing to give Winter an eyeful of cat-ass and a set of nuts that would have made him the envy of every tom in town, had he been allowed outside.

"Ah," said Winter, bringing Purrcy to his lap. "I think what you need is a girlfriend."

Purrcy leapt and darted down the hall, posting himself in front of Cade's door where he continued to meow insistently.

Winter followed, hoping the cat wasn't waking Cade. He cracked the door and Purrcy darted inside, leapt onto the bed, and disappeared into the shadows. Winter was glad; now he could throw open every door and window and air the place out with no risk of letting the cat out.

Or not. The heat of the bedroom was heavy and thick, and Winter was considering leaving the door cracked when Cade bolted up in bed, hair corkscrewed every which way. "Winter?"

"Yep. It's just me. Sorry to wake you. Your cat wanted in."

"Oh. Okay." His voice was thick with sleep but alert, on edge.

"Why don't you open your window, Gilroy."

"Why?" Cade lay back down and pulled the quilts over him.

"Because I'm getting swamp-ass just standing here."

"Then leave." He rolled over, giving Winter his back.

"You got it." Winter sighed, wondering how long he was going to remain public enemy number one. "Oh, and Gilroy?"

"*What?*"

"I think your kitty needs to get some stank on his hang-low."

"Huh?"

Winter chuckled. "I think he's looking for company of the female persuasion, if you catch my drift."

"What are you even talking about?"

"*Laid*, Gilroy. Your cat needs to get laid."

Cade pulled a pillow over his head and Winter shut the door.

He wondered how the kid would handle the funeral tomorrow - *He's really going to fucking hate me once they put her in the ground.* Winter wished he was able to attend, for Cade's sake if nothing else, but ... churches and daylight ... it wasn't going to happen.

He went into the kitchen, deciding to start there. The litter box was in desperate need of a change and he wondered if that's what the cat had been trying to tell him. *Nah,* he decided. *He just needs a good time.*

Winter could use one of those himself, and as he looked around at the stacks of dirty dishes, grimy countertops, and the overstuffed garbage can, an idea struck him: *Nadine.* Cade's filth presented Winter with the perfect opportunity to get in touch with the busty, black-haired housekeeper again. It'd been months since the two had last hooked up. *And, as an added bonus, she'll whip this place into shape so I can stand being here.* If anyone could get the stink of grief and dirty laundry out of this house, it was Nadine.

Of course, Cade would be pissed but Winter didn't care - he was pissed anyway, and at least this way he could be an asshole in an environment that didn't reek of expired bleu cheese and Civil War bandages.

Winter went into the living room, plopped onto the recliner, and left the housekeeper a message, asking if she could come out tomorrow - while Cade was at the funeral. At least the kid would come home to a clean house.

On second thought, he called back, asking if she'd like to get together one of these nights. Purrcy the cat wasn't the only one in want of a woman.

And neither am I.

Winter thought of Michael. Since returning from Eternity - and the feminine wiles of Natasha Darling - the man hadn't been himself; he obviously had an itch of his own that needed scratching.

Winter wondered how long before his boss got his bearings back - Michael's quiet intensity was starting to trouble him. Apparently, Natasha had thrown him for quite a loop. The man was on edge.

Even worse than the cat.

FULL DARK, AND NEARLY AN HOUR INTO IT.

Sydney grabbed the Walmart cookies and headed across the cobblestone walk toward Eudemonia's main building. She'd teased her hair to halo her face and cascade down her shoulders like liquid gold, and she was a dream in a tight white button-down, knotted at the midriff, and pink heels. The denim legs of her cut-offs were scissored away at the crotch, showing every last centimeter of leg and, if she bent a little, the curve of her buttocks.

Her jaw set with determination, she clicked her way through the foyer and into the lobby, set the tray of cookies on the front desk, and said, "I'm here to see Mr. Ward."

The desk girl - McKaylie, according to her name-tag - opened her mouth to speak, but Sydney plowed over her. "If you tell me he's not available, I'm going to wait right here until he is."

McKaylie hesitated. "One moment, Ms. ..."

"Call me Sydney."

"One moment, Sydney." McKaylie picked up the phone and dialed. After a moment, she began speaking - low enough that Sydney only caught snatches of conversation: "to see you ... Sydney ... she says she's not leaving unless ... All right ... I'll send her up." She hung up and gave Sydney a warm smile. "He says you can come right up. Do you know the way?"

After receiving directions, Sydney clicked toward the elevator and took it to the second floor, exiting in the east wing. From there, she sashayed past a few meeting rooms, and came to a door with a placard that read, *M. Ward*. She knocked, heard an automatic lock unbolt, and stepped inside.

And her self-assurance wilted like a blossom on a dying vine. The room was larger than she'd expected, intimidating in its no-nonsense simplicity. *Painfully dull*, she realized as she glanced around. *Almost deliberately without soul.* Furnished in wood, glass, and leather, it was the office of a man who kept his secrets close, revealing nothing of himself. She hadn't expected *flash* exactly, but this place was so sterile she might have been here to get a Pap smear. Michael himself was the only interesting thing in the room.

He stood as she entered, his rockstar-long black hair hanging loose around his shoulders. She'd never seen it not tied back and the effect was heart-stopping. There was an uncertain smile on Michael's pale and cruelly beautiful face as he said, "Ms. Doss. How nice to see you again." His voice was like a hit of morphia. " Please, sit." He gestured at a chair on the other side of the massive wooden desk.

Sydney, a sudden bundle of stops and starts, steadied herself and sank into a surprisingly comfortable chair. The room smelled not only of leather and wood, but of Michael himself - she remembered his cologne from their first and only meeting. It made her knees weak.

Michael resumed his seat and looked at her expectantly.

"I, um ..." Her mind raced, her pulse hammered, and her blood turned to tar. "I-I brought you these." She pushed the plastic tray of pink-frosted cookies toward him. They looked cheap and out of place in the stuffy surroundings of the office - like a tracksuit-wearing fat girl in a group photo of business execs. *I am that girl,* she realized with building panic. *What was I thinking wearing this?*

Michael was in a suit, the kind that flattered the width of shoulders and slimness of waist. He was taller than she remembered - several inches above the six-foot mark - and even sitting, he towered over her. And he was thin, very thin - but not unhealthily so. The term *'fashionably cadaverous,'* came unbidden to her mind.

"Thank you very much, Ms. Doss," Michael said. "But you don't need to buy me gifts."

"P-p-please," she said, furious that her childhood stutter had chosen now to return. "C-call me S-Sydney." *Fuck it all!* It had taken years to overcome her impediment and she'd be damned if she'd let it rear its ugly head now. Straightening in her seat, she cleared her throat, and planned her next words, speaking carefully. "I just ... wanted to give you ... a token of my appreciation." She glanced down at the cookies, sorely regretting them. "It's very kind of you to let me stay here."

"Of course," said Michael. "Any friend of the sheriff's is a friend of mine. I do hope-"

REDRUM!

"Oh!" Sydney jumped, her hand shooting to her throat, as the new voice, foreign and robotic, shrilled through the room.

Michael, with a look of long-suffering patience, leaned down and brought up a large birdcage. Setting it on the edge of the desk, he said, "This is Reaper."

The caged raven stared at her, its shiny black eyes considering her with curiosity. It tilted its head and let out another terrible squawk: *REDRUM! REDRUM!*

"Oh, holy Jesus, it's horrible!" As soon as she said the words, she regretted them. "Oh, I'm sorry - I didn't mean to be rude, it's just that-"

But Michael only chuckled. "He is rather horrible. Unfortunately, he only knows lines from horror movies."

"I s-see," said Sydney, trying to recompose herself.

Reaper the raven shrieked out another of its ungodly quotes.

"Hush, bird." Michael set the cage back on the floor beside him. "If he gets too talkative, I can have him removed. It's nearing his feeding time."

"Oh, it's fine." She waved a hand, trying to appear casual and, catching sight of her bubblegum pink nails, felt self-conscious all over again.

But Michael wasn't treating her like the pom-pom-waving half-wit she felt like. He clasped his hands in front of himself - beautiful hands with long, tapered fingers that could bring any woman closer with a single crook, and smiled politely, giving her lots of easy eye contact. "I do hope you're satisfied with the accommodations?"

"Oh, yes, of course. They're wonderful. Absolutely. Th-thank you again."

His eyes, the color of whiskey, watched her, and there was something in them. A sadness ... and something she couldn't peg. "You're more than welcome."

Sydney straightened herself, resolved to retain her composure. *I came here to flirt, and by God, I'm going to do it.* Smiling, she shifted her shoulders back a fraction of an inch so her blouse tightened across her breasts. She was both impressed and disappointed that Michael took no notice. She had a split-second fantasy of grabbing handfuls of his glossy onyx locks and pulling his face into her bosom - but she remained cool. "I'm enjoying my stay here very much, Mr. Ward." She leaned in now, feeling more comfortable. She reminded herself that beneath the arresting, somehow medieval package, Michael was just a man - no matter how otherworldly he might seem. "It means so much to me," she purred. "I've been through such a terrible time, and I can't begin to tell you how deeply I appreciate your kindness."

When she rested her hand over his, she felt something almost electric. She was sure he felt it too, for his eyes darkened and revealed the secret thing she'd seen in them earlier: Hunger. Need. Suddenly Michael Ward was not all brick and stone. There was a vulnerability in him - a vulnerability toward her. An erotic burn flamed through her body.

Michael cleared his throat and, with the deftness of a master magician, slipped his strangely cold hand out from under hers. An unsteady smile came to his elegant and sensitive lips. His eyes, too, were uneasy now. "Of course. Now if you'll excuse me, I have much to do." His nostrils flared almost imperceptibly and his gaze took on a subtle hardness. "It was nice to see you, Ms. Doss." The voice was cool now, professional, without heart.

That's it? Sydney felt as if she were falling down a bottomless well. *That's the end of the discussion?* But she wouldn't give up. *He's been hurt*, she realized. *He's been hurt terribly and he's afraid of getting involved.* Just like the men in the novels she read. *But he'll come around. He'll realize he wants me and over time his passion will grow. And then, eventually, he'll realize he can no longer fight his feelings.* It was going to be a process and that meant she'd need to come around more often. Through repeated exposure to her feminine charms, he'd slowly wear down.

But she had to be careful. Too much too fast and she'd blow it.

She cleared her throat. It was time to walk out now - walk out and leave him wanting more. She smiled. "Enjoy the cookies, Mr. Ward."

"I shall."

Shall? God, he was good. He really *was* like one of the men in her books.

As she rose, so did he, and Sydney did *not* ogle his slender but powerful physique. She kept her eyes fixed almost dispassionately on his, poker-faced, tit for tat. "Have a good evening, Mr. Ward." Formality at this early stage in their courtship was a must.

"And you as well, Ms. Doss."

When Sydney closed the office door behind her, she blew out a breath, pressed a hand over her heart and fanned her face. She hadn't wanted a man this badly since … well, *ever*. He'd be a tough nut to crack, but sooner or later, one way or another, Sydney always got her man. Composing herself, she headed for the elevator, not so much clicking now as drifting back toward her cabin.

THE GRIEF BROOKS HAD INFLICTED ON CADE AND HIS REGRET FOR WHAT he'd done to Samantha were almost unbearable. He lived under a chronic razor-sharp guilt that, even at the best of times, preyed on his mind, awaiting the first opportunity to pounce and remind him all over again that he was a monster, a murderer.

But none of his misery was as sharp and fierce as the threat of Gretchen's nearness. It was that, added to the already toxic mix, that brought Brooks' anxiety to the boiling point; every sound outside became Gretchen's approach, every shadow her dreaded entrance.

But though the vampiric bond with her was strong - he could feel her in his cells even now, wanting him - Brooks maintained his vow that he would not go to her. Not now and not ever, regardless of how often and how easily she seduced him in his dreams - and she was *always* in his dreams, beckoning, calling him home to her. Every time he closed his eyes, she was there, stroking him with her cold dead touch, bringing him to the brinks of horror and bliss, her strange chill breath like winter wind on his ear. '*My little tin soldier ... come home to me ...*'

But with practice, by force of will, he would sever that bond. She only wanted Cade, Brooks knew that now, and he would not help her get him. Not again.

Like Michael and his Loyals, Brooks would learn to live without violence. In time, he was certain, he would adapt and his bloodlust would subside enough that he could carry out his eternal existence with some normalcy. He knew it was possible because he'd seen Michael and his guys do just that.

The only hitch in his plan was Rafe Santangelo. Brooks hadn't the heart to abandon him. As the two men had gotten to know each other, Brooks had come to like Rafe. Looking at him now, with his dark good looks and blue eyes, Brooks could only imagine how furious Gretchen must be that he'd gotten away - it had come as no surprise to Brooks that Gretchen and her cronies had been Santangelo's captors. It only validated what Brooks already knew: Gretchen had reanimated. Not that his dreams - and the nearly unbearable need to be near her - weren't proof enough.

Brooks watched as Rafe played hand after hand of solitaire. He could see the man's hunger in the pallor of his skin, the circles under his eyes, and the slightly rusty motion of limbs. All suggested a low-grade starvation of the cells. And yet the man was content. Happy, even. Brooks wondered what had been so wrong in Rafe's life that living in a rotting cabin in the woods was the better alternative.

He didn't ask, though. He was hungry, very hungry. He'd insisted they ride it out a little longer. Later, he'd promised, they would hunt for deer.

Now Rafe groaned and threw his hand across the spread of cards. "The craving ... it's getting unbearable."

"Good." Brooks sat, his back against the rickety wood wall, knees drawn up. "It won't be much longer now."

Rafe faced Brooks. "I can't think of anything except ... blood. *Human* blood."

Brooks was silent. He wasn't ready for this conversation. Rafe already knew he was half-vampire and would remain so until he drank human blood, but what he didn't know was that until he did, his condition was reversible. It wasn't that Brooks didn't want the guy to know he still had a shot at being human again - it was that he didn't want to tell him *how* that worked. Brooks wasn't sure he ever wanted to tell him that part.

For a while both men were silent as the wind howled through the broken windows and a light patter of rain began to tap on the roof. Then Rafe said, "So, how much truth is there to vampire lore? Stakes, garlic, and all that?"

Brooks shrugged. "Some."

"Could you be a little more specific?"

"What do you want to know?"

"Well ... how long do they live?"

"Forever." The word tasted like something burnt on his tongue.

"Forever? So we can't die at all, ever?"

"There are a few ways to kill a vampire, but we're basically immortal."

"*Basically* immortal? What does that mean? How *do* you kill a vampire?"

Brooks recalled what he'd learned from Michael and his Loyals. "The five S's - starvation, sunlight, a stake through the heart, severing of the head, and … silver." He pointed to the scar on his forehead. "That's how I got this. Our wounds will heal quickly, except when they're inflicted with silver. And a mortal wound with it will kill you for good."

Rafe stared at him. "That's what caused the streak in your hair?"

Brooks shrugged. "I guess so. It wasn't there before." And it wasn't fading either. It would be there forever, a reminder of his sins.

"But it's different for me, isn't it? Because I'm not a full vampire yet."

Yet. Brooks didn't like the word and he wasn't taking the bait. "Yeah, it's different. You're not immortal."

"But I would be if I drank from a human."

"Which isn't going to happen. Later, when you've-"

"'*Had some time and I'm ready to make that decision.*'" Rafe rehearsed the litany in a tired tone. "But what if I *am* ready and it *is* what I want?"

"You're not and it isn't."

Rafe's eyes darkened. "How do you know? I don't want to go back to my old life. I like it this way."

Brooks said nothing.

"And isn't drinking human blood what we're *supposed* to do? Isn't it our nature?"

Brooks shifted. "Look, there are reasons we don't want to go after a human."

"Like what?"

Brooks bit back his irritation. "Well, if we do, it will heighten our bloodlust and we'll go out of control. I don't want to live like that. I've seen it."

"And what else? There's something you're not saying."

Brooks ran a hand through his hair and cleared his throat. "The transition into full vampirism isn't complete until you drink human blood." He met Rafe's eyes. "So right now, you're still suspended between being a human and a vampire. You're in 'retrograde.'"

"Right. I know."

"Well, once you drink human blood, you can't ever ... go back to being human. Ever."

Rafe's gaze was steady, unreadable. "So, you're saying I *can* go back now?"

Brooks nodded.

"How?"

And this was the part he hadn't wanted to tell the man. "I'm your Maker ... so as long as you're in retrograde, you'll revert back if ... if I die."

The silence lay thick between them. The rain tapping on the roof was like the tick of a thousand clocks. Brooks had known he couldn't stave off the man's questions forever but he wished they could have avoided that part a while longer. *Maybe I should have lied.*

Rafe said, "Hey, man, you're not afraid I'm going to kill you, are you?"

Brooks shrugged. "I can't say it hasn't crossed my mind. Or that I'd blame you if you did."

Rafe laughed. "Well, I'm not going to. Like I said, I don't want to go back to my old life. Maybe that's hard to believe, but I'm serious. I like the way I am now." He paused. "What about you? Do you want to go back to your old life? Do you have family? Friends?"

Family ... not anymore. Friends ... definitely not. "I have a younger brother. Cade. Our parents are dead."

"Your brother ... is he ... one of us?"

"No." Brooks winced at the idea. Talk of Cade had him shifting uncomfortably. Cade would never forgive him for what he'd taken from him.

"Are there others like us?"

"Vampires? Well, Gretchen and-"

"No, I mean, others like *us*, who aren't ... killers?"

"There are some around, yes."

"Do they drink human blood?"

"Yes."

"Well, who are they?" Rafe was suddenly animated. "Maybe we should find them and-"

Brooks shook his head. He wouldn't dare go to Michael until he was in full control of his appetites. Only when he'd amended his ways could he beg forgiveness for what he'd done. And even then, he might never be forgiven. Michael might not accept him. "No. We're on our own for the time being." He watched the flicker of hope stutter and die in the other man's eyes. "Are you saying you don't like our living arrangement?" Brooks grinned.

Rafe chuckled. "It's not so bad. I mean, it'd be nicer if you got some new threads." He glanced down at Brooks' tattered striped boxer shorts. "I'm tired of looking at your junk, but other than that..."

Brooks laughed. It was real laughter, deep and full, from the belly. It felt good.

And now Rafe knew the truth about his condition and that was a load off Brooks' mind. He didn't believe the man would stake him to regain full humanity, but there was a part of Brooks that, if he were being honest, wouldn't mind if he did.

Getting to his feet, Brooks said, "I think we've held off long enough. Let's hunt."

Rafe shot up like a jack-in-the-box. "It's about time you said something that makes sense."

They went into the night in search of blood.

Scythe had searched the entire cavern and found no sign of his cards. After forcing the two new guys to empty their pockets, the only possibility left was that Santangelo took them. And Scythe was pissed. Now he'd have to make a trip to town for a new deck - and if he did that, Jazminka would surely give him a ridiculous errand of some sort. Probably yet another blood slave for Gretchen, and Scythe was already tripping over the half a dozen new ones they'd acquired over the past few nights.

They'd found most of them in Santa Cruz, some on the streets, some at a nightclub called Liaisons, and one unlucky gal who'd been out for a late night jog. They were all young and attractive - just how

Gretchen liked them. Three males and three females, but it was the men, of course, that Gretchen favored.

But Scythe was already bored with all of them. Gretchen still wasn't in good enough shape to start administering venom, so it was up to Scythe and Jazminka - and Jazminka, bitch that she was, usually left it to Scythe.

That meant he had six hand-puppets hanging on his every word, awaiting his next move, and eager for the moment he might do something really exciting and scratch his balls or some shit.

Fucking idiots.

It would be fine, of course, if he could at least reap some of the benefits of the bond - he had his eye on a petite dark-haired stripper who went under the name DeHavalyn - but Jazminka never let her, or any of the female slaves, out of her sight long enough for Scythe to even give the girl the come-fuck-me eyes.

But the six new slaves were even now drained of too much blood, and that meant they'd be acquiring more. And the more slaves there were, the harder it would be for Jazminka to keep an eye on them. And then Scythe could make his move. Sitting in the corner, he looked over at DeHavalyn. She was staring at him while the others slept.

He glanced over at Gretchen. She, too, was sleeping. Though her appearance continued to improve - she seemed to be aging backward - she was still hideous. There was a net of wrinkles around her sunken eyes and her hair was dry straw. Scythe could see from the expression on her still-godawful, maggot-white face, that she was dreaming.

ROME, 1679.

In the weeks that followed, Gretchen and Astrid had become close with the traveling tradesman named Stefano Sabbatini - close enough that by the time he'd bitten them and claimed them as his own, neither woman had any reservations about the eternity unfurling before them, nor did they balk at the means of survival they now required. Looking back, Gretchen would later become certain the man had been dosing them both with venom, which accounted for their placid willingness to comply and conform, but at the time, the only thing that mattered was being with this man.

Gretchen was in love, and unbeknownst to Astrid, she'd begun an affair with Stefano so passionate that in the centuries that followed, nearly all of her lovers would pale in his wake. Stefano was her first, the yardstick by which all others were measured. The two stole moments together when Astrid went out - always at night now, for going into the sun was forbidden if they were to survive.

Gretchen would watch out the window of their apartment, waiting for her mother to disappear around some corner, and Stefano, as if having a secret sense that they were safely alone, would appear behind her, his breath hot on her ear, his hands in her hair, the hardness of his want pressing eagerly at her back. They would tumble into the soft bed where Stefano would teach Gretchen the ways of lovemaking, showing her things her innocent mind had never before conceived.

Often, Stefano simply stretched back, allowing Gretchen to explore his body, to memorize the textures, the smells, and the tastes of him. With her vampire senses, she drank him in, storing those sensations within her for later ruminations when they were not alone.

She was fascinated by his nudity; she enjoyed nothing more than letting her hands and mouth wander over him, relishing the tiny signals he gave when she'd reached a sweet spot. Often, this came as a soft, deep sigh, other times, a moan. But her favorite, the one that told her she was making him ravenous, was a low, throaty growl. When she elicited that sound from him, it would only be moments before he took her, abandoning his self-control and ravishing her with a hunger so powerful, so primal and demanding, that Gretchen had to bite into a pillow or a sheet or sometimes even Stefano's own throat, to silence her ecstasy.

He enjoyed taking her from behind, hands fisted in her hair, and at one point, he even introduced her to something he called Greek Love. She wouldn't have enjoyed that save for the fact that it was Stefano who was doing it to her, and because it was he, she let him have his way. But never again would Gretchen so completely give her body over to the whims of another man. Stefano was the first, and the last, to whom she ever surrendered control.

When the lovemaking was done, they would lie together, a tangle of naked limbs. These were the tender moments, the ones that Gretchen most looked forward to. In those quiet minutes, they sometimes spoke of mundane things - the gossip of the streets, the workings of Italian and international politics which Gretchen found surprisingly interesting - but more often, he told her what it meant to be a vampire, imparting pieces of wisdom from what seemed his infinite reservoir of knowledge.

And then, invariably, he would press a fingertip to Gretchen's lips, saying, "Ah, that is enough for now, vita mia. She is coming." They would dress, and then, proving his sixth-sense about these things, Astrid would return with her wares - usually new perfume, clothing, or some little trinket for Gretchen. If she ever suspected what went on between Stefano and her daughter, she gave no sign.

And then Stefano, ever the gentleman, would go out, returning later with sustenance - usually a local prostitute. He did not kill them but rather, he paid them handsomely for their blood. Most willingly obliged. There seemed no end to Stefano's supply of money - Astrid and Gretchen had quit the commedia dell'arte and were living comfortably in his support - and she often wondered that he even bothered to continue cobbling shoes at all; he seemed very able to retire.

In the beginning, Gretchen had been overcome with the guilt of the affair. She'd thought perhaps her mother had set her sights upon Stefano, but when Gretchen received no signals that the two were romantically interested in one another, the guilt subsided. But still, Gretchen and Stefano kept their passion concealed. He had insisted upon that, and Gretchen thought she knew why: Over time, she, Astrid, and Stefano had become something like a family, the dynamic of which placed Gretchen in the unfortunate position of daughter. Often, but only in Astrid's presence, Stefano called her mia figlia - *my daughter.*

For nearly a year, they lived this way and were happy. When she would look back on that time, the only cracks Gretchen would see in their smoothly polished lives were the talks between Astrid and Stefano. Speaking a language Gretchen was unfamiliar with, she never knew the subjects of those hushed conversations which usually took place when Gretchen was supposed to be sleeping. But she always knew the anger in her mother's voice. These *conversations never escalated; over time, they ceased altogether, but Astrid seemed to have become somewhat cold toward Stefano.*

But he and Gretchen only continued to grow closer, though never so close that they openly expressed their love for one another.

Stefano never gave any indication of his plans to move on and, in fact, he'd vowed the three of them would be together forever - so when Gretchen arrived home from a night at the theater to find Astrid weeping and Stefano gone, Gretchen had suffered her first broken heart. She'd fallen to the floor, sobbing.

For many nights, she'd remained in bed, refusing even to take the sustenance Astrid brought her. Only when her lack of nourishment had emaciated her frame and threatened to rob her of her life had she begun to accept the offerings. Over time, she rebuilt her strength, but Gretchen was never the same. Every night that Stefano was gone from her, Gretchen's heart grew harder until it was but a calcified stone in her chest. Astrid, on the other hand, seemed almost relieved at Stefano's departure, and Gretchen resented her mother's coldness with wild and outspoken hostility.

They began to spend their nights hunting, Gretchen often insisting on being on her own. No longer caring for decorum, she grew sloppy, killing indiscriminately and with a rage so bitter that it lay thick on her tongue, so thick that it could be counteracted only by the taste of terrified blood.

It wasn't long until the rumors began.

"Vampiros!" said the city, and eventually, for fear of being found out, Astrid and Gretchen fled.

Gretchen never saw Stefano Sabbatini again. And it would be another century before she learned the excruciating truth about what had become of him.

19

AMAZING DISGRACE

Samantha's mother had left it to Sheila to arrange the funeral, claiming she was too stressed to manage it. Apparently, she was also too stressed to attend; at the services Cade had heard she'd gone to Las Vegas to soothe her nerves. He thought this would have been the hot topic among the mourners, but it wasn't. The town of Crimson Cove was much more interested in the disappearance of Brooks in relation to Samantha's death than the fact that her own mother hadn't attended. It disgusted - and enraged - Cade.

And by the time the funeral ended and the mourners had gathered in the community hall at St. Anthony's for the reception, Cade could barely hide his fury. Now, the only thing keeping his fury under wraps was the beautiful rendition of *Amazing Grace* that Father Vincent Scarlotti played on his violin. Sheila had suggested it; it was a good call.

Vincent Scarlotti was slender and very tall with glossy dark hair - youthful-looking despite the hint of gray that declared itself at his temples. His features were rugged but pleasant and were he not a priest, he might have made a fine Hollywood heartthrob.

But it was his music that captivated the room.

Eyes closed, the priest bowed out such beautiful, soulful notes they might have been channeled directly from Heaven. As he played, time stood still - and so did Cade's pain. Tears stood in his eyes at the beauty of the music, and the heat of the room, the discomfort of his suit, and the hateful gossip he'd heard at the funeral were all momentarily forgotten. It was the only reprieve Cade had had since the morning of Samantha's death. He watched in awe as the tall man bowed out the notes with such feeling, such skill that Cade felt the music in his teeth, his bones, his soul.

But too soon the song was over and Scarlotti reverently replaced his violin in its case. The performance had been so beautiful that its absence was palpable; it took a moment for the room to catch its collective breath. Time regained its legs and the attendees began gathering themselves, quietly heading for the buffet tables to fill their plates.

Cade, who sat with Ethan and Sheila, wasn't hungry and went straight for the wine. When he returned, the Lincolnesque priest was at the podium, speaking about Samantha in velvet tones. On a table beside him was a smiling portrait of her framed in fragrant white lilies - Samantha's favorite flowers. It was a beautiful arrangement but it paled in comparison to Scarlotti's *Amazing Grace*. Cade only hoped that wherever Samantha was, she'd heard the music.

Father Vincent told how Samantha volunteered at soup kitchens during the holidays - a fact that Cade hadn't known but wasn't surprised by - and how she'd helped out with various fundraisers for the church. This *did* surprise Cade - he didn't know that she'd been involved in any church activities.

As he spoke, the priest's eyes continually returned to Cade, his gentle voice soothing, his handsome face kind. But all the same, in the absence of his beautiful music, Cade's rage slowly returned. Rage at Winter for refusing to bring Samantha back. Rage at Samantha's mother for not showing up. Rage at the town for its thoughtless conjecture and petty gossip. If only Scarlotti would play another song and vanquish Cade's pain.

But he didn't. He finished speaking and Cade went for his second glass of red wine. When he returned, a woman named Mary Considine was at the podium, tears spilling and voice quavering as she shared memories of Samantha. They'd worked together at the library and though Cade had never met her, he was sure this was the hypochondriac Samantha had told him about. He'd seen her at the funeral, hands clasped so tightly in prayer they might have been welded together. Now, as she quivered, quaked, and sobbed, he couldn't help thinking she was laying it on just a little too thick. *Or maybe I'm just being a dick.*

Sheila touched his hand as Cade downed his second glass of wine. "You look very handsome today, Cade."

He nodded. She'd already told him this twice. "I'm going to get more wine."

He headed for the bar, pausing momentarily as Ethan's neighbor, Gladiola Gelding, gossiped with two other women near the potato salad. They were dressed in all black, reminding Cade of the Three Fates, if the Three Fates were a trio of fat asses who spent their time gossiping around buffet tables at funerals.

"... it just seems awfully suspicious, if you ask me," Mrs. Gelding was saying.

"The older brother, you say?" asked one.

"And no sign of him since?" inquired another.

Gladiola Gelding shook her head with vehemence, her many chins vacillating grotesquely. "Not a trace. Murder, I tell you. Mur-"

One of the women elbowed Mrs. Gelding, eliciting a jump and a little squeak as Cade approached. They stared in silence as he poured another glass, downed it, poured another, then grinned at them a little too brightly before heading back to his table. The wine had warmed his cheeks and his belly and he was feeling loose. Angry, but loose.

"How're you holding up?" Ethan asked when Cade returned.

Cade shrugged and sipped his wine, straining to hear the whispers of the table behind him. They, too, were convinced that his brother was a murderer. Or maybe it was the boyfriend, Cade, who'd done it. She *was* living with *both* of them, you know. The slut. Perfect recipe for disaster. Someone should call that TV show, *Conversations with a Coroner,* and have this situation investigated - clearly the sheriff wasn't going to do anything about it. He's probably in on it, you know.

Cade gritted his teeth and sipped more wine.

Ethan watched the wineglass - and Cade - with obvious concern. He touched Cade's arm. "Take it easy, son. It's almost over."

Take it easy? Cade shrugged from his touch and turned his attention to Mary Considine, who continued to monopolize the podium. He had no idea what she was even talking about now, so wracked was she by hitching false sobs. Cade loosened his tie. The anger and the wine had made the heat unbearable.

Several people stopped by the table to give Cade their condolences, including his boss, Dora Langley, who looked strange and unnatural in an uncharacteristically simple black dress.

Cade greeted them all in a daze, nodding and *Mm-hmm*ing, but when the gossips from the table next to them stopped by and pretended to care, he couldn't bring himself to feign courtesy. He narrowed his eyes at them, saying nothing, and continued to stare, unblinking, until they became uncomfortable and walked away. Cade was amazed at their nerve. As he reached for his wine, Ethan cleared his throat. Cade ignored him and downed half the glass.

Father Vincent Scarlotti was making his way toward them, pausing to chat in low tones with people he knew. When he finally arrived at their table, Ethan gestured for him to sit.

"I just wanted to meet the young man Samantha cared for so much." He put a hand over Cade's and Cade's growing anger was momentarily tempered by the priest's gentle presence.

"I'm very sorry for your loss. She was a good woman, Mr. Colter."

Cade felt the sting of new tears. "She was, thank you."

"Father Scarlotti," said Sheila. "Your playing was absolutely magnificent. Thank you so much."

"That's very kind of you, Ms. Leventis. I'm happy to do it."

"How long have you been playing?" asked Ethan.

"All my life."

As the three chatted, Cade stopped listening and finished off his wine, taking petty satisfaction in the fact that by now, he was feeling more than just a little drunk. He almost hoped it was noticeable and that it was making all these assholes uncomfortable.

At long last, Mary Considine finished speaking and Mrs. Gelding got up to say a few words. This outraged Cade. Not five minutes ago, the woman was buoyant with the joy of her little whisper campaign at the buffet table and now she had the gall to act like she was grieving. She didn't even *know* Samantha and as she blathered on, dabbing her piggy little eyes, Cade's anger turned to red-hot rage, his fist tightening hard around his empty glass.

This darkening of mood was apparently not lost on Ethan and Sheila. Nor the priest, who patted his hand, leaned in, and said, "Never mind the busybodies, Mr. Colter. As the good book says, *'With their mouths the godless destroy their neighbors, but through knowledge the righteous escape.'*"

So even the priest had heard the rumors.

There was a loud *Pop*! as the wine glass broke in Cade's fist.

The room went silent.

Even Mrs. Gelding stopped talking.

"Oh!" And Sheila was at his side, inspecting his hand. "Are you okay?"

But if he'd cut himself he didn't feel it; he wasn't bleeding. Cade glanced around, embarrassed now. All eyes were on him. "I'm fine." He shoved his chair out noisily, stood, and was heading for the exit when something came over him. He paused. Maybe it was the wine, but he had a few words to say himself. Turning around, he headed to the small platform and, to Gladiola Gelding's shock, took over the podium.

Low whispers hushed through the room.

"My name is Cade Colter," he said to the stunned crowd. "I loved Samantha very much and I'll miss her more than I can say." His voice was thick with wine and fury. "To those who have come today to say goodbye, to show respect for a life taken far too soon, thank you for being here. But to the rest of you." Now he looked daggers at Gladiola Gelding, who stood watching, eyes wide, hand pressed to her breast. "Those of you who came here for entertainment, those of you who came to gossip and slander and speculate: I hope that at your own funerals, no one is as cruel to your loved ones as you've been to Samantha's today." Had he ended there, he might have retained his dignity, but the wine, combined with the murmurs of self-righteous shock, urged him onward. "I guess what I'm trying to say," he continued, "is go fuck yourselves."

The crowd gasped. Hands shot to bosoms and mouths. Mrs. Gelding's face went the color of raw dough. Sheila gaped like a beached fish. Ethan's eyes nearly bugged out of his head. Cade stepped off the platform and strode from the church, weaving from the wine, and left the mourners - and their hissing little whisper games - behind.

IN THE PARKING LOT OUTSIDE THE CHURCH, ETHAN CAUGHT UP WITH Cade before he got behind the wheel. "Come on," he said, guiding him toward his own vehicle. "I'll take you home."

Cade didn't argue.

Ethan got in and buckled up, but didn't start the engine right away. He sat behind the wheel, looking up at the tall church, not sure what to say. He glanced over at Cade who stared down at his hands, dazed and despondent - and drunk off his ass.

Ethan was at a loss. The wrong step would send the kid over the edge. He searched for the right words. "I really wish you hadn't-" But he stopped himself. Those were definitely not the right words. He cleared his throat and started again. "I was going to say I wish you hadn't done that, but you know what? I don't blame you a bit."

Cade sniffed.

"I heard what they were saying in there. About Brooks. About you. About Samantha. I was half-tempted to tell them to go fuck themselves, too." For a moment, they sat in silence. "The point is, I'm sorry. For all of it."

"Fuck them." Cade's voice was a rasp. "I don't care."

But he did care, that was obvious.

"Look, Cade. The thing is, I know this is hard. I get it. I do. It's understandable that you're having a hard time, a damned hard time, but..."

"But what? Are you going to try to tell me I should be 'handling the situation better?'" He made air quotes around the last words. "Because if you are, I don't want to hear it. You *know* what really happened to Samantha." He was slurring. "I think I'm handling it pretty goddamn well, all things considered. And as for what happened in there," he nodded at the church, "You heard what they were saying. I think I went pretty fucking easy on them."

Ethan agreed but said nothing. It wasn't what Cade had said to the mourners that concerned him - it was the way the kid was coping. Or rather *not* coping. He'd lost too much weight, he obviously wasn't sleeping, and half the time, he wasn't even showering. The outburst in St. Anthony's was just one more thing and it was painful for Ethan to watch. "You're right," he finally said. "They deserved worse. But I don't care about them, Cade. I can't ... watch you suffer like this anymore." He bit back tears, embarrassed. "I'd like you to go to one of those meetings in Santa Cruz."

"The grief support group?" Cade uttered a humorless laugh. "No, thanks."

"Just go to *one*. See what they have to offer."

Cade shook his head, tears pricking his eyes. "No."

"But why not?"

Silence.

"Why not, Cade?"

Nothing.

"Talk to me. Tell me why you-"

"Because it will make it *real*, okay?" Cade's voice was high, almost shrill. "And I don't *want* it to be real! I thought ... I thought we could bring her back ... that Winter would-"

"Bring her back? As a ... *vampire*? Cade, Samantha wouldn't want that."

"You don't *know* that!" Tears streaked down his face. "She was talking about it, saying that if we were vampires we could be together forever. And then ... after she died ... I asked Winter if he'd turn her, but he wouldn't do it. And he won't even tell me why!" Cade punched the dash, hard. A couple of times.

Ethan let him and when he finished, said, "I'm sure he has his reasons."

"*What* reasons?"

"I don't know. I'm not Winter." Ethan leaned over, grabbed a tissue from the glove box, and handed it to Cade.

"Why should Brooks get to live forever and not Samantha? How is *that* fair?"

"I'm not so sure that living forever is all it's cracked up to be, Cade."

"But anything's better than being *dead*, isn't it?"

"I don't know. I've never been dead before."

Cade brought the heels of his hands to his eyes and pressed. He wept openly and without shame. His sobs were pain-filled and soul-deep; they clutched at Ethan's heart - but there was nothing to say, nothing to do but let the kid get it all out. But he'd never felt so helpless, so impotent; he would have given anything to change things. He'd take Cade's pain himself if he could.

When Cade's sobs began to sputter out, Ethan reached over and laid a hand on his shoulder.

"Sorry about that." Cade's embarrassment was obvious. He wiped his nose.

"Not a problem. Sometimes letting it out is just what you need."

"Thanks, Ethan. And I really am sorry about all this. I know I'm a fucking mess. I know."

"You're doing just fine."

There was a stretch of silence. It was neither uncomfortable nor what you'd call companionable. It just ... *was*.

Cade blew his nose and then, in a quiet voice, said, "I'll think about it, okay? The support group, I mean."

Ethan dared not show a reaction. He didn't want to risk saying anything that might change Cade's mind.

"But I'm not promising anything."

Ethan nodded.

Cade chuckled that sad, humorless chuckle. "Of course, I don't know what I'll say … *'Hi, my name's Cade and my brother the vampire killed my girlfriend and none of the other vampires will turn her so now I'm all alone …'*"

Ethan chuckled too, and his, like Cade's, was empty. He was too drained, too hollowed out to really feel it. "Yeah, I'm sure that'd go over well. But there's plenty you *can* talk about. You can talk about your grief. Your loss. With people who understand how you're feeling."

Cade turned to face him for the first time since they'd gotten in the Wrangler. "But, Ethan … what if no one does? What if no one really can understand how it feels?"

Ethan studied him. *Is that what you're afraid of? That no one else has ever felt this way before?* "They do," he said. "I give you my word, they do. Grief is a private thing that affects people differently … but Cade … underneath it all, it hurts everyone just the same."

Cade sniffed. "You're probably right. I know you are. But I'm still not making any promises, okay? I don't know how I feel about … laying myself out in front of a bunch of strangers."

"If you'd be more comfortable talking one-on-one than in a group, I'm sure Sheila can find a good counselor for you."

"No. It's okay. I don't think it would make any difference. And besides, support groups are free. Shrinks aren't." He looked at Ethan. "And that *is* what you're talking about, isn't it? A shrink?"

Ethan shook his head. "I'm not talking about anything but options. And I wouldn't care if you found someone who charged three hundred bucks an hour. As long as he *helped* you, we'd make sure the bill got paid. Don't let money make your decision. Not this one."

Cade watched him. "You said *we*."

"Huh?"

"You said that *we* would make sure the bill got paid."

"You're damned right I did. I'm not going to let a few bucks stand in the way of you getting help."

"You'd … would you really do that for me?"

"You know I would."

But judging by Cade's expression, he knew no such thing. "I ... that means a lot to me. I'm not going to take you up on it, but it means a lot."

Ethan ran a hand down his face. "We'll deal with it as it comes. Now what say we blow this snow-cone shack and get you home?" He'd had enough angst for one day. "I want you to get some sleep, okay? And something to eat."

"I will." Cade put his seat belt on. He no longer looked drunk - emotional meltdowns had a way of sobering you up - but he probably still had a decent buzz going. Enough that Ethan wasn't about to let him drive.

"I'll have your car brought back to you later."

"Thanks."

Ethan started the Wrangler and headed for the cabin. His eyes were still misty, his ulcer flared, his head ached, and his nerves were shot to hell, but he scarcely registered any of that. His thoughts were on Cade. It was a load off his mind that the kid's anti-therapy stance was starting to crack, but Ethan approached that relief with caution. He had a feeling it wouldn't last. For now, it was enough to hope that when Cade got home he'd crawl into bed and sleep off the wine and the pain. And maybe if he slept long enough and deep enough, he might even sleep off this whole miserable day.

Ethan wanted to do the same thing himself.

20

BLUE OCTOBER

The summer, as always, tiptoed out of Crimson Cove on such silent, stealthy feet that if not for the emergence of grinning jack-o'-lanterns and arch-backed Halloween cat decorations in shop windows, you might have never known October had arrived. The nights had cooled, and by the middle of the month, the days would follow suit, but for now, the only proof of fall, aside from the spirit of the season, was that quiet dank tang that haunts the air, hovering just beyond the senses until the wind lets slip the cool, earthy smell of the coming harvest.

This, for as long as he could remember, was Cade's favorite time of year. By late September, he began to sense the season's approach, and as it arrived, it seemed to him that something in the human spirit wound down; it was a time for releasing and reflecting, and for those fleeting weeks of autumn, the world fell into a pensive mood and became a calmer, quieter place.

Since his boyhood in Gilroy, Cade had honored the season by milking out every bit of atmosphere that he could. He loved to be outside breathing deeply of the crisp breeze, and it was there, in Gilroy, in October, that he was first inspired to write. He'd wanted to capture the spirit of autumn on paper and though he never felt that he'd quite succeeded, he treasured the season doubly now because through it, he'd discovered his passion, his purpose: writing.

As the sweetgum trees outside celebrated the season with their explosions of fiery oranges, yellows, and reds, Cade had always celebrated inside with creepy trinkets: skull candy bowls, posable skeletons, light-up witches, hanging bats, faux crystal balls, fog machines, orange lights, fake cobwebs, and a jack-o'-lantern for every window. Whether in Gilroy or in Crimson Cove, Brooks - and everyone else - had accepted Cade's attraction to the macabre with a shake of the head and a good-natured roll of the eyes, letting him commemorate the season to his twisted little heart's content.

And commemorate Cade had. He liked to take his time decking the house out in darkness, doing a little here, a little there, making Halloween last the entire month. And while the days were spent decorating, the nights, of course, were for scary movies - everything from *Poltergeist* and *Pumpkinhead* to *Psycho, Scream,* and *The Shining* - every night, all month long.

October, for Cade, was more than a month. It was thirty-one days in which he could freely express his love of the macabre, the one time of year when he wasn't alone in it.

And he hadn't realized how much he cherished the unknown, how much he delighted in those darker mysteries until, by way of real-life monsters, the unknown became known and the mysteries were solved.

So this year, when October came to Crimson Cove, Cade, for the first time in his life, did nothing to bid it welcome. In fact, he hardly even noticed it. He hardly noticed anything.

For Cade, the days were painted in dark gloom and the black depression that had infected him when Samantha died had spread like a virus until every cell was poisoned. Cade saw nothing, heard nothing, felt nothing, and tasted nothing except her absence - the void she'd left behind. It was a gaping hole that hemorrhaged within him as raw and hollow as a gunshot wound - and it had only expanded since Samantha's funeral.

The shock of seeing her coffin had caused so great a rift in Cade's psyche that he'd been incapacitated entirely for three days. It had taken so long to think of Samantha as dead - dead in the fullest sense of the word, removed from Cade and this earth forever - and it was only then, at her service, that the shock and grief became real.

And on top of the grief, there were the nightmares. The tape that his unconscious mind played was worse than anything he could have purposely thought up, even after the goriest of horror movie marathons.

Dreams of blood.

Death.

Decay.

Ruin.

Long, darkened hallways that led only to Samantha's corpse corrupting in some shadowed corner and collecting hordes of bloated flies that laid eggs in her mouth and eye sockets even as she screamed at him that this was all his fault.

And the strange woman in black.

Every night, in his dreams, he saw her too, heard her wordless call.

The wasps were always there, as well - black and buzzing by the thousands, trying to get in, and often succeeding. He'd jerk awake, covered in sweat, slapping and clawing at his skin, his head slingshotting around in search of the stinging insects that were pricking his skin with thousands of tiny needles.

And daytime was no better. Since his outburst at the funeral, the citizens of Crimson Cove treated Cade like a pariah. Thankfully Dora hadn't fired him after the debacle - it had no doubt cost her some customers.

At least Brooks' business, Pinetop's, gave him no grief. Chet was running the place well and the office girl, Jana, had taken charge of the books, making it easy on Cade.

But the weight of all the other stress had resulted in a brewing hate that ran so deep and black that he could only register it in microscopic measures. He moved through the days at the bookstore, guiding customers and forcing smiles, and in the evenings, he fed the cat, tried to ignore Winter - or Dante or Rogan, or whoever Michael decided to send over - and went to bed. Sometimes he showered, sometimes he didn't, and he only bothered shaving when his jaw and neck began to itch so badly he couldn't stand it. As for eating, he only did that when someone was watching, when he had to put on a show of functionality.

Aside from the nightmares, the chronic hatred, and the black depression, the only other constant during those weeks was the silver dagger. At night he strapped it to his ankle in its antique sterling sheath. He was certain by now that the metal wasp on the dagger's hilt was somehow connected to the visions of wasps he'd been having - it didn't make sense, yet he knew it was true - but that didn't stop him from wearing it. It kept the vampires at a distance and that was what he wanted. When they bitched about it - even being within a foot of real silver offended the undead - he argued that it lessened their attraction to his particularly appetizing brand of blood, a point that had been well-taken when Dante, the dark-eyed, dark-haired Eudemonia guard, had forgotten to double up on his rations before playing bodyguard to Cade one night last week.

Cade hadn't even been writing. He'd emailed Ian Lake, his editor, briefing him on the death of Samantha, and telling him that it would be a few weeks before he'd be able to look at his manuscript. He was caught up in his own world of rote and repetition, and it had been this way until today, when his boss, Dora Langley, had finally broken her long-held silence on Cade's disheveled appearance.

She'd sent him home, requesting that he not return until he'd showered and shaved. Cade apologized but even that embarrassing confrontation had barely touched him. Personally, he didn't see how his own stink could be more offensive than the sinus-searing nag champa his boss insisted on burning during business hours. It soaked into the walls, the pages of the books, and out onto the street, reaffirming its moniker of Incense Avenue, and infuriating neighboring shopkeepers, especially Frank Merlin.

But under the barrier of his indifference, Cade knew Dora was right. In the confines of the blue Land Rover as he'd made his way home, it had been hard to deny the power of his own sour body odor.

At home, he filled Purrcy's food bowl and emptied the litter box, which was in dire need of changing. He looked around and sighed. The house wasn't as dirty as it had been, but he'd need to get on top of it before Winter took it upon himself to hire a maid again behind his back. *Tomorrow I'll clean.*

He headed to the bathroom with fresh clothes, where he paused in front of the mirror, frowning at the haggard young man staring back at him. At only twenty-four, he might have passed for middle-aged. He looked like something that had just crawled out of the gutter: his greasy hair was plastered to his equally greasy forehead and purple half-moons hung beneath his haunted eyes. His cracked, chapped lips bled too easily and his facial hair had passed the shadow stage and was swiftly moving toward a full beard. He'd lost weight, at least ten pounds by now, and given his already slim frame, he teetered on the verge of anorexic thinness. After washing up, he decided he'd try to eat something.

He splashed his face, smeared on some Barbasol, and began to shave. That done, he stepped into the shower, taking it as hot as he could stand, imagining the bacteria on his skin screaming in pain as he soaped up and scrubbed. He was feeling better - as better as he was capable of feeling, anyway - when he heard the dreadful humming buzz over the rush of the water. Dread coiled coldly in his gut. He recognized that sound. Bringing his face into the stream, he rinsed away the suds and saw nothing.

But when he felt the familiar creep of tiny insectile legs between his shoulder blades, he gasped and tried to slap at it. In his panic, he knocked the shampoo bottle from its ledge. It hit the floor of the tub and as he bent to retrieve it, he saw the wasp.

For a moment, Cade was frozen in a half-crouch. The insect perched on the faucet. Motionless, it seemed to stare back, it's bead-black eyes glittering with malevolence.

"Get the fuck out of my house." Cade grabbed the slippery shampoo bottle and slowly rose. He continued his shower, his eye on the wasp. As he stepped into the stream and raised his arms to rinse his head, the wasp took flight. It darted into the steam and drove itself directly into Cade's left eye before he could dodge it. Pain bloomed as it laid down its sting and he yelled, slapped a hand over his eye, and threw himself out of the shower, slipping and landing on the hard bathroom floor with a wet splat, taking half the shower curtain down with him. "Son of a bitch!" Scrambling to his feet, he grabbed the towel from the rack, and flung it pointlessly through the misted air, swatting at the elusive wasp.

Then somehow, the pain in his eye, the pain that had quickly engulfed the entire left side of his face, vanished. He blinked rapidly, testing his vision. It was fine. He wrapped the towel around his waist, swiped a hand across the fogged mirror, and inspected his eye.

Nothing.

Not so much as a reddened eyelid. Just like the wasp that had stung his lip weeks before, there was no evidence it had ever existed.

"What the hell?" Cade opened the door to let the steam out and searched the bathroom. But there was no wasp. He wondered if it had all been a hallucination brought on by a mind splintered by such unrest that it could no longer differentiate night terrors from reality.

Cade continued drying himself, his wide eyes questing the room for a black wasp that had apparently either fled unnoticed, or, more likely, he thought, as he touched his eye, had never been there at all.

21

DOPE SPRINGS ETERNAL

The dead man's filmy eyes, frozen open in abject terror, said more about the final horrors he'd seen than Ethan wanted to contemplate. The vic, Bert Holloway, known on the street as "Plug Daddy" - for his apparent penchant for taking MDMA rectally - was the third homicide that had come to Sheila's morgue in the past weeks. And he, like the others, hadn't merely been murdered. He'd been massacred, torn to bloody ribbons, his chest cavity cracked open like a walnut shell revealing the half-eaten heart. According to Sheila the heart had been drained of nearly all its blood, telling Ethan what he already knew: he had a vampire on his hands.

Ethan's stomach curdled as he looked down at what remained of the blackened, deflated organ, wishing like hell he hadn't had that pastrami sub for lunch. Reaching into his pocket for another Tums, he considered what he knew about the victim, looking for parallels with the others.

When he wasn't shoving illegal substances two knuckles deep into his own rectum, Holloway, aka Plug Daddy, availed himself of the sketchy pleasures of Scarlet Street and, also like the other victims, had a hard-on for damaging the merchandise. Holloway was a hitter who'd been arrested once for beating a prostitute unconscious before sodomizing her with the very socket wrench he used - as proud employee of Right Tow Roadside Assistance - to change the flat tires of grateful citizens who'd been stranded on the road.

"Do you really think Brooks might be responsible for this?" Sheila, looking skeptical, stood on the other side of the exam table. "I just can't see it."

Ethan, too, had his doubts. He knew that vampires - especially new ones - could be violent, but he couldn't attribute this kind of mutilation to the same guy he'd played pool with on Thursdays for the past year and a half. And it was more than that. With each new body, Ethan's gut told him this had nothing to do with Brooks Colter.

Sheila sighed. "How much does Cade know about all this?"

"Not much." While he couldn't stop gossip, Ethan had managed to keep the last few incidents out of the paper. So far, the victims were all from the lowest rungs of the social ladder - the kind of men who wouldn't be missed - and Ethan saw no reason to tell Cade any more than he needed to know. Plus, he wanted to avoid a public panic. Word of the Great Bear Scare, as he'd come to think of it, was already spreading. It was only a matter of time before he turned on the national news and heard one of Crimson Cove's very own uttering that famous line straight from every true-crime show ever televised: *'We just don't expect things like this in* our *town!'* And when that happened, the proverbial shit would hit the fan.

Until then, Ethan had to do his best to keep it as quiet as possible - but it wouldn't be so easy with Bert Holloway who, unlike the others, had an ex-wife who would eventually miss him. *Or his spousal support checks, anyway.* "Christ on a tricycle." Ethan pinched the bridge of his nose, warding off a headache.

Sheila pulled a sheet over the corpse. "Are Michael and his men still looking for Brooks?"

Ethan nodded. "Yep. No luck so far."

"What happens if they find him and ... and he *is* the killer?"

"I don't know. Unfortunately, the Crimson Cove Sheriff's Handbook didn't say a damned thing about the handling of vampires." Despite himself, he cracked a little smile.

Sheila did too. It wasn't the hundred-watt smile that made his heart bloom, but it was enough to make it swell a little.

"Maybe he's left town?"

Ethan shrugged. "Could be. Michael seems to think he's hanging around, though. He has a kind of ... sixth sense about these things. He and his men have been combing the woods and the outskirts of town, but there are a million places he could be hiding out."

"What about Scarlet Street? That's the only thing the victims seem to have in common." She grimaced down at the sheet-covered lump on her table. "That, and they're all scum."

"They're keeping an eye on the area. So am I." While the victims may have all been patrons of the prostitutes, it was impossible to know where they'd been killed. The first had been found between two downtown Dumpsters, the next in a field outside the city limits, and "Plug Daddy," had been unceremoniously tossed in a ditch on Frenchwood Lane, just a few blocks from Ethan's house. They'd all been miles from Scarlet Street.

And then, of course, there was missing Peddler Puck's worker, Rafe Santangelo, who Ethan had yet to viably connect to any of this. It was his feeling that the man's disappearance was somehow related; he just couldn't figure out how. *Probably, his body just hasn't been discovered yet.* But Rafe Santangelo, as far as Ethan could determine, had no record and no association with Scarlet Street.

Still, after Bert Holloway, the odds couldn't be ignored. Ethan wished he could shut down Scarlet Street. When he'd tried before, the prostitutes had simply taken to other streets and worse: public parks. No, shutting down the street wouldn't do any good. "I wish this town had a shelter," he said for the hundredth time.

Sheila stepped beside him and slipped an arm around his waist. "Enough of this morbid stuff. How about spinach ravioli for dinner?"

This snapped him back. "That sounds incredible."

"And maybe some champagne." The suggestion in Sheila's eyes brought a pleasant rush of warmth to Ethan's cheeks. And other places. She pecked a kiss on the edge of his jaw. "I like you when you're scruffy."

"I didn't get a chance to shave."

"Have you talked to Sydney, by the way?"

At that, his growing enthusiasm shriveled right up. "I haven't."

"Maybe I'll stop by and see how she's doing."

Ethan sighed. "I wish you wouldn't."

"Why's that?"

Ethan hesitated. *Where to begin?* "She's not as sweet as you think she is." He hoped she wouldn't ask for examples. He didn't want to relive the myriad humiliations of being married to Sydney. Like the day he came home to find she'd burned all of his sweaters because she'd decided knitting wasn't a manly pastime - or how she'd maxed out his credit card, twice, ordering holy knickknacks from *The God Club's* online catalogue, all allegedly blessed by Reverend Bobby Felcher himself.

As it turned out, he didn't need to mention any of this. Sheila laughed and said, "I don't think she's sweet at all. She doesn't fool me."

Ethan sighed relief. He should have known Sheila saw through the woman.

"I do feel a little sorry for her though," she continued. "I just thought maybe it would be a good gesture if we made sure she's doing all right." She paused. "But Ethan, if you don't want me to-"

"No, no. It's fine. Really." Ethan realized he was being cynical, unforgiving. Sheila was neither of those things and he loved her for it. He pulled her close and kissed her forehead. "If it'll make you happy, go ahead and stop by."

"If you're sure."

"I am." Another kiss, this one on the lips. "You're a better person than I am, Sheila. A bit too optimistic perhaps, but I wouldn't want you any other way."

Sheila broke from his embrace, retrieved his Smokey hat from the rack, and put it on his head at a rakish angle. She gave him another kiss and said, "Now, get. I've got work to do." She swatted him on the behind as he headed for the door.

22

THE GREAT BOOK BRAWL OF INCENSE AVENUE

*A*fter his shower, Cade had planned to eat a spoon of peanut butter, but he'd fallen asleep. He hadn't even been lying down - he woke with his head on the back of the couch, mouth open, spoon and peanut butter jar forgotten at his side. Purrcy had taken advantage of the situation and licked the spoon clean then curled up on his lap for a nap of his own.

If any nightmares had come, Cade didn't remember them, and as he woke, he hoped the trend would continue. He glanced at the clock. "Shit." After grabbing his keys, he pushed down his hair, and headed back to work.

Business at the Labyrinth was steady during the summer months, but book sales slowed way down once fall arrived, making Dora's psychic readings the main source of income. When he returned, Dora disappeared into the reading room with a client. Cade manned the front desk, plugging books into inventory on the computer. It was a tedious task but the monotony soothed his anxious, scattered mind.

He'd been late returning but Dora didn't lecture him about punctuality. Cade apologized anyway and got to work. He wasn't trying to be a dick - his job at the bookstore was the only thing keeping him sane - but he just couldn't seem to get his shit together. It was the lack of sleep.

Because of the nightmares.

They kept him up till all hours.

He was thinking of them when a customer, a twenty-something jerk in motorcycle-cop sunglasses and a leather jacket, approached the desk and slapped down a copy of Daphne du Maurier's *The Birds and Other Stories.* "Explain to me," he said in clipped tones, "how you justify charging more for this book now than when it was published in 1952." He jabbed a finger at the printed price on the cover of the book.

Cade blinked at him. "1952?"

"Yep. You're charging literally almost ten times as much for it now. And it's used!"

"Well ... it's been over fifty years, so ... inflation and all that." *Is this guy serious?*

"I'm not paying any more for it than it says right here." He jabbed at the original price.

"I can't sell this to you for thirty-five cents, sir. Our used paperbacks are all two-ninety-nine."

"I'm not paying that."

Cade stared. "I can't sell it for anything but two-ninety-nine." And that was true. Dora had made that very clear; she didn't haggle with customers.

"But that's ridiculous!"

Cade shrugged.

"Even if it were ninety-nine cents, that's still not fair, but at least it's *reasonable.*"

"Two-ninety-nine for a used paperback in good condition is not unreasonable, sir."

"Well, *that's* subjective. I am *not* paying that much." He stood there, unwilling to bend, nostrils flaring, eyes no doubt blazing behind the mirrored glasses.

"Then I guess I can't help you." Cade looked back to the computer screen and kept working.

"That's it? That's the extent of your customer service ability?"

"I guess so."

"This is bullshit!" His voice carried through the entire store and he slammed a fist on the desk, startling Cade.

"Look, sir, I'm sorry but it's two-ninety-"

"Fucking California!" The guy's cheeks burned red and spittle flew from his mouth. "In Missouri, this would *never* happen. In Missouri-"

"As I'm sure you're aware, sir, this isn't Missouri." Cade's skin hummed with barely-contained rage now. "And thank God for *that*," he mumbled under his breath.

The haggler spoke in grave tones. "I want to speak with your manager. Right. Now." He punctuated the last syllables with a finger-jab on the desk.

"She's with a client. If you'd care to wait-"

"No. No, I will *not* wait!"

Cade's temper was a rabid pit bull on a threadbare leash. His voice shook with anger. "Then there's nothing I can do for you, sir. I-"

"Listen to me, you little faggot, and listen good." The guy leaned in, speaking through gritted teeth. "I will *not* be taken advantage of by some highfalutin' California queer like you. *Capiche?*" Then he paused in mid-sneer, cocking his head. "Hey, aren't you the guy whose girlfriend was murdered? I saw it in the paper. Your brother killed her, right? Or maybe it was *you*."

That's when Cade snapped.

His fist smashed into the guy's nose, rocking his head back and sending his glasses flying. The man staggered back, bleeding through his fingers as Cade hurdled over the desk, knocking books down and sending paperwork flying. He lunged at the guy and both collapsed onto the floor. Cade got hold of him and continued pounding and punching and screaming. "Fuck you!" His fists came down hard against the man's face, the side of his head. "Fuck you!" And Cade was swept away, riding the wave of fury like a ship on a storm-rocked sea. As he pummeled, slideshow thoughts flashed across his mind, thoughts of Brooks, of the vampires, of Samantha, of everything that had been taken from him, of everything that he hated. "Fuck you!"

He took a hard hit to the face, then another, but the other man never gained advantage. "Fuck you!" Cade's fists hammered and pounded like machines.

A scream as Dora Langley tore out of the back office. "Cade!"

But he barely heard her. "Fuck you!" Now he had his hands in the haggler's hair. "Ugh, oomph, ouch, fuck," said the man as Cade slammed his head onto the hardwood floor.

Dora's voice: "Stop this! Now! *Stop!*"

Cade didn't stop. He took an elbow to the lip. Stacks of books lining the aisles toppled and crashed as the man twisted around onto his belly and tried to drag himself to freedom.

Cade kept hitting, his fists coming down on the back of the man's head - and then Dora was at him, trying to drag him off, but he was fastened to the guy like Velcro, hitting, hitting, screaming, screaming, unaware of the tears and blood that ran down his face. "Fuck you! Fuck you, you son a bitch!"

"SON OF A BITCH!" BACK AT THE SHERIFF'S STATION, IN THE BREAK room, Ethan stared at the television screen, transfixed by the bright flapping purple-painted lips of national news anchor woman, Paula Papadopoulos, as she regaled the entire nation with the details of the Crimson Cove murders. "Son of a bitch!" His voice echoed through the room and within seconds - surprise, surprise - the phone began ringing. He shot to his feet, fuming, his hands clenched hard at his sides. He'd hoped this wouldn't happen. Now that it had, all eyes would be on Crimson Cove. Particularly on the Sheriff's Department.

Dwayne Purkiss, out of breath, threw open the break room door. "Got an emergency, Sheriff."

"You can say that again, Purkiss."

The large man frowned. "A brawl on Incense, er, Ensign Avenue."

Ethan blinked. "A brawl?"

Purkiss nodded, his multiple chins quivering. "At Langley's Literary Labyrinth. Sounds bad."

Ethan's eyes went wide. "The bookstore?"

More nods. "The manager just called. Looks like the Colter kid went apeshit on a customer and is beating the piss out of him as we speak."

Ethan swiped his Smokey hat off the table and brushed past Purkiss. "Son of a bitch!"

BY THE TIME ETHAN ARRIVED, BOTH BLEEDING MEN HAD BEEN separated by Dora Langley who, like a WWF referee in flowing gypsy garb, had somehow managed to intervene, sending each offender to his own corner. The bookstore, which was a shambles in the first place, now looked as if a tornado had touched ground.

He was in no mood for more drama. Pointedly ignoring Cade, who hunched in a chair with a swollen eye, his knuckles as bloody as the nose beneath the wad of paper towels, Ethan dragged the other man - who'd fared far worse than his opponent - to the back room where, over a ridiculous crystal ball at Dora's fortune-telling table, he took down the man's statement.

The man, a Justin Morse from St. Louis, was hellbent on pressing charges which, from what Ethan could tell, he had every right to do. But after explaining in vague terms what Cade had recently been through, Ethan talked the guy down. Of course, it helped that Mr. Morse was hiding an armload of bench warrants. The man did not press charges and Ethan let him go. He would not, however, be so easy on Colter. Emerging from the office, he headed toward Cade, his jaw set.

Cade, stanching his bloody nose, watched as Justin Morse stomped out of the bookstore and out of their lives. "You're just letting him *go?*" Cade stood, incredulous. "But he-"

"Yes, I am," Ethan interrupted.

"But-"

"Go get in my car. Now."

"Huh?" Confusion and shock vied for supremacy on the kid's swollen, bloodied face.

"*Now.*" Ethan's tone was flat, low, and very clearly stated there would be no bullshit, and after a beat, Cade obeyed and stomped out, slamming the door behind him.

Ethan turned to Dora Langley, who was righting fallen books and collecting strewn papers. "I take it this is the first time something like this has happened?"

Dora stood, plastic hoop earrings swaying - *clickety-clack* - as she nodded. "Yes. I don't tolerate this kind of behavior and he well knows it!" Her frizzy hair was that faded in-between color - not quite blond, not quite brown; the color of indecision and procrastination.

"I'm sure he knows," said Ethan.

Dora stepped closer, her long skirts whispering as her whipcord body moved. "Sheriff." Her grating voice was hard to take but the concern in her eyes was genuine. "I know Cade's been through a lot but … I've had it up to *here* with him!" She gestured, junk bracelets jangling and clanking. "That young man used to be the light of this store! I think people used to come in just to see him! And he was just so nice and *so* handsome. But now … well …" A dark cloud doused the fire in her raccoon-wide eyes. "I don't know how to help him," she went on, softer now. "He comes in late, unbathed and unshaved. He's unfocused … and now … now, he's fighting with customers." She looked as if she might cry. "I don't even know if I can keep him on after this."

"I understand." Ethan, too, was running out of patience with the kid, and this was the final straw.

"Maybe there's someone he could talk to or-"

"Let me try to handle it." Ethan had a plan. And he knew Cade was going to hate it. *Oh, well.* "I'll be in touch."

"Thank you, Sheriff." Dora Langley chewed the end of her finger, looking distraught.

Ethan tipped his hat to her and headed out.

Inside the cruiser, Cade sat in the passenger seat, paper towel pressed to his nose, looking sulky. His lips were already swollen. They reminded Ethan of tires with too much air in them.

Ethan started the engine, put his seatbelt on, and turned off Ensign Avenue. He drove in silence a few moments, waiting for his anger to ebb enough that he could speak, but it was Cade who finally broke the quiet.

"Where are you taking me?" His voice was nasal and muffled behind the paper towel.

"Well, first, I'm taking you home where you're going to clean yourself up," said Ethan.

"I don't need-"

"The hell you don't. You're bleeding. You look like the wrath of God, son."

"Gee, thanks a-"

"After that," Ethan interrupted, "we're stopping at the station to drop off the cruiser. And *then* you and I are taking a little trip to Santa Cruz."

"Santa Cruz? Why?"

Ethan kept his eyes on the road. "You're going to a meeting." He turned onto Main. "Grief recovery."

"What? No! I don't want-"

With a violent jerk, Ethan veered the cruiser to the side of the road, braking in front of the Ancient Ways Occult Shop. He turned, leveled his hard gaze on Cade, and when he spoke, his voice was edged with rage. "Fine. You don't want to go? Your other option is court-ordered anger management. Those are your choices, son. Take your pick."

"But that guy didn't even press charges! He-"

"You either go to this meeting in Santa Cruz or *I'll* press charges and a judge will take it from there."

Cade's eyes darkened, narrowed, and brimmed with naked fury. "But *he* started it. He-"

"And *you* threw the first punch. In the eyes of the law, that makes *you* the aggressor."

Cade sputtered, then shouted, "Well, the *law* is fucking bullshit!"

Ethan shrugged. "Look, I don't even give a shit who threw the first punch at this point. You need help, Cade." His voice softened now, the anger bleeding out. "You're not yourself. You need to talk to someone. You haven't made any effort to attend the meetings and you said-"

"I said I wasn't making any promises."

"Well, you're going." Ethan watched as Cade's rancor withered. In its place came something sober, something desperate - a vulnerability that made him look like a little boy. Tears filled his bruised eyes and dripped down his cheeks. He hung his head as a sob hitched in his throat.

And Ethan felt lower than pond scum. Was he doing the right thing? He thought so.

Cade wiped his eyes and sniffed, the bloody paper towel wadded in his hand.

"There will be other people there who have lost someone they loved. I think it'll give you some perspective. You don't even have to say anything. I just want you to go in and listen."

Defeated, Cade nodded.

"They have two meetings a week, both at six o'clock. I want you to attend a few of them. I'll even go in with you if that's what you want." He dreaded the thought but was willing to do it if it meant Cade would get help. Ethan reached over and gave the kid's shoulder a squeeze. "It won't be as bad as you think."

Cade remained silent, all out of rage. He just sat there, head hung, tears dripping.

"Now let's go get you cleaned up." And while Cade was doing that, Ethan would call the group in Santa Cruz to let them know they could expect one, possibly two, new attendees tonight.

23

GRIEVING IS BELIEVING

*E*than pulled up to a large Victorian at the end of the street. "Last house on the left."

"It's in someone's *house*?" Cade had been expecting a church or community center, and that was bad enough, but this - someone's actual home - made it worse, more *intimate*.

"Looks like." Ethan parked the Wrangler on the street - to Cade's dismay, the driveway was already full. "So, you want me to come in with you?"

Cade shook his head. "I'm all right." But he made no move to exit the vehicle.

"You sure?"

Cade nodded, wondering how bad he looked. His whole face hurt like hell. "I'd rather go alone."

"You got it. I'll wait here."

But still, Cade didn't move. "I'm sorry about this, Ethan. I mean, that you have to deal with all this. I know you have other stuff you'd rather be doing. I didn't mean for what happened to ... happen. I was just *so* mad, you know?"

Ethan nodded. "I'll say this: You gave that guy one hell of a pounding. If I weren't so pissed, I'd be proud." He tried a smile.

"He asked for it."

"No doubt. But the thing is ..." Ethan cleared his throat. "This has to stop. Enough's enough. You can't just sit in sorrow and fester. If you don't start doing constructive, healthy things, you're never going to get better." He nodded at the old Victorian. "And I think this may be a good place to start."

"Maybe."

"I want you to give it a fair shot. Keep your mind open."

"I'll try."

Ethan looked at his watch. "Better get in there."

Cade exited the Wrangler, and made his way up the steps. His heart took great, clumsy leaps in his chest as he pressed the bell and waited. Glancing back at Ethan, Cade realized he was lucky that someone cared enough to bother with him. His own brother obviously didn't. Ethan was as close to family as he had now. And would ever have again.

He grimaced when he caught his reflection in the door's glass. His face was all bruises, cuts, and contusions. A blood-crusted gash through his lip. He was ready to say *fuck it* and turn right back around when the door swung open and a friendly-looking woman smiled at him. Her gaze flickered only momentarily over the ruin of his face, then quickly went back to his eyes. Well *eye*; only one was open and functioning. "You must be Cadence."

"I ... yeah. But just call me Cade, please."

"I'm Sara. Sara Delaney." The woman led him into the living room where about a dozen other people either sat or stood, looking somber. Some didn't seem to notice him, some stared at him outright, but most had the good manners to look away - just a little too quickly - from his swollen, battered features.

The diversity of the group surprised Cade: there was an Asian couple, a well-dressed black couple, and several singles of either gender. One couple stood out to him in particular, probably because of the woman's face. Though gaunt and pale like her husband's, her eyes were haunted by a pain-filled hopelessness that seemed to vibrate off her. She sat on a loveseat next to her despondent husband, hands twisting around a tissue, eyes downcast.

Cade scanned the group for a common bond among them. They'd all lost a loved one but beyond that, they appeared to have nothing in common. A space had been held for Cade on a large sofa and he lowered himself into it, next to a strikingly pretty black woman who sat rigidly erect, hands clasped tight in her lap. She smelled vaguely of cinnamon.

He felt eyes on him, and knew why. *I probably look like I got kicked down a dirt road.* He caught the gaze of a guy roughly his own age leaning forward in a folding chair near the piano. Smiling would split his lip open - not to mention, he wasn't sure grinning was appropriate grief support group behavior - so Cade nodded. The guy nodded back.

"This is our phone list," said Sara, holding up a notebook. "I'm going to pass it around. If you'd like to add your name and number, please do. If you don't want to, feel free to pass. We do this so that we can contact each other between meetings if we need to talk." She pushed a curl of dark hair from her cheek. "If someone's story resonates and you'd like to talk with them more, you can get their number from this, which we'll leave on the desk, at the end of the meeting." She handed the notebook to the man next to her. He wrote on it and passed it to his neighbor.

"We don't really have a group leader," continued Sara, "but since there are several new faces tonight, I guess I'll start." She sat down in a folding chair, her slender frame like a wisp of smoke in her long, gray skirt. "There's no judgment in this room. I encourage you all to freely say what you think and what you feel, knowing that someone here has felt or thought the same thing at some point. We shed a lot of tears some nights, but we often battle the darkness with humor." She looked around the room. "Anger, too, and that's okay. God knows there's plenty of anger. But this is a safe space. The only rule here is to be good to one another." She paused, looking at each member in turn. "What's important is that each of you know you're not alone, that life can and *will* get better. There's healing to be had. There's life after the death of our loved ones, and everyone here has gone through or is going through what you are."

"Hear, hear," said a man in a black turtleneck who sat on the stone fireplace hearth.

"We usually start with introductions, telling a little bit about why we're here, but first I'd like to share some news." She looked torn between joy and despair. "They've caught Jennifer's killer." Her face crumpled. "After nine long years, they've caught my little girl's killer."

"Oh, Sara." The woman next to Cade stood and wrapped her in a tight hug. Sara collapsed into it and Cade's discomfort sharpened. He felt like a voyeur, witnessing something private. Several others spoke up then, offering an odd, clumsy mix of condolences and semi-congratulations.

"It's a mixed bag," Sara said when the group silenced. "On one hand, it's a relief. It's *justice*. But on the other hand ... well, it doesn't change anything, does it?" She dabbed her eyes with a tissue. "It doesn't bring my baby back."

Introductions and sharing began, starting with Muriel, the regally beautiful black woman sitting next to Cade. He listened as she told the group about her younger sister's murder. She spoke the same way she carried herself: rigid and dignified. Strong.

Others were not so composed. Some cried. One woman was only able to speak in a whisper, her voice quaking as much as her hands. But Cade listened closely, putting his heart into it, as the members introduced themselves and spoke of whom they'd lost.

What hit Cade the hardest were the stories about children, some lost to disease, others runaway teens, some found murdered, others never found at all. These last, Cade thought, were probably the worst. As black as his own despair was, he couldn't fathom not knowing if your child was alive or dead, happy or hurting. The notebook came to him and Cade added his name and number to the list, riveted by one man's story about his drug-addicted runaway teen daughter who'd wound up murdered for the sixteen dollars in her pocket.

He was beginning to feel out of place, like the death of a mere girl-friend might seem a mockery to the parents grieving their children, but when Kendon, the guy about Cade's age, revealed the death of his boyfriend, no one looked at him funny; no one seemed to question the depth of his grief. Cade was relaxing a little, but when Kendon revealed how his boyfriend was killed - attacked in an alley by some wild animal - Cade felt the blood drain from his face and he looked down at his hands. Even his fingernails had turned white.

The cinnamon-scented woman next to him, Muriel, laid a hand over his and gave it a too-familiar pat, and Cade felt bad for wishing she hadn't. The hugs and hand pats were going to take some getting used to.

Kendon wrapped up and the group moved on, but Cade couldn't focus on their stories. His mind was on Kendon's boyfriend, attacked by a wild animal. The man had been brutalized, mauled, torn, and shredded. *Just like Samantha.*

When it came time for Cade to speak, he panicked. He wasn't sure how to start. Every eye in the room bored into him like hot little pokers and Cade went squirmy inside. The group was patient with him, giving him small nods of encouragement and finally, in a shaking voice, he told them about Samantha. Said she was the first victim of the bear attacks in Crimson Cove, which everyone had heard about. As he spoke, he glanced at Kendon, who's eyes narrowed with interest.

Muriel, the woman next to Cade, also seemed too curious. Something about the way she stiffened told him she was listening hard, dissecting his words with microsurgical precision. Cade hurried on, fumbling as he rushed through the story, glossing over the details of the brief - and mostly dishonest - story of Samantha's death. When he was finished, he glanced at Kendon. The guy's gaze flickered to Muriel and again, something in the woman's posture shifted. Though he could only see her peripherally, Cade knew she was returning Kendon's look. Something was passing between them and Cade didn't like it.

The group, realizing he was finished, smiled at him, and began murmuring their support. They understood, they said. He was in the right place. Welcome to the group. Cade was surrounded in a warm bubble of support. It should have felt nice, but it didn't. It was violating. Cade's story was a lie - well, most of it, anyway - and he feared being exposed. He cut another guilty glance toward Kendon, who was absorbed in the next story.

Someone handed Cade more tissues. He didn't see who. Unable to bear any more loving, supportive looks, he'd turned his attention back to his hands.

But invariably, his eyes swept back to Kendon. Something about the way the guy had looked at him earlier, as if he - and Muriel - saw through Cade's story, made him uneasy ... and when the meeting was called to a close, Cade wasted no time getting out of there.

24

CRYPTEASE

Night had fallen.

Obviously, Scythe wouldn't be getting any alone time with the stripper named DeHavalyn, and waiting for Gretchen to get presentable enough to fuck was like watching the world's slowest striptease. *Or, rather,* he thought, *cryptease. Heh.* He grinned at his own wit.

Sitting on his air mattress, he watched her in the near-darkness, noting her improvement. While she'd looked like a mummified cadaver before, she'd now advanced into aging-crone territory. It wasn't exactly enough to rotate the angle of the dangle, but with every passing night, the idea of unleashing Vlad the Impaler and giving it to her good and hard grew less revolting.

And just lately Gretchen had been giving him that look, the one that said she was getting randy, too. He half hoped she'd hold off another week or two - he wasn't into hag-humping - but after a year, he didn't care how fucking ugly she was; as soon as she said the word he knew he'd be on her like a hobo on a ham sandwich.

He reached down and adjusted his massive erection, gratified, as always, by the feel of its impressive length and girth in his hand. *Christ! Hurry up and get hot, Gretchen!* He let out a frustrated sigh.

And Gretchen's painstakingly slow progress wasn't the only thing gnawing on his nerves. They'd acquired even more blood slaves and the cavern was getting as tight as a virgin sucking a lemon. Scythe was constantly tripping over this one or that one and it was getting increasingly difficult to keep his cool.

There was good news, though. One by one, they'd been acclimating the slaves to Gretchen's venom - in the past days, she'd finally been able to produce some small amounts - and as her poison infiltrated their systems, the slaves' loyalty would shift to her and away from Scythe, who'd been dosing them nightly up till now. He was getting real sick and tired of being stared at by the human equivalent of lovestruck puppy dogs, especially because, by now, the slaves were getting addicted to the venom and it was beginning to show. They were starting to look like heroin addicts with their hollow eyes and gaunt faces. They were even getting that junkie smell to them - like something inside of them was rotting. And in this case, it really was. That's what venom did - killed the body slowly, cell by cell.

But things were returning to normal, and soon, Scythe thought, Gretchen's group would be back among the living - as it were. He just had to get through the next little while without losing his shit.

He'd do this by focusing on the positives. And there were plenty of positives. In the past couple of weeks, he'd begun to see signs that all of them were preparing for a return to civilization: Scythe had gotten a new pair of gleaming patent leather biker boots, some new wife beaters - the kind that stretched perilously thin across his muscles - and some pomade for his hair.

Jazminka now frequently returned from her trips to town with fabrics and other materials and had begun tailoring clothes again. She'd made a new pair of the thigh-high boots she was famous for. The woman was incurably addicted to big, complicated come-fuck-me boots, and was well-known among the local vampires for her ability to kill a man in six seconds or less - without spilling a drop of blood - with a single high kick of her stiletto-sharp heels. Scythe was glad to see that the boots were back but he couldn't help thinking they made her look like a steampunk prostitute.

It was a good sign, though. He'd known things were really getting serious, however, when she'd begun wearing her dark, swooping, warrior-like makeup and combing her hair straight up again, as if it were screaming off her scalp. This, with the addition of new boots, did nothing to improve her ongoing battle with the hanging lanterns.

Most exciting of all, Gretchen was giving off signals that life in the cave was coming to a close. She'd had Jazminka mend her red corset - the one made from Gretchen's dead mother's bones - and had started fussing with her appearance a little in a mirror that Jazminka had brought back from town. Occasionally, in her croaking crone's voice, she even mentioned new ideas for the eventual reopening of the Crimson Corset. Instead of female stripper mermaids in the great glassed-in water tanks in the club's main bar, she mused that perhaps they could draw a stronger female clientele by training some of the men to strip-swim for the patron's pleasure.

Scythe suspected her reasons for wanting to do this had something to do with her general anger toward the male sex - which had undoubtedly worsened since Michael and his men had staked her. When it came to swinging dicks, Gretchen had an especially wide sadistic streak, and Scythe shuddered to think what humiliations she had planned for him.

And there would be plenty, he was sure, for the only male exempt from her sexual savagery was her old business partner, Emeric. She frequently spoke of locating the old sack of bones now, and Scythe resented that, but he tried not to think about it. *Freedom is fast approaching*, he reminded himself - and he couldn't wait to taste it.

And with all the new recruits, it wouldn't be hard getting around Michael Ward's group. *They'd be idiots to fuck with an army this size.*

But Scythe had a feeling that wouldn't stop them. He only hoped that Gretchen would soon turn the blood slaves, and then she'd have *real* Loyals. Vampires, not a bunch of venom-addicted humans.

And watching Gretchen as she sat on her mattress in the shadows, her gaze intent and far away, he was certain this was her plan.

25

KICKING AND SCREAMING

*L*eda Marlene Murrow, known on Scarlet Street as Screamin' Leda, led her gentleman friend into a shadow-blackened alley between two empty shops which were currently occupied by other girls and their clients. The buildings had mattresses but she liked doing business on her feet; things moved quicker in a standing position.

Screamin' Leda had earned her moniker not only for her sexual vocals but because in her former life, she'd been a voice-over actress who could shriek bloody murder with the best of them: Sissy Spacek, Jamie Lee Curtis, Maisy Hart, and Delilah Devine had nothing on Leda in her heyday. Her screams could be heard in a respectable array of outdated horror movies.

But Leda had never managed to break into the movies. She was bombshell-beautiful, but couldn't act her way out of a wet paper sack. So after a decade, she'd gone back to Crimson Cove, her hometown.

But she hadn't returned to her childhood home alone. The excesses of Hollywood life - the pills, the coke, and the heroin were her constant companions and no mere change of scenery could have pried Leda from the hungry, insistent grip of her addictions. In Crimson Cove, unlike Hollywood, you didn't just make a phone call or go to a party to get high. In a town like Crimson Cove, you had to *work* for your fix - this had been part of the appeal when she'd first returned home; naively, she'd thought inaccessibility alone would keep her clean.

But those illusions were soon shattered.

For a while, she'd worked the floor at Joan's Jewelry on Ensign Avenue, but when she was caught swiping a tennis bracelet to fund a fix, everything changed and finding honest work was impossible. When her car was repossessed and her landlord was threatening eviction, Leda decided to use her God-given assets to keep a roof over her head.

When she'd met the other working girls on Scarlet Street Leda realized she'd found her tribe. These women were her sisters. They'd taken her in, shown her the ropes, and despite public opinion, they were good, decent people.

Though many girls - and guys - had come and gone, a core group remained on Scarlet Street. That group was comprised of four women and two men, each named for either his or her sexual specialties - as were the cases of Bareback Danny, Reacharound Joe, and herself, Screamin' Leda - or some distinguishing characteristic or defining past experience. Roach Clip Rachel was named for her love of pot, Barbwire Jane for the barbed wire tattoos that snaked around her legs, and Cyanide Suzi, the tiny Asian beauty who was rumored to have replaced an abusive ex-boyfriend's coke with the deadly poison.

The Lifers, they called themselves, and Screamin' Leda was part of that tiny society.

She was on high alert as she and her client slipped into the darkness of the alley. There was a killer on the loose, and the Lifers knew it was no bear. It was a man - Rachel had seen him. But so far, he'd only attacked abusive johns, leaving the hustlers or whores alone.

Rachel's description of the killer had been vague: Pretty tall, broad shoulders, short or slicked-back hair of indeterminate color. It wasn't much to go on, but he'd been several yards away and Rachel had just taken the buckle end of the belt from an especially violent client

THE SILVER DAGGER

named Nessie, who, apparently, was the killer's intended victim. And kill him, he had. It'd been all over the papers.

Still, Leda was cautious. The man who now shoved a hand into her panties and rooted around as if in search of a dropped peanut was a stranger to her, but she was pretty sure she'd seen him before with Barbwire Jane and, as far as Leda knew, it had been business as usual.

"Take it easy," said Leda, after the guy tugged down her panties, spun her around, and shoved her hard against the brick wall.

"Shut the fuck up." The man clinked and fumbled with his belt.

"Fine, but if you want it rough, that costs extra."

"I said, shut the fuck up!"

Leda felt the explosive blow of his giant fist to the back of her head, pain rocking her from all sides as her face smacked the brick. Simultaneously, he shoved himself inside her.

His fist was in her hair now, gripping tight. "Just. Shut. The. Fuck. UP!" And with each syllable, he smacked her head into the wall hard enough she teetered on the brink of unconsciousness.

There was just enough awareness in her to do the only thing she could, the thing that had - almost - made her famous. Leda screamed. She screamed as if she were in a Hollywood studio, tasked with convincing a worldwide audience that the danger was real, and god damn, it was close. Her shrieks shrilled down the mouth of the alley, ricocheted off the abandoned buildings, and ripped the quiet night open like an infected wound.

As her head swam, the man was suddenly yanked off of her, out of her. Her knees buckled and she hit the ground hard, but that pain was just a flick of the Bic to the wildfire of agony in her head. She realized she was sobbing as warm blood dripped into her eyes. Then she was aware of the men - scuffling shadows, grunts, the swing of a leg, the hammer of a fist. It wasn't Danny or Joe beating her client, it was someone Leda had never seen, someone she couldn't make out through the blur of blood and throb of pain.

A quick pistoning of fists, a rapid-fire *rat-tat-tat* of blows to the john's face, then the assailant did something Leda had never seen in her life, not even in the horror movies that had borrowed her screams: He crouched over the unconscious john and ripped the man's throat open with his bare teeth.

Blood sputtered and flew as he clawed at the john's shirt, his chest, tearing away flesh and digging inside to pry the ribcage apart. The crack and pop of breaking bone was followed by gristly sounds of mastication as the attacker buried his face in the blood-wet cavern of the open torso.

Leda never stopped screaming her Hollywood scream and this, she thought later, was probably what brought the madman to his senses.

He looked at her.

And she looked at him.

Not a glance, but full on, and even as her vision swam and her mind reeled and her body quaked with terror, she memorized the face behind the mask of blood. Not because she had the wherewithal in that moment to consider such things as lineups and police sketches, but because right then, he was the only thing she could see. And she knew that even if she squeezed her eyes shut, he'd still be there, burned onto her corneas like an afterimage of the sun.

26

HOME BITTER HOME

When the cravings came, they came strong, but at least now there were nights that Brooks Colter and Rafe Santangelo were somewhat satisfied with the blood of wildlife. It was, Rafe imagined, like detoxing from drugs.

In the weeks they'd spent together in the dilapidated cabin, Rafe had come to think of Brooks as his brother, and in many ways, it was as if they were married, finishing each other's sentences and reading those silent cues invisible to all but longtime life partners. Sometimes they even bickered like an old married couple.

But most of all, Rafe and Brooks were friends, and whether it was simply because they'd been stuck in the cabin alone together for too long or because Brooks was his Maker or a little of both, Rafe had developed an undying loyalty to Brooks, a respect and admiration that rivaled any son's devotion to his father.

Rafe's only complaint was the hunger, and he knew it wore on Brooks as well - probably even more so because Brooks *had* tasted human blood. But they got by, and Brooks had some pretty effective strategies to stave off the gnawing need to feed.

During their first week in the cabin, they'd begun ripping up the rotted floorboards in the bedroom, hollowing out two spaces in the earth - a bed for each of them. Sleeping in the ground, Brooks said, would ease their cravings because of the calming minerals and ores natural to the soil of Crimson Cove. This was something Brooks said he'd learned from a vampire named Michael last year before his own transition. The idea had worked. Rafe never felt so calm as when he was entombed in his earth-bed, clearing his mind with some simple meditations Brooks had suggested. Sometimes at night, when the cravings were bad, Rafe went there to lie down and always emerged with renewed self-control.

But a proper feeding, Rafe knew, was eventual. While he had yet to imbibe human blood - and complete his transition - reversing the process was out of the question. First, he could not, *would* not, kill Brooks, and second, he liked what he'd become. He'd spent a lot of time contemplating how he might obtain human blood and become a full vampire without violence. Oddly, he had no moral objection to killing now - there was plenty of scum that the world would be better off without - but he respected Brooks' chosen way of life. Rafe thought that if he could get some blood from the hospital, that would do the trick. Brooks said it would, but he was still adamant that Rafe shouldn't be hasty, that he should wait to be sure full vampirism was what he really wanted.

But this was *exactly* what Rafe wanted. In his human life, he'd had no hope, but as a vampire, he had plenty. Being a vampire, even a *half* vampire, had changed him on a molecular level - changed him for the better. Rafe experienced contentment and self-confidence for the first time in his life. It could only get better from here, but there was no telling Brooks that.

Tonight, after taking sustenance from a family of opossums that had nested beneath the cabin, Rafe and Brooks used Scythe's old deck of cards to pass the time with a game of poker. Over the weeks, they'd acquired other means of entertainment: Clue and Monopoly board games stolen from Peddler Puck's, some jigsaw puzzles, and a vast supply of books. Rafe had also acquired a small collection of dirty magazines - *real* magazines which he was delighted and surprised to find in circulation in these days of internet porn and adult chat rooms. Along with his other appetites, Rafe's new state had brought his sex drive to the boiling point, and there were nights he would have given anything for just one hour with a woman. But for now, the magazines would suffice.

They'd also acquired new shoes and clothing, and some sparse home furnishings to make the place more livable - a couple of area rugs, some pillows for their earth-beds, and a few colorful prints to brighten the rotting walls. They'd looted an assortment of toiletries, too - colognes, shampoos, and body washes - for their trips to Scarlet Falls, where they bathed several times a week.

Brooks, in a hoodie, had heisted most of the stolen items himself. On one of their earliest trips to town, they'd seen MISSING flyers for Rafe. Neither could risk being seen but Rafe's face was all over town.

When they tired of cards and board games Brooks and Rafe occupied themselves old-school-style with hours-long sessions of *Would You Rather?* and *What If?* These games of Q&A led to long talks and those conversations had knitted the two as closely together as fraternal twins. Though both men had been guarded in the beginning, now it wasn't unusual for them to discuss just about anything.

Except Rafe's past.

"Brooks and Cadence," said Rafe. "Those are unusual names. Good names, but unusual."

Brooks shrugged. "My parents were unusual people, I guess."

"You haven't said much about them." Rafe rearranged his cards, realized he had a winning hand.

"Haven't I?"

Rafe laid his cards down. "Full house."

Brooks set his own cards aside. "My dad was a cop. He got shot after pulling a guy over for speeding. Turned out the dude was a big time drug dealer. Just a case of the wrong place, the wrong time." He lifted his shoulder in a half-hearted shrug, a forced show of stoicism.

"How old were you?"

"I was sixteen. Cade was ten."

"That sucks."

"It did." Brooks sat against the wall, drawing his legs up and resting his elbows on his knees. "We did all right though. My mom was in real estate and did a good job taking care of us. She never remarried. I don't think she ever got over Dad." A smile lifted one corner of his mouth. "For a long time, I wanted to be a cop. I think Cade did, too."

"Why didn't you?"

Another shrug. "Life just took us different ways. I was better at fixing cars. Cade liked writing." His eyes lit up. "He wrote a book, did I tell you that?"

"You did," said Rafe.

Brooks looked down. "He's got real talent." His face, half-concealed in shadow, hung in the darkness like a half moon.

"Do you still see your mom?" asked Rafe.

"She's dead, too." The words poisoned the air around him. "It was ugly. Cancer. She was in Gilroy with Cade. Afterward, he came to live with me in Crimson Cove. All we had left was each other."

A weak, "Sorry about that, man," was all Rafe could offer, and that sounded lukewarm, trite even.

"It is what it is."

For several minutes, the only sounds were the wind, the rustle of leaves in the trees outside, and the distant trickle of the stream a few yards from the cabin. Occasionally, a night bird called and Rafe's stomach rumbled with the growing hunger for blood.

Brooks smiled. "He was all arms and elbows, that kid."

"Cade?"

Brooks nodded. "I don't think he grew into them until he was almost twenty. He's a few inches shorter than me, but for a while there, I thought he'd never stop growing."

"Have you ever thought about ... you know, going back and talking to him?"

Brooks shook his head. "No. He hates me."

"But maybe you're wrong. Time heals and all that."

"I don't think so. I know him. This is different."

But Rafe could see that the idea of seeing his brother held some appeal.

Brooks continued staring at the floor. "Maybe one day." He looked up at Rafe. "What about you? Isn't there anyone you want to see?"

"Nope."

"No family?"

"A mom, a dad, and one brother, all total assholes."

Brooks laughed. "What about your girlfriend. Do you miss her?"

"*Ex*-girlfriend. And no. I don't miss her, not even a little."

"That bad, huh?"

Rafe made a noncommittal sound: "Meh." He wasn't sure he wanted to open that can of worms.

"It must've been bad," said Brooks, "given how eager you are to leave it all behind. But you must have *something* to go back to, right?"

"Nope." Rafe fell silent, but something inside him urged him on. "She cheated on me."

Brooks said, "That sucks, man. I'm sorry. I didn't mean to pry."

"With my brother."

"You're *shitting* me."

"I wish I were. It was humiliating." Rafe shifted, uncomfortable with the memories. "He's older than me and was pretty much all I had. My father's a milquetoast and my mom's a drunk. A real mean one, too. She used to beat the piss out of Ken - that's my brother - and me. Especially me. Ken was her favorite and she made no bones about showing it.

"She even opened up on my dad a few times. He never left her, I don't know why. It might sound kind of corny to say he's an 'abused husband' but I think that's exactly what he is. He's scared to death of her, that much is obvious. Anyway, long story short, my brother was my only real family, and he was my friend, too. Maybe even my best friend. But he was unhappy in his marriage, so ... well ..."

"So he hooked up with your *girlfriend*?" Brooks' eyes looked like they might bug right out of his head.

Rafe shrugged. "Fiancée, actually. We were engaged. I was an idiot not to see it. I was just thrilled they got along so well. Of course, I didn't realize *how* well they were getting along until one day when my mom called me, slurring her words at one-thirty in the afternoon. She said, 'You know your brother's fucking that bimbo of yours, don't you?'"

"Holy shit." Brooks looked equally riveted and revulsed.

"Yeah," said Rafe. "My mom got a call from Ken's wife. Apparently, she'd found texts between Katie and my brother and called my mom, losing her shit. I didn't believe it, of course - not until I saw the texts myself. I was stunned stupid. When I confronted my brother, he admitted it. So did Katie. Ken's wife intervened and he broke it off with Katie. Not that I care. I haven't spoken to any of them since."

"*Any* of them? Not even your mom or dad?"

"Especially not them." Rafe laughed; there was no humor in it. "I think the worst part of the whole thing was that my mom blamed *me* for it. She said it was my fault for bringing trash into their lives and ruining my brother's happiness. My dad, of course, just went along with it. '*Whatever you say, dear,*' that's my old man's only philosophy."

Brooks' face was a kaleidoscope of confusion, shock, and a hundred other things.

Rafe gave a tight smile, spread his hands, and said nothing. There was nothing more to be said and reliving it hadn't helped a bit. He felt hot, sick, and humiliated. His face had to be as red as a stop sign. He looked down at the space between his feet. "And you want to hear the really fucked up part? *That's* not even the reason I don't want to go back to my old life."

"It isn't?"

"No. I've gotten over all that. Fuck them, you know."

"Right, but ... then why don't you want to go back?"

Rafe ran a hand down his face; this part was even harder to talk about. "When I was thirteen I was diagnosed with a severe anxiety disorder. Some sort of PTSD. The shrink thought it was brought on by the punishments my mom used to dole out." His voice roughened. "No, they weren't just punishments - that makes it sound like I got grounded for getting bad grades or backhanded when I mouthed off.

What she did ... it was worse than that. *Much* worse. And it had nothing to do with my mouth or my grades." But Rafe wasn't going to get into all that. He couldn't go there.

"Anyway." He cleared his throat. "Over the years, the anxiety worsened. It's pretty much crippled me my whole life but these past couple of years it got so bad I could hardly leave my apartment. That's why I was working the graveyard at Peddler Puck's - because I was left to myself, I didn't have to interact - and even then, I couldn't always bring myself to leave the house. I started missing a lot of work."

"What about medication?" Brooks asked.

Rafe gave a bitter laugh. "I've been on every anti-anxiety and anti-depressant and anti-what-the-fuck-ever known to man. I've done group therapy, psychotherapy, hypnosis, cognitive behavioral therapy, and your basic run-of-the-mill counseling. I've even tried some of the really desperate shit - aromatherapy, color therapy, healing crystals, feng shui and, in an especially low moment, essential oils. I spent about five hundred bucks on those worthless oils and not only were they completely ineffectual, they didn't even smell good."

"Holy hell," said Brooks. "There must be *something* that would help, at least a little, anyway."

"Some of those things helped a little at first," said Rafe. "Some did nothing at all, and some made things worse - but none of them ever brought any real relief." He pinned Brooks in a sober gaze. "Do you have any idea what it's like to be out to dinner or sitting in a movie theater or even just hanging around at home and suddenly, you feel like you're dying? It's like you can't get any oxygen even though you're actually breathing way too hard, and you can't do anything to stop it.

"It's like the world goes topsy-turvy and all of a sudden, you're afraid. But you're not just afraid - you're terrified. Shit-your-pants fucking terrified and you don't even know why."

Rafe paused, considering. "It's like a train's coming at you and you're tied to the tracks. You can't move, you can't even breathe, you can't do anything but wait for the train. It's all you can think about because when a train is heading for you, what else matters? And the worst part is, there *is* no train. You *know* there's no train - that it's all in your head, just some glitch in your wiring or something - but that doesn't change the fear.

"And people don't get it. I think that's part of why Katie ... did what she did. She couldn't understand why I couldn't just think my way out of it. People throw that word around - anxiety - like it's the same thing as running late for a hair appointment or receiving a bill you're not sure you can afford. But if you get a bill you can't pay, then yeah, you're going to have some anxiety, but that's justified. It's *normal*. But disordered anxiety, *real* anxiety... it's a different animal. It's irrational, and knowing it's irrational doesn't make it better - it just makes you feel like you're crazy." He paused and shook his head, realizing he'd been rambling. It felt good to say it though and Brooks seemed interested enough. Rafe sighed. "So, yeah, that's my life, and I gotta be honest: I've pretty much hated every goddamn minute of it." He laughed but it was hollow.

"Jesus, man," said Brooks. "I had no idea."

"Yeah, well, you wouldn't because the second that Scythe guy gave me venom, it started getting better. And when you came along and bit me, the anxiety disappeared altogether." He gave Brooks a stilted smile. "I guess now you know why I hassle you so much about turning me. The way I see it, being dead is the only shot I've got at having a normal life."

"I can understand that," said Brooks. "I still want you to think about it, though. Maybe being a vampire isn't what you think it is. You might change your mind and right now, you still can."

"The only way I can go back is if I kill you, and that's not going to happen." Rafe grinned.

"Or someone else could kill me."

"I'm not going to let that happen, either."

"You never know," said Brooks. "I just think you should leave your options open. One day, you might be glad you did."

"Vampirism *is* my only option. And I've got nothing to lose."

Brooks seemed ready to argue but he didn't. What was there to dispute?

For a long time neither man spoke. Rain ticked on the wooden ceiling and wind whispered in the trees and howled through the broken windows.

Then Rafe said, "Anyway, you're lucky. You have people to miss. I don't miss anyone."

"You're right." Brooks stared at the rotting floorboards, eyes faraway, lost in his own thoughts. After a few minutes, he rose. "I think I'll go to the Falls and take a bath. I stink."

"I'll hang back here." Rafe wanted to be alone and he had a feeling Brooks did, too.

"Maybe I'll bring us back a couple of bunnies or something."

"Make it three. Big fat ones, too."

Brooks chuckled. "I'll do my best."

Rafe watched his Maker leave the cabin. For a long time, he remained where he was, alone with his memories, keeping company with the patter of rain and the creak of distant crickets as wind sobbed through the broken windows like a frightened child. He had no idea how much time he'd passed this way, but eventually he got up to go take a leak.

That's when he realized Brooks hadn't taken the soap with him. Or a change of clothes.

27

SIRE DUTY

The lock to Michael's door clicked open and Winter stepped into the office, immediately struck by the way his boss kept his eyes averted, looking at his computer screen as if absorbed in something of great importance.

On the edge of the desk perched Reaper, who pecked at some seeds Michael had left for him. The black raven cocked his head at Winter, blinked, and said, *"They're all gonna laugh at you!"*

"I'm used to it, Reaper, trust me." Winter spun an office chair around and straddled it cowboy-style.

"Did you see anything?" asked Michael.

Winter had been sent to the deserted Crimson Corset nightclub with Rogan and Dante - Batman and Robin, as he liked to call them - to search the place; it was as abandoned tonight as it had been since they'd shut it down. "No sign of Vampire Barbie or any of her toys."

"You checked the underground tunnels and-"

"And all the rooms, yeah. Not so much as a speck of dust has moved in that place."

"You are sure?"

Winter shrugged. "If you can find her, I'll hop up on this desk and dance bare-assed for you. And you don't even have to tip me, either." He grinned.

But Michael took no notice of Winter's smartassery. "Maybe she's fled. After this much time, it is a possibility."

Was the man in denial? "Doubt it," said Winter. "She's close."

Michael studied him. "What makes you so sure?"

Winter grinned. "Because my balls are tingling."

"Charming." Michael grimaced and went back to whatever he was doing on his computer.

Tough crowd tonight.

Reaper hopped toward Winter, cocked his head, and stared up at him with a bead-black eye. *"Number one fan!"* he squawked.

"Oh, you like me now, do you?" Winter stroked the raven under the beak.

As Reaper flapped his wings, trying to jockey onto his shoulder, Winter studied his boss. Michael hadn't been the same since they'd returned from Eternity. There was an edginess about him. He'd never been the most easygoing guy and his sense of humor left a lot to be desired, but this was different. The man was as wound up as a jack-in-the-box. Winter lifted the bird to his shoulder where it began nibbling at his ear and polishing its beak. "Have you called Natasha back?" He suspected it was Natasha Darling who was throwing Michael off his game, but the guy gave nothing away.

He only shook his head. "No. I haven't had the time."

Winter knew Michael and Natasha had a romantic history together and during the Eternity trip there was no question they'd rekindled their old flame, however temporarily. Michael had likely broken his long-held vow of celibacy. He was celibate, he said, because he was an addict and one indulgence led to another - like a set of falling dominoes. And now, Winter thought Michael was probably beating himself up about it. "Is everything all right, Boss?"

"Eve was weak!" cried Reaper.

Michael looked up, his face placid. "Of course. Why do you ask?"

"You just seem ... I don't know ... out of sorts." Now the bird was hopping around wildly on Winter's shoulders and he tried vainly to shake him off.

"Taking that trip was not a good idea. I have fallen behind."

Finally, Winter lured the bird onto his finger and lowered him to the desk where he pecked at his seeds. "You know." He tried to sound casual. "If something's on your mind, I've got two good ears. Or if you'd rather, you could talk to Dante."

"Why would I talk to Dante?"

"Well, it's just that ... apparently, he had a drug problem back in the day and-"

"Are you worried that I've developed a substance abuse problem?" A smile found Michael's lips but his eyes said, *Watch your step*.

Winter shifted. "Of course not, but you know ... addiction is ..." He wished he'd never brought it up. "I'm just saying, if you're struggling with something, of a ... er, *private* matter, Dante's a good listener. He's been there, you know?"

Michael didn't move a muscle.

Winter shifted uncomfortably again.

Michael smiled then, but his eyes were all steel. It confused the senses - like being tickled with a razor-blade. "I shall take that under advisement." His eyes snapped back to his computer screen.

Winter stood. "I'll leave you to it, then." *Note to self: Don't bring up Natasha Darling.* "Who's on Sire duty tonight?"

"If you're asking me who's staying with Cade Colter, the answer is Chynna. You may go relieve her if you'd like." Judging by his tone and lack of eye contact, Winter had misstepped and Michael wasn't going to let it go so easily.

"Yeah, maybe I'll drop by and see how they're doing." Winter maintained a breezy tone. "Hey, how come you haven't seen him since we got back?"

"Seen who?"

"Cade. You haven't darkened his doorstep. I think you're giving him a complex, Boss." Winter grinned, again trying to lighten the mood.

"As I've said, I am behind on my work." The way Michael nearly flinched at the mention of Cade brought at least some of the mystery into focus: he couldn't face the kid. It had been his order that Gretchen be staked and not beheaded. *He holds himself responsible for what happened to Samantha.*

"I sent him my condolences." Michael looked up. "Did you deliver the flowers?"

"Yeah." Winter didn't mention that after reading the card - *Sorry for your loss. Yours, Michael* - Cade had tossed them in the trash. "All right then." Winter stepped to the door. "If you need me, you know where I'll be."

"*Plug it up, plug it up!*" cried Reaper.

"I'm going, I'm going." Winter held his hands up in mock surrender.

"Tell Chynna to stay there," said Michael, "I'd like you both to be there tonight."

Winter felt himself redden. This wasn't the first time Michael had arranged it so that he and Chynna shared duties. He hadn't thought his attraction to the woman was so transparent, but then, Michael's senses were keen.

Winter appreciated what his boss was trying to do, but romance wasn't in the cards; He liked the bachelor life and couldn't see getting involved in anything serious. Not now, and maybe not ever. "You got it, Boss." He stepped out of the office, leaving Reaper to his seeds and Michael to his brooding.

IF WINTER WAS UNEASY ABOUT MICHAEL'S BEHAVIOR, HIS ANXIETY doubled when he got to the Colter cabin, where the tension was so thick he could have cut it with, well, a silver dagger.

"Maybe you can talk some sense into him." Chynna was poised at the far end of the sofa, arms crossed, her silver-blond hair pulled back, emphasizing cheekbones that needed no emphasis. In her anger, she somehow struck Winter as almost alarmingly beautiful, but Cade's appearance alarmed him more.

The kid's eye was black and swollen shut, his lip fat and split and crusted with dried blood. He sat on the opposite end of the sofa and now grumbled in Chynna's general direction, "I don't see why it bothers you so much."

"Whoa." Winter let out a low whistle. "What the hell happened to your eye?"

Cade shrugged. "I got into a fight at the bookstore today. It's not important."

"That's a relief." Winter stared at him. "Based on all the bad vibes in here, I half wondered if Chynna hadn't socked you one." He tried a grin.

No one laughed, and Winter sat between them with a sigh. He looked from one to the other and this close to Cade, he knew why Chynna was complaining: The silver dagger was somewhere on Cade's person. Winter could feel the sickening heat of it.

Chynna said to Winter, "He refuses to take it off and put it away."

"It isn't hurting anything." Cade sounded like a sulky teen. "And besides," he said this to Winter. "You have one, too." He glanced down where, under the cuffs of his faded blue jeans, strapped to his boot, Winter kept a blade of his own.

"Mine's not real silver," Winter said.

"And yours is." Chynna leaned forward and said to Cade. "I can feel it from over here."

Cade said, "It probably doesn't contain much pure silver. The blade is just plated, so-"

"It's still silver." It wasn't like Chynna to be so antagonistic - or petulant - but Winter knew what silver did to vampires: it made them edgy, hyper, like someone waving a gun in your face.

"You like silver," said Cade, nodding at Chynna's signature hoop earrings.

"Not *real* silver!"

"Enough." Winter held up his hand. He turned to Cade. "So … what's the deal, Gilroy?"

Cade, tired and browbeaten, said, "If Gretchen comes back - or Brooks - I want to be able to defend myself. That's all. But *she-*"

"That's why *we're* here, Cade - to defend you." Chynna leaned forward again but now her eyes were kind, compassionate.

"Yeah, well when Dante was here, he almost attacked me." Cade remained slumped back, silently stubborn.

"But he didn't, did he?" said Chynna. "And we're not Dante. Dante's ... different."

"No, he's not. He's a vampire. You're *all* vampires."

Winter's eyes roamed to the kid's hip where, beneath his shirt, he knew the dagger was strapped. "Here's the thing, Gilroy," said Winter. "Even with the dagger, you're no match for Gretchen if she comes back for you. For one thing, she wouldn't come alone, and for another-"

"It's no different than bug repellant," said Cade. "When you hose yourself with bug repellent, insects stay away. Silver does the same to vampires. Except you," he added, making it clear he was tiring of the constant presence of vampires.

"Bugs?" asked Chynna. "Now we're *bugs*?"

Cade sighed. "All I'm saying is-"

"I *know* what you're saying, and-"

"Whoa, whoa, whoa." Winter held up his hands. "Look." He faced Cade. "How about this - when we're here, put the dagger in the drawer. That way, it's close enough to grab but not so close it bothers the guards." He glanced at Chynna. "Fair?" He turned back to Cade, then to Chynna again, a man watching a tennis match.

"I'll agree to that," Chynna finally said. Then she faced Cade, her tone softening. "The thing is, if you were hurt or in trouble and we needed to get to you, we couldn't. It's hard enough being in the same *room* with it."

"Fine." Cade stood, stalked into the kitchen, unstrapped the dagger with more vigor than necessary, and tossed it in with the silverware. "Everybody happy?"

Chynna visibly relaxed.

Cade returned, collapsing onto his end of the sofa. He'd shaved and showered, and even done a little housekeeping - but his thinness worried Winter. He refrained from lecturing the kid though; he'd been harassed enough for one night.

"Yes, I think we're all happy now." Winter felt like a father who'd forced an unsatisfactory compromise on his squabbling offspring. For a while, no one spoke. Winter cleared his throat. "So other than that, Mrs. Lincoln, how was the opera?"

"It wasn't an opera," said Chynna sourly. "It was a play."

Winter suppressed a groan and sank into the sofa, clasping his hands behind his head. "Another tough crowd, I see. I just can't catch a break."

"What?" asked Chynna.

But Cade cut in. "I want to be able to defend myself," he said. "As it is, I'm constantly tripping over vampires who are trying to protect me from other vampires. It doesn't make any sense."

"I hope," said Chynna, "that you aren't lumping us all together in the same box. Gretchen's Loyals and Michael's are two very different-"

"I know. I get that, but remember Ozryel? The traitor? Who's to say there aren't others?"

Winter did remember Ozryel - he was a plant, one of Gretchen's posing as one of Michael's. He'd nearly handed Cade to Gretchen on a platter before they'd found him out … but Chynna and her tigers had taken care of that little problem.

Chynna sighed. "I understand, Cade. I do. But-"

"Do you?" Cade shot forward, staring past Winter at Chynna, fire in his eyes. "I'm a total target. Even the two of you have to double up on blood before coming over so you can stand to be around me without killing me. I'm a sitting duck. And now my own brother is one of them. I don't trust *anyone*. I can't." He looked from one to the other. "I won't be a passive participant in my own death. With or without your consent, I'm going to defend myself. I have that right." He stood and pushed his hand through chestnut-brown hair in need of a cut. "I'm going to bed." And with that, he headed to his room, but not before pointedly retrieving the silver dagger from the kitchen.

A few moments after the bedroom door slammed shut, Chynna looked at Winter. "I'm worried about him. He's not himself."

Winter sat forward, staring at his boots. "He hasn't been sleeping or eating."

"It's more than that," she said in low tones. "He's ... hateful." Her almond-shaped silvery-gray eyes implored him.

"In his defense, Dante *did* almost go after him a few nights back. He was lucky to have that dagger."

"Well, Dante shouldn't be allowed around any human, let alone a Sire. He's never had great control. That was a bad call."

Winter realized that now. "He won't be coming back."

Chynna sighed. "I'm afraid of what he might do - Cade, I mean."

Winter studied her. "What do you mean?"

"He's losing the ability to differentiate us from Gretchen's Loyals. He's demonizing *all* vampires. He doesn't trust us." She shifted. "He *knows* I'd never attack him but when I asked him to put the dagger away, he got so ... argumentative. So angry. I thought for a minute he might ..."

"Might what, Chynna?" Alarms sounded in Winter's head. "Do you think he was going to ... try to hurt you?"

She shook her head. "I don't know. I've just never seen him so ... *nasty*."

"He's been through a lot." Winter glanced toward the hall, and spoke low. "And he's pissed because I wouldn't turn Samantha."

Chynna's eyes widened. "He wanted you to *turn* her? After ... she was dead?"

Winter nodded. "He's been up my ass about it since we got back from Eternity."

"Did you explain that-"

"No. I didn't tell him why I wouldn't do it."

"Why not?"

"Because I think he'd want me to do it anyway."

Chynna said nothing.

Winter sighed. "I think we'd better *both* be here with him from now on. Just in case."

Chynna gave him a look that said, *Oh, please.* She arched a thin brow. "I can handle Cade. Winter, you know that."

And it was true. Chynna wasn't just a babe - she was a badass in arm-candy packaging. It was that blend of beauty and badassery, Winter thought, that made her so damned attractive. He realized he hadn't moved over when Cade left. He and Chynna were still shoulder-to-shoulder on the sofa and Winter felt suddenly self-conscious. Not self-conscious enough to slide over, though. Chynna smelled fresh and clean, like a breeze off the ocean. It soothed him.

"I don't like where he's headed," she added. "And the fight. That's not like him."

"I'd sure like to get my hands on the chuckle-fuck who did that to his face," said Winter.

"From what I hear, the other guy got it worse. And he was bigger than Cade."

"Really?" A surge of pride momentarily crowded out Winter's worry. He laughed. "That kid's got more balls than brains."

"He's a time bomb and I can hear him ticking."

Winter looked at her and when he saw the anxiety etched on her features, his pride took a nosedive. She was right: there was more going on with Cade than grief, and it was serious. The kid was going to explode and when he did, Winter had a feeling it was going to make a hell of a mess.

28

OF GRIEF AND GUILT

The visions came regularly now, especially at night. She saw the same few rooms, a black-and-white cat, and occasionally, the faces of those surrounding the young man who held the dagger. And more than once she'd briefly tapped into his moods, his thoughts, and his emotions through his contact with the dagger. He was lonely. Broken-hearted. Frightened.

But most of all, he was angry. So very, very angry.

Once, she glimpsed him as he watched himself in a mirror, studying his reflection as one might study the face of a stranger, and in his eyes was all the pain of the world, in his soul, the burning emptiness of despair and the jagged agony of grief and guilt.

So much grief, so much guilt. She often felt it when he made contact with the dagger, yet there was nothing to give even a hint of the blade's location.

And she could not bring him to her. The young man was not receptive to her silent calls. Though she possessed the ability to draw to her those she desired, she held no sway over him. Some minds simply weren't penetrable - but the real reason he was inaccessible was because of the dagger. By its very nature, the dagger - and therefore, those in possession of it - eluded her. She was certain he'd sensed her, perhaps even seen her, but making any real contact - let alone drawing him to her - wasn't possible.

But the woman in black was not discouraged. She stared down at her runes, at the tall black candles burning around the circle she'd cast. Over the past weeks, she'd done many such location spells and though this one, like the others, had offered no new insight, she knew that if she persisted, the dagger would reveal itself to her, for she was its rightful owner.

It was simply a matter of time - and she had nothing but time. For if the woman in black knew anything at all, it was how to wait on the silver dagger.

She'd been doing it for centuries.

29

RISE AND GRIND'S

Ethan's morning started rough. After being up half the night with the latest murder - a john had been attacked on Scarlet Street and was now at the morgue under Sheila's watch - Ethan had slept in. Hurrying to work, he'd spilled his morning coffee down the front of his shirt when the Wrangler slammed into a pothole - one of the many crater-sized pits which he'd already complained about to the city council.

And it didn't appear as if the day was going to improve from there. He'd barely stepped through the door when the desk sergeant, Dwayne Purkiss, who'd steadily gained twenty pounds each year, held up a small sticky-note and said, "Message for you."

Ethan's stomach tightened. Personal messages from the residents of Crimson Cove were rarely good news. "Thanks." He swiped the note from Dwayne's giant paw and headed to his office. After starting a fresh pot of coffee, he sat down to read the note. On it were three itemized lines in Dwayne's chunky scrawl: *Rachel. 12:30 at Rise and Grind's. Meet at the back - wants privacy. Info regarding bear attacks.*

The bear attacks? Shit.

And he knew who Rachel was - a working girl on Scarlet Street, where last night's murder took place. *Double shit.* This wouldn't be

Ethan's first tangle with "Roach Clip Rachel." They weren't enemies but Ethan, a cop, and Rachel, a prostitute, weren't exactly friends, either. He dreaded hearing what she had to tell him. *She must have seen something.* It wasn't a comforting thought.

Ethan looked at the clock, nervous as a cat at a waterpark.

CADE WOKE TO A MOURNFUL MEOW AND A ROUGH TONGUE ON HIS cheek. Purrcy perched on his chest, watching him with anxious eyes. Cade scritched the cat's head and glanced at his alarm clock, trying to bring it into focus. His injured eye had all but swollen shut, but finally, he made out the time. Shocked, he saw that it was past ten. He'd slept in and was already late. He'd been lucky that Dora hadn't fired him for punching the customer the other day.

Then he remembered he had the day off - and that was even worse. The hours stretched out before him and he had no idea how to fill them. He considered staying in bed, but Purrcy was insistent, meowing to be fed.

"Shush." He threw off the sheets, stood, and made his way to the kitchen, nearly tripping over the cat who eeled between his feet, herding him toward the food dish which, Cade realized with shame, was empty. He filled it as Purrcy gobbled it down, then took ibuprofen for his throbbing face.

Feeling no desire to do anything else, he returned to his room and got back in bed. He couldn't remember any nightmares at all last night and wanted to return to that peaceful, quiet slumber.

But he couldn't sleep. His mind had already started spinning and spiraling, mauling the usual topics: Samantha's death, Winter's refusal to turn her, and Brooks, the murdering son of a bitch.

Since the day of the tragedy, Cade had spent countless hours fantasizing about different outcomes. He replayed the day of the murder over and over, thinking that if only he'd come home sooner - or never left at all, or at least told Samantha of his suspicions about Brooks, none of this would have happened.

And why wouldn't Winter turn Samantha? Cade had thought this one over so hard he might have burned holes in it. He wished he'd pushed Winter harder, or asked another vampire to do it.

But it was too late now. Samantha was buried.

Cade gritted his teeth, his jaw aching with tension. At the very least, he should have driven that dagger straight through his brother's heart. This, too, was a scenario he'd spent countless hours creating and polishing.

He longed for the music of Father Vincent Scarlotti. The man's violin-playing was the only thing that had stilled Cade's pain and he would have given anything now for just one song. It didn't even have to be *Amazing Grace*. He closed his eyes and tried to recall the music. Even the memory of it watered down his fury.

Until his cell rang.

He grabbed it from the night stand, not recognizing the number.

"Hello?"

"Is this Cade?" The voice was female; Cade didn't recognize it.

"Yes."

"This is Muriel."

Muriel? Cade was at a loss.

"From the Life After Loss group."

Then he remembered: the pretty woman he'd sat next to at the grief support meeting, the one who smelled like cinnamon.

"I got your number from the list," she said, "I hope you don't mind me calling."

"No, of course not."

There was a beat of awkward silence then she continued. "I heard about the bear attack last night and I wanted to make sure you're okay."

"The bear attack? Another one?" Cade hadn't heard. His heart began to trip-hammer.

"Yes. It was on the morning news." After a beat, she went on. "The real reason I called was to invite you to a meeting between meetings. Kendon and I sometimes go out for coffee, you know, just to talk. It's more personal. We'd like you to join us."

"I ... I'll think about it."

"Well, we were planning to get together today."

Cade wasn't prepared for this. "I, uh ..."

"We could come to you if the drive's a problem. We wouldn't mind meeting you in Crimson Cove."

"Um, sure. Where do you want to meet?" Cade wondered if she was as friendly with every newcomer. He recalled the way she and Kendon watched him at the meeting, and didn't think so; their interest in him was obviously personal. *But why?*

"You pick a place and time, and we'll be there."

"It would have to be later this afternoon."

"That's not a problem. We're flexible."

"How about ... four?"

"Perfect."

Since Rise and Grind's was the only coffee shop Cade knew, he gave her the address and ended the call, both wary and intrigued. And he couldn't help feeling a little resentful of the way the woman had caught him off guard and put him on the spot. He wasn't in the mood for company, especially the company of virtual strangers, but at least it would pass the day.

And make Ethan happy.

On that note, Cade rang the sheriff, curious about the latest murder. Ethan didn't answer.

RISE AND GRIND'S, ONE OF SEVERAL SMALL COFFEE SHOPS ON MAIN, WAS a little box of a place nestled between a quaint bookstore called Hit the Page, and Lily's, a clothing shop that catered to young women with anorexic figures and questionable tastes. Ethan, ten minutes early, walked to the rear and squeaked into a vinyl-upholstered booth facing the entrance.

A few patrons sat huddled over their laptops or phones, sipping their steaming javas, espressos, and whatever else the place had to offer. In another month this part of Main Street would resume its

Night-of-the-Comet vacancy, but even now it was clear that autumn had settled in, dismissing the tourist season with a chilly wave of her hand.

The walls of Rise and Grind's were splattered with obnoxious reds, greens, and blues, accented by paintings of abstract jungle animals attired in full hipster gear. Above Ethan, a poorly painted lion in a striped shirt, bow tie, and knit cap peered down at him from over the top of his Buddy Holly reading glasses, and from all corners, calypso music jazzed and jived. Ethan wasn't sure he'd ever used the word "tacky" in his entire life, but if ever asked to describe the place, that cherry would be popped.

Against the wood-topped front counter stood a yawning, stick-thin guy in a beard net who needed delousing. A server - also in need of a good scrub-down - came to take Ethan's order. Having no clue what the kids were drinking these days, he elicited a look of blank confusion from the server by asking for coffee in basic black. After a hesitation in which the young man digested this unpretentious request, he went on his way and Ethan returned to ogling the ugly walls. The more he looked, the more he had to admit that some of the color schemes worked surprisingly well, and just as he was mentally composing the boldest design yet in his "Aunt Vanessa" sweater collection, he saw her heading his way. He recognized her at once; she was impossible to mistake.

Rachel Jones, aka, "Roach Clip Rachel," had mocha-colored skin and intense ebony eyes. She was as beautiful as she was frightening - and it wasn't just her height, which stretched past the six-foot mark. Ms. Jones, who might have otherwise been a runway model, was the most capable - and dangerous - woman on Scarlet Street. The johns respected her, as did the law. Rachel Jones took no shit, and allowed no shit to be given to her girls.

Today, she wore a torso-hugging crop top and leopard-print leggings, and if that left any doubt of her profession, her ratted wig and dramatic Cleopatra makeup closed the case.

"Sheriff." She offered a hand; her nails were the color of blood and filed into stilettos which, Ethan was sure, came in handy on the street.

After an amiable handshake that promised there would be no trouble between them, she settled across from him, her shiny, high boots drawing stares and begging a tongue-bath from every hipster in the joint.

Ethan couldn't help smirking. "You always did know how to make an entrance."

Rachel gestured evocatively at her own body. "This is my brand, Sheriff. I'm sure as shit not selling Girl Scout cookies." Her perfume - a blend of honeysuckle and musk - reached out with soft, feminine fingers, casting a spell of seduction.

But Ethan wasn't buying what Rachel was selling. "Point taken." He leaned in, eager and anxious. "All right, so what's this about? You've got information about the, uh ... bear attacks?"

Her expression turned to mock consternation. "Aren't you going to at least buy a lady a drink before you plow into her like that?" She *tsked*. "Business as always, I see. You know what they say ... all work and no play ..."

Ethan sighed and motioned the server over.

After placing an order for a specialty slice of chocolate cake and a coffee concoction Ethan had never heard of, Rachel met his eyes, her face turning serious. "It's not a bear, sheriff."

Shit. There were a few ways Ethan could respond: shock, disbelief, or interest that was either eager or reluctant. He opted to remain poker-faced, indifferent, and find out how much she actually knew. "Not a bear?" He kept his tone flat, unreadable.

"You heard me. It's a man doing this." Her gaze was bold and steady. "But you already know that, don't you?"

Ethan, knowing she'd detect the slightest tell, refrained from fidgeting. "What makes you say that, Ms. Jones?"

The server returned and as the coffee and cake were placed in front of her, Rachel studied Ethan - and he knew that she saw through him.

When the hipster was out of sight, Rachel stirred sugar into her coffee, her eyes fixed on Ethan. "Let's cut the shit, okay? You *know* it isn't a bear, Sheriff. You've known all along."

Ethan seesawed momentarily between playing dumb and coming clean, but there was no point prolonging the foreplay - it was obvious the woman had seen something. His only hope now was that the word "vampire" wouldn't enter the picture. He held up a hand in surrender. "We've got to keep a lid on this, Rachel. For legal reasons." He spoke low. "Not to mention, people will panic. I need you to keep this quiet. I know you have influence on Scarlet Street."

Rachel, following suit, lowered her voice enough that the calypso music overhead blanketed her words. "I can promise you I won't talk, Sheriff, and I don't think Leda will either. But that's the problem: she won't say anything to anyone."

"Leda?"

Rachel nodded and took a bite of cake. "She was with the john who got attacked last night. She saw it all. But she's not talking. The guy, the killer ... he saved her life, see? The john was getting rough with her and that's when it happened. I think Leda feels kind of ... loyal to him, see? I told her to go to the police, but she won't. She doesn't think the killer will hurt her or anyone else that isn't beating a woman senseless."

Ethan couldn't help thinking the same thing. So far, all the victims were sleazebags, the kind who belonged behind bars. "First things first, did *you* see the guy?"

Rachel shook her head and sipped her coffee. "Not last night, no."

"But you *have* seen him?"

"Not really."

Ethan blinked at her. "Care to elaborate?"

She shrugged. "A while back. All I saw was a tall guy with broad shoulders. I couldn't even see his hair color, but it was either really short, or slicked back. He was far away and it was dark."

Ethan sighed. "All right. About Leda ..." He drew a pad out of his pocket and poised his pen. "You say she saw him up close and personal?"

Rachel nodded. "Yep, but she's the only one. Suzi saw a figure running away. Danny and Joe both thought they saw him hanging around on the night of one of the attacks, but neither could see anything except that he was tall."

"I need a description of this guy, Rachel."

"That's why I'm here. I can't get Leda to talk, but maybe you can."

"How?"

She shrugged. "This is where my job ends and yours begins, Sheriff."

"But if she won't even talk to you ... shit." Ethan leaned back, wheels turning.

Rachel leaned in, lowering her voice to barely audible tones. "The guy, the killer ... he rips the johns to pieces with his bare teeth."

Ethan stiffened. "Well, I'm sure he uses some kind of weapon."

Rachel shook her head. "That's not what Leda says. She told me he dug the guy's heart right out of his chest with his bare hands and took a big bite out of it. She watched him do it, see?" She bit down on another forkful of cake and Ethan marveled at the strength of her stomach.

"I guess I'll have to see if I can get her to talk then. What can you tell me about her?"

"What do you want to know?"

"Her full name, where she lives, where she hangs out. Does she have a day job?"

"We don't really talk about all that, Sheriff. And I don't think most of us have day jobs. Your best bet is to swing by Scarlet Street."

Ethan sighed. "What does she look like?"

"Blond, about five-two or three, maybe a hundred and five, a hundred and ten pounds. You'll know her by the sandals. No matter what else she wears, she's got those ugly-ass gold sandals on." Rachel laughed. "Most of the girls wear boots, but Leda believes in comfort."

Ethan jotted the information down.

Rachel turned serious. "Just don't tell her I talked to you. She'd be pissed if she knew. You've got to pretend you've figured this out on your own."

"You have my word, Rachel."

"And, for God's sake, don't show up in your cop car." Rachel took the final bite of cake and finished her coffee.

"I wouldn't dream of it."

"Talk about a public panic."

"No doubt. Look, I'll try to find her tonight and talk to her, but Rachel, I'd advise you to conduct your business elsewhere for the time being. Scarlet Street isn't safe right now."

"Don't you worry your handsome little head about that. We take care of ourselves just fine."

"I have no doubt, but-"

"And where would you have us go? Would you prefer we started hanging around the tourist shops?"

"Don't tempt me to arrest you." Ethan studied her. He liked her and couldn't resist offering advice. "Have you ever thought of … you know, doing something else?"

She laughed without humor. "Out of the mouths of babes."

Ethan shrugged. "I wish I understood why you do it, but I don't."

She patted his hand and chuckled. "You don't have to understand it, Sheriff. You just have to live and let live." She paused, sincerity in her eyes. "I appreciate your not giving us too much hell. We all do."

"If I thought I could stop you, I would. God knows I've tried."

Rachel shook her head, smiling. "You're full of it, Sheriff. I don't believe your bullshit any more than you do." She laughed and stood. "I better be off. Thanks for the coffee."

"Any time."

She started to walk away, then turned back. "And if you ever want to assault someone with your deadly weapon, you know where to find me." She raised a perfectly-arched brow.

"You're playing with fire, Ms. Jones."

She lifted a shoulder and smiled. "Just putting it out there."

"Thanks for the offer, but we both know that's not in the cards."

She gave him a wink. "Have a good day, Sheriff."

Too late for that.

As she left the coffee shop, Ethan's phone chirped. He checked it and groaned. It was Cade, no doubt calling for details about last night's murder. Ethan ignored it.

30

BAD COMPANY

Later that afternoon, Sydney Hunter-Doss reluctantly packed up her laptop, and left Suspire - the restaurant at Eudemonia. She'd taken advantage of the wifi to send out her resume, but was far more interested in catching a glimpse of the hunky hotelier than finding a job.

But Michael Ward was nowhere to be seen. As usual. Sydney thought he must be a night owl who spent the daylight hours in bed or something. She sighed, wishing she were in bed with him right now.

Heading back to her cabin, she paused on the cobblestone walk, seeing someone at her front door. It was Sheila Leventis. Sydney put on her biggest, fakest smile, called out, "Yoo-hoo!" and waved.

Ethan's fiancée turned and waved back. She carried a large basket and when Sydney approached, she held it out. "Some housewarming gifts. From Ethan and me."

The basket contained lemon-fresh Pledge, a scented candle, Zip-Lock bags, Windex, and Mr. Clean magic erasers. Sydney, who'd always had a thing - a fetish, really - for the muscle-bound cartoon mascot, particularly appreciated these last items. "Oh! How cute! You didn't have to do this!"

"We wanted to," said Sheila. "I know this isn't exactly a permanent home, but we hope you'll be happy here for now."

"That's *so* sweet of you guys!" Sydney tucked her laptop under her arm and hugged Sheila tight. She knew Ethan had nothing to do with this - he probably wasn't even aware of Sheila's visit, let alone the gifts - but it was nice that *someone* cared. "Are you on your lunch break?"

"I am. It's a little late, but-"

"Would you like to come in and see the place, maybe have some coffee?"

Sheila looked at her watch. "I suppose a few minutes wouldn't hurt."

ASIDE FROM THE WIDE BLUE-EYED STARE OF GIANT BLOND JESUS ABOVE the mantel, the place was pink, pink, pink, and Sheila hoped her expression didn't betray her distaste. "Where would you like this?" she asked, holding up the basket.

"Just set it on the table." Sydney scooped instant coffee into mugs of hot water. "Feel free to look around."

There wasn't much to see, but Sheila gave the place a perfunctory walk-through, oohing and ahhing at the little touches - all pink - that Sydney had sprinkled here and there. Standing in the tiny bathroom wondering how anyone raised their arms to brush their hair, Sheila jumped when Sydney appeared behind her.

"Coffee's ready." Her plum-colored lips spread into a bright smile.

"Thank you."

They returned to the living area, sipping coffee and chatting about mundanities as Giant Blond Jesus - who looked more like a beach bopper than the Messiah - looked on.

Sheila began. "It's a cute place, Sydney. I like what you've done."

"Thank you! It doesn't have electricity, so that's kind of a bummer. I miss Reverend Bobby and *The God Club*." She gave an exaggerated pout. "But to be honest, it's kind of liberating not having television."

"I can understand that." It was one of the reasons Sheila liked working in the morgue: the silence. "So," she continued, hands around her coffee mug, "how's the job hunt going?"

"No bites yet." Sydney sighed. "But I haven't really been putting my heart into it, to be honest. I've just been so ... *traumatized* by what Dickhead has put me through." She lifted her gaze to Giant Blond Jesus as if making sure He was bearing witness to the difficulties she endured.

"Well, what kind of work would you like to do?"

Sydney shrugged. "The kind that will pay me." She lifted her mug and sipped noisily. "But not a phone job. I *loathe* talking on the phone. Oh, and babysitting. Babysitting is out. I hate children even more than phones. Sticky-fingered little bastards." She mumbled this last part to herself, as if recalling some unsavory incident. "And old people." She shuddered. "They're creepy. And they smell funny."

Sheila had an idea. "There's a clothing shop called Poise and Ivy downtown that's hiring sales associates. I know the owner, Jolene. I could put in a good word if you'd like."

Sydney blinked at her. "Hmm. Maybe." She seemed genuinely insulted at the idea.

Sheila was beginning to regret her visit.

For a moment, they sipped the dreadful coffee in silence, then Sydney sighed and said, "I know I should hate you, but I don't."

Sheila almost choked. "Why should you hate me?"

Sydney shrugged. "Because you're marrying Ethan. He's *such* a catch!"

Sheila felt uncomfortable. "He is."

"Speaking of which, when are the two of you doing it, anyway? You know, getting *married*?" Sydney prodded her with an expectant smile as if they were close girlfriends sharing secrets - but it rang false. The woman was just plain prying.

Shifting, Sheila set her coffee mug on the table.

"Oh, it's just so *romantic*!" Sydney went on, as phony as a beauty queen promising world peace. "I'm *so* happy for you, and even though I shouldn't be, I'm happy for Ethan, too! I pray the two of you will be covered in the blood of Christ!"

"Um ... thanks." Sheila wondered what god-awful religion Sydney was part of that being covered in blood was considered a good thing.

"So?" she probed. "When are you two tying the knot?"

"I don't have a clue," said Sheila. "We've been meaning to set a date for a while but, you know, things get in the way. We've both got a lot going on right now and Ethan-"

"Of course it comes down to Ethan," Sydney interrupted. "I might have known *he's* the one dragging his feet." She nodded exasperatedly. "As women, *we* need to start calling the shots. Men have been doing it for centuries. It's *our* turn. You just tell him you're ready." She paused, looked smug, and sipped her coffee. "Unless, of course, you're one of those old-school stand-by-your-man types who doesn't believe in asserting herself. You have the *right* to do that, you know."

Don't rise to the bait. Sheila brought her cup to her face to silence the retort that hummed on her lips. She resented women like Sydney, women who thought that feminism meant castrating men and disregarding them - and that those who didn't follow suit were traitors to their sex. Sheila believed in women's lib as much as the next gal, but she also believed that such life-altering choices as being wed should involve both partners equally. She was just fine getting married whenever the *two* of them decided to do it. *And it's my right to feel that way.*

Sydney sighed. "I really think that's what came between Ethan and me. He can't handle a strong, independent woman. He couldn't even cope when I accepted the Lord. I think he was jealous of Him." Another loving glance at Giant Blond Jesus.

By now Sheila was irritated and itching to get out. *I should have listened to Ethan. This visit was a bad idea.* She'd hoped that showing kindness to the woman would smooth out some of the awkward kinks since Sydney would be in Crimson Cove for a while - but her plan wasn't working. At all. Sydney didn't want kindness. She wanted revenge. *Against a man she walked out on.*

Sydney continued. "In truth, it wasn't as if Ethan and I had a lot in common, so maybe it wouldn't have worked out anyway." She looked at Sheila, gave her an impish smile. "But the *sex*! Oh, dear Lord! The sex was *amazing* - as I'm sure you know!" She giggled and fanned her store-bought bosom. "The first time Ethan made love to me, I couldn't believe how *big* he was!"

Oh, God, tell me she didn't really say that.

Sydney burbled on. "I'll tell you one thing, if I knew then what I know now, I would have done it with him more often!" She let out a braying laugh, then gave Beach Boy Jesus a disproportionately coquettish glance.

Sheila cleared her throat, determined to keep things amicable. And steer the conversation away from Ethan. "Well, there are plenty of good men out there. Have you eaten at Suspire yet - Eudemonia's restaurant?"

"Mm-hmm." Sydney nodded absently, her gaze remaining dreamily Jesus-bound. "I shouldn't even be thinking about men and sex after what Drake did to me." She scowled at the mention of her second ex-husband, then snapped back to attention. A little smile lifted the corners of her brightly-painted mouth. "But you know what? I *am* thinking about it." She brayed again. "It's ridiculous, but I am!" She leaned in conspiratorially, a sparkle in her eye. "Now tell me everything you know about Michael Ward!"

Sheila's stomach clenched. "Michael ... Ward?"

Sydney nodded. "Yes, the owner of this place. I've only met him twice and he's not very easy to talk to, but oh, dear *Lord*, is that man *gorgeous!*"

Sheila knew what Michael was - and if Sydney was sniffing around him, that would only lead to trouble. "Well, I don't really know much about him. He pretty much keeps to himself. He's very private."

"*Right*? I think that's part of the appeal. I want to get inside that gorgeous head of his and figure him out." Sydney giggled. "Do you know if he's involved with anyone?"

Sheila set her cup down carefully. "Well, I don't think he dates or anything like that. At least, I've never seen him with a woman."

Sydney gasped, raising a hand to her gravity-defying breasts. "OMG!" She did not say '*Oh my God*,' but used its actual acronym - *Oh-Emm-Gee*. "He's not *gay* is he?" An accusatory glance at Giant Blond Jesus.

Sheila was momentarily tempted to say yes and get Michael off the hook, but she couldn't do that. She glanced at her watch. "Oh! I really ought to go. I only meant to take a half hour lunch break." She stood. "It's been great, and I love what you've done with the place."

Sydney got to her feet, her metallic gold tights glinting. She pulled Sheila into another hug. "Thank you *so* much for the gifts! Thank Ethan for me, too."

"Of course." Sheila patted the woman's back and broke the hug.

"Again, thank you *so* much!"

Sheila left Sydney's cabin with a nagging sense of impending disaster. She was worried about the woman poking around Michael.

But he's a big boy. He can take care of himself.

She just hoped Sydney wouldn't pry too hard; she shuddered to think how she might react to the reality of vampires - and what she'd do with that information. Sydney Hunter-Doss didn't strike Sheila as the kind of woman who held onto secrets very long, and in Crimson Cove, Sheila had learned, keeping secrets was essential to survival.

31

POKER FACE

*T*hat afternoon, as Cade entered Rise and Grind's, he couldn't help thinking Muriel and Kendon were a comically unlikely pair. They sat across from each other, the well-dressed, middle-aged black woman, and the disheveled young white guy - and it wasn't just their physical appearances that set them apart. While Muriel had a straight-backed, almost regal air, Kendon was loose and relaxed, an arm slung casually across the back of the booth.

As Cade approached, Kendon slid out and sat next to Muriel, and after a quick round of greetings, Cade took the empty seat across from them, self-conscious about his shiner; his eye was swollen entirely shut.

"We're glad you could make it, Cade." Muriel smiled and touched his hand, the kindness in her warm brown eyes reminding him of melting chocolate. This, combined with her cinnamon scent, made Cade realize he was hungry - no, famished; he hadn't eaten all day. In fact, he wasn't sure he'd eaten anything since yesterday except a spoonful of peanut butter.

"Pretty nice place," Kendon said, looking around at the hideous decor. "Do you come here often?"

"Not really." Cade had only been here on one or two occasions. He wasn't enough of a coffee-lover to spend much time in the place. The music alone - calypso - was reason to stay away.

"What do you recommend?" Muriel slipped on a pair of reading glasses, opened a menu, and looked it over.

Cade opened his own. "If you're hungry, they have pretty good desserts and stuff." He immediately decided on a jumbo cinnamon roll and an iced mocha, but kept his menu open, prolonging the silence before genuine conversation would need to be made. As he read, he felt eyes on him and glancing up, caught Kendon's gaze. The guy looked quickly, almost guiltily, away.

This was going to be awkward and Cade wished he'd made an excuse not to come. He wasn't a good conversationalist. It was one thing talking to customers at the bookstore - they were there for books, and Cade knew books. But this was different. He didn't know *what* he was supposed to discuss with these two. His grief, he supposed, and he wasn't up for it.

But it's too late to back out now, he told himself. *Just get through it.*

Muriel and Kendon discussed various menu items and when a waiter came to take their orders, she decided on tiramisu and Kendon opted for a salted caramel latte.

Cade placed his order last and when the waiter was gone, Muriel said, "I shouldn't have anything to do with such things as tiramisu, but, special occasion, right?"

Cade wondered what, exactly, the occasion was. He cleared his throat. "I don't mean to sound ungrateful - it was nice of you guys to come up here and all - but what exactly is a … 'meeting between meetings'?"

Muriel cleared her throat. "It's just what it sounds like. Kendon and I met at the Life After Loss group and after talking, wanted to start our own, alongside the regular group."

When Cade said nothing, she continued. "We found that we have some specific things in common. Things we felt comfortable discussing only with each other."

"I guess I'm not following," said Cade.

Muriel and Kendon exchanged a glance. "Well," said Muriel. "Most of the folks at the Santa Cruz group lost loved ones to natural causes. While no one's grief is any greater or lesser than anyone else's, it's sometimes difficult to relate to."

Kendon spoke up. "It's hard to identify with someone who lost a loved one to illness when you're grieving someone who died under … *other* circumstances."

"*Other* circumstances?" Cade shifted. "What do you mean?"

Silence as the two stared at him. Cade felt like a specimen under a microscope.

"Well," said Muriel. "Murder, for example." Something flickered in her melting brown eyes, something knowing and dangerous.

"Murder? But my girlfriend wasn't murdered. Not in the usual sense, anyway. And what about the lady who heads the group?" Cade had forgotten her name. "Didn't she say her daughter had been murdered? How come she's not here?"

"Sara," Muriel supplied. "And yes, her daughter *was* murdered. But there was no mystery about what happened in that case. Kendon and I are trying to understand the crimes that were committed against our loved ones. In my case, it was my sister. In Kendon's, his boyfriend."

"But I know what happened to Samantha. It was a bear attack. Like I said at the meeting."

Two sets of eyes watched Cade but neither Muriel nor Kendon spoke.

They know I'm lying, Cade thought. *They know it wasn't a bear attack.* But did they know he knew? He couldn't tell and decided it was best to give nothing away. "So, these meetings between meetings. What exactly do we do at them?"

"Well," said Muriel, "we talk. It's not so different than the Life After Loss group, except here, we're able to speculate more freely about what we think may have happened."

Kendon sipped his latte and set it aside. "We're not so sure most people would accept some of our theories."

Cade knew this was his cue to ask, *'What theories?'* but he didn't. He wasn't sure he wanted to know. This whole thing was getting too close for comfort and he had no idea how to bridge the gap between his knowledge and theirs without saying something he shouldn't.

Something about vampires.

So he remained silent, studying them, Kendon with his young, handsome face and mop of light brown hair, and Muriel with her fine-boned features and probing dark eyes.

And they watched him too, their thoughts so clear they might as well have shouted them. They were trying to read him, trying to gauge how much they could say, how far they could step.

But Cade remained poker-faced and when a pair of waiters arrived, he was grateful for the intrusion.

As they were being served, Cade caught a look between Muriel and Kendon. It seemed to say, *That's enough for now.*

Muriel thanked the waiters and tasted her dessert, moaning satisfaction.

Cade stared at his cinnamon roll, no longer hungry.

After a beat, Muriel said, "We also do grieving exercises. If you're interested, I think they might help you." She reached into her bag and unfolded sheets of paper for each of them.

Cade glanced at the itemized list. It included writing a letter to the deceased, starting a "feelings" journal in which you documented your emotions daily, and-

"That last one was the hardest for me."

Cade read the final exercise. It suggested removing the belongings of the deceased - when you felt ready, of course. Cade did not feel ready.

"Me too," agreed Kendon. "Getting rid of his things felt like ..."

"A betrayal." Muriel looked at Cade. "But when the time is right and you feel ready, it's very healing."

"Cathartic," added Kendon.

"Exactly."

Cade half-listened to their dialogue, still confused and a little shaken. He couldn't escape the feeling there was more going on here than met the eye, and he was intrigued. Despite his caution, he felt an inner stirring, a kind of internal tug drawing him to this very odd pair.

They knew something, but what?

Cade couldn't decide whether or not he wanted the answer.

AFTER KILLING THE ENGINE, CADE LINGERED IN THE DRIVEWAY, HANDS around the steering wheel, his mind still racing.

They'd spent the rest of the hour discussing healing exercises and Cade still hadn't made up his mind about Muriel and Kendon. But he was convinced they knew more than they were saying. *But what?*

He ran a hand over his face. He was tired. Very tired. If not for fear of nightmares, he'd go back to bed. Instead, he remained in the Land Rover, staring. From here, he could see Fernando, the fern he'd brought with him from Gilroy when he'd moved to Crimson Cove. After Purrcy had attacked and nearly killed it, Cade planted it outside among others of its kind. Fernando had belonged to his mother. Looking at it now, Cade remembered the joy, the sense of possibility, that he'd felt on that drive from Gilroy last year.

Last year. It seemed decades ago.

There was none of that joy now, only constant questions and the crater-sized hole in him, the searing burn of Samantha's absence.

And the persistence of his own dark thoughts, rampaging:

Brooks, who was out there somewhere, probably killing people.

Gretchen, who was no doubt biding her time, waiting for the perfect moment to strike.

The night terrors he couldn't escape, not even when he was awake.

The fact that everyone in town hated him.

And now, Kendon and Muriel ... whoever they were.

Cade felt like a marionette whose strings had been severed, and he was falling, falling, awaiting the moment when he'd crash to the ground and shatter into a thousand pieces. He wished he'd never come to Crimson Cove. He had nothing here, not even Brooks.

It won't always be like this, will it? He doubted it was true that time healed all. It seemed more likely that the damage he'd sustained was irreversible, that his mind and heart were broken for good. He couldn't conceive of a future where he was ever happy again.

He realized he was gripping the steering wheel with brute force, that his jaw was clenched so tight he could have cracked teeth, and for what must have been the thousandth time, he replayed the day of Samantha's murder, wishing he'd done it differently, silently begging God - or anyone who might be listening - for a do-over.

But God wasn't listening, obviously, and for the first time in his life, Cade considered suicide. He wondered if he had it in him to put a bullet in his skull and end it all.

He wasn't sure.

All he did know was that all of his problems had one thing in common: vampires. Fucking vampires. They weren't natural, they were freaks of nature, a biological glitch, and he wished them dead, all of them.

Thoughts of the undead brought his mind circling back to his meeting with Muriel and Kendon. What did they know? Did they know anything about vampires?

Cade was so mired in the quicksand of his own thinking that at first, he didn't hear the buzz. It started low, soft, and then rose. It was the sound of tiny, beating wings.

His blood went thick and he tried to deny the ominous noise, but when a single onyx wasp crawled out from the heating vent, Cade flushed with terror. The insect paused on the dash to rub its front legs together like a greedy banker, the smooth shell of its body glittering in the sun.

Cade didn't move, didn't even breathe. *Coincidence*, he thought. *This has nothing to do with the nightmares.* There was nothing so unusual about wasps this time of year, right?

So why was he terrified?

The wasp began washing its head - it seemed to be biding its time.

Then a second wasp crawled from the vent.

Slowly, Cade reached to unbuckle his seat belt. He didn't know how well wasps could see or if they could hear, but he moved as if on tiptoes, afraid of alerting them. As the buckle unsnapped, he watched wide-eyed as a third, and then a fourth, clambered out of the vent to join the others on the dash. One darted, startling Cade, and disappeared into the back.

Cade's hand found the door latch and just then, from beyond the grates of the heating vent, from somewhere deep within the engine, came a low growling hum - the building buzz of a thousand wings. That sound swelled like a balloon about to burst.

Panicked, Cade yanked the door latch.

But it wouldn't open.

"Fuck!"

He tugged, slamming his shoulder against the door - it wouldn't budge.

"What the-"

And then, like a toxic black cloud, a thousand wasps exploded from the vents, rushing him, clinging to him, drowning him.

Slamming himself against the door, Cade screamed, feeling thousands of legs on his skin, under his clothes, on his face, even in his eyes and nose. He was covered in a crawling black quilt of wasps; he screamed and slapped as they invaded his ears, his nostrils, his mouth, tickling, walking, humming, and buzzing.

"Fuck, fuck, *fuck*!"

And then, as a body, they laid down their stingers, and pain, like a million burning paper-cuts, pierced him.

With a gagging shriek, he hurled himself against the door.

It flew open and Cade hit the dirt outside. He clawed and slapped at himself, scuttling away from the Rover, still screaming.

But the wasps were gone.

Not only from his skin, but from the SUV.

He looked down at his arms, felt his face.

Nothing.

The searing pain of the stings had evaporated and the only sound now was the Rover's *ding, ding, ding* telling him the door was open.

He steadied himself on weak, shaking legs - *I'm losing my mind. I'm losing my goddamned mind!* - and stood there, shocked, trying to catch his breath, not daring to get close enough to the vehicle to snag the keys out of the ignition.

32

KNIT ME WITH YOUR BEST SHOT

For Sheriff Ethan Hunter, there were two ways to knit a sweater: nice and slow when relaxing after a long, hard day, or fast and furious, as he did now, to keep his mind off unsavory things. It was an hour before sundown, an hour before he'd head to Scarlet Street in search of the working girl known as Screamin' Leda, and he couldn't help feeling he was headed for trouble. His gut was a snarl of writhing snakes and the source of his fear, he supposed, would be having his worst suspicions confirmed: that Brooks Colter was responsible for the murders. *Then what?*

He paused. *Just focus on the sweater.* His fingers worked with the nimble expertise born of years of practice, but he wasn't able to give himself to the soothing repetition. Partly, he thought, because he was trying to duplicate a color scheme he'd seen at Rise and Grind's Coffee House and it just wasn't working. When Ethan made a sweater, he did it right - bright colors that jumped out, commanding the eye. But these particular shades of red, green, and blue were apparently better suited to coffee shops. Not that it mattered. Ethan had no one to give the sweater to. It would go straight into one of the boxes at the back of the closet.

He'd taken up knitting shortly after joining the police force almost twenty years ago, after seeing his first dead body. It hadn't been your run-of-the-mill peaceful-looking stiff either, but the victim of a horrendous traffic accident. The driver, who'd been drunk, had wrapped his car around a telephone pole. His body had been gutted and the steering wheel had severed his head, which Ethan had found some twenty feet away, gazing up at the heavens in betrayed disbelief. As he'd approached, he hadn't been able to escape the feeling that the severed head was staring right at him. And worse than those sightless staring eyes was the man's mouth. His tongue had been half-bitten off, lolling out from what could only be described as a raw wound filled with shattered teeth.

It wasn't until they'd towed the car and begun extricating the rest of the driver that they'd seen the kid.

No, not a kid. A baby.

The toddler had been crushed beyond all human recognition in the back seat and the sight still haunted Ethan. For weeks, he hadn't slept more than an hour or two at a time, always jerking awake in sweat-soaked sheets, grisly memories assailing him like a shower of gunshots. After a few nights of that, he'd turned to what so many others in his field did - booze. But drinking did little to blot out Ethan's horror. He needed to do something with his hands.

He'd tried a hundred things. Puzzles proved too boring, Rubik's Cubes too frustrating, painting too difficult, and journaling too involved. Then one day, in the waiting room of his doctor's office, he'd picked up a knitting magazine.

Later, he'd ordered a few books online and got busy. Knitting, it turned out, was just what he'd been looking for - the perfect balance of hand and mind coordination. It was easy, but not so easy his thoughts could wander. Once he'd gotten the hang of it, he found that it relaxed him. He'd been doing it ever since.

The only side effect was that after a couple of years, he found himself with more sweaters than he knew what to do with. Not having the heart to toss them - he was proud of his creations - Ethan had invented his Aunt Vanessa, knowing it wouldn't do for the town sheriff to be outed as having such a decidedly unmanly hobby. He'd since given many gifts in Aunt Vanessa's name and it filled him with pride when he spotted a loved one in one of "her" sweaters.

Aside from the few who'd uncovered his secret, Ethan was pretty sure no one questioned the existence of Aunt Vanessa in Oregon. In truth, Ethan didn't even know anyone in Oregon - but the fictional spinster allowed him to enjoy the fruits of his labors, and by now the little white lie came easily and he saw no reason to come clean.

He'd finally fallen into a cozy rhythm with the sweater at hand when a brusque knock at the front door made him jump. He recognized that knock - it bore the unmistakably resolute tenor of his neighbor, Mrs. Gelding. Like a man caught in an illegal act he quickly disposed of his knitting paraphernalia before getting up and peering out the peephole.

Gladiola Gelding beamed at him through the fisheye lens. Ethan groaned, forced a tolerant smile, and answered.

Mrs. Gelding didn't wait to be invited in. She pushed him aside, a tray of muffins in hand, and barged into the living room, her one-sided conversation trailing her like a loyal hound. "Can you believe this heat? And the humidity! Just this morning, I was telling Peggy - that's my niece in Milkwort Falls, you know - I was telling her, I said, 'Peggy, I don't think we've had such heat in October since I was a girl!'" Mrs. Gelding dropped the tray of muffins on the coffee table then inflicted herself upon Ethan's favorite chair. "I almost had a heat stroke in the kitchen baking those muffins for you!" Her beady eyes followed him.

"Uh, thanks." For a moment, he stood there - sitting seemed an act of surrender - but finally, defeated, Ethan eased himself onto the sofa. Mrs. Gelding was a steamroller, flattening folks into whatever shape most suited her, and Ethan didn't have the energy to fight it. He asked, "How are you, Mrs. Gelding?"

She wasted no time getting to the point. "Well, I can tell you I'd be a lot better if it weren't for all these bear attacks!"

A greasy sliding feeling oozed into Ethan's stomach.

"It's all anyone is talking about at the Senior Hall, you know." Mrs. Gelding's piggy eyes sparkled with excitement. "Well, that and your young friend's outburst at the funeral." She shook her head. "Kids these days are so disrespectful. Millimials," she said, and Ethan could only guess she meant *millennials.*

"He's been through a lot, Mrs. Gelding, and in his defense, I heard some of the ugly gossip that-"

But Mrs. Gelding was having none of that. She steamrolled on. "The point is, I've never even *heard* of a bear attacking innocent people for no good reason. Never! I *do* hope you've figured something out."

"We're working on it."

She sighed. "I suppose it's not my place to tell you how to do your job, but you might consider letting the public know what you're doing about this. We don't feel safe!"

Ethan frowned. "When there's something new, we'll announce it. In the meantime, we've made it very clear that we're doing everything we can to-" he paused. *Why am I explaining myself to her?* "We're on top of it, Mrs. Gelding." It was getting dark. He looked at his watch pointedly and said, "Mrs. Gelding, if you'll excuse me, I-"

"Well, I just don't know if that's going to be enough. I think the public *deserves* to know more."

And what she meant, Ethan knew, was that *she* wanted to know more. There was nothing Gladiola Gelding loved more than being the star of the Crimson Cove Senior Citizen Center on Bingo night, the woman to whom all gossipers flocked.

Ethan cleared his throat. "Like I said, there's nothing new to report. Now, if you'll excuse me-"

But Mrs. Gelding plowed over him with the efficacy of a squat little bulldozer, reiterating the concerns of everyone from the Senior Hall to her niece in Milkwort Falls. Resigned, Ethan tried to appear sympathetic.

Sheila's headlights cut through the living room window as Mrs. Gelding prattled on, taking no notice even as Sheila entered the living room.

As the woman blathered, Ethan and Sheila exchanged glances. His said, *Help!* And after a whimsical smile, Sheila's said, *I've got this.*

"Hello, Mrs. Gelding!" Sheila spoke a little too loudly, cutting the woman off as she perched on the sofa's arm beside Ethan.

"Oh, hello, dear." It was but a small speed bump in Mrs. Gelding's sermon and as she opened her mouth to continue, Sheila sighed loudly and looked at Ethan.

"Boy, am I glad to be home." She shook her head. "We had another groaner in the morgue tonight."

Ethan suppressed a snort.

Mrs. Gelding blinked at her. "A ... *groaner?*"

Sheila nodded. "Yep. A lot of people don't know this, Mrs. Gelding, but sometimes, dead people make noises. It's just air escaping the lungs, of course, but when you're in that darkened room alone with the corpses, it's pretty alarming." Her gaze settled on the tray of muffins. She took one, bit into it, and groaned, long and low. "Mmmm. These muffins are excellent, Mrs. Gelding. Nothing gets the stench of formaldehyde out of my nose like your muffins. Thank you." She pushed the tray toward the other woman. "You shouldn't have made so many, though. Please, have one."

All color had retreated from Mrs. Gelding's chubby cheeks. Scandalized, she shook her head. "No, thank you, dear. I have plenty at home."

Ethan was barely able to suppress laughter when Sheila continued.

"And twitching, too. Usually in the smaller muscles." She popped the rest of the muffin in her mouth. "I'll never forget the first time I saw a twitcher." Sheila grinned at Mrs. Gelding. "I thought for sure there'd been some mistake and the guy was still alive."

"Yes, well ..." said Mrs. Gelding. "It's a dreadful business, I'm sure."

"You get used to it," said Sheila. Her gaze cut to Mrs. Gelding, going grave. "Well, *some* of it, anyway. Not only do they groan and twitch, but, sometimes-"

"Well." Mrs. Gelding cleared her throat and hefted herself from the chair. "I suppose I'd better be off, but you think about what I told you, Sheriff."

Ethan got to his feet and walked her out. "Goodbye, Mrs. Gelding."

After closing the door behind her, he broke into laughter. "We need to do that more often."

"Works every time." Sheila held an uneaten part of muffin to his lips and he bit into it.

"She does make damned good muffins, though."

"She really does."

Ethan sighed. It was already dark out. "And I've got to go." He gave Sheila a quick kiss and stood.

"Go? Go where?"

He slid into his jacket and patted his pockets for his keys. "Long story short - to see a prostitute."

"Just be home in time for dinner. I'm making spaghetti."

He loved not having to explain himself to her. "I wouldn't miss it for the world." *She cooks, gets rid of nosy neighbors, and understands my job. God, I love this woman.* "Have I asked you to marry me yet?"

"You have, and I will." She smiled. "Whenever you're ready."

"We'll talk about it soon. I promise." Ethan went in for another kiss.

33

NIGHTSTRIFE

*I*n the first half-hour of darkness, Chynna stepped into the massive compound that housed her white tigers. She carried a pumpkin for each. When Hyacinthe, the blue-eyed female, caught sight of her mistress, the great cat lunged from the tall rocky platform. She loped toward Chynna, nearly knocking her over as she leapt up for hugs, wrapping her massive arms around Chynna's neck. Both pumpkins fell to the ground. "Where's your brother?" Chynna stroked the cat's great white head. In response, Hyacinthe nuzzled Chynna's neck, running her rough tongue up the side of her face.

"Yuck," said Chynna, lifting a shoulder to wipe it away. But she didn't mean it. She loved kisses from the cats.

Then Absinthe, her beautiful green-eyed male, peered out from the cozy cave beneath the lounging platform and he, too, bounded toward her, the heavy muscles under his velvety black-and-white pelt catching the moonlight and making him shimmer like satin. Bombarded by the tigers, wrapped in their giant hugs, Chynna laughed and took turns stroking them. This was her favorite part of the night.

"I've brought you pumpkins." Recognizing the word, both cats dropped down to sniff their treats. Absinthe batted at his, rolling it around like a massive ball, and chasing after it. Hyacinthe, on the other hand, crouched and began gnawing hers, holding it between her giant paws. Then Absinthe, wanting to play, pounced on his sister, earning a swat and a low growl.

"Play nice." Chynna smiled. Six years ago, when the tigers had been cubs, she'd adopted them from a run-down rescue outside of Las Vegas after her last pair had succumbed to old age. Chynna had always owned cats; in the 1920s, she'd worked as a tiger trainer for the circus and hadn't been without a pair of them since. She wished she could have a few more, but she knew that wasn't possible. There simply wasn't room. It wouldn't be fair to the tigers.

As Absinthe clawed at a tree and Hyacinthe massacred her pumpkin, Winter entered the compound, swaggering toward Chynna, his white grin and white marine-cut hair matching the t-shirt that barely confined the mounds and bulges and bundles of muscle beneath. Despite herself, Chynna flushed and her heart did a little flip-flop.

"I'm starting to think Michael's trying to set us up or something." Winter stood next to her, hands in his pockets. His eyes, a deep and exciting blue, were on the tigers. Everything about Winter was larger than life - his size, his voice, even his gaze - but now, he seemed self-conscious, a nice break from his usual cockiness.

"Set us up? What do you mean?"

Absinthe sauntered toward him, and Winter stroked the cat behind his ear. "Hey there, big fella."

It impressed Chynna that he knew which cat was male and which was female.

"He wants us both on Sire duty again tonight." The soft wind brought Winter's scent to her - woodsy, rugged, and tantalizing, and she was aware of his eyes on her. It wasn't a leer, but a healthy male appreciation of the female form.

My form. In the darkness of the compound, she reddened. "Then Sire duty it is." But she wondered if Winter was right. It seemed unnecessary for both of them to watch over Cade and if Michael really had noticed the recent flirtation between Chynna and Winter, she'd feel like an idiot. She was past the point in her life for silly romances. "I'm sure he's just being cautious."

Winter shrugged, watching as Absinthe wandered back to his tree. "Well, if he *is* trying to set us up, he's not being very subtle about it."

Chynna wished he'd drop it. "He's just worried about Gretchen. If she comes for Cade, she won't come alone."

"Who the hell knows *what* that guy's ever thinking about."

Chynna detected something in his tone. "What does that mean? Are you concerned about something?"

He shrugged. "I don't know. Michael just ... he hasn't been himself. Haven't you noticed?"

She hadn't, but then she hadn't seen him much recently. "Not really. How do you mean?"

"I don't know. He used to have that BDE, you know, and-"

"BDE? What's that?"

Winter chuckled. "Big Dick Energy. Self-confidence."

"I see."

"But lately, he seems unsteady. Uncertain. It's not like him."

Chynna knew what had happened between Michael and Natasha in Eternity and reminded Winter. "I'm sure it knocked him for a loop. For all his coolness, I don't think Michael knows how to handle real emotions."

"You're probably right."

And Michael wasn't the only one who'd changed since the trip. She'd never been self-conscious around Winter before, but now she felt more like an awkward teenager in his presence than the self-possessed woman she believed herself to be. And her reaction to Winter's ménage à trois with Natasha's younger sisters, the Darling girls, during that trip was out of character - *I was jealous, plain and simple.* She didn't like what that meant. It meant she cared.

She glanced at Winter, wondering how he felt about her. She didn't know, but she doubted he'd ever want anything more than a casual fling with anyone - that was just who he was - and Chynna wasn't interested in a fling.

They watched the tigers in silence, words seeming to hang

unspoken between them, and this, Chynna thought, probably *was* Michael's plan all along. Maybe because he couldn't be with Natasha Darling he was trying to create romance between Winter and Chynna.

If that's what was happening, she wished he'd mind his own business.

Winter cleared his throat. "We should go."

Chynna nodded. "Absinthe, Hyacinthe!" The tigers looked up. "*Ven!*" Responding to the Spanish command, the great cats loped toward her.

THE WRANGLER WAS ONE OF MANY VEHICLES HUGGING THE CURB AND, parked beneath the darkness of a burnt-out street lamp, Ethan had a perfect view of Scarlet Street. He fiddled with the radio, his eyes searching for a blonde wearing gold sandals. So far, he'd seen just about everyone but Screamin' Leda and he began wondering if maybe she'd taken the night off. Or maybe she was with a client.

Though he'd told himself he wasn't there to make arrests, it wasn't easy sitting on his hands as the local sleazeballs slinked in and out of the shadows of Crimson Cove's tiny slum, the drunkards pissing on the sides of buildings before disappearing into dark alleyways, sometimes alone, sometimes with one of the girls.

Or guys. Though he knew male prostitution wasn't at all uncommon, Ethan was always surprised by it. He watched one of the hustlers step out of the abandoned butcher shop and sit on the curb. The shorty-shorts, leather vest, and snakeskin cowboy boots distinguished him as a worker, not a client. The guy lit a smoke and hung his head, the cherry of his cigarette glowing in the night. He was young. Early to mid-twenties.

Ethan wondered what had gone so wrong that a life like this was the best alternative. The answer, he knew, often came down to drug addiction, but in a world with so much help available, he couldn't quite comprehend it. *'Some people can't be helped,'* Sheila had once told him, *'Some people don't want help.'* Ethan knew she was right - and he wondered if Mr. Shorty-Shorts was one of them.

A flash of high-beams in his rearview and the sound of thumping bass sent Ethan sinking into his seat. It was no one he recognized. He watched the glittering black Sebring roll up to the curb in front of Shorty-Shorts. The music softened as the young hustler stood, made his way to the passenger side, and bent to talk to someone. Out of sheer habit, Ethan memorized the plates. Shorty-Shorts nodded, stepped back, and turned in a slow circle - apparently offering the potential john a full view of the product.

Johns - as in plural, Ethan realized as overlapping male laughter sounded from the Sebring.

The hustler, his posture conveying weary acceptance, just stood there as the men - probably college students from Santa Cruz - laughed and hooted.

Ethan turned down his radio and strained to hear the conversation. He only made out snippets:

"... fag like you ..."

"... right up your ass ..."

"... fucking queer ..."

Someone in the back seat threw a milkshake. It exploded all over the hustler's leather vest and Ethan, a hand already poised on the door handle, swore under his breath as the Sebring disappeared in a screech of tires and jeers. He jotted down the license before he forgot it - *they'd better hope they don't have so much as an unpaid parking ticket -* then hopped out of the Wrangler and headed toward the young hustler, who was wiping ice cream off with a scrap of old newspaper.

"Rough night?"

The hustler looked up at him with the angelic face and blue eyes of a Dresden doll. Nothing in them told Ethan that the guy detected a cop in his presence.

"No more than usual." He offered a dimpled smile that the rest of his face wasn't in on. "Are you ... *looking?*"

"Not for what you're selling." Amid the reek of sweat, booze, cigarettes, and piss, Ethan was reluctant to sit down on the curb, but if he wanted to get anywhere with the guy, he needed to convey camaraderie. He sat. "But we're all looking for something, right?"

Mr. Shorty-Shorts remained standing, cautious. "I guess. But what are *you* looking for?"

"Do you know a woman named, Leda Murrow? They call her-"

"Screamin' Leda."

"That's the one."

A long silence. Then: "You a cop?"

Ethan sighed. "As a matter of fact …"

"Fuck. Look, man, I don't want any trouble, I just-"

"Take it easy. I'm not here to give anyone trouble. I just have some questions for Ms. Murrow." He glanced up at the guy. "I don't see her and was hoping maybe you could help me out."

The hustler looked like he wanted to bolt.

Ethan held up his hands. "I give you my word. No trouble." He held the young man's gaze. When the guy's shoulders relaxed, Ethan said, "I have some questions about the attacks."

"You mean the murders? What do you want to know?"

"Have you seen anything?" When the man remained silent, Ethan sighed. "Have a seat. You're making me nervous." He patted the curb beside him.

With obvious reluctance, the guy sat, and this close, Ethan realized just how young he was - if he was legal, it was barely.

"I haven't seen anything."

"Are you sure? Even something that didn't seem like a big deal at the time could be-"

"No, I mean, I haven't seen *anything*. I haven't so much as heard the guy's footsteps. Honest."

Ethan sighed. "I believe you. But Leda has. Do you know where I might find her?"

Mr. Shorty-Shorts shrugged and lit another cigarette. "Not a clue. She was beat up pretty bad. Probably took the night off."

"Do you think she'll be here tomorrow?"

"Couldn't say."

"Any idea where she lives?"

"Nope." The hustler blew out a cloud of smoke and tapped ash.

Ethan looked around for someone else who might help him but saw no one. His eyes came back to the young hustler. He was fit, clean-shaven - not the kind of guy who looked like he had a drug problem. The only thing that separated him from any other American male his age was the haunted eyes - a look of loss that made him seem older than he was. Ethan had seen that look recently. In Cade, he realized.

"Those guys in the Sebring. Does that happen often?"

Shorty-Shorts stubbed his cigarette out, half-smoked. "Gay bashers. They're common enough. Just part of the territory, I guess."

Ethan said nothing. He understood certain choices intellectually, but at an emotional level, he was at a loss. He'd learned the hard way that there wasn't much a man could say to change anyone's mind.

But there might be something he could do. "Until this guy is caught, I want you to be careful." Ethan stood, reached into his wallet, and pulled out his card. "Take this. If you ever need anything ... here's my number and email."

The hustler eyed him, then reluctantly took the card. "Thanks ..." He read the print. "Sheriff Hunter."

"Call me Ethan. And you are?"

"Danny."

"Take care of yourself, Danny."

"You too."

Ethan headed back to the Wrangler convinced of two things: his visit with Screamin' Leda wasn't going to happen tonight, and that he'd never again hear from Danny the hustler.

FROM BENEATH HIS BEDROOM DOOR, CADE HEARD THE SOUNDS OF VIDEO games and occasionally, the low voices of Winter and Chynna in the living room. He wasn't in the mood for company. He lay on his bed, a melting ice pack over his eye, Purrcy purring between his knees, thinking about the grieving exercises Muriel had suggested.

He'd try writing a letter to Samantha, he decided, but he wouldn't get rid of her things. He deserved the pain it brought to see her shoes and sweaters in the closet, her hair and makeup supplies on the dresser.

That was the part that Muriel and Kendon didn't understand, the part Cade couldn't tell them: it was his fault Samantha was dead; he may as well have killed her himself. Living in a house haunted by her possessions should be the least of his punishments.

And Brooks still haunted the place too. Everywhere Cade turned he was reminded of his brother. From the lingering smell of his aftershave to the truck and the bullet bike in the drive, to the health magazines that came in the mail, Brooks' presence was as alive as Samantha's. If anyone was a ghost in this house, it was Cade himself.

"Fucking douche-canoe!" Winter's voice from the other room made it clear he wasn't winning whatever game he was playing and Cade was tired of hearing it.

He got up and went to the dresser in search of his earbuds. After rooting around, he found them under Samantha's sweaters. He lifted one of her shirts to his face, panicking a little when he couldn't detect her scent.

Then Purrcy hopped off the bed and leapt into the open drawer, settling himself onto her folded clothes. The cat looked up and gave a questioning meow, seeming to ask, *Where did she go?*

"She's gone, buddy." Tears pricked Cade's eyes and he left Purrcy alone, returning to the bed where he grabbed his phone, searched for some violin music, and turned it up loud. He'd hoped it might soothe him the way Father Scarlotti's playing had, but it didn't. It wasn't the same somehow. He switched it to hard rock.

Tears streamed freely as guitars assaulted his ear drums.

THE SANGUINE RIVER, WHICH THE TOWN WAS FOUNDED ON IN THE GOLD rush days, ribboned through the center of Crimson Cove, dropping off some eighty-five feet where it pooled into a vast basin that shivered like black silk in the night before winding its way back to the ocean. From the cliff above the waterfall, you could park your car and view the entire town, but given that there wasn't much to look at in Crimson Cove, most people - usually horny teenagers - only went there to get drunk, smoke weed, and make out. The area was known as Scarlet Falls and here, in the basin, was where Rafe Santangelo and Brooks Colter came to bathe. Tonight, Rafe had come alone. Brooks said he'd go later.

But standing beneath the rush of water to rinse his face and hair, Rafe didn't think he would. More and more, Brooks wanted to be alone. Maybe it was the nightmares. Rafe had lost count of how many times the other man had woken him, screaming, sheathed in sweat. Sometimes, he just moaned - low, deep moans that teetered between terror and sexual ecstasy which were, to Rafe, somehow even more terrifying than the screams. But whatever he was dreaming, Brooks never talked about it.

And he had withdrawn. He'd begun taking long lonely walks, claiming he was going hunting or heading to the Falls for a bath, but Rafe couldn't help noticing that he came back from most of those hunting expeditions empty-handed and returned from his showers unwashed.

Rafe, on the other hand, did not enjoy solitude. Or rather, he did not enjoy being separated from Brooks. He felt like a clingy toddler who had to go everywhere with Daddy. He wondered if that might change if he fully transitioned, and thought it probably would. He was sure a lot of things would change - and for the better. All it would take was a little sip of human blood.

But Brooks insisted Rafe wasn't ready. Sighing, Rafe pushed all thought of transition - which now verged on obsession - out of his mind.

Squeezing body wash into his palm, he finished lathering himself, glancing up at the cliff that overlooked Crimson Cove. This late on a weeknight, it was unlikely anyone would show up, but Rafe couldn't risk being busted.

He didn't want to be identified. He had no intention of going back to his old life and hoped he'd be written off as dead and eventually, forgotten. That was part of why he wanted full transition - so there would be no turning back. Then Brooks could stop talking to him about "choices." Rafe knew he had choices - and he chose to be a vampire. A *real* one.

He wondered where Brooks was now. One of these nights, he decided as he began toweling off, he'd follow him and see where he went on his lone late-night jaunts.

"IT'S OKAY," SAID SHEILA. "IT'S BOUND TO HAPPEN FROM TIME TO TIME."

But Ethan was mortified. "Yeah, well, it's never happened to *me* before."

She was curled against him, head on his shoulder, her fingers strumming the sprinkling of hair on his chest. "Don't sweat the small stuff - and it's all small stuff."

He cringed at the word *small* and felt Sheila stiffen as she realized her gaffe.

"You know what I mean," she said.

Ethan couldn't help laughing. Sheila laughed too. It broke the tension. When the chuckling subsided, Ethan sighed. "I just hope you know that … it … it isn't you."

She raised her head and met his eyes. "I know." And as she placed a soft kiss on the corner of his lips, Ethan's heart galloped anew and he silently damned his anatomy for its insubordination.

She lay her head back down, her face soft and warm against his skin.

It wasn't that he didn't want her - he did, and badly. But he couldn't get his mind off the murders.

And Brooks Colter.

And Cade.

And the press with its growing interest in the alleged bear attacks - that damned Jojo McFerrell was showing up everywhere these days, looking for a scoop.

And, of course, Sydney.

Sheila had told him about his ex-wife's interest in Michael and that it wouldn't do for her to start snooping around. Pawning her off on Michael had been a bad idea.

Ethan felt powerless, inadequate. He was failing his friends, failing his job, failing the whole community - and there wasn't a damned thing he could do about it. As the body count rose, his self-respect dropped. He felt bottomed out. Useless. And now, even his dick wasn't working. It was the ultimate betrayal. He sighed.

"Do you want to talk about it?" Sheila's voice broke his treacherous train of thought.

He shrugged. "Talk about what?"

"All of it. You've been holding a lot in. Speak it, and it loses power."

"Is that true?"

It was her turn to shrug. "I happen to believe it."

Ethan was silent for a minute, trying to decide where to begin. At last, he said, "I just don't think Brooks is doing it. The murders, I mean."

"What makes you think that?"

"I ... don't really know. But my gut says he's not the perp."

Sheila looked up at him. "Then I'd trust that."

"I'm trying to."

"Any idea who it might be?"

Ethan sighed. "A vampire. It *has* to be a vampire. Gretchen and her goons ..."

"You don't sound convinced."

"I'm not. If Gretchen were hanging around, why haven't we seen her? She's not the type to go unnoticed." He paused. "And it won't be long before the news of the murders spreads across the country. It's juicy stuff and I can't hold it back much longer." He shuddered at the implication. "Then the real panic will start. I'll lose my job, the department will be a laughingstock. People will start digging and the whole world will think we're idiots for blaming this on a damned bear. And what if they find out the truth? That it's vampires?"

"I don't think they'll ever figure that out. I don't think they'd believe it if they did."

"But what if they do?"

"You're getting ahead of yourself, Ethan. You're losing perspective. It's barely a blip on the national radar and chances are, it'll stay that way. And as for vampires, well, in the whole history of humankind, no one has *really* believed in them yet. No one *sane*, anyway."

Ethan nodded, knowing she was right but still wishing the whole damned thing would go away. For a while, they said nothing, then Ethan broke the silence. "And then there's Cade. I don't like where he's headed. He's shifty. Unpredictable. And he looks bad. Unhealthy." He paused. "I think he might be dangerous. To himself, I mean."

"What bothers you more - that he might be dangerous or that he's in pain?"

Ethan considered, trying to untangle his feelings. "Both."

"I'm glad you got him to go to that meeting. He's planning to attend more, right?"

"He has. He texted me earlier that he met up with a couple of the group members for coffee today. Of course, I don't know how much it can help if he's only doing it because he thinks he *has* to. I've made it pretty clear he doesn't have much choice."

"Of course it's better if he *wants* to go, if his mind is open, but you know, just getting exposed to it will help. Something someone says will resonate with him eventually. Maybe it already has."

Ethan nodded, hoping she was right.

"Would it make you feel better if I checked up on him occasionally too?"

"Not really." As it was, Ethan was calling, texting, or stopping by several times a day.

"I will, anyway. Couldn't hurt."

"Thanks."

For a long moment, neither spoke. Then Sheila snuggled closer, her naked warmth and silky skin sparking unexpected life into Ethan's treasonous body.

"Anything else you want to talk about, Sheriff?" Her breath, like warm, silky fingertips, trailed across his bare chest, sealing the deal.

Ethan swallowed hard, his heart picking up speed. "I think there's been enough talking for one night."

She kissed him. "I think so, too."

By now, Scythe had lost count of how many recruits they'd acquired and he was beginning to wonder if they were ever going to stop. The cavern was a tangle of gaunt bodies and sallow faces, all watching Gretchen with adoration. *Like the good little junkies they are.* Scythe smiled to himself; they were all under *her* venom now. He watched them sitting there, awaiting their next fix, glad he was finally free of them.

When given regularly, vampire venom wreaked havoc on the human body, forming a dependence so powerful that it could only be likened to heroin addiction. The body began to slowly rot as more and more venom was needed, and over time, when the addiction was too strong to sustain, the addict was either given a large enough dose for full transition, or was cut off and left to die of venom withdrawal.

The slaves weren't that far gone yet; they were still feeling pretty good and looking upon Gretchen as a demigod, their Almighty Dealer.

And Scythe didn't know how she could stand it. Or at least, that's what he told himself. In truth, he kind of missed being the center of attention. He was invisible to them now, but that wasn't important.

The important thing was that the blood slaves were doing their jobs. Lately, Scythe, Jazminka, and Gretchen had been able to gorge themselves on hot, coppery sustenance, relishing it, practically bathing in it - and nothing beat feeding straight from the tap.

There were times Scythe had drunk so much he thought he might puke - but the moment the nausea passed, he moved onto the next supplicant and kept drinking. The free-flowing blood had given Scythe new life - he felt stronger, healthier, and more alive than he had since he and Jazminka had first disappeared into the woods. The downside, of course, was that his sex-drive was sky-high, and with nowhere to put his erotic energy but into his own hand, Scythe was getting irritable.

DeHavalyn, the smoking-hot stripper, remained under Jazminka's constant watch and Gretchen still showed no signs of wanting to fuck.

But she was definitely on the mend.

Her hair had regained its satiny luster, her skin its marble-smooth sheen, and her eyes their emerald clarity. Even her tits, confined to the now-repaired red corset, seemed to have perked back up. Gretchen was, according to Scythe's calculations, just days away from full recovery. The only remaining evidence of fragility was a lingering exhaustion that settled in after feeding, at which point she fell immediately asleep. But after each short nap, she woke a little stronger - and ready for more blood.

Less than a week, Scythe told himself, *and we'll be back in the Crimson Corset, for sure.*

Now, he'd settled into a cramped corner and laid out his new deck of cards. As he began a game of solitaire, he looked up at Gretchen. She sat against the far wall, surrounded by a clutch of adoring slaves, looking back at him. A man lay beside her, his head in her lap, and she began stroking his dark hair, her fingers suggesting lewd things.

In Scythe's fraying, acid-washed jeans, Vlad the Impaler immediately began to swell and thicken. Gretchen's gaze traveled down, settling on his burgeoning excitement. She touched her tongue - pink at last, instead of leathery gray - to her freshly painted crimson lips.

She looked back to his face, and her eyes said to him, *'Soon. Very soon.'*

Scythe couldn't wait.

34

THE WOMAN IN BLACK

Todd Hawkins and Jimmy Langdon, both thirteen years old, were official runaways now. They'd hitched a ride in the back of a truck and, not wanting to be spotted, had hopped out when the driver stopped for gas. They ran into the night and were currently approaching the outskirts of Santa Fe, nearly forty miles from their foster home in Chimayó. They each carried a backpack containing only what was necessary: clothes, food, what little money they were able to get their hands on, and a couple of flashlights and pocket knives.

"But what if someone sees us and turns us in," Jimmy said, "and we end up back at Josh and Tina's. Josh will *kill* us!"

Santa Fe had tons of people, Todd reminded Jimmy, who'd been worrying since they left. He played it cool, talking like it was no big thing, but deep down, he was worried, too. Jimmy had never run away from a foster home before, but Todd had, and it was up to him to take the lead. "No one's going to even *notice* us in a city as big as Santa Fe," Todd said.

But Jimmy was right. If they were seen and picked up, they'd end up back in Chimayó - and no way was he *ever* going back to Josh and Tina's. The alcoholic couple had only taken the boys in for the money the state gave them, and after the last beating - all because Todd left his sneakers on the floor of his *own* bedroom - Todd had had enough. He'd waited until the couple passed out, then he'd woken Jimmy, and they'd left. Though only a couple of months younger than Todd, Jimmy had become something of a little brother to him - he couldn't leave him behind.

The moon was high, bright, and bone-white, lighting their way as they walked south along the quiet road, keeping an eye out for someplace to crash. It was late, they were tired, and the city was still miles away, so first thing tomorrow morning, they'd start walking again and make it to Santa Fe long before evening. What they'd do when they got there, Todd wasn't sure. He hadn't worked that part out yet. They'd be homeless for a while, sure, but eventually they'd figure something out. Anything was better than the foster system. If Todd had learned anything in his short life, it's that there were a *lot* of Josh and Tinas out there, all disguised as angels who wanted to "help the children," and there were things far worse than being homeless. *At least I look older than I am*, he thought. *I could get a job someplace maybe.* Or, if that didn't work, he and Jimmy could make little trinkets and sell them. He'd seen lots of pictures on the internet of people doing that in Santa Fe.

"Hey, Todd, look."

Todd followed Jimmy's finger toward a lone casita in the distance. It stood against the sky, painted white by the moon, with not a single light burning inside; the place looked deserted and for a moment, Todd was transfixed. It seemed a sign right from heaven.

Or Hell. Todd clipped off that random thought. No, this was the right place. He wasn't sure how he knew, but he *felt* it. This was where they needed to go.

"Should we-"

"Yeah, come on."

They started toward it and as they neared, the little house looked more and more abandoned. And creepy. *Of course it's empty. Who the heck would live all the way out here?* Todd was so excited he suddenly had to pee. No one would ever find them here. They could walk to the city for what they needed and stay right here, just like in that old movie *The Outsiders* that Tina was always watching, when Ponyboy and Johnny killed someone and had to hide out in an old church. But this was even better than a church! The boys ran toward it.

When they came to the broken flagstone walk leading to the front door, Todd suddenly stopped, putting an arm out and bringing Jimmy to a halt beside him.

"What is it?" Jimmy whispered. "What's wrong? Do you think someone's in there?"

Todd shook his head. "No, I don't think so. It's just ..." He didn't know. There was something about the casita, a *vibe* or something, that rooted him in place. He had the sudden irrational sense that something had brought them here - something dark and dangerous.

But that was nonsense. It was obvious the place was empty and this was just the lucky break they needed. It was perfect! Todd shook off the strange unease. He was just nervous because he was afraid of being caught and sent back to Josh and Tina. *Right?*

He wasn't so sure.

And he also couldn't be a *hundred* percent sure no one was living here.

Slowly, he approached a window and looked inside, cupping his hands around the dirty, cracked glass, adjusting his eyes to the moonless dark within.

Nothing but dust and cobwebs and an old chair that probably hadn't been sat in for a hundred years.

Jimmy, looking in a different window, said, "It's empty, Todd. For sure empty."

Todd knew it, too, so why was he suddenly chickening out? He stepped away from the glass and made a deal with himself: If the front door was open, they'd go in and stay. If it wasn't, he'd take that as a sign and they'd keep walking until they found someplace else. He half-hoped it would be locked as he stepped onto the porch and put his hand on the knob.

It turned easily.

The door yawned open and once more, Todd found himself unable to move. *It wants us to come inside - that's* exactly *what it wants. It's what* she *wants.*

She? She who? The unbidden thought made no sense; Todd didn't even know who "she" was, let alone why "she" would want them to come inside.

"Todd?" And when Jimmy sidled up next to him, clinging to his arm, and said in a little boy's voice, "I'm s-scared," Todd found his resolve.

"You're always scared. Come on." He hiked his pack higher on his back and they stepped inside.

More cracked flagstone on the floors. Some rotted wooden pillars. The creepy old chair. Dust everywhere - the smell of it thick and cloying, and just under that, the faint odor of something long dead. *Rats.* Todd knew what dead rats smelled like and was sure that's what he smelled now.

"Todd? I don't like it here. I think-"

"Shh." Until they searched every room they couldn't be positive they were alone, and Todd shrugged off his backpack and found his flashlight, glad he'd packed it. Flashlights, he'd learned from his previous escapes, were necessities. Of course, they'd also been the reason he'd been caught hiding out in a barn two foster homes back.

But this time was different. He wasn't going back to Josh and Tina's. He wasn't going to be caught and he wasn't going back into the system. Not this time and not ever again. He didn't know how he knew it, but since coming across the old casita, he'd never been so sure of anything in his life.

With Jimmy's hand plastered like a leech onto his arm, Todd played the beam across the dust-covered room, lighting on an old fireplace, and then beyond that, other rooms. Bedrooms, two of them, he realized as they made their way through the tiny house. And both empty of everything except one very old dresser with nothing in it. They moved toward a closet door. It creaked as he opened it and Jimmy gasped and stiffened as a very large rat scurried past them. That explained why the death-smell was so much stronger in here -

there must have been a dozen dead rats rotting somewhere in this room.

Todd played the beam in the closet.

Suitcases. Nothing but suitcases, stacked on shelves. And without knowing how he knew it, Todd knew they were full of old clothes.

Her clothes.

The unexpected thought made him shiver. *Knock it off,* he told himself.

Nothing hung on the racks and there was no sign of anyone living here at all, so Todd didn't know why he should think the suitcases were full of clothes - specifically, old, black, moth-bitten *women's* clothes. His imagination was running away with him - it did that sometimes, but just to be safe, Todd made yet another deal with himself: He would pull down a suitcase and check inside and if there was anything in it but old black clothes, anything at all, it was a good sign and they could stay. And if it *was* old black clothes, well ... well, he'd think about that later.

And then, he promised himself, as soon as he was done, he'd find the bathroom; he needed to take a leak so bad his eyeballs were swimming in it.

As he reached up for a suitcase on the shelf, Jimmy's hands dug into his free arm. "Todd? Todd? Oh crap, Todd! Oh crap, oh crap, *ohcrapohcrapohcrap!*"

"Will you *stop*? What are you-" Todd whirled around, the beam of his flashlight slicing the air - and landing on a staring white face.

She stood, her strange blue eyes empty and unblinking, in a long black dress, watching them from the doorway.

Panic! "Oh," said Todd. "We thought ...I'm sorry ... we ..."

The woman in black reached up and pulled a long silver hat pin from her veiled black hat and with a lizardy movement, ran the sharp tip of it across her glistening tongue.

"Oh, God!" Jimmy pulled Todd into a desperate crushing embrace as the woman glided - not walked, but *glided* - toward them, the pointed toes of her stove-black shoes barely touching the floor as she drifted closer, her eyes wide and unblinking.

Jimmy was screaming now but Todd was silent and transfixed, his mind alive with images so real they might have been his own memories: The woman in black pricking him and Jimmy with her hat pin, making them bleed, making them hurt. Torturing them.

But these weren't memories - they were pictures of things to come, and in the same way that he knew her intentions, he knew *why*, too: *She wants our pain, our fear. That's how she feeds herself, and when she's drained us dry, she's going to kill us.*

Todd's aching bladder emptied itself and, at last, he screamed.

35

DEAD PERVERTS SOCIETY

The next morning started off with a bang, and not the good kind.

Word had spread fast and by the time Ethan arrived at the latest murder scene, locals were swarming the dead man like ants on a Jolly Rancher. At first, no one recognized the corpse, which wasn't surprising, since the face had been smashed to pulp, jelly, and bone shards. Only when a police photographer moved in for a close-up of the teeth did they learn that the victim's eyes had been torn from their sockets as well.

The victim. Somehow, Ethan didn't think the term applied to this man. His body had been discovered early this morning by a Mrs. Shelly Stratton in the bushes outside the bedroom window of her eight-year-old daughter. The corpse had a pair of binoculars strung around his neck and his pants were at half-mast, making it pretty clear what he'd been up to at the time of death.

There was nothing *victim* about it, and were it not for the fact that the rib cage had been broken open and the heart bitten into like the others, Ethan would have been glad to see him dead.

But as it was, he had another vampire murder on his hands, and if that wasn't enough to get the gastric acid burning a hole in his stomach, Jojo McFerrell arrived in his lime-green Volkswagen Bug and started asking hard questions. Before the tight-cheeked little reporter could get any details, Ethan ordered everyone but law enforcement away, and within an hour of gathering the dead guy's garland of intestines from the Stratton family's bushes - the eyes hadn't been found - and hauling the corpse to the morgue, Sheila called with a positive ID. Easy enough, given the vic was not only a convicted felon, but a Valley State Prison escapee, wanted by California for the very crimes that he'd been committing at the time of his death.

Popping a Tums, Ethan now sat at his desk in the sheriff's office, poring over the case, trying to see something he might have missed, something that might give him a clue to the killer's identity. The fact that the dead pervert's eyes were missing confirmed Ethan's suspicions that the perp was some sort of justice warrior - so far, he'd only killed drug-dealers, woman-beaters, and other lowlifes - but this, the missing eyes, sealed the deal. The victim was a peeping Tom so the killer had taken his sight - you didn't have to be a criminal profiler to see the symbolism.

But it bothered Ethan. Bothered him because it didn't sound like Brooks and it sure as hell didn't sound like Gretchen. It sounded like someone out of control, a baby vampire perhaps. Except that baby vamps lacked venom control and whoever was doing this was obviously controlled - otherwise at least one of the victims would've been accidentally turned. But the killer wasn't envenomating his prey, just mutilating them and draining their hearts which told Ethan that these crimes were about blood first, but they were also about vengeance.

He was tired of thinking about it, tired of reading over the reports. Until he talked to someone who knew more than he did - namely, Screamin' Leda - he had no other leads. Tonight, he planned another trip to Scarlet Street. A simple background check had given him Leda Murrow's address, but when he'd stopped by earlier, there'd been no answer. *Probably better to meet her on the street, anyway.* People tended to clam up when cops showed up on their doorsteps. And at this point, her silence wasn't an option. Ethan needed to know who this guy was, and he needed to know now.

He looked at his watch, willing the night to fall.

CADE WAS AT WORK WHEN HE GOT A CALL FROM MURIEL. HE ALMOST didn't answer but his curiosity won out.

"I just heard about the latest, uh, bear attack," she said, "and wanted to check in on you."

The murder. Of course that's why she'd called. Cade wished he hadn't answered. "I'm fine," he said. "Why wouldn't I be?"

A long, awkward silence. "We just want you to know that if you need to talk-"

"I know. I appreciate it. Thanks. Look, I'm at work and I really can't talk now."

"Oh, of course." Muriel cleared her throat. "I hope to see you at the next meeting."

"I'll be there." And he meant it. Whatever it was that Muriel and Kendon knew - or thought they knew - Cade wasn't about to confirm it for them by hiding.

He ended the call and sighed. A part of him wished the woman would just come right out and say whatever it was she obviously wanted to say - but another part of him hoped she never would. Mostly, he just hoped she'd go away.

THAT NIGHT, IN HIS OFFICE AT EUDEMONIA, MICHAEL WARD SAT AT HIS desk and though his eyes were on the computer screen, he wasn't seeing the monthly reports in front of him. Another call from Natasha Darling had come tonight. He'd ignored this one, too, and that only seemed to make her more determined to contact him. His desk phone blinked red, indicating she'd left a message, but he didn't want to listen to it, didn't want to hear her saying she was worried about him ... didn't want to hear her smooth, sexy, velvety voice...

He felt like a cad. Natasha was his oldest friend, and she'd been good to him. *Too good.* That was the problem. And *friend* had never been quite the right term to describe their relationship. There was more than friendship between Michael and Natasha. Much more.

With her, Michael could not control himself. Even after all these years of moderation and meditation, Michael had no self-control when it came to the woman - as evidenced by their brief affair in Eternity only weeks ago. A few days in her presence and his vow of celibacy had been easily broken. Michael was ashamed - and worse, he was angry. He'd known better than to toy with fire. And though she was a fine and upstanding woman, Natasha Darling was, to Michael, just that: fire.

They'd first met in New York in November of 1783, the day General Washington led the Continental army into Manhattan. It had been a great celebration, the streets filled with revelers, human and vampire alike, all drunk on wine or alcohol-laced blood. It was a night of excess and debauchery.

His affair with Natasha had been a dangerous one. Dangerous, because Michael hadn't then realized he was an addict and that one indulgence, like the first fallen domino, would lead to another and another, ultimately bringing down his carefully structured self-control. After that first affair with Natasha - and the havoc it entailed - he'd taken a vow of celibacy, taken up meditation, and moved to Crimson Cove where the earth was laden with calming elements and ores. Here, he could lead a peaceful existence, a *normal* life. And for many, many years, he'd done just that.

And then he'd gone to Eternity with Natasha Darling, and everything Michael had come to believe about himself had proven to be no more than foolish illusions built on decades of self-deception.

Even now, despite his shame and self-loathing, he was thinking of her in those dangerous ways - the glass-smooth texture of her bare skin, the soft scent of her hair, the feel of her lips and breath against his neck, his chest, his abdomen ... and lower. His mouth watered and a low, steady growl sounded from deep in his chest.

A hard rap on his office door startled him. He checked the camera monitor. Sydney Hunter-Doss, in far too little clothing for Michael's comfort, stood on the other side, beaming up at the camera, another plate of cookies in hand. He was going to have to have a talk with the receptionist about letting the woman through. Michael's fingers hovered over the buzzer as he debated allowing her entrance.

SYDNEY KNEW SHE WASN'T BEHAVING LIKE A WOMAN STRONG IN CHRIST as she stood at Michael's office door in nothing but heels, tiny pink hot pants, and a white stretch crop top that barely contained her feminine endowments, but she didn't care. If the Lord hadn't wanted her to take advantage of her female charms He wouldn't have made her so darned cute!

The door unlocked and Sydney vowed that this time, she would not stutter, sweat, or otherwise make a fool of herself. That promise was broken the moment she stepped inside.

"Ms. Doss." Michael's voice, so like a narcotic, hit her bloodstream and Sydney's knees immediately turned to rubber. He wore a black vest over a deep red shirt that accentuated his thinness. And Michael was very thin, almost gaunt, but not at all unattractive. He was a handsome slash of pure man, *real* man, who seemed too long and tall and sharp for this small office. "Please, sit. I trust you've been well?"

Before her legs could betray her, she took a seat across from him. "I ... yes. I have been. And you?" She smiled, sliding the plate of cookies toward him, then tugged at her blouse. She couldn't seem to sit still.

"Busy." He eyed the treats, his sensuous mouth curving up at one corner - and there was that satanically handsome smile she fantasized about. "I'll need new pants if you keep this up."

"Wha- what?" It took Sydney a moment to realize he was referring to his waistline rather than an ejaculatory accident brought on by her scanty outfit. Despite her vow, she began to sweat. "Oh," she squeaked, then giggled nervously. "Of course."

His black-lashed amber eyes were on her, invading her in a delicious new way, mining her, that ghost of a smile still haunting the edges of his lips.

"P-please, have one." She pushed the cookies closer. It was strange, she thought, how he frightened and attracted her in equal measure. Strange ... and exciting. She chewed her lip, aroused and unnerved, and continued to fidget.

"Perhaps later. I have a great weakness for sweets and I'm afraid if I start, I won't be able to stop." Even his eyebrows - fiendishly arched and devil-black - were handsome. Now, he cocked one at her sly-like, pumping heat into her groin. "And you wouldn't want me to make an animal of myself, would you?"

God, yes! Please! Sydney wanted this man and she wanted him bad; she was pretty sure he wanted her, too; the signals were undeniable. But she was unsettled by his sudden interest. She couldn't figure it out. She'd tried everything known to womankind to get his attention - lipstick, heels, boots, butt-hugging shorts, skirts, a bust-enhancing bra, no bra at all - and nothing had worked. Until now. Now, for some reason, he saw her, *really* saw her, and it was both terrifying and exhilarating.

From nowhere, Sydney gave a hyena-like giggle, this one punctuated at both ends by piggish snorts. She promptly clipped it off and wished herself dead.

But Michael seemed not to notice. He was still looking at her, his face unreadable.

Then something flashed in his eyes and suddenly Sydney felt herself lock up, go still, play dead. She wasn't sure she was breathing. *What's happening to me?* She couldn't even slide her gaze away from his. She'd been a jittering, stuttering mess since coming - patting her hair here, tapping her foot there, giggling, wriggling, and sweating - but now she stopped as abruptly as a period at the end of a run-on sentence.

Michael was motionless, too, except for his eyes. Those were moving. They slid from her face to her throat, settling there a moment before traveling the expanse of her breasts, her bare arms and her hands, then moving back up, slowly, very slowly.

She felt the heat of that gaze where it touched her skin and she wanted to squirm under his hot hungry scrutiny - but still, she could not move. She didn't know what was happening, but if this wasn't a bona fide state of paralysis, it was a close cousin. *Oh my God, a stroke! I'm having a stro-*

Michael smiled then, stopping her thoughts with a slow wolfish leer that was both eerie and erotic. The blend was exquisite.

Too exquisite.

With effort, Sydney was finally able to swallow. She heard the click of her dry throat as a hot flush crept up from the pit of her belly, hardening her nipples. Then, with both ecstasy and horror, she recognized the yummy little buzz in her nether regions that signified a burgeoning climax. *Oh my God!*

Michael's eyes remained on hers, and in them was a teasy roguish knowing; he knew what he was doing to her ... and somehow, he was doing it on purpose.

Sydney's leg muscles tightened and her hands dug into the chair arm as the bliss broke out like a delicious shivery rash all over her body. Her eyes never left his as her breath hitched and, with little more than a stiffening of the spine, a shudder of breath, and a rapid-fire flutter of lashes, Sydney peaked, reaching orgasm right there in the office with no stimulus but Michael Ward's piercing amber eyes.

The ecstasy ebbed as quickly as it had flowed, leaving behind a buzz in her lips and heat in her cheeks, and then, finally, Michael blinked, breaking the stare.

And just like that, the moment was over. Sydney was freed from that strange, erotic paralysis. She lurched and sucked in air, seeing stars.

Unbelievably, Michael took no notice of her strange attack of passion. He was suddenly back to business, all starch and sophistication. He cleared his throat, turned his attention to his computer screen. "I appreciate the cookies," he said without a hint of distraction, "and I do hope your stay with us is satisfactory. Please let us know if there's anything else we can do for you." It was as if nothing had happened, nothing at all.

"Wha ... what?" Sydney was stunned, reeling. *Did I imagine the whole thing?* But she knew she hadn't.

Michael repeated himself and were it not for the slight flush of his cheeks, the subtle flare of his nostrils, and the barely-there flicker of fire in his eyes, she might have believed she'd dreamed the whole thing.

"Is there anything else I can do for you, Ms. Doss?" His smile was perfectly polite, all business.

Sydney was gobsmacked. "N-no. Thank you."

A sexual charge still hung in the air, saturating the room as powerfully as the scent of coming rain, but if Michael felt it too, he didn't show it. "Then if you'll excuse me," he said, "I really should get back to work."

It took her a moment to find herself. "Oh, yes ... of-of course." *Get it together*! And then she realized she was wet, wet enough to show. She felt a jolt of panic but stood, knees pressed tightly together, and on shaking, boneless legs, somehow made her way to the door.

"I'll be sure your plate is returned." Michael's eyes never left his computer screen. "Thank you again, Ms. Doss." That voice, like satin draped on steel, sparked a confusion of emotions in her.

"At ... at your leisure, M-Mr. Ward." And, as if yanked crudely from a dream, she left the office and drifted through the halls of Eudemonia, trying to grasp what had just happened.

By the time she found her way outside, her shock and confusion had abated enough to make room for a growing intrigue, a deepening greed for more of whatever Michael Ward had just served her. *If he can do* that *with his eyes, what can he do with those strong, long-fingered hands? And those beautiful, sensitive lips?*

As she shakily mounted her front steps and slipped her key in with a quaking hand and an addled mind, she was more determined than ever to find out.

36

EPIPHANIES

That evening, Ethan parked beneath the same burnt-out lamp, leaned back in the driver's seat, and sighed. It was a slow night on Scarlet Street and as the minutes ticked by, he grew more and more convinced that Screamin' Leda had taken another night off.

Just when he was about to take a spin around the block to wake himself up, he caught sight of a blonde. She stepped out of the old butcher shop and headed his way. Gold sandals. It had to be her.

As she neared, her eyes locked right on him.

She appeared at his window, all five feet two inches of her, slender of build and pretty of face, despite the bruises at her temples and the slightly swollen lip. "I hear you've been looking for me." Her voice was soft, but her eyes were hard.

"I have," said Ethan.

She side-eyed him. "I'm not sure I can help you."

Ethan was in no mood for games, so he jumped right in. "The man who killed your client. What did he look like?"

She sighed. "He was big."

"Big?"

Leda nodded. "Tall." She held her hand up to demonstrate.

"Was he a white guy? Black? Asian maybe?"

"Couldn't say." She averted her gaze. She was lying.

"Any distinguishing marks? Moles, tattoos, scars?"

"I couldn't tell you that either."

Ethan regarded her a moment. "I find it very hard to believe, Ms. Murrow, that you didn't notice anything more than his size given how up close and personal he was."

She shrugged. "Believe what you want." She leaned into his window and her flowery perfume momentarily masked the cloud of urine and booze that hung over Scarlet Street.

Ethan saw the track-marks in the crook of her elbows.

"If I'd seen his face," she said, "I'd tell you." Another shift of the eyes, another lie. "And like I said, he was big. Tall. Broad shoulders-"

"And let me guess, short or slicked-back hair of indeterminate color," Ethan finished, reciting the vague description he'd already gotten from Rachel Jones.

Leda smiled sardonically. "That's the one."

"I hope you're taking this seriously, Ms. Murrow. The man who attacked your client is a murderer. I can't help you unless you help me."

Leda laughed. "Help *me*? Since when has the law given two squirts about anyone like me?"

"Believe it or not, Ms. Murrow, I *am* trying to help you. Until we find this guy, you and your friends are in serious danger. I'd like to protect you, but I can't do that unless you give me more to go on." He watched as she fingered a small silver locket that hung around her neck. "You know what I think?"

"What do you think, Sheriff?"

"I think you're protecting this guy."

"And why would I do that?"

"Because he saved you - or that's how you see it, anyway. I think you don't mind having a killer around so long as he doesn't bother *you* any, and that, Ms. Murrow, is foolish."

She shrugged. "Maybe you're right. Maybe I don't want him to get caught. Or maybe I'm telling you the truth. Maybe I didn't see his face.

Maybe there's nothing else to say about it. Now unless you're here to arrest me, I have to get to work." Her eyes narrowed. "*Are* you here to arrest me?"

Ethan considered. Maybe a night behind bars would loosen her lips - God knew there was plenty to charge her with. "Well, we can do it the easy way or the hard way. The choice is yours."

Uncertainty flickered in her eyes. "Why don't you cut to the chase, Sheriff?"

"All right. You either tell me everything you know about the man who committed these crimes, or I *will* book you for solicitation."

"Good luck proving-"

"And possession."

Leda stared at him.

"I don't think the needles I'd find in your purse are for insulin, Ms. Murrow." He smiled. "Don't look so surprised. You don't think I'd come here without having done my homework, do you?"

Leda's ruby lips tightened. "What kind of blackmailer would you be if you hadn't?"

"Indeed. So, to get to the point of our visit tonight, you can either start talking and I can continue looking the other way, or you can keep it up and find out what it's like to deal with a sheriff who isn't such a sweet and charming guy." He flashed her a winning grin.

Leda sighed, resigned. "Fine. What do you want to know?"

Ethan leaned over and opened the door. "All of it. And don't leave out a thing."

She climbed in the Wrangler. "It's true that I don't know who the guy is. I'd never seen him before ... until that night."

"All right. Go on." Ethan reached into the glove box for a pad and pen. "Age, height, eye and hair color, defining characteristics, anything you can remember." He poised his pen, ready to start writing.

But as Leda launched into a description of the murderer, his hand froze and his throat went dry and grainy. The hair stood up on his arms and the back of his neck. He recognized, very distinctly, the man she described.

It couldn't be, could it?

But it was - Ethan had no doubt.

Not bothering to write anything down, he listened, tossed back and forth between shocked disbelief and abject horror as the puzzle pieces came together, fitting perfectly and terribly to paint a macabre and astonishing picture.

When Leda was finished, he said, "Thank you, Ms. Murrow. You're free to go."

She got out and disappeared into the night, but Ethan sat there, dazed, thinking, trying to figure out his next move.

There was only one person who might - one person he could speak to about this.

Ethan started the engine.

THANKS TO THE SPRINKLING OF RAIN THAT WOULD MASK HIS SCENT, Rafe Santangelo followed Brooks Colter through the woods without fear of detection, keeping behind him, staying close to the trees. And as he'd expected, Brooks was not headed to Scarlet Falls as he'd claimed. He'd gone in the opposite direction, sometimes running, sometimes pausing just long enough to pick a forest creature off and feed, but always heading toward town, always with that same determination.

Rafe had lost all track of time; it seemed he'd been shadowing the other man for hours. But he wasn't tired - that was part of his new condition. He could go all night if he had to - he imagined how it would be even better when he became a full vampire. But the guilt of what he was doing was sharp. Following Brooks was dishonorable, an invasion of his privacy, and Rafe felt shitty about it.

Not shitty enough to turn around though. Rafe was being driven by more than curiosity. He was being driven by worry, by fear, and as determined as Brooks Colter was to get wherever he was going, Rafe Santangelo was just as determined to find out where that might be.

SYDNEY HUNTER-DOSS, WHO HAD A SECRET PENCHANT FOR THE EROTIC fiction of Sylvia Day, sat curled up on the couch beneath the battery-operated lamp, book in hand, ignoring the glowering gaze of the Savior who surely did not approve of her literary pleasures.

Twice, Sydney had gone back to Eudemonia with another trumped-up excuse to see the elusive Michael Ward - this time, she intended to lure him into *her* territory by claiming she needed his help moving the dresser - but both times, she'd come away with nothing. He was busy, the desk girl said, and wouldn't be available until later. How much later, she didn't know - business and all that.

So, discouraged but refusing to sulk, Sydney had made do with an evening alone. It was a cozy end to a pretty good day, but she couldn't quit thinking of Michael. She was obsessed by thoughts of the man, and tomorrow, she planned to buy a new outfit and get her hair done at a cute little corner shop on Main called *The Hair Affair.*

There was no question that she would remain in Crimson Cove. Not only was Michael here, but the town had grown since she'd been away and was more interesting now.

And returning to her hometown felt like a new beginning. She was on friendly terms with her ex-husband and his fiancée and that made life a lot easier. Eventually, she knew some jackass would dredge up ancient history - no doubt there were plenty of locals who were just *scandalized* that she'd have the nerve to return to Crimson Cove after what she'd put Ethan through - but Sydney didn't care. It was her life and she meant to live it *her* way.

She smiled and continued reading about the kinky adventures of Sylvia Day's latest heroine - and engrossed as she was in the story, she didn't at first register the long shadow that crossed the room. It paused a moment then shifted away just as Sydney looked up.

Curious, she set down the book and moved to the glass. Pushing aside her pink curtains, she stared out and caught a glimpse of a figure darting between the trees - there and gone.

Sydney went back to the couch and tried to shake it off, but she couldn't escape the impression of a face pressed against the glass, of someone watching her, probably some pervert who was staying in a nearby cabin. It unnerved her. Tightening the belt of her new pink robe, she slipped on shoes, and grabbed her phone. She stepped onto the porch, into the hazy rain, and searched the shadows.

For a long moment, there was nothing.

And then, between trees some thirty yards away, she spied movement.

"All right, Gilroy, enough of the silent treatment. Say what you gotta say." Winter stretched his arm across the back of the sofa and propped his size fourteen jackboots on the ottoman, blocking Cade's view of the television.

Cade knew he should have stayed in his room tonight. "I don't know what you're talking about."

"Don't play dumb with me. You've been doing everything you can to avoid me and we both know why."

"If you know why, then why are you asking me?"

"Because obviously, you need to say it. Clear the air, get it off your chest. Kick me in the nuts if you need to. I think I'd respect you more if you did. This passive-aggressive bullshit is getting old."

Cade's anger flared. "*Respect* me? You think I give a shit if you respect me?"

Winter shrugged.

"Okay, fine, you want to hear it?"

"Yep." Winter sat forward. "Give me your worst. Clear the air. Say what you need to say."

"Okay, to begin with, you're a fucking asshole."

Winter's eyes didn't waver. A jaw muscle bulged. "I guess that's as good a place to start as any. Go on."

"You could have brought Samantha back but you wouldn't do it." Tears hovered in Cade's eyes - not tears of pain, though, tears of rage. "You wouldn't do it and I hate you for it."

"Is that it?"

"No. It isn't. You let her be buried while Brooks runs around a free man. How many people has Gretchen killed? And you guys let *her* live! But Samantha ... you wouldn't even-"

"Look, Gilroy, you don't un-"

"I know - I don't fucking understand. You've told me a thousand times, but you won't tell me *what* I don't understand." Cade's voice shook. "And I'll never forgive you for it. Never. I hate you."

Something came into Winter's ice-blue eyes. Regret maybe.

"Is that what you want to hear, Winter? Do you feel better knowing that I fucking hate you - that I'll always fucking hate you - or should we just go back to ignoring each other again?"

"Jesus." Winter blew out a breath. "I think I'd have preferred you just kicked me in the balls."

Brooks stood in the shadow of an ancient redwood, watching the cabin he used to share with his younger brother. Lights burned, and Winter's Hummer stood in the drive like a great white sentry. This wasn't Brooks' first trip to his former home but he had yet to catch sight of Cade - he hadn't worked up the nerve to get any closer than he was now - but tonight was the night. He needed to see him, needed to know he was okay.

He slipped through the shadows, heading closer, crouching low, his heart pounding. A soft warm rain misted the night and above the scents of trees and damp earth, Brooks caught the familiar smell of a fire burning within the cabin. He moved as close as he dared; he didn't want Winter to catch his scent. The rain would hopefully mask his odor from the vampire within. Tamping down his anxiety, he came to the cabin's side window on silent feet.

He stepped into the flower beds, his shoes mired in mud, and rose on tiptoes to stare between a crack in the drapes. He was surprised by the state of the living room. It was filthy. Books and magazines were strewn across the floor, and even from here he saw the layer of dust that coated the furniture. Purrcy lay curled on the sofa between Cade and Winter. They were deep in discussion.

Brooks smiled at the familiar sight of his brother, but it crashed when he saw Cade's black eye. *What happened?* Then Brooks detected the mood in the living room - whatever they were talking about, it wasn't pleasant. Brooks hunkered from sight just below the window and listened.

"... help you get past it. That's good." This was Winter.

Brooks strained. His hearing had sharpened since the transition, but the patter of rain diluted their words.

"... don't know if I'll ever get past it but ... meetings twice a week, and Ethan says ..."

Winter mumbled something.

Then Cade, the pain in his tone tormenting Brooks: "... don't really want to talk about it anymore ..."

Tears pricked Brooks' eyes. He raised his face, peered inside.

His brother sat on the couch, staring sightlessly at his hands. Someone had hurt him. Not only did he have a black eye, but also a swollen nose and a split lip.

Brooks was frightened by Cade's appearance. He'd lost weight. Not a little, but a lot. His skin was sickly gray, and there was an empty, haunted quality in his sunken eyes.

Brooks hadn't expected this. Grief, yes. Anger, yes. Even hatred. But not this. Not total ruin. And that's what he was looking at: the ruin of his little brother. *And it's my fault.*

Then Cade's gaze slid toward Brooks, locked onto him.

Brooks' heart stuttered and his breath caught. Surely, Cade saw him ...

But no. There was nothing. No recognition. No surprise, no anger, nothing. Just that glassy emptiness.

Then Cade looked away; he hadn't seen Brooks at all - the living room lights made that impossible. He'd looked past him - no, *through* him - and in that moment, Brooks felt his brother's pain, suffered his loss, endured the agony that he himself had inflicted. Until tonight, Brooks had the luxury of denial, of believing that Cade would somehow be okay - and that one day, just maybe, he might even forgive.

But Brooks knew now that would never happen. That depth of pain wasn't forgivable.

Cade said to Winter, "You should've turned *me*, then *I* could have turned her."

Turned her? Samantha?

Cade continued: "And you still could do it. I know you could. But you won't."

"Jesus Christ, Gilroy, are you ever going to stop riding my ass about this? I told you, I won't do it."

"Why?"

A pause. "It's complicated."

"Complicated how?"

"Just ... look, it can't be done. Get it out of your head, all right?"

"This is bull-"

"Look, you don't even know if that's what she would have wanted. Maybe she didn't *want* to be a vampire, Gilroy. Maybe-"

"It's better than being dead!"

"No. It isn't."

Brooks lost track of the conversation then. His mind was spinning. Cade was asking Winter to turn Samantha and Winter was refusing.

Brooks stepped back, disappearing into the forest. *I can fix this*, he thought, baffled that it hadn't occurred to him sooner. *Yes, I can fix this*. Hope, after such a long, long time, surged and flowed through him, invigorating him. *I can fix this and I will! How did I not think of this!*

At a dead run, Brooks sprinted toward town, unaware that he was being watched.

RAFE SANTANGELO FELT LIKE THE SCUM OF THE EARTH. HE'D INFRINGED on a personal moment and as Brooks took off running, Rafe headed back to their cabin deep in the woods, leaving the man alone to fight his private war. He'd watched for too long. He couldn't help it. He hated seeing Brooks in such pain and wished he could do something for him.

But that didn't make it right to spy. Grief was not a spectator sport, and Rafe vowed that he'd never do that to Brooks again. He hated himself for it.

And that's what I deserve for not minding my own business. He was just glad he'd left before Brooks had seen him.

The rain was coming heavier now and Rafe, too, broke into a run, eager to get back to the abandoned cabin, the place he called home.

"ALL RIGHT, GILROY, HERE'S THE THING." WINTER LEANED FORWARD and clasped his big hands together. "I wasn't lying when I said it was too late to turn Samantha ... but there's more to it than I've told you."

Cade remained silent; he didn't want to risk saying anything that would change Winter's mind about what he was finally ready to disclose.

"If I'd been there when Samantha was killed, I would have turned her, Cade. I would have. But by the time I even heard about it she'd been dead for hours. And the thing is ... when someone's been gone that long and you bring them back ... well ..." he looked at Cade, his arctic-blue eyes full of regret. And fear. "Well, they don't come back the same."

"Of course they don't come back the same. They come back as vampires. I know that!"

Winter shook his head. "No, you don't know. Once someone's been dead more than a few minutes, they don't come back as a vampire - not the kind of vampire you'd recognize, anyway. They have no souls."

"What are you talking about?"

"Their souls have left. Or their spirits, or energy, or whatever you choose to call the force that keeps people alive and makes them human. That force usually remains intact for a few minutes. Maybe. In that time, as long as the body is still ensouled, the transition is fine. But if the soul has departed and you pump an empty corpse full of venom, well, you don't end up with a vampire. Not exactly. You end up with something else. Something darker. Something we call a ghoul."

"A ghoul?" Cade leaned in, as eager as he was frightened to hear more. "What the hell is a ghoul?"

"They go way back. They're the most basic form of vampire. You've probably read about them in old Eastern European legends."

"So… what's the difference between a vampire with a soul and one without?"

Winter frowned. "Where to begin? Well, for one thing, an ensouled vampire usually retains the memories and same basic personality he or she had before they were turned. And often, the same moral code. That's not the case with ghouls. With ghouls, the body was dead for too long and they come back as something that has little, if anything, in common with who they used to be. The body has begun to decompose, as has the brain, leaving them with very little, if any, reasoning ability, and none of their human qualities. They're not people by any means. They're subhumans with no moral sense, just pure instinct - and their only instinct is to feed."

"So … what you're saying is …they're like … zombies, but instead of brains they want blood?"

Winter considered. "I guess that pretty much sums it up. It's a real boner-killer, I know, but there it is." He put a hand on Cade's shoulder and met his eyes. "If I'd brought Samantha back, she'd be a walking corpse - an unthinking, unfeeling machine in search of blood. She wouldn't have been Samantha, Gilroy. It was too late for that. And ghouls are dangerous. Deadly. Even to other vampires. A mortal wound from a ghoul can kill us."

"So there's more than the basic five Ss that can destroy a vampire?" Cade stared at Winter, his mind reeling. "Why didn't you tell me this before now?"

"Because I know you, Gilroy. You wouldn't have given a damn about the consequences. You wouldn't have taken no for an answer. It was easier just to tell you it couldn't be done and leave it at that."

For a moment, neither spoke.

"I'm sorry, Gilroy. Truly. I'd change things if I could. I wouldn't deny you this if there was any way around it. I need you to know that."

Cade tried to envision Samantha as the thing that Winter had described. A ghoul. He shuddered. For the first time, he felt they'd done the right thing by letting her go. There was at least a little bit of peace in that.

SOMETHING WAS WRONG, VERY WRONG, AND FOR THE FIRST TIME IN HER life, Sydney felt she was in the presence of the supernatural. The rain came hard, plastering her hair to her scalp, but she neither noticed nor cared. She was too intrigued by what she was seeing; she was a woman obsessed.

The tall shadow dashed between the trees, moving with almost inhuman speed. She followed him, hanging back, out of breath. He'd have lost her but he paused now and then, raising his head like a dog scenting the air before sprinting off again - always east, past the guest cabins, through the parking lot, toward the highway.

Mesmerized by the urgency with which he moved and the desperation of his heavy breathing, she now hunkered maybe ten yards back between tall shrubs, watching with growing horror and disbelief as he scurried lizard-like up a low hill, then disappeared into the darkness. This was not a human being, but some kind of animal. An animal in the shape of a man.

For a moment, Sydney was paralyzed. Every cell in her body screamed at her to turn around, but she could not. She sparked into motion, running toward the hill, slipping in mud, encompassed in terror but driven by the need to see more - the need to know who - *what* - it was she was pursuing. She came to the rise and began to climb, pulling herself upward, hands and feet slipping, sliding, and sinking into the soft wet earth, proving what she already knew: that no normal man could have scaled the hill so easily.

Yet she'd watched him do it.

The highway came into view and she spotted a different man a few yards away. This one stood under a street lamp at the edge of the road on the opposite side, thumb out, seeking a ride. But she didn't see the man she'd followed. Frantically, she looked around.

And then she saw him.

He lunged from the shadowed border of trees, flying through the air like a great, dark beast of prey. The hitchhiker screamed as the man crashed down on him.

Peering out from over the rise of the hill, Sydney's blood drained and a scream built within her and her legs turned to lead. The crack of bone echoed off the mountains beyond the highway as the man broke open the hitchhiker's ribs and reached inside. As he ripped out the hitchhiker's heart and bit into it, her scream exploded into the night.

The killer looked up. Their eyes met, and only then did Sydney realize, *truly* realize, who she was looking at.

37

LIFE (AND DEATH) AT LA VOLIÈRE

*G*retchen was spent. Wonderfully, deliciously, painfully spent. Scythe had pounded her like a champion and it was everything she'd been waiting for - everything she knew *he'd* been waiting for. It didn't bother her that they'd done it on a mattress in front of her new slaves. Gretchen liked an audience - she always had.

Satisfied, she pushed Scythe's sweaty, hard-muscled body off, then rolled over and sighed. *Ah, Vlad the Impaler.* She'd missed that vein-marbled weapon of mass destruction that hung between his legs more than she'd missed the man himself. In fact, were it not for his magnificent manhood, she didn't know if she'd have kept the lunkhead around as long as she had.

But the long-awaited fuck-session with Scythe went far beyond carnal satisfaction for Gretchen. It had been a test, the ultimate test, and her body had passed with flying colors. She knew now that she was back, fully recovered, strong enough to return to the Crimson Corset and reclaim her position as queen of the underground. Queen of Crimson Cove.

Michael and his Loyals would do everything they could to keep her from reopening the club, but she'd begun building an army that was now nearly three times the size of his ragtag band.

She smiled - *tomorrow, it all begins tomorrow* - and closed her eyes, letting herself drift. Tonight was for rest. For revival. For preparation. All her hungers satiated, Gretchen slept, and within moments, she dreamed.

New York, 1779.

La Maison de Volière stood tall and proud on a rolling green just outside Manhattan. It was a modest mansion of forty-odd rooms and a stone and brick façade that spoke of culture and refinement. Within the mansion, and atop the mansard and towered rooftops, grace and elegance combined with a number of unusual features that had made La Volière *a place that many in society hoped to visit. Rumors - some true, most unfounded - of the grand but bizarre architecture within made the mansion a frequent topic of discussion among those who dwelt in boring but polite society.*

The builder, Francois Alouette, an eccentric lover of birds, had sunk the entirety of his fortune into the great house, building massive and ornate cages into the very walls of the mansion. Upon the roofs were a series of huge wrought-iron domes - ornately designed aviaries where he kept collections of indigenous birds, carrier pigeons, and even peacocks. The peacocks' cries were infamous for sounding like the screams of dying children and one of the rumors about Monsieur Alouette was that he collected orphans to feed to his pet vultures. This, of course, was nonsense, but those who did not receive invitations to his lavish soirees delighted in perpetrating such tales.

Francois Alouette had not cared; he only cared for his beloved birds.

Alas, not a decade passed before the avian enthusiast succumbed to consumption and died virtually penniless, leaving his birds to fend for themselves. Another five years passed. Some birds died, but many had been set free in time and, to this day, they nested in bright noisy clutches upon the property.

La Volière, still tall, still proud, remained much as it had once been, complete with its indoor cages and massive rooftop iron domes. When Astrid VanTreese first saw the place, she'd been entranced and had bought it to serve not only as home to her and Gretchen but as a grand salon for vampiric society. Astrid VanTreese, who was born to be royalty, was quickly accepted as Mistress of Vampires in New York.

She'd had the mansion cleaned and painted, and the gilt restored. She'd retained the huge indoor cages for both the safety - and display of - the blood slaves and supplicants who came to her. She'd covered the walls with beautiful tapestries and paintings, and her nightly parties, complete with live musicians, were soon among the most talked about events in New York society. But Astrid's parties were invitation-only, and catered solely to the undead.

With Italy behind them, Astrid and Gretchen were more successful than they'd ever been, but Gretchen, knowing where their wealth had come from, resented their lavish lifestyle, and while New York was kind to them, she never forgot Stefano Sabbatini - the man she'd loved, the man whose fortune financed them. She never stopped wondering what had happened to him and if he might be looking for her.

Astrid, however, had moved on and now had eyes for another man, Michael Ward - a new vampire and former soldier of the American Revolutionary War. Astrid caught wind of a murderous vampire in the city and eventually located him and took him in, teaching him through meditation and calming earth minerals how to control his blood lust and live humanely. It had taken some work but she'd tamed him.

Michael, now reserved, polite, and mysterious, was nothing like Stefano, and though Astrid loved him, Gretchen would not accept him as Stefano's replacement. Michael loved Astrid in return, there was little doubt of that, and this was another thing Gretchen resented. Why should her mother be so happy when she, Gretchen, still suffered the loss of her own true love even a century later?

By now, Gretchen's heart had calcified but pain was her constant companion. Of anger, too, there was plenty - especially once Astrid found such happiness with Michael. Gretchen began defying her mother at every turn, behaving in ways she knew Astrid would not approve, in ways meant solely to bring shame upon her mother. She took lovers during the parties at La Volière, sometimes seducing two or even three different men per night and leading them into the lavish rooms upstairs where she would slake her most carnal desires.

Those desires grew, evolved, and soon - to Astrid's great mortification -

Gretchen was flaunting her sexuality openly, luring her lovers into the main parlor and having her way with them, often in front of an audience.

Astrid was furious and Gretchen was unrepentant.

If unwholesome rumors of Astrid VanTreese's daughter began to circulate among vampiric society, Gretchen neither knew nor cared. While her mother had found true love with Michael Ward, Gretchen had learned to take a different satisfaction in sex, approaching it fiercely, indeed, spitefully.

And she'd found a surprising number of men who enjoyed her erotic antics. Often, she entered a crowded room, stood with her back against a wall, lifted her skirts, and commanded the man of her choice to his knees, requiring that he crawl to her and pleasure her with his mouth. When she was satisfied, she would shove him away, smooth down her skirts, and leave without a word, already in search of the next pleasure.

She began taking great delight in the suffering of her men. This was where Gretchen fully came into her own. She enjoyed tying them down, torturing them, humiliating them in front of others. Drunk on absinthe-laced blood and high on her own lust, she became violent, beating her lovers, using them to burn off her own seething hatred toward a cruel world - and the man who'd left her alone in it, the man who'd betrayed her.

It was a lifestyle that would follow Gretchen for the rest of her days, and soon, word began to spread. Humans and vampires alike became aware of Gretchen VanTreese's cruel and unusual brand of lovemaking, and men, fools that men are, began to seek her out, offering great dividends for her services.

And this was where Astrid drew the line. She would not allow her daughter to exchange sex for money. The discord between her and Gretchen became unbearable. But despite her mother's resistance, Gretchen continued this behavior on the sly, spiriting the men away and taking them to the rooftop, to the cages, where she practiced her craft in privacy. There were many men, but Gretchen never fully gave herself - not from her soul - to anyone after Stefano Sabbatini. The men she spent her time with now were toys, mere playthings that lent her temporary reprieve from her own emptiness.

But it wasn't long before Gretchen learned that her frustration had been misplaced. As much as she quarreled with her mother and resented her happiness, Gretchen didn't know true hatred - pure, black, unbridled hatred -

until the night she overheard the conversation between Astrid and Michael Ward. The conversation that would forever alter each of their lives.

Sunrise neared and the party was over. Astrid and Michael had retired to their shared chambers and Gretchen, who always stayed up later to remove evidence of her rooftop exploits, paused in front of her mother's room at the sound of hushed, secretive voices from within.

Crouching, Gretchen peered through the keyhole and saw Astrid's massive bed, its heavy scarlet curtains pulled back. She could make out the forms of Michael and her mother in the soft glow of a bedside candle. She turned her ear to the keyhole, straining to hear.

"I don't know what to do about her," Astrid was saying. "I'm becoming frightened of her. She's been different ever since ... Stefano ... and it's gotten worse."

"You are sure she doesn't know what really happened to him?" came Michael's velvety tones.

Gretchen perked up.

"I don't see how she could," said Astrid, "but the way she seems to resent me ... perhaps she senses it on some level."

Senses it? Senses what? Gretchen leaned closer, fully intrigued, her heart hammering.

"Perhaps you should tell her the truth."

"Absolutely not." Astrid was aghast. "She wouldn't believe I had her best interests in mind. I know my daughter, Michael. She'd only see it as an attack on her happiness."

"But if she knew the man was dangerous, that he was putting you both in danger, perhaps then she would understand."

Putting us in danger? Stefano?

"That he was controlling," Michael went on. "Abusive."

"But she wouldn't see it that way. She never saw his control over us as anything but love. Specifically, love for her. Love that she needed. Michael, she truly believed he loved her."

Gretchen's breath stopped and her hands trembled.

Michael was silent a moment. Then, "Surely, she knew that you and he were ... together all that time."

Rage filled Gretchen as it always did at the thought.

"She must have." Astrid sounded distant, distracted. "But to tell her that I killed him ... the man she loved ... it would destroy her. And she'd destroy me."

Killed him! Gretchen's breath hitched. Her stomach clenched as the world tilted and spun. Killed him?

"Michael?" Astrid asked. "I want you to promise me something. If anything should ever happen to me, take care of her. Please?"

"I give you my word ..."

The rest of the conversation was lost to the hammering of her heart, the thrumming rush of blood in Gretchen's ears. She tried to stand but it was as though the floor had opened up and she was falling, endlessly falling. Hot tears spilled from her eyes but she didn't notice.

Astrid had killed Stefano. Killed him.

Killed him!

On shaking legs, she managed to rise, a piercing, blinding headache throbbing behind her eyes, her vision swimming. She couldn't breathe. She put a hand to the wall, steadying herself, trying to comprehend - and trying to convince herself she'd misunderstood, that somehow it wasn't true.

But she knew it was true. It all made sense now. The way Astrid had watched Gretchen and Stefano so closely - too closely. And the way Stefano had simply disappeared without a word to either of them.

But he hadn't simply disappeared. He wouldn't have. He loved me! Gretchen's blood turned as hot and thick as molten lava as shock gave way to fury. He loved me more and Mother couldn't stand it!

No longer able to stifle the sobs, she stole down the hall, to her own room, and threw herself onto her bed where she wept as she'd never wept before.

And hours later, after the unbridled keening, wrapped in hate and consumed by vengeance, she rose and moved to her vanity and sat trembling and cold all over, brushing her hair, studying her own reflection, thinking, thinking. Planning.

Astrid would not get away with this. Gretchen wouldn't let her.

She looked upon her reflection. There was something in her eyes that hadn't been there before. Something deeper than anger and blacker than hate.

Something murderous.

And no longer sane.

Ethan, still shocked by Leda Murrow's revelation, raced toward the Colter cabin, hands fisted around the steering wheel, knuckles bleached white. He felt fevered, his face sheathed in a cold sweat. He sped through town, vehicles moving out of his way as if by magic. He barely slowed at stop signs and red lights, his thoughts ricocheting off the walls of his mind as the conversation with the prostitute played on a loop, screaming at him.

At first, he hadn't believed it, thought the whole thing was coincidence, some kind of macabre mix-up, but the more he thought about it, the closer he got to his destination, the more certain he became. He'd know for sure when he arrived.

Just as the Colter cabin came into view, his phone rang.

"Mother? Mother?" Careful not to wake Michael, Gretchen gently shook Astrid's shoulder. There was still half an hour until sunrise, but both were fast asleep already. "Mother?"

At last, the woman opened her eyes. Recognizing her daughter, she sat up, pulling the sheets around her. "Gretchen?" She spoke in a whisper. "What is it?"

"The rooftop. There's someone up there. They're hurt."

Astrid blinked bleary eyes. "Hurt? On the roof? Who-"

"I don't know but we must hurry!"

Astrid glanced at Michael.

"There's no time, Mother. The sun is coming up soon. We must go now!" To Gretchen's relief, Astrid flung herself out of bed, not waking Michael. Michael was a complication Gretchen didn't need. Astrid pulled her white satin dressing gown tight and followed her daughter hurriedly into the hall and up the winding back stairs that led to the rooftop aviaries.

Gretchen's heart pounded with exhilaration at what she was about to do.

"Ethan!" Crouching low behind a massive redwood on the Eudemonia grounds, Sydney hissed into the phone.

"Sydney? What's going on? What is it?" Ethan's voice crackled. The connection was shoddy - she'd been lucky to get through at all. "It's him, Ethan!" She'd managed to outrun the dark man - *the killer!* - but she knew he was close behind. "I saw ..." She still couldn't believe her own eyes. "I saw him by the highway." She gasped, trying to catch her breath, trying to speak coherently. "I ran. He's coming, Ethan. He's coming for me!" Tears and rain streaked down her face and her heart thundered in her chest so hard it hurt.

"Who?" The connection crackled. "What ... you see?"

Shit! "Ethan? Can you hear me?"

His voice came distorted, broken. "Damn it ... Sydney, what ... talking about? Who's coming? Who ... see?"

"Fuck!" She wanted to slam the phone against the tree.

"Where ... you?"

"Eudemonia," she said as loudly as she dared. "I'm at Eudemonia, Ethan! Please, hurry!"

No response. The connection was lost. "Ethan? *Ethan?*"

And then she became aware of a deepening darkness around her, as if a cloud passed over the moon. But it was not a cloud and there was no moon. She looked up and her hammering heart skipped a beat. Her breath caught in her throat and the rain and sweat that covered her body turned to ice.

He stood over her, eyes blazing with hate, chest heaving, lips curled back in a malicious sneer.

"Oh, God, oh, God, please, no ..." She scrambled backward, slipping and sliding as he approached, his hard white fists flexing at his sides.

"Sydney? Hello? *Hello?* Damn it!" Ethan threw the phone against the dash. It shattered. "Damn it!"

Eudemonia! She'd said she was at Eudemonia. And something about the highway.

He'd just pulled into the Colters' drive, but now he yanked the wheel, stomped the gas, then peeled out. "Son of a *bitch!*" Tires slinging mud, engine roaring, the Wrangler barreled back the way it had come, back toward Eudemonia, toward Sydney.

THEY EMERGED FROM A SMALL CORNER GAZEBO THAT HOUSED THE BACK stairs, onto the rooftop of La Volière.

"Over there!" Gretchen pointed toward the largest of the iron bird cages that stood upon the mansard roof. "He's hurt very badly, Mother."

Astrid hurried toward it, her nightgown fluttering behind her, Gretchen on her heels.

They arrived at the iron bars and Astrid looked around wildly. "Where ...?" She turned to face her daughter and that's when Gretchen pulled the filleting knife from her skirts. It was slender and sharp, very sharp. It wasn't real silver, but that didn't mean it wouldn't cause serious damage.

Astrid's eyes widened. "Gretchen? What are you do-"

Gretchen thrust the blade upward, its pointed end pressing against the softest part of her mother's throat - just below the chin. But Gretchen did not break skin, not yet.

Astrid, head high, looked down on her daughter with stunned, frightened eyes. She looked like a fox under the fang of a hound and Gretchen delighted in her terror; it came off her in waves now, and Gretchen breathed it in. "Gretchen?" Astrid's voice, as thin as the blade at her throat, trembled.

"You killed him," said Gretchen. "You killed Stefano."

Astrid swallowed. "Gretchen. You don't understand. I-"

Gretchen applied pressure. The blade dimpled skin and brought a drop of blood. "Be silent!" She knew her time was limited. She had no illusions about her mother's strength and she couldn't allow her any advantage. "Get into the cage or I shall cut your throat here and now."

"The ... cage?" She was buying time.

Gretchen applied more pressure.

Astrid winced.

"Get in."

Astrid stepped inside the giant prison. Gretchen quickly slammed the door and locked it.

"He was going to expose us," Astrid said from the other side of the bars, "to save himself. He'd already gone to the police and-"

"Be silent!" Gretchen clamped her hands over her ears, the knife clattering to the ground. "He wouldn't! He loved me!"

"Stefano Sabatini loved neither of us! He loved no one, do you hear me? He wasn't capable." Astrid wrapped her fingers around the iron rods that imprisoned her. "The city found out that the undead were walking among them. Stefano identified us as vampires! He planned to flee the very night that I... that I killed him. That's how I found out what he'd done. I found him packing and-"

"Liar!" Gretchen stepped away from her mother, away from the ugly lies.

"He was malicious. He made no apology. He told me they were coming for us and ... and he laughed." Tears welled then spilled from Astrid's eyes. "He laughed and laughed, Gretchen! We had to flee."

"No." Eyes wild, Gretchen shook her head. "Lies. All lies. You killed him. You killed him. You didn't have to, but you killed him!" Gretchen wept, face buried in her hands.

"You're right. I did not have to kill him. But I won't apologize for it, either. He betrayed us. He betrayed *you*."

"No! You're lying!" Gretchen threw herself at the bars, reaching in, grappling for her mother's throat, but Astrid dodged her. "Liar!"

And Astrid said no more. As her daughter sobbed, she watched her, the panic in her eyes evaporating until only sadness remained. "You are the one in prison," Astrid finally said, "not I."

And in that moment, Gretchen *did* feel imprisoned.

It turned her pain to outrage and she spat at her mother.

Astrid only stared.

Gretchen looked over at the easterly hills where a vague pinkish haze was just beginning to show behind the peaks of the mountains. She straightened and spoke in firm tones. "Scream as loud as you want to, Mother. No one will hear you." Then she smiled, reconsidering. "Well, perhaps Michael will, but it's not as if he'll be able to save you." She held up the keys to the cage, rattling them just inches from Astrid's face. "You deserve this, Mother."

Then she turned and left the rooftop, never looking back at her mother, never looking back at all.

"What the fuck's this about?" Winter stood at the living room window of Cade Colter's cabin, watching as Ethan's red Wrangler peeled out of the drive and bounced down the dirt road back toward town.

Cade joined him, watching the taillights disappear. "Was that Ethan?"

"It was." Winter faced Cade. "Something's up, Gilroy. Something funky. I can smell it. Will you-"

"Got it." Cade had his phone out and began dialing the sheriff's number. After several rings, he shook his head. "No answer."

"Something's not right." Winter dug into his pocket and pulled out his keys. "I'm going after him."

"I'm coming with you."

"Fine." Winter had a feeling there wasn't time to argue. He was out the door in record time, Cade on his heels.

It wasn't long before the first rays of the sun breached the horizon and when the screams came, they were delectable.

Gretchen sat in the parlor, enjoying the cool air that sifted between the heavy drapes from the open window, feet propped on a velvet ottoman, relishing the sounds of her mother's agonizing exit from this earth.

And Michael's desperate screams as he tried - and failed - to save her.

Gretchen heard his frantic footsteps running for the shadows as the sunlight grew too strong to endure. She was suddenly tired herself, but she wouldn't rest - not until it was over.

And it was over far too soon. When the screams stopped, Gretchen sighed and stood, a smile on her lips. That smile only widened when Michael appeared in the doorway, reeking of ash, his sooty face wet with tears and sweat. "You did this." His voice was pure poison.

Gretchen stared at him, unflinching.

In a quick fluid move, Michael was at her, a large hand around her throat. He lifted her off her feet, his jaw set, eyes blazing. "You did this!"

Gretchen allowed the smile to sneak back to her lips.

"I will kill you." He shook her.

Gretchen sucked in air. "Kill me, will you? And break your promise to my mother?"

Slowly, his eyes changed and he set her on her feet and one by one, his fingers relaxed. "What are you talking about, Gretchen?"

She smiled. "You promised to take care of me should something happen to her. Are you or are you not a man of your word, Michael?" She raised her chin, exposing her throat. "We shall see, Michael. We shall see."

Michael was a stone statue, silent and marble-white, his fists like granite at his sides.

And Gretchen knew he would not kill her, knew he could not kill her.

"Leave this house at sundown," said Gretchen, "and I'll spare your life. Test me and you'll suffer the same fate as my mother."

Michael stared at her for long moments, disbelieving. Then, seeing she meant what she'd said, the still-flickering glint of fury in his eyes died out and his shoulders dropped in resignation. "You're a monster." It was the last thing he said to her before leaving the parlor - the last thing, in fact, he'd said to her until crossing her path again many, many years later.

GLOCK IN HAND, ETHAN ABANDONED THE WRANGLER AND RACED through the woods behind Eudemonia. The rain came hard and he slipped several times, skinning his knees. Sydney hadn't been at her cabin.

She'd said something about the highway.

His clothing fully soaked, he ran faster than he ever had, ducking under branches and hopping over bushes, finally darting back through the parking lot, toward the highway.

THE SILVER DAGGER

Michael did leave at sundown the next night, and Gretchen did not see him again for many years, but she heard rumors. So many rumors.

The night after Astrid's death, Gretchen had returned to the rooftop to collect her mother's remains. Bones, teeth, and amazingly, some hair were all that was left of her. Later, when she'd taken one of the blood slaves, an Amazon-sized Slavic, as her personal modiste, Gretchen had her mother's remains fashioned into jewelry and accessories, which she wore with great satisfaction. The Slavic woman, Jazminka, would also help Gretchen transform La Volière into a veritable palace of perversity and pleasure.

The mansion was Gretchen's domain now, and under her management, the salon had become the kind of place that catered to a larger - and much darker - base. The new patrons came to La Volière solely for the sex rooms, blood orgies, absinthe, and opium, and Gretchen, having declared herself Vampire Queen of New York, gladly indulged them.

As for Michael Ward, he never did return to La Volière. The death of Astrid VanTreese had pushed him over the edge. Gretchen later learned that he'd succumbed to what was known in the vampire community as Rage Killing, and was responsible for the horrendous deaths of dozens of humans.

But Gretchen sensed his nearness. Some nights, as she stood upon the rooftops of La Volière overlooking the vast rolling green, she could feel his eyes upon her - watching over her from some shadowed corner of the property, keeping his promise to Astrid.

She never caught a glimpse of him, but her suspicions were verified when Gretchen moved across the country to California after the mansion was destroyed in a fire, and Michael soon followed.

Gretchen woke from the dream smiling. She blinked, looked around the cave, and saw Jazminka, who remained her personal modiste after all these years, sitting on the edge of the mattress beside her, watching over her as she slept.

It was time. Time to return to the Crimson Corset. And bring full transition upon the blood slaves.

"Tomorrow night," she whispered to her right-hand woman. "Tomorrow night we go home."

"Yes, Meestress." A smile like a slithering serpent, crept to Jazminka's lips.

Still satiated on sex and blood, Gretchen closed her eyes.

And her thoughts drifted back to Michael Ward.

He'd called her a monster once and he'd been right. But what he hadn't known at the time, what he'd soon found out, was that he himself was capable of just as much carnage and bloodshed as she. Perhaps even more. Hovering on the edge of unconsciousness, she wondered just how many murders the man had committed.

"Stop!" Ethan aimed his Glock, finger on the trigger, still not believing his eyes.

In a small shadowclad clearing at the edge of the property, Michael Ward held Sydney's limp body up by her hair with one hand, the other suspended in mid-air, prepared to punch a hole straight through her chest.

"I said stop!"

Michael's feral eyes flashed on the sheriff, and his white face, a gaunt mask of wild horror, sent sparks of ice down Ethan's spine.

"Stop, or I'll shoot!" The world went eerily silent, the only sound the tick of rain - like a time bomb counting down to explosion. Ethan felt sick inside.

Wet with rain and blood, Sydney coughed, and Michael, still hesitating, glanced between her and Ethan.

Ethan took a step closer, his shoes squelching in the mud. "Let her go, Michael. Nice and easy." He couldn't tell if the man was even cognizant, but thought he saw recognition flicker in those wild, animal eyes. "Let her go and no one gets hurt."

The gurgle of Sydney's breath said it might already be too late for that.

Another careful step closer. "It's me, Michael. It's Ethan. Step away from her and I'll lower the gun." Ethan had a clear headshot; one wrong move and he'd pull the trigger. It wouldn't kill Michael, but it'd sure as hell slow him down.

"Just step away." Ethan's voice was calm, but inside he was a quivering mass of nerves. He'd never seen Michael - or any vampire - like this before. The man's body was like a spring-loaded steel trap, a feather's breath away from snapping.

Slowly, carefully, Michael began lowering Sydney to the wet forest floor.

"That's it. Now, step away, nice and slow." Ethan's heart hammered hard and his extremities felt heavy and numb. His hand quaked on the trigger. "Nice and slow, Michael. Nice and slow." Another step closer.

Michael faced Ethan, a rigid dark figure, arms at his sides, breath coming hard.

"It's all right, Michael. Just take it easy." Despite his fear, he took another slow step closer.

But it was one step too many.

Michael snapped to sudden life, lunged away, loped into the shadowed forest, and disappeared with such speed it was like watching a movie on fast-forward.

"Wait!"

But Michael was gone.

"Goddamnit!"

Sydney coughed and Ethan ran to his ex-wife, vaguely aware of new voices behind him through the pounding rain and rush and thrum of blood in his own ears.

"Sheriff!" Winter's voice.

But Ethan took no notice. His ex-wife lay on the wet earth, her face covered in mud and blood. She'd been beaten to near death. Her breath was jagged and rattling, her face a ruin. Her pink mud-covered robe had fallen open and she was missing a shoe. He crouched and fumbled for his radio.

"Did you see the guy?" asked Winter. "Did you see who did this?"

Cade stood beside him, out of breath, his eyes like wide, glowing embers.

"It's Michael," said Ethan. "He did this."

Winter looked like he'd taken a punch to the gut. "Michael? But-"

Sydney coughed again and blood exploded from her nose and mouth. Her breath hitched once, twice, then came to a sudden, terrifying stop.

"Shit!" Ethan exploded into motion, pumping her chest, but Winter bulled in, shoving him out of the way.

The big white man felt for a pulse.

"CPR!" shouted Ethan.

"Too late for that, Sheriff."

"Wait!"

But before Ethan could stop him, Winter draped his body over Sydney's and sunk his fangs into her throat.

Cade, eyes bulging, stepped back, slipped in the mud, and landed on his ass.

Ethan was frozen to the spot as he watched the massive vampire administer venom.

When Winter raised his head, blood dripped from his lips and chin, glittering so black in the moonlight that it was somehow profane against his ice-white skin. "Just enough to heal her," he said, wiping his mouth with the back of his hand.

But nothing happened. Sydney's breath never came.

The world went silent again save for the tick of rain.

Ethan looked desperately at Winter. Raindrops glittered in his white crewcut like jewels. "Nothing's happening!"

Winter stared at the woman. "Well, shit."

Ethan was aware of Cade beside him, watching, stunned, silent.

Then Winter looked up, his pale eyes stuttering over Ethan's face. "It's too late. She's gone."

"Gone?" The word held no meaning for Ethan. "What do you mean gone?"

"We need to make a decision," said Winter, "and we've got to do it quick. Her body's dead but it's probably still ensouled. We can still-"

"Just save her!" Ethan's voice cracked like a whip.

Winter did. He hunched over the dead woman and pumped her lifeless body full of venom. Enough to bring her back.

Not as she once was, but as one of the undead.

38

GRAVE EXPECTATIONS

*T*he heavy, wet earth made his task harder, but Brooks Colter had succeeded. He'd worked steadily, silently, without shovel or spade, slinging mud like a digging dog. It had taken some doing, but when his fingers found the groove of the coffin lid, he'd pried it open and gone to work, injecting Samantha Corbett's corpse with as much venom as he could produce. He'd given her two heavy rounds, and still, nothing was happening.

She just needs a little more. Brooks, all but venomless, now rested under the shelter of a tree, his back against the cold wet bark. He was drenched in rain and sweat, and his muscles ached and burned. Before his transition, there was no way he'd have been able to achieve what he had tonight, but even so, his body was exhausted. Apparently, expressing mass amounts of venom took a lot out of a vampire. *That, and digging up a grave with your bare hands.*

But it would be worth it. If he could bring Samantha back, he could ease Cade's suffering and set things right. She'd be a vampire but at least she'd be alive. *Well, kind of alive, anyway.*

He glanced at the dug-up grave. That curious sense of fullness was slowly returning to his incisors, indicating he was just about ready to try again. *One more dose, a big one, and then hopefully ...*

But it should have worked by now, right?

Brooks hadn't a clue.

Maybe, he thought, the longer a person was dead, the more venom they needed and the longer it took for them to reanimate. It seemed logical, but he didn't know the rules. Michael and his gang had never said anything about envenomating a person who'd been dead several weeks.

Or maybe it's me. Maybe I'm doing it wrong.

No. He was doing it right. He'd felt the same tingle in his incisors when he'd envenomated Rafe, the same liquid warmth as the venom was expressed. *That same blissful, almost sexual, release.*

He felt like he was being watched and glanced around the cemetery. He was alone - it was only his nerves. He was grateful for the privacy of the night.

But there's only so much of it left. There was no more time to waste. He glanced back at the great mound of freshly turned earth, dreading giving her another dose. It was a sickening process, but he had to try. *Just one more time.*

He stood, wiped mud from the seat of his jeans, and trudged back toward the open grave, pausing at the temporary grave marker that read SAMANTHA CORBETT. Even now, the whole thing seemed unreal, like a crazy dream. He couldn't have *really* killed Samantha, right?

But he had. And it was time to make it right.

Pulling back the hood of his wet red sweatshirt, Brooks took a deep breath, and lowered himself into the open earth. The smell hit him and again, he wretched, but this time, nothing came up; he'd already emptied all contents of his stomach during the first two doses. Teeth clenched against the rising nausea, he stared down into the open coffin - at the woman he'd murdered. He barely recognized her.

Samantha Corbett looked like an old ruined doll. Damp green-black moss grew on her discolored skin and Brooks resisted an urge to wipe it away. Sheila Leventis had done the best she could, but Brooks could still see the cuts under the makeup, which had begun to run in the rain. The corpse's mangled throat was concealed by a stained white scarf, and her eyes had sunken in. Her head bulged in a strange way, and dirty cotton, like cobwebs, clogged her mouth and protruded from the breaking seams of thread that stitched her lips together. Brooks had thought morticians used glue these days, but apparently, Sheila was old-school.

"I'm sorry, Samantha," he said for what must have been the hundredth time tonight. "I'm so sorry." He bit back bitter tears and hooked an arm under her. Bracing himself against the fetid damp smell of rot, he lifted her from the casket.

She was surprisingly light, as if she'd been hollowed out - and she probably had. Her head lolled back, exposing the leathery gray flesh and the stitching on her throat. Those stitches creaked and strained, nearly breaking apart and, supporting her head with his hand, Books took a deep breath, lowered his face to the putrid flesh, and bit down.

It was like biting into a piece of rotten fruit. The taste of embalming fluids made his stomach spasm, but he pushed down hard on his rising gorge and once again, expressed as much venom as he could.

And just when he thought he had no more in him, he concentrated and pushed harder until, finally, the last of the hot silky liquid came in tiny spurts, each one smaller than the last, until he'd emptied himself into her entirely.

Coughing, spitting, wiping madly at his mouth, he scrambled out of the grave and onto the wet grass where, on all fours, he began to heave, retching desperately. Nothing came but a long string of bile and drool that swayed back and forth from his lip before finally snapping.

Seized by rolling nausea, unable to move, Brooks spat out the taste of formaldehyde, the taste of decay. The rain beat down harder now and the wind thrashed the weeping willows, howling through the cemetery like everything in Hell had been set free.

Slowly, the sickness began to subside. Brooks got unsteadily to his feet and looked down into the coffin, his face crumpling, tears spilling from his eyes.

Nothing was happening. Nothing at all.

"Goddamnit. Why? Why won't you come back?" He'd done all that he could. He had no more venom to give and no more time.

It was too late.

Too late.

"I'm so sorry, Samantha. I'm so sorry." Crying, he laid Samantha Corbett back to rest, and began the arduous task of replacing the dirt over her grave.

39

NEW TRANSITIONS

Sydney's eyes popped open; she saw nothing but trees and sky. Rain was coming down hard. She lay on her back on the wet ground.

She didn't feel right.

Something was wrong. And something had happened. But what?

Michael.

He killed a man! The memories crashed back and Sydney screamed - she screamed so hard she thought her lungs might rip loose from their moorings.

A large hand clamped over her mouth and three faces invaded her line of sight, all gaping down at her. In her panic, she scarcely recognized them.

"Be silent," said the man covering her mouth. He was huge, all muscle, with white hair and cool blue eyes. She recognized him but couldn't remember his name.

Her body hummed and buzzed in a frightening, foreign way as more memories came flooding back: *Michael Ward attacked me. He tried to kill me!*

She needed to get away from here. *Now!* She struggled to get free but the big man was strong. *Winter. His name's Winter.* One hand was planted over her abdomen, locking her in place, and his other still covered her mouth. Sydney beat at his muscled arms, scratched, and tried to wriggle free, but his body was as hard and unmoving as concrete.

"Be calm!" he ordered, but Sydney could not.

She was in danger. If Michael came back ...

She bit down as hard as she could on Winter's hand.

"Ouch! Christ on a tricycle!"

It worked. Winter yanked his hand back and Sydney rolled out from under him and began belly-crawling away, sliding in mud.

She didn't get far before Winter was on her again, crushing the air out of her. She screamed and he pushed her face down, muffling the sound, then brought his lips to her ear. "Listen to me. Be quiet. You're safe. You're fine. I am not going to hurt you."

"M-Michael..." she managed.

"Michael is gone."

Michael. Gone. Her panic eased some but her thoughts still raced. She was breathing hard, coughing on rain and mud. "Let me up," she said. "Please, let me up."

He did.

Sydney rolled over and sat up, looking around. Ethan and a young man with a black eye stood nearby, wet with rain, eyes full of alarm. There was something about the young man. *Something.* Even in her panic, she wanted to get closer to him.

Then Winter was beside her. He held his hands out, a show of peace. "Just take it easy, okay? No one's going to hurt you. You're safe."

His voice was strangely comforting but she couldn't stop hyperventilating.

"I'm going to take you back to Eudemonia and we'll explain everything, okay?"

Eudemonia. Michael. Murder.

Panic.

She screamed and tried to run but slipped and began to drag herself away.

"Oh, for Christ's sake." Winter grabbed her ankle and pulled her easily through the slippery mud back to him. "Help me hold her down."

Ethan and the young man started forward, but Winter said, "No, not you, Cade. You stay back."

Ethan pinned her by the arms as Winter quickly peeled off his shirt and shoved it into her mouth, amputating her screams. Then, as casually as a man slinging a sack of potatoes, he hefted her up, and threw her over his shoulder caveman-style. "I guess we're going to have to do this the hard way."

Winter made nothing of her weight, nor the punching, kicking, and scratching, as he trotted toward Eudemonia.

Sydney watched Ethan and the young man follow close behind, and for the first time since awakening, despite her fear and fury, she became aware of a strange, new hunger.

40

UNDEAD AND UNWELL

*I*n the great library at Eudemonia, Cade looked out at the rain, his stomach feeling oily and sick as he tried to wrap his mind around what he'd learned.

Michael was the killer. Peace-loving Michael, who just a year ago, refused to behead Gretchen VanTreese. It infuriated Cade that so many innocent humans had died at Michael's hand when Gretchen was still around.

Brooks wasn't the murderer after all. There was some comfort in that.

Lightning flashed, brightening the night and turning the trees into dancing phantoms. Cade stepped away from the window and lowered himself into a black leather chair.

Winter, his face a battleground of warring emotions, sat on a matching sofa. He looked too big for the room despite the high ceilings. Ethan paced in front of the fire.

The three of them had been silent, each man alone with his thoughts, but now, Winter spoke. "It all makes sense."

"How do you mean?" Ethan sat down on the hearth, drying off by the popping fire, his tired, drawn face the color of cold ash. "What makes sense?"

"Michael hasn't had a thing to do with Cade since we got back from Eternity." Winter's eyes were faraway.

"And?"

"Cade's a Sire. Michael's been in a state we call Raging. Basically, his bloodlust is off the hook. He wouldn't have been able to resist a Sire's blood and he knew it. That's why he was avoiding him." Winter shook his head. "I should have known."

Ethan began pacing again. He'd been like a caged lion since they'd come inside. "Maybe I'd better go check-"

Winter cut him off. "Emmeline's got it under control. Sydney's out cold. Just let her sleep."

They'd knocked her out with tranquilizers and she was sleeping now, under Emmeline's watch, in one of the bedrooms.

Ethan sat down again and for a while, all three returned to their private worlds until Ethan broke the silence. "Any word from your guys?"

Winter shook his head. "Nothing yet. Michael's smart. They won't find him if he doesn't want to be found."

Dante and Rogan, who'd been sent out to scour the area for Michael, had been gone for over two hours.

Cade, unable to sit still, returned to the window. Lightning flashed and the forest and rain flickered silver-blue. It wouldn't be long before the sun came up. He stood in the alcove of the large bay window and stared out into the night, wondering how the world outside could be so normal when his own world was crashing down. He found himself thinking of the tall, dark priest, Vincent Scarlotti. Now, more than ever, he longed for the soothing music of his violin. *I could really use one of your songs about now, Father.* He wondered how often the man played and where he might hear his music again.

In the fireplace, a pine knot exploded like a gunshot, making all of them jump.

"You don't think Michael will come back to Eudemonia?" Cade asked.

"Not a chance." Winter's voice brimmed with too many emotions for Cade to clearly read. There was pity in there, anger and guilt, too, but more, much more. "He'll be too ashamed of himself." Winter shook his head. "And now I know why he kept putting Chynna and me on duty together."

"What do you mean?" asked Ethan.

"I thought he was trying to set us up. Turns out, he was trying to distract us - keep us out of his hair so he could ... do what he was doing." Winter rubbed his eyes. "Fuck almighty, the signs were all there. I should have seen them a million miles away."

Ethan, pacing again, said, "Don't beat yourself up. I suspected just about everyone *but* him."

Winter shook his head. "Yeah, but you weren't there in Eternity. You didn't see him during the battle at the Biting Man Festival. He wasn't himself. He went ... primal. It's no wonder he hasn't taken any of Natasha's calls."

"You think that's what set him off?" asked Cade. "Natasha?"

Winter nodded. "No doubt. They go way back and at Biting Man, I kind of figured he'd broken his vow of celibacy with her." He gave a humorless laugh. "I was happy for the guy. I thought he needed nothing more than a good lay. But as he says himself, an addict is an addict is an addict. One vice leads to another. It escalates and ... apparently, leads him to ... *this*."

The room fell silent again as each man sat alone with his thoughts. Then Ethan sighed. "Look, I can't sit here and do nothing. Maybe I should go look for him."

"No way," said Winter. "He's raging. He'll tear you to pieces."

"But-"

"No." Winter pinned him in a deadly-serious gaze. "We need to handle this our way. If anyone can find him, it'll be Dante and Rogan. But like I said, I doubt he wants to be found, so there's nothing to be done. At least not now. You ought to go home and get some sleep, Sheriff."

"Not until I check on Sydney."

"I told you Emmeline-"

"I'm not leaving until I see her." Ethan said this in his cop voice and reluctantly, Winter nodded.

From the bay window, Cade said, "Mind if I tag along?"

But Winter shook his head. "Nope, sorry, Gilroy. Not going to happen."

"Why?" Cade looked at him.

"You're a Sire," Winter explained. "And Sydney's a new vampire. A female, no less. You shouldn't even be under the same roof right now."

"But you said she's unconscious."

"Sorry, Gilroy. We can't risk it."

"Fine." Cade watched Ethan leave the room.

ETHAN KNOCKED ON THE BEDROOM DOOR, AND EMMELINE'S BLUNT features peered out.

"Winter gave me permission to see Sydney."

She eyed him suspiciously. The former suffragette was stout, stocky, and smiling, but despite her usually sweet demeanor, Ethan suspected the devil shivered when the woman finally lost her patience.

At last, she opened the door and let him in.

The room was lowly-lit and crypt-quiet. Heavy black curtains covered the windows, and an antique dresser was bare of everything but a vintage lamp sporting blood red blossoms on the glass shade. The air was thick, silent, and uninviting.

Sydney lay on a large bed, buried under heavy, patchwork quilts. Two chairs rested against the wall. Emmeline sat and resumed working on a crossword puzzle. "Keep your distance, Sheriff."

Ethan nodded, ulcer flaring as he recognized the symptoms of vampirism in his ex-wife. She looked dead. She *was* dead, really. With the others, he could pretend they were human. It was easy to do - he hadn't known them before their transitions. With Sydney, it wouldn't be like that. He patted his pocket unconsciously in search of a Tums. He was fresh out. "How is she?" he asked Emmeline.

The ex-suffragette didn't look up from her word puzzle. "About as well as can be expected."

"She looks ... better." Better wasn't quite the right word but it seemed appropriate. Sydney's wounds had healed and there was no sign of blood on the collar of a fresh white night dress; this was not the blood-covered woman he'd found only a couple of hours ago, so she did look better, he supposed. Dead, but better. "Has she been lucid?"

Emmeline shook her head. "Not yet."

"What happens when she is?"

Finally, the woman looked up and smiled, her round face framed by short dark hair. "Your guess is as good as mine, Sheriff."

Ethan stepped closer to the bed, and his ex-wife's eyes shot open. Ethan gasped.

Emmeline was on her feet. "Don't get any closer. She smells your blood."

Sydney's empty gaze shifted around, searching the ceiling.

"Can she hear us?"

Emmeline's arm came out, keeping Ethan at bay. "Not a clue."

But Ethan barely heard the woman. He was transfixed. Aside from the dead expression, Sydney's features were the same, familiar, but there was that pale mannequin-like smoothness of skin that all vampires had that made them equally beautiful and frightening. Ethan hadn't loved Sydney in a long time - if he ever had at all - but seeing her like this brought a flood of regret. *It's my fault. I gave the order to turn her.*

Because otherwise she'd be dead for good.

"I think you'd better go, Sheriff."

"With all due respect, Emmeline, that's not going to happen." His ex-wife's eyes found him. "Sydney?"

But the woman on the bed stared past him, through him.

Emmeline allowed him to move closer and he smoothed a finger down the side of his ex-wife's face. It was like touching a corpse - cold, dry, and marble-smooth. Unnatural. And somehow ... *unclean.* He wiped his fingers on the sheets to relieve the unpleasant sensation.

"That's enough, Sheriff. I'm afraid I must insist. You need to go."

He gave her a nod. "I just wanted to check up on her. You'll contact me if anything changes?"

"Of course." Emmeline visibly relaxed when Ethan stepped away from the bed.

Sydney's breath caught.

Emmeline bustled over as the other woman's breathing turned fast and hard.

"What is it?"

"Stay back," Emmeline ordered.

"What's happening?"

Emmeline ignored him, speaking in soothing tones to Sydney. "It's all right. I'm here, sweetie."

Sydney's eyes went wider, her face tense, and her breath came even harder and faster now.

"Get out, Sheriff," Emmeline began. "She's-"

Sydney made a sudden gagging sound then shot up. Startled, Ethan jumped back; Emmeline threw herself over Sydney. "Get out!"

But it was too late and Emmeline couldn't hold her.

With a growl, Sydney exploded off the bed, foam flying from her mouth. She lunged at Ethan and knocked him down. They hit the dresser and the lamp toppled, shattering. She clawed his face as Emmeline grabbed, unable to get hold of her. Ethan's arms came up to shield his face. Hot red pain seared his hand where her razor-sharp fangs sank in.

Ethan screamed.

Fabric ripped as Emmeline grabbed the back of Sydney's nightdress and sent her sprawling across the hardwood floor. The crazed woman hit the wall, shrieked, and leapt to her feet, cat-quick.

But it was too late. She'd drunk his blood, completing her transition into full vampirism, and within moments, she groaned, hunched over, then collapsed. She twitched then went still. For several seconds, she remained curled up on the floor unmoving, and then, she jerked back to life.

She looked around with wild eyes, slowly getting to her feet.

"Sydney?" Emmeline stepped closer and Sydney bolted, colliding with the door frame as she dashed into the hall. It didn't even slow her down.

"Stop!" cried Emmeline. She ran after her.

Ethan followed. Blood ran into his eyes painting the world red but he saw Sydney at the end of the hall. She crashed into the banister, then fell down the staircase.

Ethan rushed down the stairs as Winter burst out of the library behind them. The big vampire moved with impossible speed, charging past Ethan and Emmeline. "Stop!"

And like a toy unplugged, Sydney did.

Slowly, she turned and looked up at Winter. Recognition filled her eyes and her face, a tense visage of mad fury, began to relax. "You." Her whisper was like a husk of something dry and dead. "You."

Ethan watched, stunned, as his ex-wife turned from a rampaging thing into something docile and lost.

Tears sprang to her eyes. "What ... where ..." She looked around - at Emmeline, at Winter. When she looked at Ethan, her eyes blazed with hunger and she was back on that slippery slope between madness and sanity.

Winter stepped in front of her, blocking Ethan from her view. "Look at me, Sydney. Don't look at anything but me."

She obeyed.

BACK UPSTAIRS, EMMELINE LED ETHAN INTO A BEDROOM FAR FROM THE one where Winter had taken Sydney.

"Holy Jesus." Ethan sat on the edge of the bed, cupping one hand over the other, trying to stanch the blood flow as Emmeline rummaged through drawers in an adjoining bathroom for a first-aid kit. He felt woozy, his stomach flaring with ulcerous pain. His face burned where Sydney had clawed him but the bite on his hand throbbed worse. "Shit." Blood dripped onto the floor.

Emmeline came with gauze and adhesive tape. She hesitated in the doorway, eyeing the crimson droplets uneasily before stepping just close enough to hand him the bandages; her bloodlust was apparent. He began carefully wrapping the wound. It continued burning and he was suddenly struck by a horrifying thought. "Good thing she doesn't have venom."

Emmeline's expression was flat. "Actually, she does."

Ethan looked at her. "But, I thought-"

"Her wounds were too serious. She wasn't going to make it. We had to give her human blood."

"So she's ... full vampire?"

Emmeline nodded.

Ethan looked at his hand. "You don't think ... she envenomated me, do you?"

"I doubt it." She remained in the doorway, keeping her distance. "But even if she did, it couldn't have been much. You'd know by now if she'd expressed enough to ... turn you."

Ethan's stomach twisted at the thought. More blood, like the last bit of an unspooling ribbon, dripped from his hairline into his eye. He wiped at it with his free hand before his lashes could gum together.

"Does it burn?" she asked.

"Well, yes, but-"

"Tingle?"

Ethan thought about it. "Maybe a little."

"Worst case," said Emmeline, "you got a little venom in you and you'll heal faster. Maybe feel a little hyper for the next twenty-four hours or so. Nothing serious."

"I guess." Ethan didn't like the idea of it. He felt violated. He finished wrapping and held up his hand. "All done."

Emmeline's smile was tight. "Good. But it won't be long before the others pick up on the scent of blood." She nodded at the weeping cuts on his face. "Use this." She handed him a damp cloth.

"Thanks." He stood. "I guess I'd better get out of here."

"Clean those wounds when you get home." She paused. "And tell Winter to take the Sire home. It's not safe."

Those were suggestions Ethan was happy to take. He wanted nothing more than to get home to Sheila, pop some Tums, and nurse a few Killian's.

41

HOMEWARD BOUND

The wind kept up its unearthly howls and the rain continued slashing at the trees as thunder ripped the night open and lightning, lizard-quick, slithered across the sky. Outside the wrought iron gates of the Crimson Cove Cemetery, hard gusts blew wet leaves and litter down the sidewalks as the gutters rushed rampant ... but within, save for the rain and wind in the weeping willows, the cemetery was silent.

Despite the storm, the graveyard smelled of something long dead. It was strong enough that had anyone been there to catch the odor, they would have covered their face and recoiled. The mingled and fleeting scents of wet cemetery roses and lilies were a faint perfume beneath the unmistakable reek of chemicals and death.

It was strongest near the recently disturbed earth of Samantha Corbett's grave - a smell so fetid, so putrid and cloying you could almost feel the grime coating your skin, the delicate lining of your sinuses and throat. Even your soul.

As the dead thing made its way through the soil, like a mole burrowing ever closer to the surface, that stench grew stronger, stronger, only to be stolen by the wind like a hushed whisper.

So driven by hunger was the rotting ghoul beneath the earth, so compelled by its mindless need to feed, that it felt no pain, suffered no discomfort from the cold dirt. It moved on instinct alone, clawing its way to freedom, closer, closer, and in only moments now, the corpse of Samantha Corbett would escape its earthen prison.

And from there, it knew exactly where to go.

42

DAYLIGHT CRAVINGS

Sheila reached out and slapped the alarm, surprised to find Ethan awake. She could just make him out in the early morning shadows. He sat in bed beside her, silent. "Couldn't sleep, Sheriff?" She smiled and moved closer, draping an arm over his waist and nuzzling into him.

Distracted, Ethan mumbled something about insomnia.

"After last night, I thought you'd snooze like a baby." Sheila smiled.

Their lovemaking had gone on until nearly sunrise, beginning around three in the morning; she'd woken up when he got home but hadn't had a chance to speak to him - or even lay eyes on him. He'd said nothing, just turned her over and taken her from behind again and again in the pitch darkness. He'd been insatiable, an animal, boring into her as if he'd intended to come out on the other side. At first, she hadn't been sure what to make of it, but he'd been so intense, so passionate, that soon she was as into it as he. Now she was sore all over and not looking forward to getting out of bed.

Ethan remained silent as she looked up at him. "A penny for your thoughts?" And only then, in the gray light, did she notice the marks - vague pink lines that started at his forehead and dragged down the sides of his jaw. She sat up. "What happened to your face?"

He chuckled. "Where to begin?"

Sheila saw that his hand was bandaged and felt the beginnings of panic. "What went on last night, Ethan?"

He sighed and cleared his throat. "Long story short, Michael's the killer and Sydney's a vampire now."

Sheila chuckled, but it was strangled and dry. "Whatever you say, Ethan. Now tell me what really happened."

"Michael's the killer and Sydney's a vampire. That's really what happened." He wasn't smiling.

Sheila's stomach knotted. "You're serious?"

"Yep. That's how I got this." Ethan indicated the marks on his face. "And this." He held up his bandaged hand. "And this. When Sydney came to, she lost control."

"And Michael ... he's the killer?" It was too much. She couldn't process it.

Ethan nodded.

"Why didn't you tell me this last night? I had no idea!"

He shrugged. "I didn't want to think about it anymore, I guess."

"Ethan ... I can't believe it."

"All true." As he began telling her what happened, it only became harder for her to wrap her mind around it. She wouldn't have believed such a tale from anyone else.

Michael was the killer.

And Sydney was a vampire.

After wolfing down two and a half asiago bagels, a couple of protein bars, and two tall glasses of orange juice - a breakfast more than twice the size he usually ate - Ethan started the shower and stared at his reflection in the mirror while the water warmed. Despite getting exactly zero hours of sleep, he was bright-eyed and bushy-tailed. The claw marks on his face had already faded to a mere soft pink. *Maybe the damage wasn't as bad as I thought.* He unwrapped his hand and saw that it, too, was healing remarkably fast.

All things considered, he felt good. Still hungry somehow, but good. He was ready for the day and eager to get a handle on the Michael situation, and despite Winter's insistence that he stay out of it, Ethan had no intention of sitting back. He'd start with a one-man search of the woods. Raging or not, vampires were virtually useless during the day and it was possible that Michael had found a shadowed, deeply forested area to sleep away the sunny hours.

Not that it was sunny enough outside to kill a vampire - only direct sunlight did that - but it *would* slow one down. The sky was a dull shade of gunmetal gray that leeched the color out of everything and clouds half-heartedly spat a few drops of rain as if they'd exhausted themselves and were building strength for the next storm. And another one was coming, even bigger this time. The morning news said it would roll in this evening.

Ethan scratched the fading bite mark on his hand - it itched like hell - then stepped into the shower, ticking off a list of items he'd need for his solitary manhunt: the cross from one of Sheila's necklaces, the old Bible that sat ignored in his nightstand. He didn't have any silver, but that was fine. The weapons were to protect himself, not kill anyone - though given Michael's crimes, Ethan could have justified it. It occurred to him that he didn't actually know what he'd do if he found the man. He couldn't throw him in jail - nor could he let him go. *I guess I'll cross that bridge when I get there.*

Then his thoughts slid back to food and sex. He wanted more of both. Lots more. If he hurried, he and Sheila might have time for another round before she headed to the morgue. He'd been rough with her last night - something he'd never been before - and he could tell she wasn't sure what to make of it. But it had been good, damned good, and as he thought of it now, his cock, as if making amends for its recent failures, stood at full, proud attention. He looked down at it. *Well, aren't you an eager beaver this morning.*

He chuckled and continued soaping and scrubbing.

Though it had been drizzling most of the day, when the real storm came to Crimson Cove, it was as if an angry god had lost his temper and begun kicking over buckets of rain water, grinding out the sounds of thunder with heavy heels, and throwing bolts of lightning.

The east wind pushed the storm across town in vicious, angry sheets that streamed off the Colter cabin's roof, gurgled along the gutters, and rushed noisily to the ground. Outside, trees and bushes dipped, shuddered, and swayed, tossing off rain like dogs shaking themselves dry.

Inside, Purrcy hid beneath the sofa and Cade stood at the kitchen window, watching as whirlwinds of cold water raced through the trees, assaulting everything in sight, including Fernando, the fern. Cade worried the poor thing might be ripped right from its roots.

Lightning flickered too close and thunder clapped and roared like applause. Cade stepped away from the window and back into the living room to try once more to comfort his stressed-out cat. He crouched and stared under the sofa. "Are you all right down there? Want to come out yet?" Purrcy blinked wide eyes at him, but remained in place. "Have it your way."

Cade wondered where Brooks was, and if he had shelter. When he caught himself thinking about it, he told himself he didn't care, that his brother - no, his *ex*-brother - deserved whatever he got.

Though there were still a few hours till sundown, the room was dark and Cade switched on a lamp, grateful that the power wasn't down - not yet, anyway. His phone service was working as well.

He went into his room, flipped on the computer, and tried to do some edits on his novel. But every few lines, he'd find himself thinking of Samantha. Or Brooks. Or Michael. Occasionally, his thoughts drifted to Muriel and Kendon. The woman had called him earlier but hadn't left a message. He wondered what she wanted. No, he decided. He didn't want to know.

As the snare drum sounds of rain hummed and shooshed along all sides of the cabin, he remembered the wasps. It brought gooseflesh to his bare skin and made him feel vulnerable. He tried to ignore it, tried to focus on his book, but the sense that the insects were drawing nearer only grew stronger.

Then he felt things moving on him.

Insectile legs.

Crawling up his thighs.

On his arms.

His face.

He jerked and slapped at them.

Nothing was there, but the terror, though brief, was acute. It brought a slimy sweat to his face. Suddenly cold and needing to take a leak, he started for the bathroom, ignoring how the swish of wind in trees outside was like the beat of a thousand wings and the taps of rain on the window glass like a horde of wasps seeking entrance. *Calm the hell down.* As he relieved himself, he took slow, deep breaths. His imagination had run away with him. Again. He had to do something to occupy his mind before he lathered himself into a full-blown panic.

Go through Samantha's things. He dreaded the thought. It was something he'd been putting off; he hadn't been ready to deal with it. *But it's time to start thinking about it.* Cade shook off and flushed, intent on beginning the traitorous task.

But he wasn't sure where to start. There were pieces of her everywhere and the sight of her perfume collection and toiletries, which used to bring him comfort, now only tormented him. They were cruel reminders of how quickly normal life, happy life, could be obliterated by the swift, cruel hand of death. He picked up a bottle of her favorite perfume - *Lavande d'Amour* - and turned it over. It seemed so fragile. A single slip and the whole thing would shatter. *Just like life.*

His finger rested on the pump but he couldn't bring himself to mist the air with her signature scent. It would bring back sweet memories, yes ... but that sweetness would turn sour. He couldn't do it. But neither could he carelessly toss the bottle out; it was too heavy in his hand, as if it wanted to remain where it was. As if *she* didn't want him to throw it out. He glanced at the trash and tears blurred his vision.

He wished Muriel had never given him the idea of throwing out

Samantha's stuff. He felt like shit for even considering it and, setting the perfume bottle back down, he left the bathroom wondering how much longer could he live surrounded by her things. When was it appropriate to move on?

Just then, there was a hard knock on the front door, followed by a peal of thunder.

Who the hell would be paying him a visit in this weather? He threw back his curtains and glanced outside. A black Lexus stood in the driveway. He didn't know anyone who drove a black Lexus. Cade pulled on a shirt and headed to the front door.

THE NOW-STEADY DRIZZLE HADN'T MADE ETHAN'S FOREST ADVENTURE any easier; in fact it made it miserable. As he continued his search for vampire hideouts, he wished Crimson Cove knew autumn was supposed to be crisp and cool, or at least soggy and cool. To be fair, it was probably no more than 72 degrees, but it felt more like 85 as he trudged through the woods.

It's a fool's errand, he thought as he headed deeper into the woods behind Crimson Lake. Even if he did find Michael, he had no plan of action. *So, what's the point?* Idly, he thought he should've brought a stake. But he couldn't have used it. *Mmm, steak.* The very thought made his mouth water. *Maybe I should barbecue a couple steaks for dinner. And convince Sheila she's dessert.* He grinned to himself, wondering what the hell was going on with his sex drive all of a sudden. He was as horny as a fourteen-year-old boy and had had to think away a woody at least three times already despite the morning sexfest with Sheila.

He adjusted his erection then rubbed his itchy hand against the fabric of his trousers. The heightened sex drive was probably just his natural response to almost being killed by his ex-wife. That made sense, he supposed, but he couldn't help wondering why God made human beings so fucked up.

He halted and pulled a bottle of water out of his back pocket and drank the dregs down. Still thirsty, he dropped the bottle, slung his day pack off his back and opened it. "Damn it to hell and back." He'd run out. He picked up the empty, tossed in in the pack, then slung it back over his shoulder, and as he did so, something caught his eye.

Something that stood out in a copse of pines. A stone chimney. *An old cabin, maybe?* He was too far away to be sure, but with new hope he shouldered his pack and headed toward it.

He was right. It was a dilapidated redwood structure, slightly skewed with age, and from the looks of it, inhabited only by woodland creatures. The place had a bad case of scoliosis and the windows were boarded up.

As he neared, he stepped right into a little creek, hardly more than a hoseful of water, but his Nike sank into the mud and with a squelching sucking sound, it stuck. Ethan tripped, losing the shoe and landing on his hands and knees. "Goddamnit!"

Turning, he fought with the mud and finally freed his shoe. What was once white was now shit-brown inside and out. He did his best to clean it in the miserable little stream then somehow managed to get it back on his foot. "Damn it."

Grabbing his pack, he turned to look at the cabin. It was dinky, but something about it - the front porch, maybe - reminded him of the Colter cabin. He approached the four rickety stairs and tried a step. Then two. The third one cracked under his weight and he skipped it.

The wooden porch was rotting away, but there was something about the place that made him think someone had been here. *Squatters?* That wasn't likely. Still, hand on his holstered .38, he couldn't take chances. The front door was shut and he saw nail holes indicating it had been boarded up. But it wasn't now. He rapped smartly on the weather-beaten door. "Anybody home?" He knocked again. "It's the sheriff. Anybody there?"

He waited, listening carefully, and heard nothing. Not a creak, not a whisper, not a goddamned thing.

He tried the doorknob. It turned freely, but the door didn't budge. Something was holding it in place inside. He hammered on the door. "This is the Crimson County Sheriff. Open up."

Silence.

He turned the knob and began pushing. He felt something heavy move out of the door's path, and finally, got it about a foot open. "Hello?"

No answer. He dropped the pack and fished out his rubber-handled flashlight and shined it into the dark room.

Nothing stirred, but there were a few pieces of furniture in the room - a few folding chairs and a card table where a game of Monopoly stood waiting. Piles of clothes covered the chairs.

He left the pack outside and slid through the door and instantly, he smelled wood rot and mildew - and aftershave.

He shined the light over the small room. The fireplace was as damaged inside as out - the missing stones from the chimney had fallen into the firebox. But on the stone hearth were men's toiletries carefully laid out. Razors, deodorant, combs, a couple different kinds of aftershave. *Well-groomed squatters.*

Michael? But as he looked at the labels on the aftershave bottles, he didn't think so - these were Old Spice and Drakkar Noir. Michael was a more upscale type of guy and no way had he had enough time to acquire all this stuff, anyway.

Ethan stepped around a gaping hole in the rotting floor and approached an interior door. He played his light inside the smaller room and to his surprise, saw a couple bright prints hanging on the moldy gray wall. They looked new. Sunflowers in a bright blue pot and a street scene in Victorian Paris.

And then he saw the hollowed-out spaces in the middle of the floor, side by side, like two empty plots. Ethan moved closer and crouched, shining his light down the first of them. "You've got to be shitting me," he whispered.

Brooks Colter lay, eyes closed, as pale and eerily still as a wax statue. A new scar began in his right eyebrow and twisted into his hairline. His dark hair was streaked with a shot of silver there, and his features seemed to have sharpened; he'd become even handsomer in un-life.

Ethan moved the beam over the elder Colter's hooded sweatshirt, jeans, and muddy tennis shoes. Brooks didn't stir and Ethan checked out the occupant of the other space.

The guy in this one was big and dark-haired, and Ethan recognized him at once as the missing Peddler Puck's worker, Rafe Santangelo. Santangelo, too, slept the sleep of the dead, but somehow didn't possess quite the same mannequin-like appearance as Brooks. Whereas Colter looked like a well-preserved corpse, Santangelo just looked like a regular guy in a deep sleep. How the two of them had come together, Ethan hadn't a clue.

"I'll be a son of a bitch." Ethan switched off his flashlight for fear of waking the men. Looking at his watch, he pulled his phone from his pocket. First he texted Sheila, telling her he'd be working late - probably until well after sundown. Then he texted Winter, letting him know what - and more specifically, who - he'd found. Winter wouldn't get the message until after sunset of course, but Ethan sent him the GPS to the decaying cabin, asking him to come as soon as he could. Ethan had no idea how Brooks might react when he woke up and saw him there - he might need back-up.

Dragging a folding chair in from the other room, Ethan positioned himself at the foot of the vampire's earthen beds. There was no way he was leaving until Brooks and his buddy woke up and he could talk to them. How he would pass the next several hours, however, he didn't know. Looking around, he saw a small stack of dirty magazines shoved into a corner. *No way.* He was having enough trouble keeping his mind off sex today without the aid of porn.

Against another wall were some paperbacks. *That's better.* Ethan got up to look them over. There were none of the more embarrassing titles that he secretly enjoyed - only sci-fi and fantasy: Isaac Asimov, Robert Heinlein, Ray Bradbury. Ethan chose a copy of *The Halloween Tree* and returned to his folding chair and began reading, waiting for sundown.

43

HIGH STAKES

"It's time we had a talk, Cade." Muriel and Kendon from the Life After Loss grief support group stood on the porch. Even in a glistening wet rain slicker, she gave off an air of regality. Kendon, in an oversized raincoat, stood beside her, his gaze flickering nervously over the Adirondack chairs on the porch.

Muriel, however, had no trouble making eye contact. She stared at Cade with an intensity that bordered on invasive.

"A talk?" Cade's pulse did a little tap dance. *What the hell does she want from me?* "A talk about *what*?"

"The murders," said Muriel. "Specifically, the murder of your girlfriend."

Cade stared at her. Thunder crashed.

"There have been more, as I'm sure you're aware," she continued. "It's time to do something about it." Her voice was as steely as her eyes and the wind delivered traces of her cinnamon scent.

"I don't ..." but something made Cade stop - perhaps it was the way she looked at him, as if to say the jig was up. She meant business. Cade nodded and stepped aside.

Kendon helped her out of her slicker, shrugged out of his own, and draped both across an Adirondack chair before entering.

More thunder boomed as Cade closed the door behind them. "Please, sit down." He gestured at the sofa and realized his hands were trembling.

Muriel and Kendon sat down and before Cade could offer them a cup of coffee, Muriel said, "We're well aware of what really happened to Samantha, Cade, and we think you are, too."

Cade glanced between the two of them. He considered playing dumb but the iron certainty in Muriel's eyes made it clear she wasn't here on a hunch. *They know. Somehow, they know everything.* Anxiety coiled coldly in his stomach. With blind fingertips, he felt for the recliner and perched himself on the edge of its arm.

Muriel smiled warmly. "You're a smart young man, Cade. I saw that from the beginning."

"The ... beginning?" Cade looked to Kendon. The other man offered no help.

Muriel nodded, slow and sure. "You've sensed that we know something about Samantha's death and it frightens you. You shouldn't be frightened. We mean you no harm."

He remained stock-still and placid-faced. Sweat had broken in his armpits and groin and he felt his pulse beating in his neck, but he believed her: They meant him no harm. Still, he couldn't afford to tip his hand. "I know you have some interest in what happened to my girlfriend - I saw the looks you two exchanged when I talked about her at the meeting - but I'm not sure-"

"Like I said, smart." Muriel tapped her temple and smiled. "Perceptive."

Cade looked from Muriel to Kendon. "What's your interest in her?"

"We have no particular interest in *her*, Cade," said Muriel. "But in her death, we have plenty."

Cade stared stonily at her. "What's your interest in her death?"

Muriel, a rigid upright slash, nodded. "I'll get to the point."

"Please do."

"I won't ask you what you know, not yet. I'm going to tell you what

I know - what *we* know - and then you can decide how much of your own story you want to share."

Cade crossed his arms. "Fair enough."

Muriel closed her eyes and, released from that steely dark gaze, Cade was able to breathe easier.

"I suppose I'd better start at the beginning." But for a long moment, she didn't speak.

Kendon spoke up. "I think the best way to say it is-"

But Muriel silenced him with a raised hand. "As you know from the group meetings, Cade, I had a younger sister who was killed."

"I remember."

"Her name was Marion. After the death of our parents when I was just seventeen, I was left to raise her on my own. I was ill-prepared to take care of a child - Marion was nearly ten years my junior - and I'm afraid I probably didn't do a very good job." Another long silence.

Cade wasn't in the mood for the woman's entire history. "I'm sorry to hear that but what does this have to do with my girlfriend?"

"Be patient. This story deserves some time." This in a take-no-prisoners voice.

Cade nodded.

"As a teen, Marion rebelled. She was dabbling in drugs and running with a bad crowd. When she was nineteen, I kicked her out because I knew that tough love was the only way to get her straight." She paused, reflecting. "It worked. For the next twelve years, she remained clean. She put herself through school, and ended up with a good job. I was proud of her. But that's not the part that concerns you. I only tell you that to help you understand my relationship with her. The story *really* starts when Marion met *him*."

"Him?"

Muriel nodded. "His name was Roberto, and they met at a nightclub here in Crimson Cove. She began an affair with him and quickly backslid, falling into her old destructive habits - but it was different this time. Worse. At first I thought the man had addicted her to heroin. You see, I worked - and still work - as head nurse at Oceanview Psychiatric Institute where I specialize in drug-induced psychoses. Marion's symptoms were consistent with heroin addiction. I was certain that was what I was looking at. But I began to dig and eventually got the truth from her, and I learned that it had nothing to do with heroin. Her vice was something worse, something deadlier. Something I didn't believe - *couldn't* believe - for a very long time."

She paused, watching Cade, waiting for a reaction that he refused to give her.

"The club I'm referring to, of course, is the Crimson Corset. Perhaps you've heard of it?"

Still, Cade said nothing, but his throat went dry as desert sand.

"The Crimson Corset was Pandora's Box and my sister not only opened it, but stepped right inside." Muriel leaned forward, pinning Cade in her gaze with an almost physical force. "And it wasn't heroin she became addicted to. It was another substance, venom, and it came from a woman named Gretchen VanTreese." Muriel continued watching Cade, her eyes flint-hard and unblinking. "And it was then, three years ago, that I learned of the existence of vampires."

Even though he'd seen it coming, the word dropped like a bomb, the room seemed to darken and Cade turned cold. "Vampires?" He tried to sound incredulous but it came out an uncertain squeak.

"Yes." More staring.

Cade swallowed and searched frantically for what to say next, but Muriel didn't let him flounder for long. "Gretchen, who'd been using Marion for blood, eventually grew bored and disposed of her. And by disposed of her, I mean that she murdered my little sister. Brutally. So I went on a mission. I was convinced there were others like me who'd lost loved ones to vampires. I began seeking out these survivors. Grief support groups seemed the logical place to start."

Kendon cleared his throat. "And that's how she met me."

"You?" asked Cade.

The younger man nodded. "My boyfriend, Martin, and I were leaving a club one night just outside of Santa Cruz and were attacked. The man - or rather, the vampire - tore Martin to shreds with no weapon at all. I got away and went straight to the police, but when I told them what happened, they thought I was in shock and having some kind of psychotic break. No man could do what had been done to Martin, they said, especially with only his bare hands and his ... *teeth*. An animal did it, a bear, they said, and in my distress, I'd gotten confused and imagined it was a man. That's what they told me." Kendon leaned forward, his eyes shimmering lakes of blazing anger and naked pain. "But I was there, I *saw* what happened. It wasn't a bear. It was a man. No, not a man - a *vampire*."

Muriel nodded.

Cade felt a wave of vertigo. If these people knew about Gretchen, about Samantha ... What about Brooks? Did they know about him?

Kendon leaned forward. "Anyway, I started to think maybe I *was* crazy. I started drinking and ended up in legal trouble and a judge ordered me to see a psychiatrist. The psychiatrist agreed with law enforcement, saying I'd invented the murderer. He said it was because I needed someone to blame. It was a coping mechanism, he told me, and not all that uncommon. But I knew better. So I clammed up, deciding I'd never tell another living soul what I witnessed that night. I became unresponsive to my therapy and the psychiatrist referred me to a grief support group - Life After Loss in Santa Cruz."

Muriel picked up. "I listened to Kendon's story about the animal attack and thought nothing of it at first, but then something piqued my interest. More than once, Kendon referred to the animal as *he* or *him*. I started to wonder if his boyfriend had been murdered, and if so, why Kendon was covering it up." She squeezed the younger man's hand. "The more I listened, the more convinced I became that I was onto something, so I made it a point to get to know Kendon - and get to the truth. I showed him he could trust me, and when the time was right, I pointed out that there were pieces missing from his story. I told him I wanted to know what really happened that night." She paused, watching Cade. "I sense the same missing pieces in your story, Cade. I know a bear didn't kill your girlfriend, and I know that you know it, too. I knew it the first time you came to the meeting. I saw the way the blood drained from your face when Kendon told his story, and I knew."

A thick, cloying silence. Cade knew what they were trying to do.

They were trying to establish trust. They'd told their stories and now he was supposed to tell his. But that wasn't going to happen. He only said, "I'm not sure how you want me to respond."

"I understand." Muriel smiled. "You're not sure about us just yet. Let me assure you that our only motive is to help you."

"Help me? Help me how?"

"By doing the only thing we can at this point - by bringing the vampire who killed your loved one to justice. By bringing them *all* to justice."

"Justice?" His voice cracked.

She hesitated. "By catching them and ... exterminating them."

Cade's eyes widened and he almost laughed. "You're ... vampire slayers? You two? Like *Buffy*?"

"I guess you could say that," said Muriel. "But it's not just the two of us. We're growing. As of now we have nearly a half dozen members. But we need more."

"So ... you're asking me to ... join your group of vampire hunters and ... help you kill some bad vampires?"

"Is there any other kind?"

Cade opened his mouth, snapped it shut. If they didn't know about the good guys - Michael's guys - he wasn't about to tell them.

"All vampires are evil, Cade. They have no souls."

But Cade knew better than that, too. Winter had just explained that most vampires were ensouled.

"You know that better than anyone, don't you?" Muriel asked.

Buying time, Cade said, "Vampire slayers. For *real*?"

"The Exterminators," Kendon said. "That's the name of our group."

Cade laughed and it surprised them all. "The Exterminators? It sounds like a pest-control company." But he immediately regretted the joke. Neither Muriel nor Kendon saw the humor. Their faces remained deadly serious.

"That's right," said Kendon.

Mind racing, Cade cleared his throat. He needed to get out of this conversation, away from these lunatics. "I, uh ... well ... I'm sorry, but this is all just a little too much for me. I-"

"Are you denying the existence of the walking undead?" asked Muriel. "Even after what happened to Samantha? After what we *know* you witnessed?"

Cade blinked at her. "You don't know what I witnessed." He was getting angry now.

She smiled. "But I do. I also know what happened between your brother and Gretchen VanTreese last year."

Shit. How did she know about Brooks? Despite his efforts to play it cool, Cade's jaw dropped. "But … how …?"

"I've done my homework," said Muriel. "What happened to your brother is exactly what happened to my sister. Except, of course, that Marion was killed. The point is, I know what I'm looking at."

So there was no doubt. She knew about Gretchen and Brooks and the vampires of the Crimson Corset - but she couldn't know that Michael was the murderer. If she knew about his group at Eudemonia at all, she wasn't saying. But did she? Had she been watching them? Had she seen Winter and Chynna traipsing in and out of his house? "How did you find out where I live?" He suddenly realized he'd never told them.

"Crimson Cove is a very small town. I simply asked around and-"

"Well I wish you hadn't done that." His heart hammered in earnest now. Muriel was dangerous. "I don't appreciate being spied on."

She smiled gently. "Understood, but please try to see this from our point of view. There's a problem in this town, Cade, a big one. How many more murders are going to happen at the hands of vampires while law enforcement lays the blame on lions and tigers and bears?"

Law enforcement. Cade thought of Ethan, then of Brooks and Michael and Winter. Of Dante and Rogan and Emmeline. Muriel's group wanted to kill all vampires - not some, but *all*. He needed to keep Muriel and Kendon - *The Exterminators* - far away from Eudemonia. But first, he needed to find out how much they really knew and that required playing dumb. "You said there was a vampire problem in this town and that they used to hang out at the Crimson Corset. But the Crimson Corset is closed down and no one even knows where Gretchen VanTreese went. She's ... dead." The lie didn't come easy.

"But there are others."

"Others where?" Cade plowed onward, hoping to lead her far away from Michael and his Loyals. "You said Kendon's boyfriend was killed in Santa Cruz. Does that mean vampires are all over the place, roaming the entire state, the country? The whole *world*?"

"They probably are, but we can only kill one at a time. All we know right now is that there's definitely a vampire here in Crimson Cove. The same one who killed your girlfriend, the same one who's killing the others."

A vampire, she'd said. As in just one. So they weren't aware of Michael or anyone at Eudemonia. Nor were they aware that Brooks had killed Samantha. But Cade's relief was short-lived. If they figured it out, they'd execute both of them.

And Cade wouldn't allow that.

He glanced at the clock. He needed to get them out of here before dark, before Winter or Chynna showed up. "Look, this is a very entertaining theory but I'm afraid I don't buy it. I mean, *vampires*? I'm sorry but I can't listen to any more of this."

Muriel looked incredulous. "You're going to deny it? All of it?"

"There's nothing here to believe. It's outrageous." He was fidgeting, acting nervous. And he *was* nervous. "Look, I'm sorry, but I need to ask you to leave now. I've got a lot to do and-"

Muriel held up a hand. "Understood." She gave Kendon a nod and they both stood.

Cade got up and headed toward the door, but Muriel stopped in front of it and turned to face him. "You know where to find me if you change your mind."

The two held a brief staring contest. Cade said, "Change my mind about what?"

"About telling us what you know. About telling us the truth." She made no move to leave so Cade reached past her and pulled the door open.

"You have my number, I assume?"

Cade glanced at the darkening sky. There was no more time; he needed them gone, and now. Night was coming. Winter was coming, Chynna too, probably. "I've got it, yes."

"Good. I hope you use it."

"Goodbye."

And without another word, Muriel and Kendon left his house.

Cade shut the door behind them, stepped to the window, and watched them leave. He hoped never to see either of them ever again.

44

YAWN OF THE DEAD

Brooks yawned, waking to the sound of rain beating on the rotted roof of the cabin ... and the looming face of Ethan Hunter gazing down at him. He jumped. "What the-"

"Nice place you got here, Colter." Ethan sounded amused.

Brooks sat up. "What are you doing here?" But he knew why the man had come. *To arrest me for killing Samantha.* A tangle of emotions overcame him. He was scared but also relieved; he was tired of hiding, tired of running away. *Time to face the music.* He lifted himself from his makeshift sleeping chamber, half expecting Ethan to pull his gun.

But the sheriff didn't move. He sat in a chair, looking as cautious of Brooks as Brooks was of him. For long moments the only sound was the rain spilling through the roof and dripping onto the rotting cabin floor.

Finally, Ethan spoke. "I'm not here to arrest you if that's what you're thinking."

Brooks' muscles, cramped with tension, relaxed. "You're not?"

"Nope."

The tick of rain, the sound of distant rolling thunder. Slowly, cautiously, Brooks pulled up a chair and sat. "Why not?"

The sheriff shrugged. "For one thing, you're a vampire." He nodded at Rafe's earth-bed. "Is it safe to assume your compadre is too?"

"He's ... not exactly. He's in retrograde."

Ethan tipped his head. "Retrograde?"

"I accidentally envenomated him but I've seen to it that he hasn't had human blood yet. His transition isn't complete."

"So, what have the two of you been surviving on?"

"Wildlife, and nothing but." Brooks met Ethan's eyes. "I give you my word."

"I believe you."

"You do?"

The sheriff nodded. "I do. And what about Gretchen VanTreese? Have you ... seen her?"

"No. And I hope I never do."

Ethan watched him closely. "Are you sure about that? You should be crawling out of your skin to get to her, shouldn't you?"

Brooks sighed and leaned forward, clasping his hands between his knees. "It was hard at first. I wanted to go to her, but ... I didn't. I don't want anything to do with her. She's done enough damage."

"You're right about that."

"I wouldn't even know where to start looking for her anyway. I know she's out there, I can sense her, but ..." Brooks shook his head. "I'm just not interested in hunting her down. Not at all." He didn't mention the many nights he'd spent fighting back that urge.

"Do you think she's close?"

Brooks shrugged. "No idea. This is still pretty new to me."

Ethan sighed. "Well, I think it's time you come home."

Brooks stared at him. "I can't go home. Cade-"

"I don't mean *home* home."

Confused, Brooks asked, "Then where?"

"Eudemonia."

"Eudemonia? But Michael ... does he know what happened? He'll kill me if-"

"Michael won't be a problem, trust me."

"How's that?"

Ethan shifted in his seat. "Let's just say things have changed since you've been gone."

The look on the sheriff's face told Brooks something wasn't right. "It isn't about Cade, is it? Is he-"

"Cade's fine. Well, as fine as can be expected."

Brooks' throat tightened. "I'm sure he hates me."

Avoiding that topic, Ethan continued. "Anyway, I've discussed it with Winter. He's on his way here now. You and your friend are going to stay at Eudemonia for a while and, uh, get your bearings." He met Brooks' eyes. "As long as you keep this ... vampire stuff under control from here on out, I won't have to arrest you." He paused. "And evidently, you've done a pretty good job so far."

"Yeah, well, I learned from Michael," said Brooks. "I remembered what he told us about his lifestyle and ... I applied it. I don't want to live like a savage." He thought of Samantha, of what he'd done to her, and winced. "I don't want to kill anyone else, Ethan. Not ever." His voice cracked.

Outside, lightning flashed and thunder grumbled, closer now.

Brooks sniffed and pulled back. "Ethan, I want to see Cade. I need to."

The sheriff shook his head. "Not yet. Not for a while."

"But-"

"It's not a good idea right now." This, in the voice that meant business.

Brooks didn't argue but was determined to see his brother again. Maybe it wasn't a good idea to try to talk to him yet, but no one could stop his secret visits to his old home. Tonight, he decided, he'd go look in on Cade again.

Headlights flashed outside, their beams breaking through the cracks of the decaying walls, and brightening the room.

"That'll be Winter," Ethan said. "Why don't you wake your friend and let him know what's going on." He paused. "And Colter?" Ethan stared at the space between his feet. "I missed you."

Fresh tears pricked Brooks' eyes. "I missed you, too."

45

ESCAPE FROM DOMESTICITY

From the shadows of the forest, Michael Ward watched as Winter led Brooks Colter and another man from the old crooked cabin to the white Hummer. They were followed by Sheriff Ethan Hunter - and that's when Michael realized what had drawn him so near to the dilapidated cabin. *Blood. Human blood. Ethan's blood.* The men piled into the vehicle, the engine roared to life, and Michael ducked as headlights slashed through the shadows.

Watching his quarry slip away was almost painful. When the engine's sounds faded he stood, scanning the forest. The wind had the trees shimmying like dancing drunks. Save for the hiss of wind and patter of rain, the woods were silent. There was nothing more here for him. He did not want to live in the wilderness, surviving on animals, nor could he return to Crimson Cove. Not after what he'd done - not after what he knew he would continue to do. Even now his hunger was ferocious - he'd put off feeding for too long - and he intended to fully gorge himself tonight. It was just a matter of finding the next kill.

Santa Cruz. It was his best option; it was crowded with people. There, he could feed freely. Like a sign from the heavens, lightning lit up the night. *Yes, Santa Cruz.* Though his clothes and hair were sodden, he was not cold, but suddenly warm, suddenly alive. More alive than he'd been in ages. Raising his head, taking in the heady scents of rain and wet earth, he tried to detect the blood of some forest creature, just something to tide him over.

But even the wildlife had taken deep cover from the storm. Pushing his long wet hair out of his face, Michael began walking, and then, as his hunger sharpened, he ran. If he hurried, he could make it to Santa Cruz before sunrise.

In his raging state, it did not occur to him that he might miss Crimson Cove or any of its inhabitants. As the hunger cut deeper into him, there was little of the human mind left; he thought only of the kill, the blood. Hot, salty, coppery blood.

He ran and ran, defying the driving wind - defying the civilized nature he'd been forcing himself to adhere to. *Lies, all lies.* He was a killer, had always been a killer, he knew that now - and reveled in it.

So, he ran from Crimson Cove, from the lies he'd told himself there, knowing that nothing would turn him around this time. He'd gone too far - too deep - into the truth of his own nature.

46

KNOWN UNKNOWNS

Cade said nothing to Chynna about his unexpected visit from Muriel and Kendon. Nor did he mention it to Winter when he showed up a couple of hours later - and, Cade decided, he never would. Winter had arrived with news of Brooks, and that took precedence anyway.

They'd found him in the woods and taken him to Eudemonia. According to Winter, Brooks was his old self, not the undead killing machine that Cade - and everyone else - had worried he'd become.

Cade could tell by Winter's and Chynna's hopeful glances that he was supposed to be happy that his brother had rehabilitated himself and could now live a productive life as one of the good guys, but Cade couldn't find that joy. All he felt was that same volcanic anger. "So," he said, interrupting Winter's monologue, "he kills Samantha, and *then* decides to do the right thing. How thoughtful of him."

Winter sat forward in the recliner. "You have to understand Gilroy, the bloodlust is strong in the beginning. We all make mistakes and being that Samantha had AB Negative blood, it's not a surprise. Brooks wasn't prepared and-"

"I know, I know." Cade held up his hand. He'd heard it all before.

Chynna sat beside him on the sofa, Purrcy curled in her lap. She touched Cade's hand. It was a pleading touch, the kind that asked understanding. "Samantha's death was a tragedy. No one's disputing that, Cade. But what happened to her ... that's probably *why* your brother learned to get himself under control. Because he couldn't live with-"

"So you're saying it's a *good* thing he killed her? So he could learn an important lesson about self-control?"

"No ... no, of course not, but ..." Her silvery eyes flashed to Winter for help.

"Look, Gilroy." Winter leaned forward, his large hands clamped on his knees. "If you're going to blame someone for what happened, blame Gretchen VanTreese for turning him."

"Or Michael," said Cade, "for not lopping off her head when he had the chance."

Winter averted his gaze. "He did what he thought was right."

"But he was wrong," said Cade. "Wasn't he?"

Winter didn't argue and Cade sensed that he agreed with him.

Purrcy batted an impatient paw and Chynna resumed stroking him under the chin. "None of this brings Samantha back," she said. "I think the important thing now is that Brooks is trying. And as for Gretchen, well ... I guess we'll deal with her when we locate her."

"Deal with her how?" asked Cade.

Winter and Chynna looked uncertain.

"She needs to be stopped," Cade said, cutting his gaze from one vampire to the other. "And not the way Michael stopped her, but *truly* stopped. For good. You said if there's anyone to blame it's her, so we should find her and do something about it. Something *permanent* ... while Michael's out of the picture."

The only sounds were the tick of the clock, the tap of the rain, the purr of the cat, and a distant roll of thunder.

"But we don't even know where she is," said Chynna.

"She's probably long gone," added Winter.

Cade wondered if either would go against Michael's wishes and kill her if they had the chance. He wasn't sure. His thoughts drifted to

Muriel and her group, the Exterminators, but he clipped them off. *Not an option.*

Gretchen probably really was long gone. Winter said that even Brooks hadn't seen her, and Cade believed it.

She'd be a fool to remain in Crimson Cove - and Gretchen VanTreese, Cade thought, was no fool.

VAMPIRES. IMMORTALS. BLOOD SUCKERS. THE UNDEAD. NOT ONLY WERE they real, but Sydney Hunter-Doss was one of them. It was too much to comprehend and her emotions clashed hard enough that her sanity threatened to crack. She had to find a way to mellow out.

She sat up in bed, trying to collect her kaleidoscoping thoughts. Glancing at Emmeline, who sat in a chair working on a crossword puzzle as if the whole world hadn't just been tipped upside down, Sydney wondered how well the woman had adapted to her own transition so long ago. Given the stiff-spined air of cool competence, Sydney couldn't imagine the former suffragette having trouble handling anything.

Vampires. Immortals. Blood suckers. The undead.

And I'm one of them.

Not possible. It's just not possible.

But it was - and that meant that everything she'd ever believed was wrong. *What about God? And Jesus?* She couldn't even go there.

She cleared her throat. "When will he be back?" she asked Emmeline.

The other woman looked up from her puzzle. "Winter?"

Sydney nodded. As aghast as she was at the implications of her new existence, she was equally - and suddenly - obsessed by the giant blond bodybuilder who'd turned her. Being away from him was like falling down a hole.

"He's gone for the night, I'm afraid."

"But *why*? Where is he?"

With a maternal smile, Emmeline stood and fluffed Sydney's pillow. "Just rest, dear. There's plenty of time for questions later." She grabbed the glass from the night stand and held it in front of Sydney - and even as she sipped the blood, she couldn't believe she was doing it. Sydney closed her eyes and relished the coppery tang of life and with every swallow, peace tightened warm arms around her. The blood - and Winter - were the only things that made sense, the only things that mattered.

Finished, she slumped back into the pillows and stared out at the night beyond the window. The blood had soothed her, but it did nothing to erase the feeling that this was some kind of test, perhaps a test of faith that the Lord trusted her to face - and overcome. *No, this isn't God's will. It can't be.* Surely, God wouldn't bestow such a curse even on His most faithful. This was something else. This was ... unholy, evil.

Sydney's eyes welled with tears. *I can't do this,* she thought. *I won't succumb to it. It's not natural.*

She had no idea how - not yet, anyway - but she was going to get out of it. She wouldn't - *couldn't* - live like this.

She thought of Winter - *He did this to me*! How could she have thought she needed him, *loved* him even. It was all his fault.

He should have let me die.

But he hadn't, and Sydney should hate him for it. *I* will *hate him! That's what he deserves*!

Then and there she made a vow that despite her irrational adoration of her Maker, she *would* not love him. She would find a way to turn off her feelings.

She started by shifting her thoughts to Michael Ward, the man she'd fallen in love with - *genuinely* fallen in love with - before all of this happened.

Yes. Michael. It was he, not Winter, who deserved her love. *In spite of what he's done ...*

BROOKS COULDN'T SIT STILL. AT EUDEMONIA, HE AND RAFE HAD THEIR own rooms and plenty of sustenance - deer's blood from Chynna's latest kill for Rafe, and some human O positive for Brooks from a stash of blood bags the vamps kept in the basement. It was nice to be out of the decaying cabin, but Brooks' nerves were frayed and raw. He paced the length of the room, thinking, thinking. Ethan had filled him in on everything. So much had happened since he'd taken off that Brooks couldn't get his head around it: dead bodies, missing persons, Ethan's ex-wife now a vampire.

And Michael. It was so hard to swallow. He was a killer. *A killer!* The words echoed through Brooks' mind as if someone were shouting them down an endless canyon. *A killer.* And now the man had gone missing and somewhere out there, he was rage-killing.

And Cade: the fistfight at the bookstore, the group therapy, the weight loss. He was the real reason Brooks was pacing the floor; he needed to see his little brother.

Earlier, he'd asked to go along with Winter when he went to the cabin - he and Chynna were guarding Cade until Gretchen was apprehended - but Winter told him no, saying that his brother wasn't ready to see him.

But Brooks *was* ready. He needed to see Cade - and let Cade see him. He needed to know where he stood.

Brooks paused, staring out into the night. Rain poured, lightning flashed, and thunder cracked like gunshots.

No one would know if he disappeared for a while. Rafe was in his room across the hall, probably drunk on deer's blood, Ethan had left on a disturbance call, and Emmeline was with Sydney on another floor. There were others, but none who'd look in on him. *And even if they did, so what? I'm a grown man. And if Cade doesn't want to see me he can tell me to get lost. Even if he tells me to fuck off, it'd be better than this ... this ... silence. This not knowing ...*

A new thought struck: Though his weeks in the woods had taught him self-restraint, he wondered if he strong enough to resist Cade's blood - *Sire* blood?

Brooks downed another ration, his third for the night, just to be safe, then, his mind made up, he eased the bedroom door open and glanced down the hallway. The place was silent and deserted. Shutting the door quietly behind himself, he hurried down the hall, out of the building, and away from Eudemonia, toward the cabin he once shared with Cade. Not to try to strong arm his brother into a peace treaty, but just to see him. Just to find out how much his little brother really hated him.

47

REVIVAL

"Well, shit." When Ethan pulled into the lot of the abandoned Crimson Corset nightclub at the edge of town, he wished he'd brought back-up. He was responding to a disturbance call from a passerby who'd seen flashlights shining from within the tinted windows of the club. Ethan had assumed kids had broken in, probably to drink, smoke weed, fornicate, and perhaps do a little tagging - it wouldn't be the first time it had happened - but that's not what was going on tonight.

Lumber and saw horses were stacked outside the adjoining Black Garter restaurant next to abandoned circular saws. Apparently, the power wasn't yet on, and the crew was working with tools plugged into generators.

"Shit, shit, shit."

Several white pickup trucks bearing Crimson Lake Construction logos nosed up under the long awnings of the building like a litter of hungry piglets, their beds full of paint cans, tarps, shop-vacs, and enough building supplies to open a Home Depot of their own. A few men wore tool belts and stood smoking and chatting, near a sign that announced GRAND REOPENING in blood red letters lit by the floodlights. Music blasted from the cab of one of the trucks.

Ethan's stomach twisted as he pulled up near the group of loitering workers. They went silent, watching him as he rolled down his window.

"Evening, Sheriff." A burly man stepped forward, squinting around the smoke from a damp cigarette that bobbed on his lip.

"Evening," said Ethan.

"What can we do for you?"

Ethan killed the engine and the windshield wipers stopped mid-swipe. Rain sluiced down the glass. "You must be well-paid to work overtime in this weather."

The burly man flashed a yellow-toothed grin. "You know it. Triple-time. That little lady, the owner, says money's no object. She wants this place up and running ASAP!"

That little lady. Ethan's ulcer flared. "I don't suppose she's around, is she?"

Yellow-Teeth nodded toward the building. "She's in there."

"Could you do me a favor and ask her to come out? I'd like to talk to-" As if on cue, a petite figure near the club's open doorway detached itself from the shadows and Ethan's balls headed north and his stomach took a wrong turn. At just under the five-foot mark, Gretchen VanTreese looked like a little girl's favorite doll - the kind that stayed in its box and never got played with. Even so, Ethan was terrified.

With a scarlet smile, she drifted toward him, her face half-hidden under a lacy red parasol that was as fashionable as it was practical. Her long skirt and revealing top were also lacy and red, and the workers, their eyes riveted to her hourglass shape, parted like the red sea as she stepped through them, untouched by the pounding rain, toward Ethan's window. The scent of her, like rain and roses, tickled his senses and Ethan fought the urge to start the engine, punch the gas, and bolt.

"Sheriff." Her voice, so like the tinkle of wind chimes, dripped with sweet, sweet poison and with her white-blond hair pulled into long Rapunzel-plaits - not a strand out of place - she was beautiful, much more beautiful than he remembered. But it was trickery, a form of perjury, because beautiful or not, she was a lunatic. "We meet again." Her smile bore further false witness against her true nature and Ethan erupted in gooseflesh as she held out a pale slender hand tipped by crimson claw-like nails.

He couldn't bring himself to touch her. "I'd hoped you'd left town."

Yellow-Teeth lingered nearby, a bodyguard prepared to pounce. No doubt she'd pumped him full of enough venom that he'd wash her feet with his tongue if she asked. And she probably had.

Gretchen continued smiling her red smile as she withdrew her hand. "Is that any way to greet a lady? And after such a long absence! You're being rather rude, Sheriff."

"You're no lady, Ms. VanTreese."

Gretchen shrugged off his words and sidled closer to the window. "Haven't you missed me even a little bit, Sheriff? I've certainly missed *you*." Her emerald gaze glittered hungrily over his face, pausing on his lips, her eyes conveying pornographic thoughts.

He looked past her at the club, wondering how long she'd been planning her return, how many Loyals she'd since acquired, and what fresh hell awaited the residents of Crimson Cove.

And what he could do to stop her.

"I assume your license for the place is up to date."

Yellow-Teeth chuckled and shook his head - *This fuckin' guy* - and flicked his cigarette to the ground.

Gretchen splayed a hand across her breast, feigning offense. "Of course, Sheriff. You know better than anyone that I *always* dot my i's and cross my t's." She giggled then leaned in close, her gaze turning deadly serious. "And you also know there's nothing you can do to stop me from reopening." Her eyes, not sane, bored into Ethan. "Now, why don't you run along. I've got work to do, Sheriff."

Ethan didn't break the stare, but it took all he had. "I can and will make this hard for you, Ms. VanTreese."

Her red smile brightened. "Good. I like it rough."

"I've got friends at fire and health who owe me favors. Not to mention-"

Her laughter was like the tinkle of a silver dinner bell. "So we're going to play it this way, are we?"

Yellow-Teeth stepped closer but Ethan ignored him. "Yes, we are, I'm afraid."

"You're afraid?" She laughed. "Not half as afraid as you should be." Her feathery voice betrayed no malice, but her eyes - they were like toxic swamps concealing dangerous things.

"You do what you've got to do, Ms. VanTreese, and I'll do what I've got to do."

She shrugged and twirled her parasol. "You talk about rules as if I've ever been one to follow them." She clucked her tongue. "You know better, Sheriff."

Ethan started the engine, willing his fingers not to tremble. "You can expect visits from my friends."

"I look forward to meeting them. They sound utterly delicious." Her pink tongue slicked across her crimson lips in an X-rated display.

"You lay one fang on anyone in this town and you'll be answerable to me." Even to him, the threat sounded weak, and Gretchen giggled, high and mad.

"Run along, Sheriff. Surely, you've got paperwork to sort and donuts to eat. If you need me, I'll be here, running the most successful business in Crimson Cove."

"Not if I have anything to say about it."

"We shall see. We shall see."

And suddenly, the lights within the Swiss chalet structure bloomed, lighting up the night. The giant windmill fronting the building creaked and began to turn, and Gretchen, psycho that she was, giggled, pinched the fabric of her skirt, and curtsied prettily.

As the sheriff's tail lights painted the rain red, Gretchen sighed, and turned to the contractor. "You heard what he said." All courtesy was gone from her voice. "Go take care of it." She waved a hand, dismissing him.

The contractor grinned and bounded for his truck.

"And do keep it clean, please," she added.

"You got it." He started the engine, pulled out, and followed the sheriff.

48

RESURRECTION

*B*lood. Not just any blood, but *his* blood.

The scent of it rode the rain, was stolen by the wind, and had carried to the Crimson Cove cemetery, luring the unliving thing from its grave and setting it on a mindless, instinctual pursuit of sustenance, of survival.

The creatures of the forest, scenting the chemicals and rot and detecting the presence of something vile, took shelter. They peered out of their holes, from between tree branches, and from beneath bushes and shrubs, waiting in dread, and taking flight as the dead thing approached, lumbering through the rain on rotted legs. It groaned as it step-dragged through the forest, its dirt-clotted hands reaching and clenching, seeking out tender living flesh, and moving ever-steadily toward the source of the blood.

Not just any blood, but *his* blood.

49

I PUT A SPELL ON YOU

Tapping into what was known as the *Forward* - an inhumanly persuasive mental frequency that was unique to her kind - the woman in black continued sending out invisible invitations, luring the receptive and naive to her little adobe casita outside of Santa Fe. Now, along with the corpses of the two young foster boys she'd beckoned to her earlier, lay the dried husks of a half-dozen more human bodies, all drained of blood, all left to molder in the cellar.

She wiped the last of that blood from her mouth and, lowering the now-dead man's head to the floor, she rose, gliding to the center of the room where she began to light the first of thirteen tapered black candles.

It had been too long since she'd intuited the dagger, and as her strength grew, so did her impatience to locate it, to recover it - for it was obvious by now that she could not guide the thing home to her; she would have to go and get it. She only hoped that this time, the spell would reveal the thing's location.

When the last of the candles were lit, she entered the circle, knelt, and began the ceremony. She did not close her eyes - that was something that, in the many centuries of her cursed existence, had never been possible. Nor did she speak - that too was a function she'd never possessed. But from within her mind, from within that sacred circle of flickering flames, she began her silent chant, beseeching the unholy gods from whom she was descended.

50

THE WORLD WENT DARK RED

The Sanguine River, so named because of the red earth that gave the water its bloody cast, ribboned down the center of Crimson Cove, making its way toward the sea. Sometimes it glided calmly toward its destination, and sometimes, like tonight, when the wind was high and the rain came hard, the river raged, its waves angry and mountainous.

As it came into view, Ethan pulled the Wrangler to the side of the road. He was on the phone with Sheila and knew from experience there was no cell reception on Sanguine Bridge.

"There've been some new developments," he told her, feeling guilty. They'd planned a quiet evening together with movies and junk food. *And lots of necking.*

"What's going on, Ethan?"

He sighed. "I got a disturbance call at the Crimson Corset and when I got there ... well, Gretchen's reopening the place."

"*What?* Did she ... did you talk to her?"

"Yep."

"Ethan ... I don't like this."

"You and me both. Anyway, before I come home, I need to stop by the Colter cabin and let Winter know."

A long silence. Then, "What happens next, Ethan?" The apprehension in her voice was unmistakable.

"Not a clue." He sighed. "I'll keep this quick."

"Don't worry. I'm running a little behind. And Ethan?"

"Yeah?"

"Be careful, okay?"

"I will."

"Promise me."

"I promise." He scratched the nagging itch on his hand where Sydney had bit him and gazed ahead, at the narrow strip of roadway that led to Sanguine Bridge. He could barely see it for the rain. "Give me twenty, maybe thirty minutes."

"I know the drill."

"You know that's why I love you, don't you?"

"Why's that?"

"Because you get it. My job."

Sheila laughed. "Well, I hope there's a *little* more to it than that."

"Oh, there's plenty more."

"All right. So ... I'll get there when I get there."

"Perfect. Your dinner will be waiting."

"Dinner?" At the mention of food, a fireworks display of saliva exploded under his tongue and his anxiety was temporarily suspended. "I thought it was Doritos-popcorn-and-beer night tonight."

"It was, but you've been so hungry I decided to make something special."

"Mmm. Talk dirty to me." His stomach grumbled.

"Well ... I was going to keep it a surprise, but since you have to work late, I suppose you've earned it. Spinach tomato tortellini."

His favorite. "You're a saint."

"And baked clams."

Ethan practically drooled.

"With antipasto salad."

"You're killing me with this."

"And tiramisu for dessert."

"God, I love you."

Sheila laughed.

But Ethan was serious. "I mean it." Along with his new appetites for food and sex, he felt more sentimental since Sydney's attack.

"I love you, too, Ethan."

Her words brought a lump to his throat and whether because of the recent attack, the promise of home cooked Italian dishes for the rest of his life, or Gretchen's return, Ethan wanted to set an official wedding date. Gretchen VanTreese and all other drama be damned. "I want to talk to you about something when I get home. Something important."

"Sounds mysterious." There was a smile in her voice.

Ethan wondered if she knew what he was hinting at. "Not mysterious - just that ... well, we've waited long enough. Let's set a date."

"I think that's a wonderful plan." He could hear the smile in her voice.

"Great. We'll talk about it tonight."

"Perfect." She paused. "And Ethan-"

"I'll be careful, I promise." He ended the call, determined to get his visit with Winter over with fast so he could get home to Sheila. Squinting through the downpour - even on their highest speed, the wipers were barely effective against the deluge - he nosed the Wrangler toward the road and checked to see if it was clear. He could barely see anything in any of the mirrors so he rolled down the window and leaned out. Wind shrieked and rain stung his face. Headlights shone just behind him where a car - or a truck, considering the height of the headlamps - waited to let him in. Ethan rolled up the window, gave a little wave he doubted the driver could see, and turned onto the road, not wanting to hold the guy up any longer than he already had.

He started onto Sanguine Bridge. When he was about a quarter of the way across, the headlights behind him shot perilously close, the truck's engine revving. "What the hell?" Ethan tapped the brakes, just enough that his rear lights would flash in case the guy somehow didn't see him.

But the truck only crowded closer, way too close, its engine screaming. Ethan braced himself for impact but it never came. The guy backed off, then barreled forward once more, taunting him, braking just inches from Ethan's bumper, then backing off like a pitbull reaching the length of its chain.

Angry now, Ethan looked for a place to pull over - he wanted to find out what this clown thought he was doing - but until they reached the end of the bridge, there was no shoulder. "Keep it up, pal," Ethan said to the headlights in his rearview.

SHEILA HAD WANTED TO TELL ETHAN TO JUST COME HOME - SHE DIDN'T like that he'd spoken to Gretchen VanTreese. Nothing good could come from that.

And he wants to set a date in spite of all the shit going on. She smiled.

She sat at the kitchen table, excited, happy ... but beneath her elation, darker things brewed. Gretchen VanTreese's return eclipsed her joy.

She forced the vampire from her mind and brought her thoughts back to Ethan, to the wedding. But she wondered why, in the midst of all the death and drama, he suddenly wanted to set the date.

Maybe it's because *of all the death and drama - maybe he needs something positive, something permanent and good.*

But then again ... maybe it was something else.

He hasn't exactly been himself lately.

There was no denying that. He'd been different lately - not necessarily *bad* different, just different. Edgier. More passionate.

Hungrier.

Soon, her thoughts circled back to Gretchen.

She shivered.

THE TRUCK SHOT TOWARD ETHAN'S BUMPER AGAIN, JERKED TO THE SIDE at the last second, and pulled into the opposing lane, accelerating until it sidled up to the Wrangler. Ethan glanced over and was just able to see the driver - *Gretchen's yellow-toothed contractor* - before the guy wrenched the wheel and slammed into the side of him.

Metal screeched out unholy sounds, and as the contractor forced the Wrangler toward the guardrails lining the bridge, Ethan's feet did a frantic dance in search of the brakes.

But it happened too fast.

Sparks exploded as the passenger side struck the metal railing, grinding and shrieking, and with a final violent jerk of his wheel, the contractor slammed his truck against the Jeep.

Rubber screamed on the wet pavement as the Wrangler was thrown off balance - and over the metal railing, off the Sanguine Bridge.

Inertia swallowed him whole; Ethan was spinning in slow motion, falling, falling. The world went utterly silent.

Then: the smack-crunch of metal hitting water.

The explosion and powdery reek of the airbag.

And as the Wrangler sank deeper, the creak and pop of safety glass, the icy onslaught of rushing water slamming into him, hitting his face and chest with what felt like the power of a firehose. The world went dark red.

The Wrangler sank lower and lower, spinning slowly in a graceful underwater pirouette despite the crashing currents.

Ethan clawed at the door handle, shoving himself, up, up with his feet - but something held him in place, locked him tight to the driver's seat.

The seat belt!

He'd had no time to prepare, no time to suck in air, and as what little breath he had burned in his lungs, he fought with that thick strap that was meant to save his life but now had turned against him.

The river current battered him, knocking him around like a punching dummy, and the only sound was the deafening rush of water. His lungs burned hot as he fought against the need for air, and just as he thought he might surrender to that fatal instinct to inhale, the seat belt set him free.

Up! Up!

He kick-swam his way out of the Wrangler and began kicking, clawing as if dragging his body up a mountain.

Up! Up!

But the rush of water wouldn't allow it.

It tossed him every which way and he spun, fought the confusion of currents, felt himself being pushed and shoved and swallowed. He railed against it with all he had.

Up! Up!

But he could no longer tell up from down.

The breath in his lungs burned bright and painful - and then, piece by piece, appendage by appendage, his body threatened to stop listening to him. His hands tried to curl inward, his arms tried to seize, his legs tried to lock.

A curious euphoria loomed nearby, hovering just beside him, inviting him closer, promising to melt away the panic.

Just sink, it said. *Sink. And rest.*

But even as death seduced him, Ethan fought.

Fought until he thought he'd break.

Fought even as the last bit of oxygen was leeched from his blood.

Fought until he lost track of himself and was no longer sure if the battle was real or only in his mind.

Sheila blew out the dinner candles.

Something's wrong. She'd felt it ever since she'd gotten off the phone with Ethan.

But she wouldn't let herself believe it.

I'm overreacting.

She switched off the kitchen light and, upstairs, slipped into a lacy black negligee - just in case *all* of Ethan's appetites were voracious tonight. She yawned, fighting off the strain of the long day.

Something's wrong.

51

A GRAVE SITUATION

Wind blasted through the trees and rain shattered down like tumbling glass.

Brooks Colter stood between the redwoods, his eyes on the house he used to live in. Lights burned within the cabin and occasionally, a figure passed by one of the windows - Winter, then Cade.

But Brooks couldn't move. He'd lost his nerve. He knew his brother, and if he pushed himself on him, it would only make Cade hate him more.

Yet he couldn't bring himself to turn around and head back to Eudemonia. He stood there in the darkness, rooted in place.

Lighting splintered across the sky, flickering and turning the world a stroboscopic violet-white. A deafening peal of thunder followed. It sounded as if the fabric of the night had been ripped open as wind blew wildly, loaded with threat.

And on it rode a new odor - grotesque, sickening.

Brooks lifted his nose, scenting the air.

Something dead.

And something else - something chemical ... and all too familiar.

His skin tightened and an icy snake of fear slithered down his spine. Using his vampiric vision, he searched the darkness, but the shadows were thick and dense, draping the woods like funeral crepe; in the endless night, it was impossible to tell the trees from what they might be concealing.

That familiar stench of chemicals and rot grew stronger. He thought he detected movement in the dark. Motionless as a mannequin, he waited.

Waited.

And saw nothing more.

But now the scent was strong enough he nearly gagged. He had to hold his breath.

Then a *crunch-squish* - and a slow, steady *scrape* like a heel dragging across the muddy, wet earth.

Closer. It was coming closer.

A soft hissing groan to the left.

Close. Very close.

His breath coming harder, Brooks searched the darkness - but the night gave up none of its secrets.

Then a rapid-fire stabbing of lightning bolts turned night into day, and in those flickering flashes, Brooks came face-to-face with the grotesquery. He gasped, jumped back from the terrible figure that loomed just feet away from him - *Oh, my God!* - and as the world returned to black, he ran for the cabin, his heart knocking so hard he felt it throughout his entire body.

Oh, my God, oh, my God, oh, my God!

OUTSIDE THE KITCHEN WINDOW WAS A WET WHIRLWIND AS THE STORM assaulted the night.

Something was wrong, Winter could feel it.

And smell it - distant, wet, dead.

And underlying that, the pungent stench of chemicals. *Formaldehyde?*

"Do you smell it, too?" Chynna's whisper startled him. Beside him now, she placed a hand on his arm.

Winter nodded, eyes on the window. "Yeah."

"What is it?" Her tone was shot through with uncharacteristic fear.

"Not a clue." Winter glanced back to the living room where Cade sat, a game controller in his hand, oblivious to the reek of encroaching death.

"It's your turn, Winter," he called.

"Coming." Winter looked at Chynna. "Something's out there." He spoke under his breath.

"Want me to go check it out?"

Winter shook his head. "No. I'll go."

Lighting ripped across the sky and a crash of thunder rattled the windows, reverberating through the cabin.

Then, as the thunder trailed off, machine-gun pounding hammered the front door and a voice screamed, "Let me in!"

Cade shot to his feet just as Brooks exploded into the living room, terrified and dripping wet. He slammed the door shut behind him.

"I didn't mean for it happen." The guy was shaking. He looked wild and shell-shocked. "I didn't mean it. I thought ... I thought ..."

CADE GASPED AS HE CAME FACE-TO-FACE WITH HIS BROTHER AND Brooks' words died on his lips as their eyes met.

And then Cade was pushed aside so hard he almost fell and Winter was between them, one hand against Cade's chest, the other against Brooks'.

"Don't worry, I've fed," said Brooks. "Triple rations. Cade's safe." He held up his hands. "You have my word."

Cade, trying to process what the hell was going on, just stared, vaguely aware of Chynna beside him, her hand on his arm. He was transfixed by his older brother's appearance.

Brooks was full vampire now, there was no question. The smooth, pale skin was a dead giveaway, and his eyes, which used to be the color of dark jade, were paler now, brighter. While he still had the square jaw, cleft chin, and chiseled cheekbones that made him unmistakably Brooks, his feature had sharpened somehow - an effect of vampirism that Michael had explained as nature's way of making the species more attractive to their mates. *And their prey.* Yes, it was Brooks - the enhanced, vampire version, but Brooks all the same. The only thing about him that was really new was the jagged vertical scar, like a little bolt of lightning, that began in his brow and ran the length of his forehead, disappearing into his hair and streaking it silver. Cade realized this was where he'd wounded him with the silver dagger.

"Bubba." Uncertainly, Brooks stepped closer.

Cade drew back. The use of the nickname infuriated him. Brooks was a traitor, a murderer, and hearing that word from his brother's lips was almost enough to send him into a blind fury.

Winter still stood between them. He looked from one to the other, eyes cautious, poised to pounce if any sudden moves were made. "What the hell's going on, Colter?" he asked Brooks.

Brooks' mouth moved, but it took a moment for him to find his words. "Samantha."

"*What?*" Cade, Chynna, and Winter spoke in unison.

Brooks' face tightened. He looked like a frightened little boy. "I didn't know. I didn't know."

Then Cade became aware of a sudden rotting stench hanging in the air.

"Oh, shit," said Winter, sniffing. "Don't tell me you tried to bring her back."

"I didn't know! No one told me! I thought ... I just thought I could ... for Cade. I overheard you talking and ..."

Cade looked from Winter to Brooks, then over to Chynna, who appeared as confused as he was. "What the hell are you guys talking about?"

Lightning flashed, thunder rattled the windows, and the cabin's lights flickered once, twice.

Winter stepped to the window, pulled back the drapes, and stared out.

Nerves ready to snap, Cade shouted, "Will someone *please* tell me what the hell is going on?"

Chynna turned to him. "He envenomated her corpse, Cade."

Cade felt the blood drain from his face. *Samantha's out there?*

"I did it for you, Bubba." Brooks stepped closer. "I overheard you guys talking one night - you said you wanted Winter to bring her back. Winter said he wouldn't do it and-"

"And there's a reason for that." Winter's teeth were gritted, his hands balled into fists at his sides. "This is why baby vampires fuck up and die so often."

Brooks turned hard eyes on him. "Well, no one told me! How was I supposed to know? It's not like I had anyone to sit me down and tell me the fucking rules!"

Winter's fist shot out and he grabbed Brooks by the shirt collar, pulling him so close they were nose-to-nose. "Then here's a lesson for you, Colter: When you envenomate a body that's no longer ensouled, it comes back as something else, something mindless, unnatural, and very dangerous. Very. Fucking. Dangerous. I guess you didn't hear *that* part of the conversation when you were eavesdropping."

Chynna stepped closer. "Take it easy, Winter."

Winter and Brooks faced each other, Winter breathing like an angry bull, Brooks staring back at him, eyes flint-hard and glittering with defiance.

"So what does this *mean*?" Cade asked.

Winter, still holding Brooks by the collar, said, "It means she's out there, looking for blood. Probably *your* blood, if my guess is right."

A low rasping groan - guttural, dirt-clotted, and unholy - sounded from outside. The door handle shook as something tried to get in.

"Well, shit." Winter let go of Brooks and looked at Cade. "Only you can kill it, Gilroy."

"*What?*" Cade shook his head. "I ... I can't!" The ground beneath him gave way, hurtling him into a bottomless spiral.

The slow and steady THUD, THUD, THUD continued as the groaning thing outside beat on the door.

"You have to. With that silver dagger. Only real silver will do it and we can't handle silver, you know that. *You* have to destroy it."

Cade, feeling numb, said, "But it's ... it's Samantha."

Winter stepped in front of him, blocking his view of the door. "It's not Samantha. Not anymore. We have to-"

"I won't let her die again!" Cade spat the words.

Winter's eyes turned to fire. "That thing out there is *not* Samantha! I *told* you about this."

Cade recalled what Winter had told him about ghouls.

"We have to be careful, all of us," Winter continued. "Remember, a mortal wound from a ghoul can kill a vampire."

None of them were safe. Cade's head spun.

"I'm sorry, Gilroy, but it's up to you."

"But-"

"He's right," said Brooks. "That thing isn't Samantha."

Cade whirled on his brother. "I can't kill her! I won't!"

Winter dragged Cade to the peephole in the door. "See for yourself."

Cade peered through it and gasped. The horror lurking on the porch shocked him down to his bones, and above the beat of rain, the complaining thunder, and the low, wheezing groans of the walking dead thing outside, Cade heard something else - the trip-hammering thud of his own terrified heartbeat.

52

THE LAST BEAT OF MY HEART

In the depths of the Sanguine, Ethan Hunter's lungs filled with dirty water and his body sank slowly toward the bottom of the river, lower, lower, where the waters were calm. His heart sputtered, kicked out a beat, one time, two times, and - after far too long a pause - a third time.

The last time.

Slowly, his eyes fell closed.

53

AN INSIDE JOB

*C*ade Colter knew there was a Hell. There was a Hell, and he was in it.

The thing outside was a monster, an abomination, but though dead and buried for weeks now, she was still unmistakable. It was Samantha, her once-pretty features ruined by rot, wrecked by death, and bloated by gases.

Even through the peephole he could see that one eye was still sewn shut while the other, covered by milky cataracts, bulged against a half-hooded lid, peering out from between the broken, rotting strands of mortician's thread. Crusts of green moss mottled and clogged the nostrils, and the mouth was a decaying gaping wound that yawned and shut, yawned and shut, like the mouth of some terrible, dying fish gasping for water.

And her throat - *Oh, God, her throat!* - so carefully stitched where Brooks had torn it open. But now those delicate threads had loosened, exposing tough, dried tendon and other things, horrible gray, meaty things. The rupturing fissure tipped her head at an almost playful angle, like a puppy seeking meaning from its master's commands.

"S-Samantha …?" Her name came out of Cade on a sigh of blank shock. "She's hurt!" His sanity threatened to crack. "She needs help!"

"Cade, no!" But it was too late. Before Winter could stop him, Cade threw the door open and with a jerky agitation of half-decomposed arms and legs, the animated cadaver barreled through the doorway.

Pandemonium broke out.

Winter, Chynna, and Brooks erupted into motion, but not soon enough - not before the ghoul hurled itself at Cade. With a crash, it collided into him and took him down, hissing and stinking and groaning, the noxious scent of its fetid breath hitting him like a wall of embalming fluid and corruption as dirt-clotted teeth snapped closer, closer, to Cade's throat.

Screaming like an animal in a saw-tooth trap, Cade kicked and writhed and elbowed and hammered, his fists snapping fragile bone and sinking deep into the cold, rotting, snail-slippery insides of the woman he once loved.

WINTER LUNGED, GRABBED THE GHOUL, AND WITH ALL THE DECORUM OF a bouncer tossing out a rowdy drunk, hurled the thing out the front door where it crashed onto the porch, bones cracking and appendages splintering as it hit and sprawled, halfway down the steps.

He slammed the door shut, locked it. He could have killed Brooks Colter and if it weren't for more immediate matters, he just might have. He pressed his back against the door and took a deep breath.

The room still reeked of death and undertaker's fluids, and the carpet was mottled with rot, moss, and brown-black secretions Winter wanted nothing to do with.

Cade was on his feet, his eyes the size of doorknobs. His face was icicle-white and he looked ready to blow his groceries all over the floor.

And Winter wouldn't blame him. The stink was so bad you could cut it with a knife. "You need to go get that silver dagger, Gilroy. The ghoul won't stop until it gets what it wants."

Cade stood there, dumbstruck.

"What *does* it want?" Brooks peered out the front window, watching the ghoul.

"Blood. Sire blood at that." Winter slid his hunting knife from his boot. The faux-silver blade wouldn't put any mortal damage on the ghoul but the weapon felt good in his hand, sure and solid.

Chynna was wiping corpse-juice off her hands, leaving brown-black smears on her pants. "I'm going to kill that fucking thing." She had iron in her eyes. She realized what she'd said and looked guiltily at Cade. "Sorry."

But Cade, white-faced and wide-eyed, didn't seem to hear her. He stared at the door, his mind lost in some dark and desperate place.

She turned her gaze to Winter. "You think it came all the way here from the cemetery for Sire blood?"

"That," Winter said, "and this place is what's familiar to it. It probably has a little remaining memory." Realizing what his words implied, he turned to Cade and added, "But that doesn't mean there's anything of Samantha still in there. The brain retains things. Ghouls are just mindless magnets, drawn to their old stomping grounds."

"Oh, shit," Brooks was at the window, shading his eyes to see out the glass. "It's getting up."

Winter looked at Cade. "The silver dagger, Gilroy. Go get it. You've got to plant it in the fucking thing's brain."

"It's in my room."

"Go get it!"

"But-"

"Now!"

Cade obeyed and Winter turned to Brooks. "What do you have in the way of weapons?"

Brooks hesitated. "A baseball bat?"

"Get it." Winter held his hunting knife out to Chynna. "And here. You take this."

She took it. "But what about you?"

"I've got Snowfell in the Hummer." He always carried his sword with him. It was just a matter of getting past the walking corpse to retrieve it which, at a glance, didn't seem too difficult a task - there were four of them and only one ghoul - but Winter had never dealt with such a creature before. He didn't know what to expect and it didn't seem wise to underestimate it. *But we'll handle it. We have to.*

BANG-BANG-BANG! came the pounding at the door.

"We need to lure it away from the cabin," said Winter.

"Into the woods," suggested Chynna. "Easier to dispose of there."

Winter nodded. "Less messy, too."

Brooks and Cade stood ready, weapons in hand.

"I'll go first," said Chynna. "Follow me." She headed out the kitchen door. The others followed.

"I'm getting my sword," said Winter. "I'll be right there." He headed for his Hummer.

54

THE WALKING UNDEAD

Cade stood under the canopy of trees, flanked by Chynna and Brooks, watching the ghoul, now about twenty-five feet away - and drawing closer. The night was wet and bone-biting cold, but the clouds had broken to reveal the moon making everything seem to glow. The ghoul's face, as if it hadn't been dreadful enough, now looked like a mask, all hills and hollows, valleys and peaks. Cade stood, a pulse beating thick and hard in his throat. He was vaguely aware of tears spilling down his cheeks.

But those tears were mostly anger. Some primitive part of him had been awakened by the attack and stoked his fury - fury at what he had to do, fury that such an unnatural thing as the creature lumbering toward him could even *be*.

Samantha - *no, not Samantha, not Samantha, it can't be Samantha* - shambled and stumped toward them, steadily nearing, now ten feet away, arms outstretched, teetering on decaying legs. It moved faster than Cade could believe. With its rotting flesh and unsteady limbs, he'd expected something out of *The Walking Dead*, ungainly and stupid. But this was no bumbling zombie. This thing knew what it wanted. *And what it wants is me.* His entire body broke out in icy sick sweat as it lumbered closer.

"I've got your back, brother." Brooks stood, baseball bat held high, waiting.

"You can do this, Cade." Chynna was ready to pounce, Winter's hunting knife clutched hard in her hand.

But Cade wished Winter would hurry the hell up with his sword.

The ghoul was close now - close enough that Cade could almost taste the decay.

The dagger, with its ornamental wasp, made a deadly, silvery sound as he pulled it from the sheath slung at his hip. He widened his stance and flexed his fingers around the hilt.

55

SLEEPLESS IN SANTA FE

New vision struck:
    The forest.
The rain.
The cold terror of the young man now clutching the dagger.

Terror because something unholy was walking his way - something dead but not dead. The creature teetered ever closer, and the woman glimpsed its hideous face looming from the shadows.

The young man with the dagger wept.

'I've got your back, brother.' A man's voice.

Then a woman's: *'You can do this, Cade.'*

Cade. That was his name. *Cade.*

But she needed more.

The woman in black willed the young man to strike, for once the blade shed blood, all would be revealed.

56

BLAZE OF GORY

Come on, Cade thought, *come on,* wondering if he had it in him to drive the silver through the putrefying brain. "Come on." This time, he said it aloud and the ghoul paused and stared through that cataracted, half-shut eye, face expressionless, head tilted in its obscenely jaunty angle.

Did some part of that rotting brain recognize him? Cade couldn't tell. It looked more as if the thing had simply blanked out, momentarily forgetting where it was and what it was after.

Or maybe it's thinking, planning.

In his mind's eye, Cade saw it lunge, take a fleshy bite out of his neck and face, gnaw off his nose and crunch into it like a carrot before sucking his eyes into its rotting mouth like ripe, juicy grapes.

He shook off the images. Stepping back, holding the dagger in front of him, he trembled as rain, sweat, and tears ran rivers down his face and body.

Any second now, Winter would return, weapon in hand, but until he did, Cade didn't dare let the ghoul within striking distance. He flexed his hands around the handle of the dagger. "Come on." His voice was lost to the rush of rain and wind.

But still, the creature made no move.

"What's it doing?" Brooks hissed, his knuckles hard and white around the upraised baseball bat, his shirt plastered to his body.

"Not a clue." Chynna was poised to strike. "If we can incapacitate it-"

And then, with an animal grunt, the ghoul came back to its senses. It charged clumsily toward them, headlong, clawed hands slashing at air, lips pulled back in a gruesome sneer, its eye, glinting with mad lust, fixed on Cade.

"Hey!" The voice cracked through the night like thunder.

The ghoul spun, nearly toppled.

Winter rushed the thing, charged it like a bull, his sword held high, his battle cry shattering the night. With a flash of glinting blade, he swung, lopping off the ghoul's right arm. Cade felt the breath of the sword's quick passage and the ghoul's arm flew, landing near Brooks with a smack on the wet earth and a sickening twitch of fingers.

The ghoul screamed and the sounds that came out of the corpse's dirt-clotted throat seared Cade's brain like acid - a screeching, a keening, a thick, wet howling that was, and yet was not, Samantha.

Brooks' years of playing baseball were apparent when, with perfect form, he swung the bat low, and knocked the thing off its feet.

The ghoul howled as it hit the ground with a sickening squelch. Then, enraged, it gathered itself and began a rapid, unnatural belly crawl toward Cade.

Chynna lunged, crashed onto the ghoul, and began stabbing, the hunting knife stitching through the air like a sewing needle. Brooks slid in beside her, pressing the ghoul fast to the ground.

"Gilroy! Not yet!" cried Winter.

Until that moment, Cade hadn't realized he was running toward the tangle. He skidded to a stop, heart pounding, and stared down, paralyzed, shocked, as Chynna jammed the hunting knife into the ghoul's throat, tearing leathery skin, shredding dried tendon and ripping into death-toughened muscle.

As the blade dragged down the corpse's abdomen, gutting it, the sound of ripping dried flesh along with the stench of rot and chemicals made Cade's stomach seize. Embalming fluids leaked out and Cade gagged, bent over, and unleashed a spray of acidic vomit.

As he retched, the ghoul, despite its missing arm, somehow gained advantage over Chynna, straddled her, guts pouring out of its abdomen as it choked her with its mold-encrusted hand. Winter charged, drove his sword through the ghoul, hard, impaling the thing on his long blade, and Brooks took another swing. The bat connected with its head and shards of bone and brain shattered outward and sent the corpse flying. With a wet smack, it slammed into a tree six feet away, and crashed to the ground in a heap, one half of its head broken and caved.

But impossibly, it got to its feet, rising as easily as a marionette pulled by strings, and with a guttural groan, started toward them.

"You've got to be fucking kidding me." Winter growled as he charged, sword aimed.

The blade went through the ghoul, clear through, pinning it to the tree behind it. Foul, dark fluids sprayed out of the wound in a pungent mist.

The ghoul's mangled face showed shock and pain, its one eye bulging, its mouth gaping and leaking dark fluids like oil - *glug, glug*. It shrieked, writhed, and flailed its arm, kicking its legs.

"Now!" Winter yelled, his voice like a firing shot. "Right through the brain, Gilroy!"

But Cade just stood there, edgy, brittle, and paralyzed.

It was the eye.

That milky orb was on him, and wide with wounded terror. Suffering. The ghoul made an almost childlike sound, a soft whimpering. And then, even worse, it coughed - such a human sound.

"Now!" cried Winter.

But the silver dagger suddenly weighed a thousand pounds.

"You have to do this, Cade." This was Brooks.

"Her ... eye." Cade stumble-stepped back from Samantha's impaled mewling corpse. "She sees me. She's looking right at-"

"*It* doesn't see a fucking thing except its dinner," Winter cried. "Now show some fucking balls and-"

Chynna raised her hunting knife high and brought it down hard, stabbing the ghoul in the eye with a sickening wet sound. More unearthly shrieks echoed through the trees. Black fluid exploded and the ghoul's lips peeled back in a painful grimace exposing dirt-clotted teeth and a bloated, purple-blue tongue.

Chynna turned to Cade, her jaw hard. "Put it out of its misery."

But the latest wound had infuriated the ghoul. It yanked itself away from the tree, pushing, pushing, walking its way to the end of the sword, the giant crossguard disappearing into its guts as the ghoul groaned and grunted and dragged itself forward. Ribs snapped and cracked and ichor flowed as the heavy pommel disappeared inside of it. The ghoul was almost free.

"Gilroy!" yelled Winter.

But Cade was mesmerized. Though fully blinded now, it freed itself and easily scented Cade's blood and lumbered toward him, its intestines dragging behind it.

"Over here!" Brooks cried, distracting it.

The ghoul turned its blind face his way then raised its remaining arm, searching, clawing, stumbling close. Brooks sidestepped it, but somehow, it predicted his move, and with a fierce swipe of its clawed hand, ripped into Brooks' throat.

Brooks' eyes went horror-movie wide and his hands shot up. Blood spurted between his fingers, and poured down his chest.

That's when Cade exploded into motion. "No!" The silver dagger raised, lips peeled back in a feral scream, Cade charged.

Brooks dropped to his knees, gasping, as Cade collided with the ghoul. Its bones snapped like twigs under his weight.

"DIE! DIE!"

The ghoul bucked as Cade stabbed its throat, its face, the silver blade ripping, tearing and slicing skin, glancing off bone. "DIE!" Fluids sprayed out in a slick, noxious mist, coating his face, his clothes, his hair. "DIE! DIE!" The ghoul's shrieks became low moans, an otherworldly, mournful mewling. "DIE!"

Cade raised the dagger high and brought it down hard into its temple.

It cracked through skull, into brain.

But if the ghoul had stopped moving, Cade didn't notice. He brought the dagger down again and again. "DIE! DIE!" Thick wet sounds came from somewhere inside the thing's head. "DIE!" Cade kept stabbing. More bone broke - he heard it, felt it - but he continued thrusting, stabbing, screaming. His head was swimming, floating away. He was all vengeance, and when the dagger slipped free from his gore-slick hands and clattered to the ground, he pounded the thing's head with his fists, pounding, pounding, until it made a sound like a mallet striking raw meat.

Someone grabbed him by the shirt and yanked him to his feet.

"Enough!" Winter locked Cade's arms behind his back.

Cade, still screaming, kicked, his heavy wet shoes thudding into dead flesh, rotting bone.

"DIE!" He kicked the head and something gave - an inconsequential cracking sound as the skull caved completely. "DIE!"

Pain as Winter's lock tightened, but Cade thrashed, wrestled free, and threw himself back onto the ghoul, wrapping hands around its mangled throat, squeezing until bones snapped.

Winter tore him off again and, this time, sent him flying.

Cade hit the ground several feet away, rolled onto his back, and stared up at the trees, the sky, the falling rain.

"He's not going to make it!" Chynna's words rang in his ears, their meaning momentarily lost on him.

Of course I'm going to make it, he thought. *I'm fine.*

Then he remembered: A mortal wound from a ghoul would kill a vampire.

Brooks!

"Your brother needs blood, Gilroy!" This from Winter.

Cade got to his feet, his body aching, his mind swimming.

Brooks lay on the forest floor, eyes rolled back, his torn throat spurting blood.

Panic.

Quickly, Cade grappled for the dagger, found it, and dragged the blade across the palm of his hand. He dropped the dagger, wincing at the pain as blood - hot, slick, and tar-black in the night - welled up and began to flow. "Move!" He crouched beside Brooks and pressed his bleeding hand to his brother's mouth.

Nothing happened.

"He's not drinking!"

Winter and Chynna stood several feet away now, eyes glazed with hunger, and only then did Cade realize what the scent of his blood must be doing to them.

Brooks still wasn't responding.

Cade pressed his hand harder to his lips. "Come on. Please. Please, drink." But the blood only spilled down the sides of Brooks' lips.

Cade's tears came in a flood. Panic and terror burgeoned until he stood on the edge of it, ready to crack. "Drink, Goddamnit, drink!" He forced Brooks' mouth open.

Still, nothing.

"Drink!"

And then Brooks twitched, coughed.

Relief crashed over Cade. "Drink!"

And at last, Brooks did.

Cade let go of the breath he'd been holding. *ThankyouThankyouThankyou.*

Brooks' eyes fluttered open and flashed with bloodlust. His hand shot up, locking onto Cade's wrist, his mouth moving hungrily, greedily.

"That's enough," called Winter.

But Brooks was a dog with bone; he wouldn't let go.

"Stop," said Cade, feeling light-headed. *Too much blood. I'm losing too much blood.* "That's enough."

But Brooks' hand was an iron vise. He was breathing hard and sucking even harder.

"Stop!" Cade tried twisting his hand and Brooks gnawed all the harder, biting, sucking, drawing blood until Cade's vision began to darken around the edges. The world tipped and Cade's stomach did a sickening somersault.

"Enough!" Winter hooked an arm around Cade, yanking him away.

Brooks was on his feet, hands fisted at his sides, his body contracting with labored breath, murder in his eyes.

"The dagger." Winter had turned away and covered his nose, unable to bear such proximity to spilled Sire blood.

Trying to focus his eyes on Brooks and swaying from blood loss, Cade found the dagger and got to his feet. "It's me, Brooks." His words were thick, slurred. "It's Cade." There was nothing but hate and hunger in Brooks' blazing eyes. Cade held the dagger in front of him. He stepped back, wobbled, and almost fell. "Stay back."

Brooks winced away from the silver as if he were looking into a very bright light.

"It's me. It's Cade." The world began spinning in earnest now. "Your brother."

Then something in Brooks' face changed. His eyes softened, the spark of madness flickering out of them. He blinked. "Bubba …" His voice held recognition.

Cade felt himself fading. He lost his slippery grip on consciousness and hit the ground.

THE WOMAN'S VIOLET-BLUE EYES FOCUSED.

She knew.

From within the circle of burning black candles she stood and raised the netted veil of her black, moth-eaten hat. Her widow's weeds whispered across the floor as she glided toward the closet at the end of the hall.

She opened the door and brought down a small black suitcase, snapped it open, and peered inside. Within was everything she needed to get where she was going.

And at last, she knew where that was.

57

LATER THAT NIGHT

*B*y the time Michael arrived at the Santa Cruz Boardwalk, the storm had passed and now thick patches of fog drifted like ghosts along the concrete making it seem as if the Ferris wheels and roller coasters rose from clouds in some fantasy kingdom. This late, the lights were out save for the myriads of white fairy lights twinkling along the walkways and outlining the buildings. Though the rides were closed and the visitors long gone to their beds, he could still smell the faint aroma of hot dogs and popcorn drifting on the ocean breezes.

Like an insistent lover, the setting moon flirted with a patch of fog, leaving moonbeam trails, like kisses, across the water. The beach lay silent and deserted as he walked the length of the pier listening to the water lick at the pilings below, another insistent lover.

The pier was lit here and there by ugly yellow sodium lamps as Michael headed back toward the beach, pausing only to suck away traces of blood from his fingers, relishing the metallic tang as he gazed out onto moonlit water, remembering the last time he'd been here. That had been in 1906 and much had changed. Back then, it had been a place where he could clear his mind. But now, with imported palm trees shivering in the breeze, lights glittering, and the sound of traffic in the distance, the boardwalk did little to soothe him.

He'd chosen this beach city for its anonymity; the influx of tourists even at this time of year promised invisibility, but even now, in the pitch of night, he felt exposed, open as a weeping wound, and though he hadn't seen another soul roaming in the last hour, he sensed imaginary eyes upon him.

But it was only his guilt, he knew. Guilt for what he'd done - for what he'd let himself become. It wormed through his mind like a song on a loop, always there, hitting its highest notes when his bloodlust had been sated - as it was now - and only going mute when his hunger was so strong he could think of nothing but the next kill.

He left the pier and walked quietly along. Having just fed, his guilt was so razor-sharp and agonizing he almost wished for the return of the bloodlust. Almost.

But the *real* hunger wouldn't be back for a time. The indigent he'd found sleeping on the sand beneath the pier had satisfied him enough that the need for blood was just a low-grade fever - nothing Michael couldn't manage. And now, while he was clear-headed, he needed to find shelter. Somewhere he could stay unseen. Somewhere safe from sunlight. He considered the boats docked at a wharf not far away - *too risky* - and turned around, heading back toward the Giant Dipper roller coaster.

He paused in front of one of the huge old buildings housing arcades and rides. This one was topped by a turret and a sign that read, "The Haunted Castle." He stared up at the crouching gargoyles guarding the dark ride's arched entrance. They peered down on him with wide eyes, their thick grimacing lips promising terror. This place seemed an appropriate sanctuary.

As Michael began looking for a way into the building, his thoughts turned briefly to Eudemonia. He wondered how Winter and the others were getting along without him. Wincing, he turned those thoughts off quickly, unwilling to shoulder any more guilt than he already suffered.

It was time to start a new life - and this was the place to do it.

At his new home in Eudemonia, Rafe Santangelo slipped back into his underground quarters, the bag of human blood tucked covertly into the waistband of his shorts. He doubted he'd be seen but he hid the bag anyway, in case someone happened upon him in the hallway.

No one did. Not since he'd explained that he wanted to be alone, that he needed to think. Cedric, the distinguished older vampire who'd been assigned to help him should he need anything, had respected his wishes and left him alone. It had given Rafe the perfect opportunity to explore - and find the stash of human blood.

Now, in his quarters, he pulled the bag from his waistband and stared at it, heart pounding, mouth watering. Feeling like he'd just gotten his hands on a winning lottery ticket, he sat on the edge of the bed, breathing slow, willing himself to be calm. He opened the bag of blood and the smell of it hit him - coppery, sweet even, and so different from animal blood. Despite the profusion of deer's blood he'd been given since arriving at Eudemonia, his hunger kicked into a higher gear, a dangerous gear. He trembled with need, yet he did not move.

Now was his chance to finally become a true vampire ... so why was he hesitating?

Maybe because he knew Brooks wouldn't approve; he'd insisted that Rafe give it some time at Eudemonia, around other vampires, before taking the plunge.

But Rafe knew what he wanted - and what he wanted was true immortality. He'd be good at vampiring; he could feel it. *I'll be happier.*

But still, he couldn't quite bring himself to drink. It was as if his muscles wouldn't obey his commands.

Rafe knew why - and it had nothing to do with Brooks.

Once you drink this, he thought, *there's no turning back. Not ever. So you'd better be goddamned sure this is what you want.* He'd been sure up until now. But the fantasy of full transition and the reality, it turned out, were different things. *What if it's painful? What if I change my mind a year, ten years, a century from now?*

But then another part of him, a clearer part, spoke up. *Do you really think that by some fucking miracle, you'll wake up one morning and suddenly your panic attacks will just disappear forever? And if Brooks dies, do you really want to go back to stocking shelves at Peddler Puck's for the rest of your life? Do you really believe you'll patch things up with your mom and dad and ...*

Rafe knew better than all that.

This bag of blood was his escape hatch - the only one he'd ever have. The only way to stop the panic attacks forever, and the only way he would ever have a family again.

So, with no further thought, Rafe Santangelo brought the bag of blood to his lips and drank, swallowing mouthful after mouthful, relishing the coppery flavor.

And this, his first taste of human blood, was so exquisite, so *divine*, that he was amazed that he'd been able to survive so long on the blood of lowly forest creatures.

"Do you know why Jesus was crucified?" Sydney shrieked. "Because He preferred it to looking at *you*!" She hurled the bedside lamp. It shattered against the wall, missing Emmeline's big blocky head by mere inches. "Get out! Get *out*!"

And finally, exasperated, the insufferable suffragette walked out and Sydney had the room to herself. For now. She knew the woman would be back, though - she could see the shadow under the door where Emmeline was hovering, listening for the slightest sound that would give her an excuse to come back and offer more unwanted assistance.

But Sydney had all the help she wanted.

No, she wasn't hungry.

No, she didn't walk to talk about it.

And no, she didn't want to spend any more time with the others -

especially that girl Erin and her simple-minded Maker, Arnie. Erin and Arnie, like Sydney, were Winter's direct descendants, and therefore, apparently, her direct kin now - but that didn't impress Sydney one iota. Erin was a dipshit and Arnie was retarded. Sydney wasn't about to spend the rest of eternity playing Connect Four and Hungry, Hungry Hippos with them, she didn't care *who* created them.

She wiped away tears, blew her nose, and settled into her bed, wishing she could sleep.

How can this be? she thought. *How could the Lord allow such abominations as vampires to walk the earth? And how could He let me become one of them?*

The answer was simple: He didn't. Because He didn't exist. There *were* no such beings as the Father, Son, and Holy Ghost.

And where does that leave me? What did you worship when your idols blinked out of existence? And if there was no God, then what was the purpose of life?

That answer, too, was simple: there *was* none. There was no purpose and nothing mattered except making yourself happy.

Without realizing it, Sydney's thoughts drifted to Winter. *He* made her happy with those bulging muscles, his back so broad you could show a movie on it, the way those blue jeans hugged his ass and cupped his-

Stop! She squeezed her eyes shut and redirected her mind - a talent she was getting better at already. Her heart, her soul, still belonged and would always belong, to Michael.

Ah, Michael. Yes, Michael. That was a much better thought. She sank into it, gave herself to it.

Michael. Think of Michael.

She used all of her willpower to pry Winter off her mind. It was just like weaning oneself off a drug. According to Emmeline, Sydney's bond to Winter would loosen some over time. It wouldn't always be this hard.

She closed her eyes and took slow deep breaths. *I do not love Winter,* she told herself. *It's only a glitch, a trick of nature.* And it made perfect sense. As Emmeline had explained to her, if a vampire killed his Maker before taking blood, he could revert to humanity, so nature intervened. The bond between a Maker and his vampire was just science's way of ensuring the perpetuation of the species.

But that's not love. Love is Michael. Michael, who was as beautiful as Lucifer before the fall ...

She wondered where he was. She'd heard he'd run off to slash and slay the innocent. The thought of him murdering his way across town inspired pride in Sydney - she was happy he'd gotten away from Eudemonia and its Victorian constraints.

I'm getting out of here the first chance I get, and I'm going to find him. I'll break my bond to Winter then make my move.

But what's my move? She needed a plan.

According to Emmeline, Rogan and Dante would be installing shutters on the windows of her cabin, so it was obvious they didn't expect her to live here in the main building with them. That meant she'd have privacy. And that would make things easier.

But they weren't letting her out of their sight just yet. She needed to prove herself first, they said. So that's what she'd do. She'd earn the trust of her captors - and they *were* captors - and then, when they didn't expect it, she'd run.

Run to Michael. She didn't know how she'd find him exactly, but she'd find a way. Sydney *always* found a way.

Ah, my darling, Michael ... we belong together ... It's our destiny ...

For the first time since she'd been turned, Sydney smiled.

SHEILA HADN'T MEANT TO FALL ASLEEP. ONE MOMENT, SHE'D BEEN reading, and the next, she was sheathed in cold sweat, jerking awake from a nightmare.

In it, Ethan had been screaming for her, but she couldn't find him.

She felt for him in the darkness, but the sheets beside her were cool and empty. *Shit!* He still wasn't back. Reaching for the nightstand lamp - and nearly knocking it over - she flipped the light on and checked the time.

When she saw how late it was, her mouth went dry. He'd said he might run late but this was ridiculous. She checked her phone.

No texts, no missed calls, no voice messages.

Maybe something's happened.

Something ... the dreaded word when you loved a cop. *Something.* Something's *happened.*

Not willing to lose any more time, Sheila called Winter.

AFTER SLAUGHTERING THE GHOUL, WINTER RETURNED TO EUDEMONIA. Emmeline had called saying there were some business matters that needed attending to - something Winter supposed he'd be doing a lot more of now that Michael was MIA. He wasn't keen on office duties - Winter was a man of action - but as Michael's second-in-command, it was part of the gig.

So he left the Colter brothers at the cabin under Chynna's watch, and after a hot shower, buzzed Emmeline.

She immediately bustled into the office, where Winter was feeding Michael's squawking raven. "I need you to sign these." Emmeline laid down the paychecks for the staff. "And these," she plunked down some invoices. "And these, for your approval." A small stack of work orders.

Winter stared at the papers, sighed, and began reading. The words were blurry but if he squinted, he could make them out. He signed what needed signing and handed them back to Emmeline. "How's Sydney?"

Emmeline shrugged. "Distant. I don't think she's too happy with the situation."

Winter sighed. "I guess I'd better check on her." He studied Emmeline. "You know, if I'm going to be in charge around here for a while, how would you feel about my making some changes?"

"Such as?"

"Well," Winter drew the word out. "For starters, maybe you'd be better at this stuff - the office stuff - than I am. Think of it as a promotion."

"A promotion?"

"Yes. A step up the corporate ladder." Winter leaned back in his chair and grinned. "After serious consideration," he added with mock professionalism, "we at Eudemonia would like to offer you the position."

Emmeline arched a brow at him. "I know when I'm being manipulated, young man, but as it happens, I think I'd make a damned good office manager." She shrugged. "I pretty much am already ... so yes, I'll take the promotion." She held out a hand. It was as squat and blunt as the rest of her.

Winter gave it a firm shake. "Welcome to the team."

Emmeline *tsk*ed. "I'll start by handing these out to the night shift." She squared the papers and paychecks on the desk, and headed to the door, pausing when Reaper screeched out that he was her number one fan. "You, however," she said to Winter, "are in charge of that damned bird."

"But-"

But Emmeline was gone, the door closing resolutely behind her.

"Well, shit." Winter frowned at Reaper, who cocked his head, blinked his beady black eyes, and told Winter to *Plug it up, plug it up!*

"How many damn horror movies did Michael make you watch?"

Reaper answered with a series of shrill, *Redrums*.

"Got it." Winter poured more seeds into his hand and held it out. He supposed taking care of a bird couldn't be too hard, and as the raven hopped over and began pecking and swallowing, Winter realized something. He was in full charge of security now. He had complete freedom to make decisions - and there were a lot to be made. Especially regarding Cade. As terrifying as the ghoul situation had been for him, it was the least of the kid's problems. Gretchen VanTreese was out there and Winter knew better than to think she was going give up her plans to acquire the Sire. Even now, she'd be sniffing around. Winter wasn't about to give her a chance to strike.

That meant he needed to recruit more vampires. The Eudemonia group wasn't large enough to handle her. Cedric and Emmeline weren't warriors - their strengths were better suited to business than the battlefield. Dante and Rogan were invaluable, but they couldn't be everywhere. There simply weren't enough of them if - no, *when* - Gretchen made her move.

Winter needed to make a few calls. He had friends - some went back decades and others were contacts he'd made recently at the Biting Man Festival in Eternity. He was confident he could talk a few of them into joining the Eudemonia group - and they could begin hunting Gretchen down immediately.

And unlike Michael, Winter had no qualms about permanently wiping her off the face of the planet.

Just as he was picking up the landline, his cell rang.

On the other end, a panic-stricken Sheila Leventis wanted to know where Ethan was - apparently, he'd left hours ago to talk to Winter. When she told him why - that Gretchen was not only in town but was back at the Crimson Corset with a plan to reopen it - Winter clutched his phone so hard it cracked.

THE STORM HAD PASSED AND THE WATERS OF THE SANGUINE RIVER WERE calm. In the placid depths twenty feet below, the body of Ethan Hunter drifted on gentle currents, its lungs water-sodden, its heart no longer beating, its electrical impulses arrested. Under normal circumstances, the damage to the oxygen-starved brain would be irreparable.

But these were not normal circumstances.

In Ethan's blood still swirled just the smallest amount of vampire venom, injected by his ex-wife, Sydney. It was not enough to turn him, but it *was* enough to heal him - and enough to restart his system.

Slowly, his heart began to pump again - a single beat at first, then another, then a third until at last, it found an adequate, if erratic, rhythm.

Then, in the pathways of his deadened brain, a single synapse fired, then another and another, each pumping out vital bits of information until, one by one, his cells began to spark - and then hum - with electrical activity, with life.

The nerve-to-nerve and nerve-to-muscle commands came first, followed quickly by the first conscious thought - Air! he needed air - and Ethan jerked into motion and began pushing himself upward, kicking and swimming.

At last, Ethan broke the surface, coughing out endless streams of water. He took his first deep pull on oxygen - *pure, clean, life-giving oxygen!* - and, after a few gagging but wonderful breaths, he was able to swim for the riverbank.

But even as he fought his way toward it, he had no awareness of what had happened, of why he was here. All that mattered was getting to land, and when he finally did, his fingers sank deep into the beloved dirt and he dragged himself out of the river. Finally released, he flopped down onto the earth, and coughed up more water.

He dipped in and out of consciousness, willing himself to remain alert.

But he could not. His mind was too tired, his body too battered, and there was not enough venom in his system to sustain him.

Ethan Hunter blinked out of awareness, his face hitting the dirt.

IF YOU WENT INTO THE BACK OFFICE AT THE CRIMSON CORSET nightclub, you'd see a large bookcase lining the wall. If you knew about the secret passageway behind it, you could take the stairs to the underground where private rooms bloomed out from winding corridors like toxic roses on twisted vines. Among those many rooms were Gretchen VanTreese's old quarters - a large low-ceilinged room with black carpet and dull, reddish walls sporting black iron sconces and the splatter-art paintings of Sebastian Antonelli, Gretchen's handsome Italian Loyal who'd been murdered last year by none other than the Sire himself, Cade Colter.

At the center of the room, on a low, ten-foot-wide platform, sat a red velvet high-back chair where Gretchen, like a queen, used to receive her human supplicants, trading doses of her venom in return for their blood. That was her chosen means of survival - clean and easy - and Gretchen intended to return to that way of life right away.

She entered the room and made her way to that red velvet chair now, running a hand along the ornately-carved wood as Scythe stood sentry at the door, looking good enough to drain dry. He said nothing, just let her have her moment.

Home, she thought. *I'm home.*

She looked around the room.

Spiderwebs hung in dusty membranes over everything. In the northwest corner stood a 19th-century walnut Renaissance Revival hall stand with a sanguine finish; she'd bought it in San Francisco several decades ago. Against one wall was her large mahogany Victorian armoire with its heavy carved doors, and next to that, the ivory hook where Gretchen kept her array of colorful feathers that she liked to fasten into her hair. The Victorian grandfather clock, no longer ticking, loomed silently in the corner, and modern side tables of black iron and glass punctuated the room. The place reeked of dust and inactivity.

Beyond the main room were three tall archways, each leading to different rooms, one of which was her bedroom, where her 18th-century bed awaited her with its purple canopy and matching comforter - all made from the finest satins and silks. She hadn't yet visited the bedroom but knew that on her nightstand was the blue-shelled Tiffany lamp she'd had for decades, and next to that, the crystal candle jar with its silky purple tassel where she used to keep her black widow spider, Lilith. Lilith, who had scurried so affectionately under Gretchen's clothes and nested in her hair. Gretchen twisted her amethyst and onyx poison ring absent-mindedly, remembering how the spider had loved imbibing the venom Gretchen always kept inside the bezel. She didn't know what had become of her beloved pet, but could only assume that the Sire had killed her as well.

The Sire. Cade Colter. He'd become both the bane of, and the reason for, her existence. Only a Sire could reproduce with a vampire. With Cade Colter, she could create a new bloodline, half-human, half-vampire, which, ideally, would have the strengths of vampires and humans both. A master race.

And she'd gotten close, so very close. Had Michael and his Loyals not intervened, she would have succeeded.

But now I've been given a second chance. Sires were incredibly rare, and Gretchen could not, *would* not, let Cade slip past her again. *Not this time.* This time, she'd have an even bigger army of Loyals to protect her, making it easier to penetrate the barrier of guards surrounding Cade.

And having Ethan Hunter killed tonight had been a nice start. *Good riddance, Sheriff.* But it was Winter, Michael, and the others who truly stood in her way. Especially Michael. He would be the first on her hit list - after Ethan Hunter, anyway.

She would torture Michael Ward, kill him slowly, and keep him with her always, just as she kept Mommy Dearest with her. But she would wear Michael's remains in a different way than she did her mother's - Gretchen didn't want so much as one of his teeth to be salvageable when she was done with him. She would burn his body to cinders and keep his ashes - or at least some of them - in the bevel of her amethyst and onyx ring. Whatever was left of him could blow away with the wind for all she cared.

Yes, she had to take them all down, one at a time. Michael, Winter, and everyone at Eudemonia. *And now Brooks Colter, as well.* She frowned. He still hadn't returned to her which meant he'd probably joined Michael's side. She'd made every effort to call him home, yet somehow he'd resisted her. It was just like that stubborn fool to defy his own Maker.

Not for the first time, Gretchen berated herself for having turned the man. At the time, the elder Colter brother had seemed the quickest way to Cade, and Gretchen had even come to enjoy his companionship. Such a beautiful man he was, with a body that Michelangelo might have spent a decade chiseling. Gretchen loved beautiful things, and Brooks Colter was a work of art, there was no denying that, but now that she'd been unstaked, he presented a problem. He would have reverted back to full-vampire, informing those around him that Gretchen had returned. She would have preferred to execute her new plans invisibly, but because of Brooks, the element of surprise was impossible.

Never mind Brooks Colter; Gretchen had never been one to cry over spilled blood.

She was back.

Back to health.

Back to the Crimson Corset.

Back to her plan of taking the Sire for her own.

And that meant she needed to build her army. She turned to face the man in the doorway. "Scythe, darling. Bring in the slaves. And have Jazminka return with you, as well."

"As you wish, Mistress."

"That's my good boy."

Scythe nodded and left her quarters as Gretchen sank into the familiar comfort of her high-back chair. It was like coming home all over again. She thought of Emeric in his mansion in Palo Alto. It was time to find him and bring him home, too. He would be thrilled. She smiled. With his help, Gretchen's plans would go off without a hitch.

Scythe returned with Jazminka and the slaves and, despite their fear, the venom-addicted humans did as they were told, forming a single-file line that stretched out of the room and into the corridor beyond. Several of them whimpered in terror.

"Keep them silent," Gretchen told Jazminka.

Jazminka promptly slapped a whiner into silence and the others took heed.

"Scythe," said Gretchen. "Come here." She patted the edge of the seat between her legs. "This should be a pleasurable experience for me. I've earned that much, don't you think?"

Scythe grinned as she spread her legs, hooking one on either arm of the chair, then lifted her skirts to expose her bare sex. With a lusty flash of fang, Scythe dropped to his knees in front of her and began pleasuring her as, one at a time, Jazminka led the slaves to Gretchen for a toxic dose a venom. A dose that would bring them transition.

She bit into the throats of her slaves, relishing the taste of their pain, getting high on the scent of their collective terror as Scythe brought her to rapture again and again with his talented tongue.

It was ecstasy at both ends.

The *real* bliss, however, came from knowing that by the time this night was over, she would have a new and powerful army of vampires, and nothing - not even if Michael's group had tripled in number - could keep her from obtaining the Sire.

THEY'D DRAGGED THE DEAD GHOUL DEEP INTO THE WOODS AND BURIED it near an ancient redwood. Winter, Chynna, and Brooks had done the shoveling, insisting that Cade go inside and wrap his bleeding hand in several layers of gauze, enough to mute the scent of his blood. By the time he'd finished, Winter had gone back to Eudemonia, then Chynna had taken a shower in one bathroom while Brooks used the other.

Chynna had since made herself scarce so Brooks and Cade could have a talk. But there was no talking. The brothers now sat on opposite ends of the sofa, listening to the tick of the clock, and the rusty purr of the cat who lay curled up between them. There was so much to say, but there seemed no possible way to say it.

And Cade was too tired to try to figure it out. His muscles ached as if they'd turned to stone and he felt about as sharp as a bowl of oatmeal. He just sat there, lost in his own thoughts. Vaguely, he could smell soap on his brother's skin, the shampoo he'd used to wash his hair, but otherwise, Cade might have been alone. Despite a long, scalding shower of his own, he didn't feel clean and suspected he wouldn't for a while. The dirty feeling didn't just cling to him; it had seeped into his skin.

And it wasn't just because he'd been covered in human decay, either. It was because Cade was ashamed. He'd choked out there tonight and it had nearly cost everyone their lives. He hadn't been prepared to see Samantha like ... *that*, and he'd hesitated, turned stupid. He swore to himself it would never happen again. *Not ever again.*

When Brooks finally spoke, it startled him.

"You saved my life, Bubba."

And you ruined mine. Cade kept the thought to himself.

Brooks' eyes were filled with tears. "I didn't mean for it to happen. Any of it." His voice cracked. "I spent so much time trying to figure out how to tell you how sorry I am, trying to find the words that could make you understand ... but there aren't any. I don't know what to say except I'm sorry ... and that's not enough, I know." He sniffed, stroking Purrcy absently. "Please, forgive me. Please."

Cade, too, had done a lot of thinking in the past weeks, fantasizing about the many ways he could punish Brooks, but somehow, now, he could feel no hatred. Maybe it was because he was exhausted - or maybe it was because of the depth of genuine regret in his brother's eyes. Regret and sorrow. Brooks was grieving. Not only the loss of Samantha, but of Cade probably, and even his own humanity. Suddenly, he wasn't the monster Cade had made him out to be in his late night fantasies of revenge.

Cade cleared his throat. "It's going to take some time for me to ... get over it."

"I know." Brooks pulled him into a sudden, clumsy hug. "I love you, Bubba."

Cade didn't want to say it back but he couldn't help it. "I love you, too." His own tears spilled. He hugged his brother back, quickly, then stood. "I need to be alone now. Are you ... staying here or ...?"

Brooks considered. "I'd love to come back. But I think I'd better stay at Eudemonia for a while. I still need to work on my self-control a little ... but before too long, I think-"

Chynna's cell phone rang and some deep sixth sense set Cade on alert. She answered and Cade followed her into the kitchen, listening.

"I see." Her words revealed nothing, but something in her posture changed, stiffened, and Cade knew his premonition had been correct: Something was wrong.

Brooks remained on the sofa but leaned forward, looking anxious.

"What is it?" Cade asked when she ended the call. "Who was that?"

"Winter." Chynna's silver-gray eyes avoided Cade. "There's been an accident. With Ethan."

Brooks was on his feet. "Ethan?"

"What happened?" Cade's pulse thundered.

Chynna pulled out a kitchen chair. "I think you should sit down." Her voice was even and soft. She still wouldn't meet his eyes.

"I'm *not* sitting down." Cade's thoughts were spiraling. "Tell me what happened!"

Brooks stepped into the kitchen, wide-eyed and silent. It was all too reminiscent of the night their mother had told them their father had been killed. "Is he ... is he dead?"

Chynna shook her head and relief hit Cade's bloodstream like an injection. "But he's not doing well. He's at the hospital. Sheila called Winter to tell him Ethan hadn't come home. Winter sent a search out. Rogan and Dante found him by the river and-"

"The river?" asked Brooks. "What the hell happened?"

"Apparently, he was driven off the bridge and-"

"Driven off the bridge?" Now it was Cade's turn to interrupt. "By who?"

Chynna hesitated. "By one of Gretchen's. She's ... she's back at the Crimson Corset."

Unreality. The kitchen turned cold. Cade looked at Brooks. Brooks stared back. Cade had almost convinced himself she'd left town.

"We need to go see Ethan," said Brooks.

Chynna nodded. "We'll all go."

Cade hurried down the hall to his bedroom. Inside, he peeled off his sweatpants and pulled on jeans. *Gretchen's back and Ethan might die.* The words played over and over in his mind.

He pulled the dresser drawer open and grabbed the silver dagger - cleaned and sheathed - and strapped it to his hip, just in case. Whether or not it brought new nightmares - *wasps, always the wasps* - he wanted it with him. That dagger was part of him now and given that Gretchen had returned, he wasn't letting it out of his sight.

Gretchen's back and Ethan might die.

He felt helpless, out of control, and realized he was crying.

He glanced at his phone on the dresser. An idea tried to surface.

Gretchen's back and Ethan might die.

He didn't know what to do.

He grabbed his keys and again glanced at his phone. He'd need to take that, too.

And the moment the phone was in his hand, the idea that been trying to form finally did … Maybe he couldn't save Ethan, but there *was* a way to stop Gretchen.

'Call me if you change your mind.' Muriel's words were so clear in his mind they might have been spoken aloud.

No. He shook his head. It wasn't safe. It was-

He was hesitating - just like he'd vowed he never would again - as Ethan lay dying in the hospital and Gretchen roamed free.

He punched in her number before another second was lost.

Muriel answered on the first ring.

"I'm in," said Cade.

Silence.

"Your group," Cade continued in quick, low tones. "I want to join. I want to … help."

Muriel laughed. "I knew what you meant, Cade. And I knew you'd be calling."

Cade didn't bother to ask what she meant by that. His mind was racing and in just few seconds, he calculated how he was going to make this work. Muriel's Exterminators killed *all* vampires, she'd been very clear about that, but they didn't know about Cade's friends at Eudemonia. As long as he kept it that way, Winter's group would be safe. Cade could put Muriel and her minions on Gretchen's trail and they'd all be free of the Crimson Corset vampires once and for all.

This is crazy. It's stupid. I shouldn't have called.

No, it's the right thing to do. It's the only *thing to do.*

"Hello? Cade? Are you there?"

He realized Muriel had been speaking. "Oh. Yeah, sorry."

"Does that sound good? Coffee tomorrow at noon at Rise and Grind's?"

"I'll be there." He hung up. Unwilling to lose even one more second of his life to hesitation, he herded Brooks and Chynna to the Land Rover, hopped behind the wheel, and raced to the hospital, to Ethan, praying to a god he'd never prayed to before that the sheriff would be all right.

EPILOGUE

Two nights later, a shiny yellow cab pulled to a stop in front of the Crimson Cozy Inn, a snug bed and breakfast in the heart of town that offered a view of the lake and mountains. The driver turned to give a crooked-toothed smile to the woman in the back seat.

She was dressed in strict black mourning clothes complete with gloves and a netted veil that concealed her features. Through the net, he could see her eyes though, and boy, were they creepy. A strange, pale shade of sickly unblinking violet-blue. She hadn't said a word during the drive and she said nothing now, just slipped him the money he was owed - no tip, he noted - and retrieved her single suitcase.

It takes all kinds. The driver shook his head and watched her, an apparition in outdated widow's weeds, gliding up the stone steps toward the double glass doors of the inn. "Well, screw you, too, lady." With another shake of his head, he pulled out and headed home to his wife who would undoubtedly feel sorry for him for having to work so late and give him a good mercy fuck. Miranda's mercy fucks were the best fucks of all.

The driver began whistling an extra-cheery rendition of CCR's

Bad Moon Rising. He had no idea that he'd just delivered Hell itself to the quaint mountain town of Crimson Cove.

IN HER ROOM AT THE CRIMSON COZY INN, THE WOMAN IN BLACK STOOD at the window and pulled back her veil to gaze out onto the lake, the hills, the moon and the trees. She'd like it here, she thought - not that it would matter much if she didn't. She wouldn't be staying long.

Just long enough to retrieve what was rightfully hers.

The silver dagger.

Finally, after all these years, she'd found it.

She drew the curtains, and for the first time in many ages, the woman known only as The Black Wasp smiled.

CONTINUE FOLLOWING THE COLTER BROTHERS' ADVENTURES IN **THE BLACK WASP!** See the sneak preview for more more information.

SNEAK PREVIEW: THE BLACK WASP

PROLOGUE

"Oh, hell no!" Sabrina Burke slammed her cards down.

"Read 'em and weep." Jordan Santos laid his winning hand on the table, leaned back, and grinned. "You know the rules. Off with it." He nodded at the only thing she wore from the waist up: a lacy white bra that did plenty to emphasize her cleavage but unfortunately revealed not the slightest hint of nipple. They were pink, he was betting. Pink and small, probably, despite her D cups — and that was just how Jordan liked them.

"I win again." He coughed into the crook of his arm, mentally cursing whatever walking Petri dish had passed a cold onto him.

"You cheated." Sabrina crossed her arms, blocking his view.

"That's bullshit and you know it." But it wasn't bullshit. In the weeks since he'd introduced her to the joys of strip twenty-one, Jordan had quickly realized that leaving things to chance didn't pay off. His solution was to stick a couple aces from a matching deck to the underside of the table with chewing gum — and it was working beautifully.

Sabrina glanced at the clock.

Jordan, following her gaze, said, "No such luck. We still have five minutes."

The employees of the Crimson Cozy Inn were given two fifteen-minute breaks and one thirty-minute lunch per shift. Jordan and Sabrina were twenty-five minutes into their lunch and so far had both been freed of their socks, shoes, belts, and shirts.

"It's either the bra or your pants," said Jordan, grinning. "Them's the rules."

A pink flush crept up from Sabrina's cleavage and into her cheeks. "But what if someone comes in?"

"They won't. Never have before." Business was slow this time of year and the only other housekeeper — a squat, middle-aged Latina named Maria — didn't take breaks. She also never came into the break room. *And even if she did,* Jordan thought, *it wasn't as if she could rat us out.* The woman didn't speak a lick of English as far as he could tell. "Come on." He lowered his voice to what was meant to be a deep, sexy timbre, but thanks to his cold, the words came out nasal and frog-like. "Don't be a sore loser." He might have sounded like shit, but he had other weapons in his arsenal. Cocking his eyebrow into the devilish arch he knew she couldn't resist, he said, "Do it and I'll throw in some extra honey, just to show what a good sport I can be."

"What extra honey?"

"Take it off, and I'll do all your bathrooms for the rest of the day."

Sabrina hesitated. "All of them?" She hated scrubbing toilets, probably because it dirtied her nails or some shit.

"*All* of them," he said.

At last, she sighed, resigned. "Fine." She reached to unhook her bra and Jordan was mesmerized by the way her breasts pressed against the cups, fully prepared to pop out and say hello at any moment.

He reached under the table to adjust a ruthless erection. "That's the stuff," he purred.

Then the sound of humming wasps filled Jordan's ears and he lost his train of thought.

"Room 106." Even to him, his voice sounded hollow and far away.

"What?" Sabrina paused, staring at him. "Are you okay? You look stoned or something."

"Room 106," he repeated. "She wants room service."

Jordan forgot all about Sabrina's breasts and his erection wilted as quickly as if he'd been doused by a bucket of ice water. He was vaguely aware of the strange fog that settled over his mind as he got to his feet.

"What the hell's the matter with you, Jordan?"

But he barely heard her. He pulled his pants and shirt on, moving like a blank-eyed automaton, dressing himself to the humming horde of invisible wasps.

Sabrina yanked her own shirt on. "If you didn't want to play, you could have just said so. Are you even listening to me? Where are you going? Fine. Be a fucking douche, see if I care."

And the next thing he knew, Jordan stood at the door of room 106.

He hadn't yet knocked when the woman on the other side bid him entrance. *"Enter,"* she said, but not with words, never with words. Her commands were silent and seemed to come from the center of Jordan's own mind.

The door clicked open and for a moment, he hesitated. There was terror, yes, but under that was something cloyingly sweet and seductive, something soothing... and irresistible.

Yes. Irresistible.

He stepped inside and the door shut firmly behind him.

There was nothing unusual about the room — the beige carpets and blue curtains were replicas of the others. Even the cheap framed prints affixed to their respective walls via theft-proof security hangers were duplicates of those in the other rooms.

Only she, the woman herself, lent any distinction to the place. She sat near the window, a dark figure, ramrod straight in her chair. A few black wasps hovered around her, occasionally lighting on the black netted veil that concealed her face. Jordan had never glimpsed anything behind that veil except the flash of strange blue eyes. Otherwise, the woman was a blank. She may have been hideous, she may have been beautiful, but somehow, he didn't think she was either. It seemed to him she didn't *have* a face, that hidden under the veil was nothing at all, not even a lump of flesh where a face *should* be. Just... blackness. Emptiness. Absence. The end. Nowhere. *Nothing.*

Nothing except those eyes ...

"*Approach,*" said the non-voice, and again, the young housekeeper obeyed, his heart chugging in his chest like a runaway train.

"*Kneel.*"

His panic burgeoned and swelled. He wanted to scream, wanted to run, wanted to do anything but what the woman bade him — but he could not. When he opened his mouth to protest, language was unknown to him and, without his consent, his legs folded and he was on his knees, at the horrible woman's feet. Her long black skirts filled his vision and this close he could smell her: dust, and things long dead, as if she kept the carcasses of rats hidden in the many folds of her old-fashioned black mourning dress.

Wasps crawled out from under her skirts, clinging to the edges to watch him with glittering black eyes. A few more came from her sleeves, and then more and more until the woman seemed to be *dripping* the fucking things. They were always there, those wasps, but — thank God — they'd never taken any real interest in Jordan. They seemed only to want to watch, to stand sentinel.

"*Come closer.*"

Jordan's windpipe narrowed to a pinhole but he obeyed. He knew what was coming, knew there was nothing he could do to stop it, and knew that when it was over he'd somehow forget it entirely. *Until the next time she calls me ...*

And how long would these torture sessions continue? How much more did the woman need from him? Jordan's mouth was so dry he could've struck a match on his tongue. "P—please ..." he rasped. It took such brute strength to utter the word that he might have been trying to lift a piano.

The woman took no notice. She was humming. It wasn't a human hum, but a low buzz somewhere deep in her throat, as if, even inside of her, her legion of wasps were clamoring for escape.

She lifted a pale hand to extract a long sharp hatpin from her veiled hat. It made a slow silvery sound as it slid free. She licked the needle-sharp tip with a gray leathery tongue and Jordan waited, frozen, knowing what came next: with that pin, she'd pierce the

SNEAK PREVIEW: THE BLACK WASP

tender flesh of some hidden region of his body. She would suckle from him, yes, but that wasn't the worst part. The worst part was her poison. It would enter his veins through the hat pin where she'd licked it and it would slowly poison him, feeding her as he suffered. And afterward, Jordan would silently stagger to his feet and leave room 106 with only a gaping hole in his memory.

And then, tomorrow, it would happen again. And again the next day. The woman would beckon him and feed from him, and her strange saliva, like a liquid cancer, would poison him just a little more with each visit until ...

Until what? Jordan wondered.

But the answer was obvious: *Until she uses me up ... until she kills me.*

The Black Wasp is available in ebook, paper, and audio at Amazon

ABOUT THE AUTHOR

Alistair Cross' debut novel, **The Crimson Corset**, a vampiric tale of terror and seduction, was an immediate bestseller earning praise from veteran vampire-lit author, Chelsea Quinn Yarbro, and New York Times bestseller, Jay Bonansinga. In 2012, Alistair joined forces with international bestseller, Tamara Thorne, and as Thorne & Cross, they write - among other things - the successful Gothic series, **The Ravencrest Saga**. Their debut collaboration, **The Cliffhouse Haunting**, was an immediate bestseller. Their thriller, **Mother**, has been optioned for film. They are currently working on several new books together.

In 2014, Alistair and Tamara began the radio show, Thorne & Cross: Haunted Nights LIVE!, which has featured such guests as Anne Rice of The Vampire Chronicles, Charlaine Harris of the Southern Vampire Mysteries and basis of the HBO series True Blood, Jeff Lindsay, author of the Dexter novels, Jay Bonansinga of The Walking Dead series, Laurell K. Hamilton of the Anita Blake novels, Peter Atkins, screenwriter of HELLRAISER 2, 3, and 4, worldwide bestseller V.C. Andrews, and New York Times best sellers Preston & Child, Christopher Rice, and Christopher Moore.

For book deals, updates, specials, exclusives, and upcoming guests on Thorne & Cross: Haunted Nights LIVE!, join the newsletter at Alistair's website at: alistaircross.com

Made in the USA
Las Vegas, NV
02 April 2025